SWEPT AWAY BY THE ENIGMATIC TYCOON

ROSANNA BATTIGELLI

THE LIEUTENANTS' ONLINE LOVE

CARO CARSON

D1149211

MILLS & BOON

First Published in Great Britain 2018
by Mills & Boon, an imprint of HarperCollinsPublishers,
1 London Bridge Street, London, SE1 9GF

Swept Away by the Enigmatic Tycoon © 2018 Rosanna Battigelli
The Lieutenants' Online Love © 2018 Caroline Phipps

ISBN: 978-0-263-26495-1

38-0518

MIX
Paper from
responsible sources
FSC™ C007454

WEST DUNBARTONSHIRE	
D000053577	
Bertrams	08/05/2018
ROM	£5.99

SWEPT AWAY BY THE ENIGMATIC TYCOON

ROSANNA BATTIGELLI

To Nic, who has always believed in me as a writer,
read every draft, made delicious meals
and gone along with my dreams.
Here's to a new chapter in our lives, Nic! xo

CHAPTER ONE

JUSTINE SURVEYED THE peaceful tableau lazily. The waters of Georgian Bay were calmer today, and she watched the gentle undulations with pleasure, letting her senses revel in the rugged beauty before her.

The clear blue water, shimmering with pinpoints of reflected sunlight, was dazzling—mesmerizing, really. The water lilies clustered along the water's edge looked like they were straight out of a Monet painting, their crisp white petals and yellow centers resting among dozens of flat, round, overlapping green pads. Occasionally the seagulls announced their monopoly on the sky with their shrill, almost human-like cries as they swooped and glided, tail feathers outspread, but even that wasn't enough to disrupt Justine from her contemplative mood.

She breathed in the fresh July air and congratulated herself again for exchanging the smog and humidity of the big city for *this*…this nature lover's paradise on Georgian Bay. She had made the right decision in accepting her parents' offer, Justine assured herself again as she rubbed sunscreen over her legs. Their proposal had come at the perfect time.

Working in the Toronto law office of attorney Robert Morrell had become too stressful—she'd had no choice but to resign. The memory of how she had trusted him in the first place still caused her pangs of remorse. Her mouth twisted cynically. How naïve she had been, falling for a man who was going through a turbulent divorce.

After leaving her resignation notice on his desk she had immediately headed home to Winter's Haven. As she'd pulled into the driveway, seeing her parents sitting together on the porch swing holding hands had made her burst into tears. *Why couldn't she have been so lucky?* In all her years at home she had never doubted her parents' trust, respect and devotion to each other. And to *her*. With such loving role models how could she settle for anything less?

Their love and support had cushioned her for the next four days, and then the morning she had thought herself ready to drive back to Toronto, eyes still puffy and shadowed, they'd made her an offer that took her breath away.

They had talked extensively, they'd said, and had decided that the time had come for them to retire from managing their cottage resort and to enjoy their golden years. They wanted to travel around the world while they still had their health and energy. If Justine were willing, they would sign Winter's Haven over to her and move into the smallest of the twelve cottages there. Justine could enjoy her inheritance early, and they would be delighted that the business would stay in the family.

"Take your time to think it over, sweetheart," her father had said, hugging her tightly. "But we have every confidence in your skills—business or otherwise."

Her mother had nodded and joined in the embrace, her eyes misting, and after kissing them both Justine had left, her own eyes starting to well up.

A month later the lease on her apartment had been up and she'd headed home to Winter's Haven for good.

The sting of Robert's deceit had begun to subside, and although she still had down days, feeling alternately embarrassed and angry for letting herself be fooled, she had come to terms with the end of their relationship. Taking over from her parents would occupy her time and her energy, and Justine was looking forward to exploring new ideas for the business while enjoying the more relaxed pace of the area.

Now, two months after her return, Justine could flick away any thought involving Robert almost nonchalantly. Usually followed by any number of silent declarations.

I am so over it! I'm done being a bleeding heart! Done with men and their games!

Justine closed her eyes and listened to the gentle lapping of the waves. She allowed herself to be soothed by the rhythmic sounds, enjoying the touch of the sun over her body as she settled back on the chaise longue. Tilting her sunhat to protect her face, Justine felt the familiar magic of Winter's Haven ease the stress out of her, and with a contented sigh she allowed herself to drift into a peaceful nap.

The sound of typewriter keys and a telephone ring jolted her awake. She fumbled for her cell phone, by her side on the chaise. Squinting, she read the text.

Good God, Justine! Where the heck are you? Did you forget the two o'clock appointment I arranged for you?

Justine sat up, her heart skipping a beat. It was one fifty-five. She'd never make it in time.

She leapt up and ran the short distance from the beach to her house, not stopping until she reached the washroom on the second floor. She usually enjoyed taking leisurely showers after a soak in the sun, but on this occasion she was in and out in less than five minutes. Her shoulder-length hair would have to dry on the way there. And there was no time for make-up.

She hastily put on a flowered wrap-around skirt and a white cotton eyelet top, and made a dash to her car. She usually walked to the main office, but she wanted to avoid any further delay.

She had managed this place efficiently since her parents had turned over the business to her two months earlier. "I'll run this place as smoothly as you did," she'd promised them before they left for their retirement travels, and she had done just that—except for today.

Justine had never been late for anything in her life. She'd have to make sure it didn't happen again. It didn't make her look very responsible. She should have never given in to Mandy, who had uncharacteristically scheduled an appointment on her day off.

The sight of a sleek silver-green Mustang convertible in the parking lot dashed her hopes that her visitor might be late.

She took the steps to the office two at a time and entered the building, taking deep breaths. Mandy Holliday, her friend since high school and her assistant and office receptionist, smirked at her from behind the wooden desk, cocking an eyebrow toward the double doors leading to the diner.

"He's been waiting there thirty minutes. The last time I checked he was talking to the Elliots in Cottage Number One."

"Of all the times to doze off on the beach…" Justine grimaced. "I wonder why this Forrest man has insisted on seeing *me*. If he wants to rent a cottage, you could have dealt with him. I wish you had been able to squeeze some information out of him."

She adjusted the tie belt on her wrap-around skirt.

"I hope he's not one of those pompous business types. You know—the punctuality nuts, the arrogant *'you must be as perfect as I am'* professionals who—" She stopped at the sudden furrowing of Mandy's eyebrows.

"Perhaps you should reserve your judgment until after our meeting," a cool voice suggested directly behind her.

"I'll be in the diner if you need me," Mandy murmured, before retreating hastily.

Justine turned around stiffly to face her visitor. He was not at all what she'd expected. But what *had* she expected after hearing that ice-tinged drawl?

She tried not to reveal her surprise as her gaze smacked into the chest of his impeccably tailored gray suit before moving slowly upward to his face. His height topped hers by at least a foot. Her pulse quickened as her eyes took him in. A five o'clock shadow she suspected he wore permanently. Dark brown hair with burnished bits, styled like someone out of *GQ*. Chestnut eyes with flecks of gold.

She felt sweat on her upper lip. To her horror, she ran her tongue over her lips without thinking. She felt like combusting.

How could he look so cool in that suit? She almost felt like suggesting he remove his jacket or tie… And then her mouth crinkled slightly, nervously, at the thought of how such a suggestion would sound to him.

He caught the crooked smile, but didn't return it. He looked down at her imperiously, his jaw tense.

He's angry, Justine thought, unable to tear her gaze from his face. It was so *male* and rugged, with a straight nose and firm, sensual lips clearly visible under the meticulously groomed shadow. At second glance she caught a slight curl in his hair, and his eyes, unwavering, were disturbingly hypnotizing.

"I'm sorry," she said quickly. "I didn't mean to offend you. I was irritated at myself for being late. It's not like me." She extended her hand, forcing herself to offer him an apologetic smile. "I'm Justine Winter."

For a moment, he just stared at her, and Justine was about to withdraw her hand in embarrassment when he finally took it, his long fingers closing around hers completely in a firm clasp.

"Apology accepted," he replied, motioning abruptly for Justine to sit down.

She did so and he pulled up a nearby chair.

"What can I do for you, Mr. Forrest?"

"Forrester. Casson Forrester."

Her eyebrows shot up at his name. "Yes, of course. You made an appointment with Mandy to see me, but you didn't state your reasons. Are you interested in renting a cottage? Did you want a tour of the grounds and facilities before making a reservation? We may have an opening, depending when it is you want to stay." She paused, realizing she was babbling.

His lips curved slightly. "Yes, I'm very interested in the cottages. You see, I've just purchased the adjoining land on both sides of your property."

Justine frowned. "I can't believe the Russells have sold their properties—" She broke off, stunned. The Russells' ancestors had been among the original homesteaders in the area.

"I made them a convincing offer." He was unable to conceal the satisfaction in his voice. "Our transaction was mutually profitable."

Justine looked at him warily. "I don't suppose you arranged this appointment just for the sake of meeting your new neighbor…?"

He laughed curtly. "You're perceptive, if nothing else."

Justine flushed, her mouth narrowing. She didn't like the negative implication of "if nothing else." "Why don't you come right to the point?" she suggested sweetly, trying not to clench her teeth.

His eyebrows arched slightly at her directness. "I have development plans for both lakefront properties," he explained brusquely. "However, *your* property, being in the center, poses a number of problems for me. It would seem that the ideal solution would be for me to purchase this property in order to maximize the success of my venture." His eyes narrowed. "Just name your price. You'll have it in your bank account first thing tomorrow morning."

Justine couldn't prevent the gasp from her lips. "You can't be serious!"

"I'm not the joking type," he countered sharply. "Nor do I intend to play any money games with you, Miss Winter. Negotiations aren't necessary here. I'm willing to pay whatever you feel is an optimum price for this place."

Justine felt her eyes fluttering in disbelief. "I'm not interested in selling—no matter what you offer, Mr. Forrester," she stated as firmly as she could muster. "It's not a matter of money; it's a question of principle."

She stood up, both palms on the table, willing him to leave.

A muscle flicked at his jaw. He made no move to stand, let alone leave. "Kindly explain yourself, Miss Winter," he said evenly.

Justine took a deep breath. "I would not want to see the natural beauty and seclusion of this area spoiled by a commercial venture. That's what you have in mind, don't you?" She put her hands on her hips, her blue-gray eyes piercing his accusingly.

"Let me clarify my intentions."

He leaned forward, resting both elbows on Justine's desk. His face was disturbingly close to her chest. She was mortified as she noticed her black bra peeking from under the white eyelet blouse. She hadn't even thought about the selection of her bra in her after-shower haste. She sat down and crossed her arms in front of her.

"I think the rugged beauty of this stretch of Georgian Bay shoreline should be fully enjoyed—not kept a secret. I am contemplating the construction of a luxury waterfront resort and a restaurant that will enhance the experience of visitors. Nothing like high-rise condominiums; that would be unnatural in these surroundings."

He rubbed his jaw with long, manicured fingers.

"I like the thought of luxury cottages nestled privately among the pines and spruces, each overlooking the bay." He paused briefly, but as she opened her mouth to reply, added coolly, "Let me make one thing clear, Miss Winter. Even if you refuse to accept my offer, I intend to go ahead with my plans for the Russell properties."

Justine had listened with growing trepidation as she thought of the repercussions his commercial venture would have—not only on her property, but on the surrounding area. She had no intention of giving in to him. His plans would *not* enhance the existing atmosphere of this stretch of the bay—she was certain of it. The seclusion and quiet ambiance her customers depended on would definitely be compromised with all the construction and traffic his venture would generate.

She felt her jaw clenching. No, she did not intend to let him bully her into selling.

"I cannot accept your offer," she told him coldly. "*Someone* has to cater to common folk with regular incomes who want a holiday away from it all. I cannot, in all good conscience, agree to a proposal that would not only deprive my regular customers of a quiet, restful vacation retreat, but also exploit the natural wilderness of the area."

She was unable to control a slight grimace.

"Have you even thought of looking into the Georgian Bay Biosphere Reserve? Or the Provincial Endangered Species Act? Obviously, Mr. Forrester, personal financial gain is higher on your list of priorities than the preservation of nature."

Justine stood up again, hoping he would take the hint and leave.

Instead he leaned back in his chair and continued to gaze directly at her, an unfathomable gleam in his chestnut eyes. She cleared her throat uncomfortably, wondering what she could say to get him out of the office without resorting to being rude.

Stroking his jaw thoughtfully, he murmured, "Why don't I just make you an offer anyway? How does this sound to you…?"

Justine only just stopped herself from swaying. Even half the amount he was offering would be exorbitant. No wonder the Russells had sold out to him if this was the way he conducted his business transactions. For a moment her mind swarmed with thoughts of what she could do with that kind of money, and she couldn't deny that she felt the stirrings of temptation to consider his offer.

She looked at him, sitting back comfortably with his arms crossed, and the hint of smugness on his face gave her the impression that he knew exactly what she was feeling. He was counting on it that she would abandon her principles if the price were right.

Well, he was *wrong*. She might have been tempted in a moment of weakness, but she would never sell Winter's Haven. It represented a lot of things for a lot of people, but for her it was *home*. Her special healing place. Even her hurt over Robert had lessened since she had come back. There was an atmosphere here that she had never felt in the city—or anywhere else for that matter. She had an affinity for this kind of natural lifestyle, and after leaving it once she had no intentions of ever leaving it again.

Her blue-gray eyes were defiant as she looked across at him. "I'm sorry, Mr. Forrest…"

"Forrester."

"Mr. *Forrester*. I can imagine that your offer might be tempting to some, but nothing would make me sell my home and property. I belong here."

Surprise flickered briefly in the depths of his eyes. "Bad timing."

"What do you mean?" she demanded defensively.

"Your parents were almost ready to accept an offer I made on this place three months ago, then changed their minds when you showed up. It's too bad for me that you didn't time your arrival for a week later. The deal would have gone through by then," he continued bluntly, "and I wouldn't have had to waste my valuable time talking to you."

He rose fluidly from the chair.

Justine could feel her cheeks flaming. She remembered her parents mentioning an offer somebody had made—it hadn't been the first time—but that they had turned it down.

"What's *really* too bad, *Mr. Forrester*," she shot back indignantly, "is the fact that you've become my neighbor."

He smiled, but the smile didn't reach his eyes. "Not for long, perhaps," he replied coolly. "I will come up with another offer soon—one you may not be able to resist, despite your lofty principles."

"Don't count on it," she snapped.

"We'll see," he replied softly. "Any woman can eventually be bought. I don't imagine you're any different." He turned to leave with a cynical smile. "Except maybe a little higher-priced," he said, his tone cold as he opened the door and clicked it shut.

Justine stared at the door speechlessly. She slammed one palm down on the desk, furious that he had had the last word—and the last insult.

"Ouch," she moaned, slumping into her chair.

She felt emotionally drained. The last thing she had expected from her visitor today was an offer to buy Winter's Haven. *And what an offer,* she mused.

Casson Forrester obviously meant business, and money

was no object. She didn't imagine he would stop at anything until ultimately he got what he wanted. And he wanted Winter's Haven. He hardly seemed the type to back away from any venture once he had made up his mind.

Justine recalled the set of his jaw and the steely determination in his eyes. Those dangerous tawny eyes. Tiger eyes, she thought suddenly, eyes that made her feel like the hunted in a quest for territorial supremacy.

How long would he stalk her? she wondered nervously, rubbing at her sore palm. What means would he use to try to break down her resolve and get her to give in to him?

It doesn't matter what he tries, an inner voice reasoned. *There's nothing he can do to make you change your mind.*

"Nothing!" She rose to leave.

At that moment Mandy returned to the office, unconcealed curiosity on her face. "What do you mean, *'Nothing'*? Tell me what that hunk of a man wanted... Please say he's booked a cottage for a month. I'll be more than happy to forego my vacation and tend to his every need—"

"He's not worth getting excited about," Justine sniffed. "He's an assuming, boorish snob who thinks money can buy anything or anyone." She felt her cheeks ignite with renewed anger. "He's got a lot of nerve."

"I take it you didn't quite hit it off?" Mandy said, sitting on the edge of the desk. "What on earth did he say— or do—to get you so riled up? I've never seen this side of you."

"That's because no one has ever infuriated me so much," Justine huffed.

She told Mandy the purpose of Casson Forrester's visit.

"I'll never sell, though," she concluded adamantly. "To him or to anyone else."

"Hmm...it doesn't sound like we've heard the last of him, though, since he *is* our new neighbor." A dreamy look came into her eyes. "I wonder if he's married..."

"I pity his wife if he is," Justine retorted. "Having to live with such an overbearing, narrow-minded brute!"

"I'd like to see what your idea of a hunk is if you consider this man a brute!" Mandy laughed.

Justine gave an indelicate snort. "All that glitters isn't gold, you know. He may look…*attractive*—"

"Gorgeous," Mandy corrected.

"But it's the inside that counts. Trust me, Mandy, he has a *terrible* personality. No, it's not even terrible. It's non-existent."

Mandy eyed her speculatively. "Not your kind of man?"

"Not at all," Justine replied decisively, turning to leave. "If he calls again, think up any excuse you can; just tell him I'm not available. Whatever you do, *do not* set up another appointment. I've had enough personal contact with Casson Forrest… Forrester—whatever his name is—to last me a lifetime. All I want to do is forget him."

Easier said than done, she thought, driving the short distance back to her house. How could she forget those tiger eyes? His entire face, for that matter… It was not a face one could easily forget. Not that *she* was interested, but she had to admit grudgingly to herself that Casson Forrester probably never lacked for female companionship.

Or lovers, she mused, stepping out of her car. She felt a warm rush as she imagined him in an intimate embrace, then immediately berated herself for even allowing herself to conjure such thoughts.

Justine sprinted up the stairs to her bedroom, changed into her turquoise swimsuit, grabbed a towel, and headed to her private beach.

The first invigorating splash into the bay immediately took some of her tension away. And as Justine floated on the bay's mirrored surface, absorbed in interpreting the images in the clouds, the threat that Casson Forrester posed to Winter's Haven already seemed less imposing.

What vacationers liked most about the place was the seclusion of each of the twelve rustic cottages tucked amidst the canopy of trees, only a short walk to their own stretch of private beach. They also appreciated the extra conveniences that Justine's parents had added to enhance their stay. Along with the popular diner—which featured freshly caught pickerel, bass or whitefish—over seventeen years her parents had added a convenience store, a small-scale laundromat, and boat and motor facilities with optional guiding services.

Many of their guests came back year after year during their favorite season. Justine hoped that Casson Forrester's plans wouldn't change that.

She swam back to shore, towel-dried her hair, patted down her body quickly and decided she would change and eat at the diner instead of cooking. She liked to mingle with the guests, many of whom had become friends of the family.

Justine put on her flip-flop sandals, hung up her towel on the outside clothesline, and walked up the wide flagstone path. On either side myriad flowers bloomed among Dusty Millers and variegated hostas.

Ordinarily Justine entered through the back entrance after going for a swim, but the sound of tires crunching slowly up toward the front of her house made her change her mind. A new guest, she thought, mistaking her driveway for the office entrance.

She rounded the corner with a welcoming smile. The car sitting in her driveway had tinted windows, so she couldn't make out the driver. But she didn't have to. Her smile faded and she stopped walking. She knew who the silver-green Mustang convertible belonged to.

With the windows up he had full advantage, seeing her with her swimsuit plastered to her body, hair tousled and tangled. She wished she had wrapped her towel around her.

She felt her insides churn with annoyance. Frustration.

Was he going to come out of his car, or did he actually expect her to walk up to his window?

She stood there awkwardly, her arms at her sides, feeling ridiculous. Just when she thought she couldn't stand it anymore, the convertible top started to glide down. Spanish guitar music was playing.

He had shades on, which annoyed her even further. He had taken off his jacket and tossed it on the seat beside him. His shirt was short-sleeved, and even from where she stood Justine could tell it was of high quality, the color of cantaloupe with vertical lime stripes. His arms were tanned, and she watched him reach over to grab a large brown envelope, turn down the music slightly and step out of his car. Without taking his gaze off her.

"I wanted you to have a glance at this, Miss Winter." He held out the envelope.

Justine crossed her arms and frowned.

"It's a development proposal drafted by an architect friend of mine. I would be happy to go over it with you." When she didn't respond, he added, "I would appreciate it if you at least gave the plan and the drawings a glance. They might help dispel some of your doubts about my venture."

Justine stared at him coldly. "I'm not interested, Mr. Forrest. You're wasting your time." Her entire face felt flushed, the refreshed feeling after her swim completely dissipated.

He stood there for a moment, his mouth curving into a half-smile. He held the envelope in front of her for a few moments, then turned and tossed it into the Mustang. "Very well, Miss *Wintry*. Perhaps you need some time to think about it."

"Not at all," she returned curtly. "And my last name is *Winter*."

"So sorry, Miss *Winter*." He took off his sunglasses. "And mine's *Forrester*."

Justine's knees felt weak. His dark eyes blazed at her in the sunlight. She knew she should apologize as well, but when she opened her mouth no words came out. She watched him get behind the wheel and put on his sunglasses.

"But you can call me Casson," he said, and grinned before turning on the ignition.

He cranked up the music and with a few swift turns was out of her driveway and out of sight.

Now that he could no longer see Justine Winter in his rearview mirror, Casson concentrated on the road ahead. He loved this area. His family—which had included him and his younger brother Franklin—had always spent part of the summer at their friends' cottage on Georgian Bay, and the tradition had continued even after they'd lost Franklin to leukemia when he was only seven years old.

Even after his parents and their friends had passed away, and the cottage had been sold, Casson had felt compelled to return regularly to the area. There would always be twinges of grief at his memories, but Casson didn't want the memories to fade, and the familiar landscape brought him serenity and healing as well.

Determined to find a location for what would be "Franklin's Resort," he had spent months searching for the right spot. After finding out that the Russell properties were for sale, he'd hired a pilot to fly him over Georgian Bay's 30,000 Islands area to scope out the parcels of land, which were on either side of Winter's Haven.

The seductive curve of sandy beach, with the surf foaming along its edge, and the cottages set back among the thickly wooded terrain had given him a thrill. The bay, with its undulating waves of blue and indigo, sparkling like an endless motherlode of diamonds, had made his heartbeat quicken.

The sudden feeling that Franklin was somehow with him had sent shivers along his arms. Casson had always sensed that the spirit of Franklin was in Georgian Bay, and he'd had an overwhelming feeling that his search was over. He'd made the Russells an offer he was sure they couldn't refuse and had then turned his attention to Winter's Haven.

Now, as he sped past the mixed forest of white pine, birch and cedar, he caught glimpses of Georgian Bay, its surface glittering with pinpoints of sunlight. A mesmerizing blue.

Just like Justine Winter's eyes.

The thought came before he could stop it. His lips curved into a smile. He hadn't expected the new owner of Winter's Haven to be so...*striking.* So outspoken. From the way her father had spoken he had expected someone a little more shy and reticent, someone more *fragile*.

"I've decided not to sell after all," Thomas Winter had said, when he'd phoned him a few months earlier. "My daughter Justine has had enough of the big city—and a bad relationship—and she needs a new direction in life. A new venture that will lift her spirits. My wife and I have decided to offer the business to her and finally do some travelling. Winter's Haven will be a good place for Justine to recover..."

Recover?

Casson had wondered if Mr. Winter's daughter was emotionally healthy enough to maintain a business that had obviously thrived for years under her parents' management. Which was why he'd decided to wait a couple of months before approaching her with his offer. With any luck the place would be in a shambles and she'd be ready to unload it. And even if that wasn't the case, he'd come to learn that most people had their price...

At first glance Justine Winter had seemed anything but fragile. She had dashed into the office with damp hair, flushed cheeks, tanned arms and shapely legs under a flowered skirt that swayed with the movement of her hips. And as he'd sauntered toward her his eyes hadn't been able to help sweeping over that peekaboo top, glimpsing the black bra underneath...

He had felt a sudden jolt. He had come to Winter's Haven expecting a depressed young woman who had needed her parents to save her by offering her a lifeline. *Not a woman whose firm curves and just-out-of-the-shower freshness had caused his body to stir uncontrollably...*

And then she had turned to face him, her blue-gray eyes striking him like a cresting wave. And, no, it *hadn't* looked like the place was anywhere near in a shambles, with her pining away for her former lover.

He had watched her expression flit from disbelief about his purchase of the adjoining Russell properties to wide-eyed amazement at his offer. And he had felt a momentary smugness when her gaze shifted and became dreamy.

She had been thinking about what she could do with the money. He'd been sure of it.

And then her gaze had snapped back to meet his, and the ice-blue hardness of her eyes and her flat-out refusal of his money had caused something within him to strike back with the prediction that she would eventually cave at a higher price.

He had almost been able to feel the flinty sparks from her eyes searing his back as he'd left...

Casson drove into the larger of the Russell properties—*his* properties now—and after greeting his dog, Luna, he grabbed a cold beer and plunked himself down into one of the Muskoka chairs on the wraparound porch.

Luna ran around the property for a while and then settled down beside him. Casson stared out at the flickering waters of the bay. It already felt like he had been there for years.

This really was a slice of heaven. Prime Group of Seven country.

Casson had grown up hearing about the Group of Seven as if they were actual members of his family. His grandfather's friendship with A. J. Casson—who had been his neighbor for years—and the collection of Casson paintings he had eventually bequeathed to his only daughter, had resulted in Casson's childhood being steeped in art knowledge and appreciation. Not only of A. J. Casson's work, but the work of all the Group of Seven artists.

And now here he was as an adult, just days away from sponsoring and hosting Franklin & Casson on the Bay— an exhibition of the paintings of Franklin Carmichael and A. J. Casson at the Charles W. Stockey Centre for the Performing Arts in Parry Sound. The center was renowned for its annual Festival of the Sound summer classical music festival, as well as for housing the Bobby Orr Hall of Fame—a sports museum celebrating Parry Sound's ice hockey legend.

It was all close to falling into place. This exhibition was the first step in making his resort a reality. Franklin's Resort would be a non-profit venture, to honor the memory of its namesake and to provide a much-needed safe haven for families.

At the exhibition Casson would outline his plan to create a luxury haven for children after cancer treatment— a place to restore their strength and their spirit with their families, who would all have experienced trauma. The families would enjoy a week's stay at the resort at no cost.

He had no doubt that the Carmichael/Casson exhibition would be successful in raising awareness and backing for his venture. And the *pièce de résistance* was a painting from his own personal collection. It was one of A.J. Casson's early pieces, *Storm on the Bay*, and had been given to Casson's grandfather when A.J. had been his neighbor. It was the prize in a silent auction, and Casson hoped it would attract a collector's eye and boost the development of the resort.

A lump formed in his throat. He had been only ten when Franklin had died, and although he had not been able to articulate his feelings at the time, he knew now that he had coped with his feeling of helplessness by overcompensating in other ways. Helping with chores; learning to make meals as a teen and excelling at school, in sport and at university. Subconsciously he had done everything he could not to add to his parents' misery.

After pursuing a Business and Commerce degree in Toronto, Casson had returned home to Huntsville—an hour away from Parry Sound—to purchase a struggling hardware store downtown. He had been grateful for the money his grandfather had left him in his will, which had enabled him to put a down payment on the business, and he'd vowed that he would make his grandpa proud.

Within a couple of years the store had been thriving, and Casson had set his sights on developing a chain. Six more years and he'd had stores in Gravenhurst, Bracebridge, Port Carling and—his most recent acquisition—a hardware store in Parry Sound, just outside the Muskoka area.

Casson had revived each store with innovative changes and promotions that would appeal both to the locals and the seasonal property-owners. The Forrest Hardware chain had made him a multi-millionaire by the time he was thirty-four.

Losing his brother at such a young age had affected Casson deeply; he hadn't been able to control what happened to Franklin, so he had learned to take control of his own life early. He was still in control now, steering his expanding hardware chain, and yet he had no control over Justine Winter. Not that he wanted to control *her*; he simply wanted control of Winter's Haven. Her property was the last piece of the puzzle that he needed to fit into his plan.

Earlier, the thought had flashed into his mind to invite Justine to go with him to the Stockey Centre the following day—to show her that his motive when it came to the Russell properties and Winter's Haven was not one of financial gain, as she had immediately assumed. However, the fact that he'd even considered telling Justine the truth shocked him... He *never* talked about Franklin. He'd learned to keep those feelings hidden.

Why had he nearly told her?

It might have had something to do with those initial sparks between them...

Anyway, he hadn't wanted to show his vulnerability or how much this venture meant to him as a tribute to his brother. So instead he had thrust his offer upon Justine with the arrogant expectation that she would be so dazzled by the amount she'd agree to it, no questions asked.

And if she *had* asked questions he wouldn't have been prepared to open up his soul to her. Tell her that he was doing this not only for Franklin, but for himself. For all the lonely years he had spent after his brother's death, unable to share his grief with his mother, whose pain at losing Franklin had created an emotional barrier that even Casson could not penetrate. His father had thrown himself into his work, and when he was at home had seemed to have only enough energy to provide a comforting shoulder for his wife.

It was only in later years that Casson had contemplated going to a few sessions of grief counselling. It had been emotionally wrenching to relive the past, but Casson had eventually forgiven his parents. It had been during that time that his idea for a resort to help kids like Franklin had begun to take root. What he hadn't been able to do for Franklin at ten years of age, he could now do for many kids like him—including his godson Andy, his cousin Veronica's only child.

Andy's cancer diagnosis a year earlier had shocked Casson, and triggered memories and feelings of the past. Supporting Andy and Veronica during subsequent treatment had made him all the more determined to see his venture become a reality. Casson just wished his parents were still alive to witness it as well…

Franklin & Casson on the Bay was only a few days away. His plan was on target. There was one key missing.

And Justine had it.

Casson took a gulp of his beer. *Damn*, it was hot. He loosened his tie. As he contemplated changing and going for a swim, a vision of Justine Winter standing with wet hair in her bathing suit flashed in his memory. That turquoise one-piece had molded to the heady curves of her body, and her tanned thighs and legs had been sugared with white beach sand that sparkled in the sun. Her hair, straight and dripping water over her cleavage… An enchanting sea creature…

He had sensed her discomfort, knew how exposed she'd felt. If only she knew what the sight of her body had done to *him*.

Casson unbuttoned his shirt and went inside to change. A dip in the refreshing waters of Georgian Bay would cool him down—inside and out…

Casson stretched out on the edge of the dock to let the sun heat his body. There was nothing like that first dive into the bay when your body was sizzling hot. He closed his eyes for a few moments, and when he opened them, wondered if he had dozed off. Although he had slapped on some sunscreen earlier, his skin felt slightly more burnished.

He scrambled to his feet and Luna shuffled excitedly

around him. Casson heard a faint voice calling him, but when he turned there was nobody there. There was some rustling in the trees and a flash of blue, followed by the shrill call of a blue jay.

Casson looked down at the water, anticipating the bracing pleasure awaiting him. A hint of a breeze tickled his nose, followed by the faint smell of fish. He blinked at his reflection, wiping at the sweat prickling his eyes. In the gently lapping bay he imagined Franklin beside him, wearing his faded Toronto Blue Jays cap, his skinny arms holding a fishing rod with its catch of pickerel and his toothy grin. And the sparkle in his eyes…

And then the sparkle was lost in the sun's glittering reflection and the image was swallowed up by the waves. Casson dropped down to sit at the edge of the dock, his original intention forgotten. He continued to peer intensely into the water, and it was only moments later, when Luna pressed against him to lick his face, that Casson realized she was licking the salty tears on his cheeks.

CHAPTER TWO

THE RAIN DRUMMING on the roof woke Justine an hour before she'd intended. She didn't mind at all, though. Rainy days were good for doing odd jobs, renovating an empty cottage, or just relaxing with a good book in the window seat in her room. It was one of her favorite reading spots, with its plush flowery cushions and magnificent view of the bay.

Justine changed into jeans and a nautical-style T-shirt, brushed her hair back into a ponytail, and went downstairs. After having a quick coffee and one of the banana yogurt muffins she had made last night, she grabbed her umbrella and dashed to her car.

Despite the fact that she had always liked this kind of weather, Justine couldn't help but feel a twist in her stomach, remembering the rainy day she'd walked into Robert Morrell's law office for an interview. She'd been twenty-four, and had graduated *summa cum laude* in Law and Justice from the University of Toronto. That and her business electives had impressed Robert and Clare, his senior administrative assistant, who would be retiring in six months, and Robert had offered her the job the following day.

As time had progressed the initial rapport between them had developed into an easy friendship. Justine had sometimes stayed at the office during lunchtime, catching up on paperwork between bites of her sandwich or salad. And

Robert, to her surprise, had often done the same, claiming he wanted to go home at a decent hour so his wife wouldn't complain that he was "married to the job."

Shared conversations had begun to take on a more personal note during Justine's second year at the office, and when Robert had started to hint at his marriage breakdown she had felt compelled to listen and comfort him as he'd revealed more and more.

The underlying spark of attraction between them had not come to the forefront until after his divorce had almost become final. Then, with nothing and nobody to hold them back, Justine and Robert had begun dating...

Justine forced Robert out of her thoughts as she turned the corner and drove into the parking lot of the hardware store, finding a spot near the front doors. Something looked vaguely different about the place, and then she realized the signage had changed. New ownership, she had heard.

Without bothering to get her umbrella, she dashed into the store and toward the wood department.

"May I help you?"

Justine turned to find a middle-aged employee smiling at her.

"Yes, thank you, Mr. Blake," she said, smiling back. "Glad to see you're still here. I'd like to order some cedar paneling for one of the cottages."

"I thought it was you. Back from Toronto, I hear. Your dad told me you'd be taking over Winter's Haven."

Justine nodded. "I'm glad to be back."

As she handed him a piece of paper with the measurements a feeling of contentedness came over her. She *had* made the right decision, coming back home.

This was what she loved about living in a small town— knowing the names of local merchants, dealing with people who knew her parents.

She had felt the call of the big city, and had enjoyed it for a time, but the breakup with Robert and the lonely month that had followed had made her realize how truly *alone* she was. With no job and no meaningful friendships—the people Robert had introduced her to didn't qualify—she'd yearned for the small-town connections of Parry Sound. *Home.* The place she had always felt safe in, nurtured and supported by family, friends and community.

"Are you thinking of running the business on a permanent basis?" Mr. Blake glanced at her curiously.

"I sure am." She beamed. "I can't imagine ever leaving Winter's Haven again."

Mr. Blake glanced over her shoulder, as if he were looking for someone, and then gave her a hesitant smile. "Well, good luck to you. When your order is ready I'll give you a call. You can let me know then when you want the job done."

"Sounds good!" Justine leafed through her bag and took out her car keys. "Thanks, Mr. Blake, and have a great day."

Justine strode toward the exit, wondering why the expression on his face had seemed to change after her saying she couldn't imagine ever leaving Winter's Haven. She grimaced when she came to the door. The rain was coming down in torrents now, and she regretted leaving her umbrella in the car. She would get drenched despite the short distance.

She made a run for it, giving a yelp as she stepped in a sizeable puddle.

"Damn," she muttered as she inserted the wrong key in the lock. She should have brought a rain jacket, she berated herself, slamming the door at last.

Her top was plastered against her, and although she had planned to do some further shopping she was not about to go anywhere in this condition. Her jeans were soaked as well—front and back—and she couldn't wait to get back home, strip everything off and take a shower.

She backed out carefully and drove out of the parking lot. Although it was barely mid-morning the sky had darkened, and she could hear ominous rumbles of thunder. Her wipers were going at full-tilt, but the rain was pelting the windshield so hard that she could barely see through it.

As Justine drove slowly out of the town limits and toward the long country road that would take her home she tried to ignore the clammy feeling of her wet clothes against her skin.

A sudden beeping noise behind her startled her, and she glanced immediately in the rearview mirror. She could see a burgundy pickup truck, but it was impossible to see the driver.

To Justine's consternation the honking became more persistent. The truck didn't have its indicators on, so the driver couldn't be in any kind of trouble. And she didn't imagine it was an admirer. She wasn't unused to appreciative smiles from male drivers once in a while, along with the occasional whistle or honk of their horn, but she doubted that this was the case today.

The rain was subsiding—thank goodness. And as she looked in the rearview mirror again she saw that the driver had his arm out the window, signaling for her to pull over. Now she felt alarmed. Was it a cop? No, not in a pickup truck. And it wouldn't be for speeding…

He honked again and she looked back, but a sudden rush of oncoming cars made her concentrate on the road. She cautiously pressed on the gas pedal. *Too many weirdos on the road,* she thought. She swerved around a bend, and a quick look reassured her that the creep was gone.

She reached the turnoff to Winter's Haven. The rain had stopped and the sun was breaking through the clouds. She clicked off her wipers, headed directly past the office building and turned into the road through a lengthy wooded stretch that led to her driveway. She sighed, but had barely turned off the ignition when she heard the crunch of an approaching vehicle.

A moment later the burgundy pickup truck she'd thought she had seen the last of pulled up right next to her.

She was more angry than worried now. *How dare he?* Without a thought to any potential danger, she flung the car door open and got out, her cheeks flaming. The man had gotten out of his truck and was leaning against it, casually silent, as he watched Justine march stormily up to him.

"Why are you following me?" she demanded, stopping a few feet away from him. "It was bad enough trying to drive with you tailgating and honking incessantly. Can't you find a more civilized way of pursuing a woman? Highway dramatics don't do anything for me."

The man's mouth twisted and he continued to stare at her through dark sunglasses. A few seconds passed. Why wasn't he answering her? Maybe she should have stayed in the car. He might have a knife. She could scream, but nobody was close enough to hear her.

She looked at him closely. She might need to file a report if she managed to get away from him. His faded jeans and jacket seemed ordinary enough, but his bearded face, dark glasses and baseball cap might very well be concealing the face of an escaped criminal. Would she be able to run back to her car? No, she'd never make it if he intended to pursue her.

She shivered and said shakily, "What do you want?"

Another twist of his lips. "Your hubcap flew off a few miles back," he drawled. "So you can relax. I'm not about to attack you."

Justine let out an audible sigh. And then she felt her cheeks start to burn. She had accused him of *pursuing* her.

"I'm usually more civilized when it comes to pursuing women," he said, and laughed, as if he had read her thoughts. "And 'highway dramatics,' as I believe you put it, are not my style."

Justine's discomfiture grew. "I apologize for jumping to the wrong conclusion, but you can hardly blame me, can you?" Her eyes narrowed. "Your voice sounds familiar..."

For some reason, the realization bothered her.

A suspicion suddenly struck her in a way that made her knees want to buckle.

"Haven't figured it out yet?" he said, removing his sunglasses.

Tiger eyes. Damn!

With the cap, sunglasses, casual clothes and truck, and two weeks' growth of beard, she hadn't even suspected.

"It's...*you*!" she sputtered, wide-eyed.

"Nice to see you again, too," Casson Forrester murmured, with the slightest hint of sarcasm. "Actually, I spotted you in the hardware store, but you left before I could reach you. There are a few things I want to discuss with you."

"You didn't have to follow me."

"I didn't think you'd accept my call." His eyes narrowed. "Among other things, I was going to suggest you don't bother paneling or doing any other kind of work if you're going to end up selling the place..."

Justine's eyes flashed their annoyance. "That's your mistaken presumption," she retorted. "And were you eavesdropping on my conversation?"

"I didn't have to. Mr. Blake happened to mention it when I called a staff meeting."

"You *own* Forrest Hardware?" she said slowly. "And Forrest Construction...."

Of course. Forrest was simply an abbreviated form of his name, and an appropriate choice for his chain of stores in the Muskoka area—including the latest one in Parry

Sound. She had briefly noticed the new sign, but the name hadn't registered in her consciousness—least of all the connection with its owner.

She gave a curt laugh. "No wonder you can buy practically anything—or anybody—you want."

"Not always," his tiger eyes glinted. "Although it's not for lack of trying."

She shivered. And at the sudden clap of thunder they both looked up to the sky. The clouds had blocked out the sun again, and a few errant raindrops had started coming down. Realizing she had been standing there in her wet T-shirt and jeans, her hair flattened against her head except for the few strands that were now curling with the humidity, she crossed her arms in front of her.

"Excuse me," she said icily, "I'm going to have to leave." She turned away, then glanced back. "I'll look for the hubcap later."

She retrieved her keys and bag from her car and strode toward the house. When she was halfway there the rain intensified, making her curse indelicately as she ran the rest of the way. Breathing a sigh of relief as she reached the door of the porch, she closed it behind her as another clap of thunder reverberated around her.

Hearing the porch door creak open again, she turned around to close it tightly. But it wasn't the wind that had forced it open. It was Casson Forrester. And a big dog.

"I hope you don't mind if we wait out the storm in your house." He closed the porch door firmly. "Driving would be foolish in almost zero visibility. And Luna is terrified of storms." He took off his cap and grinned at Justine. "Would you be so kind as to hand me a towel? I'd hate for us to drip all over your house."

Justine blinked at the sight before her. Casson Forrester and his big panting dog, both dripping wet.

Casson took off his baseball cap and flung it toward

the hook on the wall opposite him. It landed perfectly. He looked at her expectantly, one hand in a pocket of his jeans, the other patting Luna on the head. Both pant legs were soaked, along with his jean jacket.

She tore her gaze away from his formfitting jeans and looked at Luna. She'd make a mess in her house, for sure. She sighed inwardly. Did she have any choice but to supply this dripping duo with towels? She couldn't very well let them stand there.

Anther clap of thunder caused Luna to give a sharp yelp, and she rose from her sitting position, looking like she wanted to bolt.

Justine blurted, "I'll just be a minute," and hurried inside, closing the door with a firm click. She wasn't going to let either of them inside until they were relatively drip-free.

She scrambled up the stairs to the hall closet near her room, fished out a couple of the largest towels she could find and then, as an afterthought, rifled through another section to find a pair of oversized painting overalls. He could get out of his jeans and wear these while his clothes dried.

Unable to stop the image of his bare legs invading her thoughts, she flushed, and hoped her cheeks wouldn't betray her.

She walked slowly down the stairs, and after taking a steadying breath re-entered the porch.

"I found a pair of painting overalls. You can get out of your wet clothes and throw them into the dryer," she said coolly. "There's a washroom just inside this door, next to the laundry room. If you want, I can pat down your dog."

She handed him the overalls and one of the towels.

He reached out for them and the towel fell open. His eyebrows rose and he glanced at her with a quirky half-smile. "I like the color, but I'm afraid they're a tad too small for me. But thanks."

Justine wanted the floor to split open and swallow her up. She snatched the hot pink bikini panties from where they clung to the towel and shoved them in her pocket. They must have been in the dryer together. She bent down to dry Luna, not wanting Casson to see how mortified she felt.

She let out her breath when she heard him enter the house.

Luna whimpered at the next rumble of thunder and started skittering around the porch. "Come here, Luna, you big scaredy-cat," she said. "Come on." To her surprise the dog gave a short bark and came to her, tail wagging. "Good dog. Now, lie down so I can dry you."

Luna obeyed, and Justine patted her head and dark coat with the towel. She was a mixed breed—Labrador Retriever, for sure, and maybe some German Shepherd. Her doleful eyes and the coloring around the face and head—tan and white, with a black peak in the middle of her forehead—made Justine wonder if there were some beagle ancestry as well.

"Don't you have pretty eyes?" she murmured, chuckling as Luna rewarded her with a lick on the hand.

They looked as if someone had taken eyeliner to them. And the brown of her coat tapered off to tan before ending in white paws, making it seem as if she had dipped them in white paint.

"You're such a pretty girl—you know that?" Justine gave her a final patting and set down the towel. "Even if you've left your fur all over my towel."

Justine crouched forward and scratched behind Luna's ears. Before Justine could stop her Luna had sprung forward to lick her on the cheek. Unprepared for the considerable weight of the furry bundle, Justine lost her balance and fell back awkwardly on the floor.

"Luna, come!"

Casson's voice was firm, displeased. She hadn't heard him come back.

"It's all right, she was just being affectionate," Justine hurried to explain. "I lost my footing."

She scrambled to get up, and her embarrassment dissipated when she saw him standing there in a T-shirt and the white overalls. It wasn't the T-shirt that made her want to burst out laughing. Under different circumstances those muscled arms would certainly have elicited emotions other than laughter. It was the overalls—the not-so-oversized overalls.

They fit him snugly, and only came down to just above his ankles. How could someone so ruggedly handsome look so...so *dorky* at the same time? She covered her mouth with her hand, but couldn't help her shoulders from quaking as she laughed silently. Here was Mr. Perfect—the stylish, wealthy entrepreneur Casson Forrester—wearing something that looked like it belonged to Mr. Bean.

Casson's eyes glinted. "What? You find this fashion statement humorous? Hmm... I suppose it does detract from your previous impression of me, however—"

The boom of thunder drowned out his words, and as the rain pelted down even harder Justine motioned toward the door. Once they were inside she ran to make sure all the windows were closed. The rain lashed against the panes, obliterating any view at all. She turned on a lamp in the living room.

"Have a seat." She gestured toward the couch. "I need to check the windows upstairs and change my clothes too." She glanced at Luna, who was whimpering. "You might want to turn on the TV to drown out the thunder."

After Justine had left, Casson smirked at the memory of her face when she'd turned to find him and Luna inside her porch. Her eyes had almost doubled in size, with blinking lashes that had reminded him of delicate hummingbird wings. Peach lips had fallen open and then immediately pursed. It had taken him everything not to burst out laughing.

Although laughing was not what he'd wanted to do when her pink panties had emerged from that towel… Her cheeks had immediately turned almost the same intense color, and he'd felt glad he hadn't given in to the impulse to hand them to her.

It had been her turn to smirk, though, when he'd appeared in these painting overalls. Casson knew he looked ridiculous—but, given the situation, beggars couldn't be choosers.

He grabbed the remote and found a classical music channel that would diffuse some of the thunder noise. Sitting back on the couch, he looked around with interest. The stone fireplace across from him was the focal point of the room, with its rustic slab of oak as mantel, and the Parry Sound stone continued upward to the pine-lined cathedral ceiling.

He drew a quick intake of breath as his gaze fell on the Group of Seven print above the mantel. *Mirror Lake*, by Franklin Carmichael. His eyes followed the curves of the multi-colored hills, the bands of varying hues of red, blue, purple, turquoise, green and gold and the perfect stillness of the lake, its surface a gleaming mirror.

This piece always tugged at his emotions and brought back so many memories—memories he didn't want to conjure up right now, with Justine set to return at any moment.

Casson's gaze shifted to the oversized recliners flanking the fireplace, one with a matching ottoman. Their colors, along with the couch and love seat, were an assortment of burnt sienna, brown and sage-green, with contrasting cushions. The wide-plank maple flooring, enhanced by a large forest green rug with a border of pine cones and branches, gave the place an authentic cottage feel, and the rustic coffee table and end tables complemented the décor.

The far wall behind the love seat featured huge windows of varying sizes, the top ones arching toward the peak of the ceiling and the largest one in the middle a huge bay window, providing what must be a spectacular view of the bay when the rain wasn't pounding against the panes.

A well-stocked bookshelf against one wall, eclectic lighting, and a vase containing a mix of wildflowers enhanced what Casson considered to be the ideal Georgian Bay cottage. He sat back, nodding, making mental notes for his future resort cottages.

After making a few investigative circles around the room Luna plunked down at his feet, panting slightly, her ears perked, as if she were expecting the next clap of thunder. Casson leaned forward to give her a reassuring pat and she grumbled contentedly and settled into a more relaxed position.

Casson wished *he* could feel more relaxed, but the painting overalls were compressing him in too many places. He wondered what Miss *Wintry*'s reaction would be if he stretched out on the couch. At least then he wouldn't feel like his masculinity was being compromised, he thought wryly. He checked the time on his watch. Sighing, he lay back and rested his head on one cushion.

Ah, relief.

He closed his eyes and listened to the classical music, accompanied by the rain pelting against the windows. A picture of Justine changing into dry clothes popped into his head.

Would she be slipping on those pink panties?

What was he doing?

He was here to wait for his clothes to dry and the storm to pass, not to imagine her naked…

* * *

Upstairs in her room, Justine peeled off her clothes, dried herself vigorously, and wished she could jump into a hot shower. But that would have to wait until Casson was gone. She didn't want to be thinking about him while she was… undressed. She changed quickly into white leggings and a long, brightly flowered shirt.

As an afterthought she opened her closet and moved a few boxes until she found the one she was looking for. Although Christmas was months away, she stashed away presents whenever she could instead of waiting for the last minute. The box she opened contained a dressing robe she had picked out for her dad. It was forest green, with burgundy trim at the wrists and collar, and she had embroidered the letters 'WH', for Winter's Haven, on one side. She had wanted to surprise her dad with this as a new idea—providing a robe in each cottage, like they did in hotels.

She lifted it out of the box and its tissue wrapping and hooked it over her arm. At the door she hesitated, feeling a sudden twinge of guilt, and then, before she could change her mind, she strode downstairs.

The TV was on and Luna was lying at Casson's feet. Justine held out the robe. "I thought you might appreciate this instead," she said.

He stood up and took it from her, before tossing the cushion he was holding back on the couch. "Indeed I do," he said, his jaw twitching. "Now I know you're not all flint and arrows."

Justine opened her mouth to voice a retort but his hand came up.

"No offence intended," he said. "I realize we didn't start off on exactly a positive note but, given the present circumstances, could we perhaps call a truce of some sort?"

Justine was taken aback. "We're not in a battle, Mr. Forrester. So there's no need for a truce. Excuse me. I'm going to put on some fresh coffee. Care for a cup?" She turned toward the open-concept kitchen/dining room.

"Love some coffee," he replied. "Just milk or cream, no sugar. And you'll have to excuse *me* as well. I'm dying to get out of these overalls."

He smirked and headed toward the washroom. Luna lifted her head quizzically, gave a contented grumble, and promptly settled back into her nap.

When Casson came back into the living room he had the overalls neatly folded. He placed them on a side chair and then sat down on the couch. The robe fit him well, which meant it would have been a size or two too big for her dad.

"That coffee smells great," he drawled, tightening the sash on the robe before crossing his legs.

Justine came out of the kitchen with a tray holding two mugs, a small container of cream and a plate of muffins. She caught her breath at seeing him there, one leg partially exposed. She felt a warm rush infuse her body. It was such an *intimate* scenario: Casson leaning back against the couch, totally relaxed, as if he were the owner of the place.

She saw his gaze flicker over her body as she approached. She wanted to squirm. Her jaw tensed. This was *her* place. Why did she suddenly feel like she was at a disadvantage?

She would *not* let him know that his presence was affecting her. She would treat him like any other cottage guest. Politely, respectfully. And hopefully the heavens would soon clam up and she could send him on his way. His clothes shouldn't take too long to dry.

She set the tray down on the coffee table and, picking up the plate of four muffins, held it out to him. "Banana yogurt. Homemade."

"Thank you, Miss Winter."

He reached forward and took one. At the same time

Luna lifted her head, sniffing excitedly. Before Justine had a chance to move the plate Luna had a muffin in her jaws. Startled, Justine tipped the plate and stumbled over Casson's foot. She felt herself falling backward, and a moment later landed in the last place she'd ever want to land. A steaming volcano would have been preferable.

She felt his arms closing around her. The muffin was still in his hand.

"Now that you've fallen right into my lap," he murmured huskily in her right ear, "would you like to share my muffin?"

CHAPTER THREE

JUSTINE COULD FEEL Casson's breath on the side of her neck. She shivered involuntarily. His left arm was around her waist and his right arm was elevated, holding the muffin. His robe had opened slightly in the commotion and, glancing downward, she saw to her consternation that one bare leg was under her.

She was sitting on his bare leg.

Her head snapped up. She was glad he couldn't see her face. She needed to get off him. But to do so would mean pushing down against him to get some leverage. She bit her lip. Why didn't he just give her a push? That would avoid her needing to grind into him.

She cleared her throat. Luna had downed one muffin and was eyeing the two that had flipped onto the coffee table.

"Oh, no, you don't." Casson's voice was firm. "Luna, lie down."

His tone brooked no argument. With a doleful look at the muffins, and then at her master, Luna obeyed with a mournful growl. And then Casson gave Justine a gentle push and she was out of his lap.

He set down his muffin and crouched down to face Luna. "Dogs don't eat muffins," he said emphatically, before giving Luna a low growl.

Justine knew that Casson was emphasizing his alpha male status. Luna responded with a look of shame at being reprimanded, and Justine couldn't help chuckling—which caused Luna to begin wagging her tail, her doggy enthusiasm restored.

Casson lifted an eyebrow and Justine wondered if he was going to growl at *her* for interrupting his disciplinary moment. She saw his mouth twitch and he rose, grabbed his mug and muffin and sat down again.

"And no whining!" he reproached Luna, who flopped back on her side.

Flustered, and trying not to show it, Justine sat down on the love seat. She sipped her coffee and turned to glance out the big bay window. Through the sheets of rain battering the pane she could glimpse patches of sky and bloated gray-black clouds. The water in the bay would be churning, the whitecaps foaming.

"Good muffin." Casson reached for the two still on the coffee table and handed one to her. "I hope these are for sale in the diner."

Justine took it from him and broke off a piece from the top. He seemed totally comfortable sitting in her living room, lounging with nothing on but a robe. She concentrated on pulling the paper back from the muffin and forced herself to avoid glancing at his well-muscled calves and bare feet. And the slight patch of hair in the V below his neck.

She hoped the rain would abate soon. She nibbled at her muffin and took long sips of her coffee, and then realized she hadn't responded.

"Um…yes, we do have muffins for sale in the diner. I usually make a fresh batch every morning…"

The thought of being alone with Casson for much longer was disturbing—mostly because her body was betraying her physically, reacting in a way that was not in sync with her mental perception of Casson Forrester. Her mind had reacted coolly to him from his first arrogant appearance; however, her body was becoming increasingly warm…in ways that made her want to squirm.

"What made you want to return here?" Casson asked with a note of genuine curiosity.

Justine looked up from her muffin and stared blankly at him, her mind scrambling to come up with an alternative explanation, since she had no intention of revealing the truth to him. Her involvement with Robert was none of Casson's business.

"It really doesn't matter," she said, making her voice light. "I'm just glad I returned when I did…to save our humble property from certain demise." She finished her muffin and folded the paper muffin cup several times, before setting it down on the table. "But I'm willing to forget our first negative meeting if you are. We might as well be civil to each other, since you own the Russell properties now."

She picked up her mug and sipped while gazing at him, wondering how he would reply.

Casson stood up and walked to the bay window. He drank his coffee and stared out at the storm. Justine wondered if he intended to ignore her peace offering. Her heart thudded against her chest as she watched him, standing there in the robe. The dark green suited him. His hair was thick, and slightly longer than when she had first seen him, and his short beard did not detract from his good looks. In fact, she was having a hard time deciding if he was more handsome with or without it.

Casson turned then and she started, realizing how intently she had been staring at him.

"Of course we can be civil."

He eyed her for a moment, then left his position at the window to sit down next to her on the love seat. Justine drummed a quiet beat on the arm of the seat, wondering why his eyes were glittering so devilishly. Was the room getting darker, or was it just her imagination?

What they needed was more illumination, she decided, and was about to turn on the other table lamp when a deafening series of thunderclaps shattered her thoughts. Instinctively she swiveled toward Casson, both palms landing flat against his chest. Luna yelped and scampered around the room, barking and panting.

Casson clasped her shoulders. Simultaneously horrified and shocked at her reaction—and his—she stared at him wordlessly, unable to wrench herself away. The rise and fall of his chest as he breathed made her shiver. While his eyes remained fixed on hers, his arms slid around to encircle her back.

Casson's face was suddenly closer, his eyes intense, and Justine felt herself quiver. His lips made contact with hers and involuntarily she closed her eyes. His arms tightened around her and his kiss deepened. Justine felt her lips open as if they had a mind of their own. His gentle exploration ignited sparks of desire along her nerve-endings.

As if he could sense her powerlessness to tear herself away, Casson guided her hands from his chest to the back of his neck. He pressed Justine tightly to him. She responded hungrily, caught in the moment. When she felt the intensity of his kiss diminish she opened her eyes. He pulled slightly away from her, his eyes searing hers, and with a muffled groan lowered his face to nuzzle her neck.

Justine froze, her pulse pounding as erratically as the raindrops beating relentlessly against the window panes. *What were they doing?* How could she have allowed her emotions to get out of control like that? She didn't even *like* this man, nor what he intended to do with his properties, and yet here she was, allowing him to be so *intimate* with her—as if they were a *couple*.

Casson must have felt her stiffening. He straightened and let her arms fall from around his neck. "That was a mistake," she said as steadily as she could, avoiding his gaze. "You'd better go."

She shifted away from him and crossed her arms and legs.

"Don't you want to know what I had to tell you?"

Justine looked at him in bewilderment, and then recalled his earlier words.

"After checking in on my store, I was about to officially start my holidays and head out to Winter's Haven when I spotted you in the paneling department."

Justine frowned. "Why *were* you heading out to Winter's Haven?" She looked at him pointedly. "You didn't actually think there was a chance that I'd change my mind about selling, did you? I told you before—I'm not interested in any proposal you have to make."

Casson's mouth lifted at one corner. "Perhaps you'll change your mind before my stay here is over," he said calmly, stroking his beard.

"That will never happen, believe—" She broke off, her eyes narrowing warily. "What do you mean, your stay *here*?"

"I plan to spend a week of my holiday at Winter's Haven. I'd like to see first-hand how things are run here."

"That's impossible." She gave him a frosty smile. "All twelve cottages are booked to the end of the summer."

Casson stood up lithely. "Just wait here a minute. I'll go check my clothes."

Justine watched him leave the room. Luna bolted after him and he turned, caught Justine's eye, and said, "Go back, Luna. Go lie down."

He winked at Justine and left the room.

Luna padded back and plunked herself down by Justine's feet. Despite her annoyance with Casson, Justine couldn't help being charmed by his big, friendly, generally well-behaved dog.

"Did you enjoy my muffin, you big cutie?" She laughed, patting Luna on the head, and Luna responded with a noisy yawn and rolled to one side. "Oh, now you want a belly rub, do you?" She smiled, leaning forward. "It's obvious your master spoils you."

"She deserves spoiling."

Casson's voice was behind her.

"Her original owner wasn't so nice to her. He left her on the side of the road and took off. Before I could drive up to the spot she was gone. I found her wandering in the woods. Fur all covered with burrs. She was barely a year old."

"Oh...poor baby."

Justine felt tears stinging her eyes. She blinked rapidly, but a few slipped down. Luna sat up and immediately licked her on the cheek.

Not wanting Casson to know how emotional she felt, Justine laughed and said, "Well, maybe I might just give you another muffin, Miss Luna."

"You'd better not," Casson advised. "Muffins are *not* part of her diet."

He stood across from her. He had changed back into his jeans and T-shirt, but his jacket was in his hands. He flung it on the arm of the couch and then reached into the pocket of his jeans. He held out a key that looked all too familiar to Justine.

She blinked. "Where did you get that?" she demanded. She could see the number engraved on it. The number one. For Cottage Number One—the cottage closest to her house. Justine stood up and reached for it. Casson's reaction was quick. He drew back his arm, leaving Justine grasping at thin air.

"How did you get that key? The Elliots are renting that cottage."

"They *were*," he corrected.

"But—"

"Let me explain," he interjected smoothly. "While I was waiting in the restaurant for you a couple of weeks ago I met the Elliots. Talking to them gave me the idea of renting one of your cottages. I made them an offer they couldn't refuse—an all-expenses-paid round-trip anywhere in the world in exchange for their cottage for a week." He smiled. "My timing was perfect. They had recently received an invitation from friends in Greece and declined, since they couldn't afford it. Needless to say, they jumped at my offer."

Justine gaped at him. "I can't *believe* this. They would have said something to me about it. It's against the rules to let someone else stay in their cottage without asking me or Mandy first. And *I* make the final decision."

Another infuriatingly smug smile. "I made them promise not to say anything. I told them I wanted to surprise my *very good friend* with a visit…and a *proposal*."

Justine's stomach muscles tightened. Her anger had been growing with his every word, and at this revelation she exploded. "A *proposal*? You had them believe you were going to *propose* to me?" She glared at him, her hands on her hips. "You had it all planned, didn't you? How dare you manipulate my customers to get what you want? You had no right to use the Elliots that way, for your own advantage."

"Would you have rented out a cottage to me if I had consulted you first?"

His voice was calm, which infuriated her all the more.

"Certainly not! I don't rent out to devious, untrustworthy, manipulative… Oh, what's the use?" She threw her hands up in the air. "You can't teach an old dog new tricks."

Casson chuckled. "I've been called many things by

women—mostly positive, I might add—but 'old dog' is a new one for me." His eyes blazed down at her. "Could you be more specific as to the breed?"

"Don't try to be funny, Mr. Forrester, and make light of this. I'm not amused." She stuck out her hand. "The only decent thing for you to do is to give me back the key. Besides, you now own the properties on either side of me. Why don't you stay on one of *them* to carry out your surveillance tactics?"

"You make me sound like a spy," he countered wryly. "I admit I have a good point, Miss Winter, but although I now *own* the properties I can't really observe the way things are run at Winter's Haven unless I'm actually *here*. Day and night. I thought it fair to at least tell you before settling in."

"Fair?" She filled her lungs with air and let it out in a rush.

"Look, all I want is a week to see how this place operates." His eyes narrowed speculatively. "You never know— the experience might even change my mind about going ahead with a large-scale venture. I may find that a smaller operation is more in keeping with the balance of nature in this area…"

"I have no guarantee that you will change your mind," Justine retorted, "and I refuse to be subjected to your scrutiny for any length of time. Your tactics are futile. I have no intentions of selling to you. *Ever.* Now, give me the key, please. My hand is getting tired." She glowered at him. "What you did may have negative legal implications— which, I assure you, I will look into if you do not return my key."

"There's nothing illegal about what I did and you know it," he said, putting the key back in his jeans pocket. He glanced out the bay window. "I see the rain has stopped for the time being so, if you'll excuse me, I'd like to take advantage of your dining facilities…"

He turned to leave.

"Won't you join me, Miss Winter?"

Justine was sure her face was aflame. "No, thank you," she replied icily, her blue-gray eyes flashing a warning at him. He was pushing her too far. If he didn't soon leave she would throw…throw the remaining muffin or a cushion at him.

"See you later then," he said with a slight nod. "Come on, Luna, I'll take you to your new digs. I don't believe you're allowed in the diner." When he opened the door to the porch, he called out, "Thank you for taking us in. Luna and I enjoyed the muffins…and your company."

Justine swiveled around with a retort on the tip of her tongue, but he was already out the door. Deflated, she sank back down on the love seat.

Casson felt like letting out a boyish cheer as he left Justine's place. *Step one, accomplished!* The rain had diminished to a soft drizzle, which he barely noticed as he opened the side door of his pickup truck. Luna jumped in happily, turning several times in her spot until sinking down, her big brown eyes looking at him expectantly.

Casson grinned and gave her several pats on her rump. "I suppose I should thank you for your part in this, Luna Lu."

Luna gave a soft bark. Casson laughed and reached into his pocket.

"I may not have Miss Winter in the palm of my hand, but it sure felt good having her in my lap."

And tasting her lips.

It was the last thing he'd expected to happen between them. He hadn't planned it, but he couldn't say he regretted it. How could he regret the feel of those soft, pliant lips against his? The way they'd opened to him, let him in deeper? The feel of her under that thin T-shirt, pressed against him so tightly? A mistake, she'd called it. But he had felt the electricity between them as she withdrew.

He wondered if she suspected he was using his masculine wiles to influence her and weaken her resolve about refusing to sell. That was not his intention, but he doubted she would believe him if he attempted to explain. So of course he had feigned indifference at her withdrawal, and proceeded to explain why he wanted to stay at Winter's Haven.

He drove back to the Russell house—*his* house now— and set down his briefcase on the kitchen table. He pulled out a thick folder containing the deeds to his new properties. Now that he was actually on the main property he wanted to examine the maps and surveyors' documents again. He wanted to become familiar with every curve, corner and contour of his land and shoreline.

Even on paper, the Russell and Winter properties occupied an impressive stretch of the Georgian Bay shoreline. The Russells had cleared very little of this property—just enough to snake a path through the dense forest and construct their home on the main parcel and a small cottage on the second one.

Casson peered closely at the map showing the zoning of the adjoining properties. He examined the boundaries of Winter's Haven. It was obvious the Winters had also endeavored to maintain the rugged features of their property. Even though they had eventually added twelve cottages to the land, and an office/diner, they, too, were built with minimal clearing and, like the Russell property, sat further back from the shoreline.

Casson stared at one of the more detailed zoning maps. He shuffled through the folder and pulled out an older document. He rubbed his jaw thoughtfully as he compared them. He was no zoning expert, but he was certain there was a discrepancy in the documents. The older one showed the adjoining properties before any structures had been built. The document showing the addition of the properties revealed something that made him start.

Why hadn't this been brought to his attention? Had the realtor even been aware of it?

Casson knew that both structures had been built in the fifties, and evidently had been beautifully maintained, with occasional renovations, but one thing he hadn't known was the way a section of the Winter home had been erected on a slice of land that clearly belonged to the Russells.

Casson let out a deep breath. Justine's place was sitting partially on *his* property.

He was certain she had absolutely no knowledge of this. Her parents probably didn't either. Or if they did they hadn't revealed it to Justine. It might have been an oversight that the Russells had dismissed, given that they owned so much land. *And* they had been the best of friends with the Winters. Mr. Winter had said as much, when he and Casson had first discussed the potential sale of Winter's Haven.

Casson drummed his fingers on the smooth surface of the table. He wasn't sure he wanted to share his findings with his new neighbor. Not just yet. But he would write a letter to Justine and wait for the appropriate time to give it to her.

He pulled out his laptop and quickly typed it up, ending with an invitation to meet him and discuss options. He was glad he had brought his portable printer with him—a habit, since he did so much travelling. After printing out a copy, he placed the letter and the other documents in an envelope and into his briefcase, along with his laptop.

Casson looked around. There would be time enough to enjoy his new place after a week at Winter's Haven.

With a feeling of anticipation for the week ahead, Casson grabbed his briefcase and the one piece of luggage that he had packed the night before. Heading out to his truck with Luna, he began to whistle.

He couldn't wait to settle in to Cottage Number One.

CHAPTER FOUR

NONE OF THE cottagers were in the diner yet. Justine glanced at the board indicating the special of the day—turkey cranberry burgers with arugula salad—and helped herself to a cup of coffee before sitting at one of the tables by the window. Mandy was still in the office, on the phone with a booking. Justine had waited for a bit, anxious to tell her what Casson Forrester had had the nerve to do, but Mandy had waved her away, indicating she would join her when she was done.

Justine sipped her coffee and looked out at the bay. The sky was a slate of gray, ruffled with layers of low cloud. She thought about Casson Forrester settling in to Cottage Number One and felt a shiver run through her body.

She replayed earlier events in her mind—from her realization that the jerk following her was Casson, to his barging into her home with Luna and the deafening series of thunderclaps that had caused her to end up in Casson's arms. The last thing she had ever imagined when he'd first strode into the office was that she'd be thoroughly kissed by him in her own home...*and that she'd thoroughly enjoy it.*

She wasn't sure how long she had sat frozen on the love seat after Casson had left. She'd felt like she had been tossed about in a whirlwind, and had had to let her brain and body restore its calm and balance. Her feelings had alternated between fury at being manipulated and helplessness. She'd pondered calling a local police officer she knew, who had breakfast regularly in the diner. But what could he do, really? Perhaps she needed to consult a lawyer to see if there was a way of getting Casson Forrester off her property…

Do you really want him off your property?

Justine started at the tiny inner voice that had popped into her mind. To be honest with herself, if Casson had been renting a cottage for a week or more, without any intention to take over, she would have been happy—*thrilled* would be more accurate. After all, who *wouldn't* want to have the pleasure of looking at such a fine specimen of a man for any length of time? Despite the fact that she had been duped by Robert, she wasn't so jaded that she could ignore the presence of someone as handsome as Casson.

But the fact of the matter was that Casson had an ulterior motive in staying at Winter's Haven. And even if he *had* kissed her it was her property he wanted, not *her*.

"Hey, Justine. What are you dreaming about?" Mandy smiled and sat down across from her.

Justine snapped out of her thoughts and took a deep breath. "Remember Casson Forrester, who was here last week?"

Mandy's eyes widened. "Mr. Gorgeous, you mean? The hunk I wish they'd name an ice cream flavor after?"

"Mandy! You're *engaged*, remember?" Justine couldn't help laughing.

"I'm engaged—not blind!"

"Well, Mr. Forrester has just finagled his way into staying at Winter's Haven. He wants to observe how things are run up close. I guess he figures he'll find a way to convince me to sell. He's staying in Cottage Number One for a week."

Justine paused, watching Mandy's face wrinkle in confusion. She clearly had no idea of the transaction between Casson and the Elliots.

"*What?* How can that be? The Elliots are in there!"

Justine explained, then sat back, crossing her arms. "Now, what should we do? Call Constable Phil? A lawyer?"

"Geez…" Mandy's brows furrowed. "Do we want to complicate things? Other than being hot, Casson Forrester seems pretty harmless. Ambitious, maybe, but not dangerous. Look, you're not going to sell, so why don't you just let him enjoy the cottage and in a week's time you can kiss him goodbye!"

Justine knew Mandy was speaking figuratively, but the thought of kissing Casson again gave her a rush. She felt her cheeks burn, and saw Mandy looking at her speculatively, but she wasn't ready to share what had happened…

"I hate to spring another surprise on you, Justine, but the call I just took…" Mandy sighed. "It was *Robert*. He wants to see you. He tried to book a cottage."

Justine just about dropped her coffee mug. She set it down and stared at Mandy. "What for?"

Mandy took a deep breath. "He told me that he knows he made mistakes but that he hopes you'll give him a chance to apologize."

"He's the *last* person I want to see," Justine moaned, covering her face with her hands.

"I hope you're not talking about *me,* Miss Winter."

Justine slowly let her hands slip from her face.

"And I hope you don't mind if I join you for lunch." Casson looked at her directly. "I haven't picked up any supplies for my stay yet, and I hear the locals come to eat here a lot, which convinces me I should try it." He glanced over at Mandy. "Hello, Miss Holliday. Nice to see you again." He offered his hand.

"My pleasure." Mandy beamed. "And, yes—please join us."

Justine wanted to scowl at her, but Casson had turned to look at her again.

"Only if the Boss Lady agrees," he said, amusement tinging his voice.

"That's fine," Justine said, trying to keep from clenching her teeth.

Casson pulled out a chair to sit next to Mandy.

"Actually, I'm not staying for lunch," Mandy said. "My fiancé's taking me out." She waved at Justine and Casson. "See you later."

She glanced slyly at Justine, and Justine shot her a *Just wait 'till you get back* glare.

When a waitress walked over and set down two glasses of water for them Casson thanked her and looked over at Justine expectantly.

Justine flushed. "Hi, Mel. Casson Forrester—meet Melody Green, our wonderful waitress."

After Melody had taken their orders—turkey burger for her and fish and chips for him—Casson flashed Justine a smile. "I can see why people want to stay at Winter's Haven," he smiled. "The cottage is perfect. Luna has already found her favorite spot." As Justine's eyebrows went up, he said, "Couch in the living room. She's curled up on it right now." He chuckled. "But I don't doubt she'll find a way to join me on the bed tonight."

Casson saw something flicker in Justine's eyes. He might be totally out in left field, but was that a spark of—?

"She's a nice dog," Justine said grudgingly.

"And she's very protective of her owner." Casson grinned.

"I can't imagine *you'd* need protecting."

Casson gave a hearty laugh. "I might—if the owner of

this place becomes aggressive with me." He gazed quiz-zically at Justine. "But, then again, Luna likes you. If you tried to tackle me she'd probably do nothing. Or think we were playing and try to join in." He gazed at her for a few seconds.

Justine's face wrinkled into a frown. "There would be no reason for me to tackle you, Mr. Forrester."

"*Please.* Call me Casson. After all, we'll be neighbors for the next week. By the way—I have a couple of guests coming to spend the weekend with me. I figured it was okay, since the cottage has a loft and a pull-out couch. But I did want to mention it in case there's an extra charge."

He looked expectantly at Justine. She was slightly taken aback, judging by her hesitation in responding and the sudden tapping of her foot against the table leg, which she seemed unaware of.

"Yes, a limited number of guests are allowed. There is a minimal charge."

"Great—just add it to my bill." Casson nodded in satisfaction.

"Here are your orders," Melody announced cheerfully. "Enjoy." She placed a platter in front of each of them. "Is there anything else you'd like to drink, Mr. Forrester?"

"Water will be fine, thanks." He slipped her a couple of bills. "No change needed." He smiled at Melody's look of appreciation, and then picked up one of his fries. "*Bon appétit.*" He winked at Justine.

They ate silently for a couple of minutes, and even though Casson tried not to make it obvious he couldn't help glancing occasionally at Justine. While he enjoyed his fresh-cut fries and battered whitefish, Justine was try-ing to eat a massive burger delicately. When she set her bun down in frustration he saw a smear of ketchup on her cheek and chin. He had a crazy desire to lean over and lick it off her face.

But of course he wouldn't.

Casson watched as she ran her tongue over her lips and just outside her mouth. His heart did a flip. He picked up a clean napkin and, rising slightly, reached over and gently wiped at the two spots of ketchup, his eyes locking with hers.

It was like looking into the bay. *Deep blue. A blue that could swallow you up.*

He didn't know how long he stayed in that position, half out of his seat, but when he sat down he felt like something had knocked him out temporarily. Justine's face was flushed, and she immediately looked down and concentrated on finishing her burger.

"By the way, it seems that one of your prospective guests couldn't book a cottage here, so he asked around and was told about the Russell properties being under new ownership. He came looking for me and asked if he could rent the small cottage." Casson shrugged. "I hadn't even thought about renting it, but what the heck? Might as well let someone enjoy the place."

He saw Justine stiffen. "Who did you rent it out to?" Her voice trembled slightly.

"A lawyer called Robert Morrell."

CHAPTER FIVE

JUSTINE WANTED THE floor to open up and swallow her. It was bad enough that she had an issue with Casson. Having to deal with Robert now was just too much. She had spent the last couple of months convinced she was finished with him, and had never imagined he would come to see her here at Winter's Haven. Not knowing what he was planning to do jangled her nerves. She couldn't believe he had called the office and tried to rent a cottage... He could walk into the diner at any moment...

She realized Casson had asked her a question...asked if she knew Robert. "Yes, I know him." She tried to respond in a neutral tone, so Casson wouldn't ask any more questions, but she heard her voice crack.

She saw Casson looking at her thoughtfully. The sun had nudged its way through the clouds, shining through the window, and it was reflected in his deep brown eyes. His suntanned face with its dark beard, his plaid shirt with its rolled-up sleeves and his jeans made him look like a muscled hiking guide. She felt her heartbeat accelerating.

"Old boyfriend?"

Justine stared at him. "How did you—?"

"Know? You're not that hard to read. You know that expression 'wearing your heart on your sleeve'? Well, with you, your feelings show on your face."

Justine cocked her head at him and frowned.

He nodded. "Yup. Eyelashes fluttering. Blue eyes darkening. Cheeks flushing. All the classic signs." His eyes narrowed and he leaned forward. "Did you dump *him* or was it the other way around?"

Justine wanted to squirm. Casson wasn't her *friend*, for goodness' sakes. She wasn't about to reveal anything about her past to him, and nor did she intend to enlighten him as to who had dumped whom.

While she grappled with an appropriate response Casson leaned back again and took a long drink of his water. Afterward he stood up, and with a nod said, "Sorry. I was being nosy. Nice doing lunch. I'll see you later..." He turned away and then glanced back at her. "If he let you go, he was a fool..."

Not waiting for her to reply, he walked out of the diner.

Justine followed him with her eyes until the last inch of him was out of sight. Reaching for her handbag, she shuffled through it for her keys. She left the diner and got into her car. She was glad she had already planned to go into Parry Sound to pick up her order of bread for the diner. Now, with the disheartening news about Robert, she decided she'd stay away even longer.

Justine headed first to *West Lake Cosmetics*. She loved owner Wendy's natural handmade soaps, skincare products and bath treats. She also stocked the cottages with products having names like *Muskoka Mimosa*, *Rose Rapture* and *Georgian Bay Linen*. After today's stress, she needed *something* to help her relax.

She chose a *Rose Rapture* soap and a *Citrus Wave* bath pod, and looked forward to pampering herself later with a long, soothing bath. But first she'd have to relieve Mandy for the afternoon shift.

Justine left the shop and moments later stepped into *The Country Gourmet Café and Gallery* to pick up the loaves she had ordered for the diner and two walnut loaves for herself. She thanked Chris, the friendly owner, then headed back to Winter's Haven and tried not to think about Robert.

Everything looked fresh and clean after the earlier downpour. Justine rolled down her windows, lifted her face to the warm breeze and thought about Casson's last words. *If he let you go, he was a fool...* Her heart catapulted at the memory, just as it had done when he had uttered the words.

She replayed the conversation in her head as she drove, and wondered why Casson had wanted to know who was responsible for the ending of her relationship with Robert. *Robert!*

He was the one who had decided to break things off. Unable to face working with him every day, Justine had resigned immediately and fled to Winter's Haven for a few days, needing the support of her parents. She had been stunned when they'd made her the offer...

She'd gone back to Toronto and fortunately had only had to wait a month for the end of the lease on her apartment. But it had been the hardest month to get through. She'd had lots of time to process the failed relationship. To go over every painful detail of how Robert had taken advantage of her trust, her naiveté. She winced at the memories, and a rash of anger ignited and spread under her skin.

She *had* been naïve. She had allowed Robert to draw her in, letting her care for him while his marriage deteriorated. Robert had used her, milking her genuine concern and thoughtfulness until she had been practically frothing over him. She had believed his intentions to be honorable, and his betrayal had hit her like a winter gale from Georgian Bay.

By the end of the month she'd accepted that it was over and had become determined not to allow anyone to use her again. She'd realized it was a godsend that her parents had offered her the opportunity of taking over the business.

It had been time to leave the city and go home.

When she'd driven into Winter's Haven two months ago, and breathed in the fresh scent of the woods and the bay, she'd known she had made the right decision. The chapter of her life with Robert Morrell in it was finished.

Until now.

Justine took a deep breath and let it out slowly. She dropped off the loaves to Melody, took over the office from Mandy, and tried to focus on business tasks. Every once in a while she looked up, wondering anxiously if Robert would suddenly appear.

Justine was relieved when the time came to close up the office. When she got home she kicked off her shoes, put away the bread, and eagerly reached for the bag inside her purse. She was more than ready for a relaxing Citrus Wave bath. And, although it was not yet eight, she started to fill up the tub. She began to undress—then heard the doorbell ring.

Her heart skipped a beat. Was Casson here with another strategy to entice her to sell? He *had* said, "I'll see you later…"

Justine slipped her T-shirt back on and flew down the stairs to the front door. Through the window curtain she could make out a profile.

Wrong man.

When Casson entered his cottage he made a pot of coffee and satisfied himself that the place was ready for his guests' stay. His cousin Veronica would be arriving around noon the following day, along with her son Andy.

Casson smiled. Andy was such a good kid. When he was born, five years ago, Ronnie had asked Casson to be his godfather and he had been thrilled. Ronnie was like a sister to him—the sister he'd never had.

Casson's jaw tightened. She had separated from her husband Peter over a year ago. Peter had been unable to deal with the day-to-day challenges of his son's illness, and had found solace in the comforting arms of a woman who was "there" for him.

But Ronnie had rallied and Andy was now in his second year of his treatment. He had recently finished another round of maintenance chemotherapy, and when Ronnie had texted Casson with this news he had immediately invited them to spend a weekend with him at Winter's Haven. To his delight, Ronnie had called to accept.

Casson poured himself a big mug of coffee before going out to sit on the back deck. Watching the blue waves, he found his thoughts returning to Justine, and the alarm he had glimpsed in her eyes when she'd found out Robert Morrell was renting his cottage.

His jaws clenched. Had the creep hurt her in some way?

He'd find an excuse to check on Robert tonight. And Justine, just to make sure she was okay. Whether it was his business or not, and despite the fact that he might very well be wrong in his suspicions, Casson needed to know what Robert Morrell wanted with Justine.

CHAPTER SIX

JUSTINE HESITATED. WHY had Robert waited until this evening to come and find her? She jumped as Robert tapped the door knocker. She could ignore him...but he probably would have seen her approaching through the lace curtain.

He knocked again. She bit her lip and opened the door slightly, the chain still in place. She didn't offer a greeting; she just gave him a cold stare.

"Justine... Look, I wouldn't blame you if you slammed the door in my face. I just... I just had to try to make things right with you." His voice had a slight tremor. "Even if we never see each other again."

Justine pursed her lips, unconvinced. She wasn't sure if he expected her to let him in, but she felt reluctant to let him step foot in her house. After all, she had never invited him to Winter's Haven before they'd split up—no, before he'd dumped her—so why should she allow him into her private space *now*?

And besides, did she really want to hear what he had to say?

Justine shivered, even though the evening air was warm and still.

She cleared her throat. "Why would you want to do that now, Robert?" She hoped her voice was cool, uncaring—

unlike the way she had responded when he'd told her it was over.

Robert cringed visibly at her tone, as if she had just struck him across the face. "I want to apologize, Justine. Please—just let me try to make amends. I made a mistake in the way I treated you. You deserve more than an apology…"

He looked like a puppy dog, Justine thought, with doleful eyes that were begging for a little mercy. Justine felt herself waver. Robert sounded genuinely sorry. Maybe she needed to hear him explain his less than cavalier behavior toward her…

Nodding, she slid the door chain off. "I don't have a lot of time," she lied.

Relief flooded Robert's face. He stood hesitantly as Justine opened the door wider and then offered a grateful smile as he entered her home. He looked around appreciatively. "Nice place," he said, eyebrows lifting as his gaze settled on the bay window. "Beautiful view."

She gestured toward a recliner, away from the love seat…

Robert nodded and passed in front of her. And then she heard the water still flowing into the bathtub.

"Good heavens!" She threw him a panicked look. "I forgot to turn off the water."

She bolted up the stairs two at a time. She drew out a long breath of relief as she turned both taps off. The water level was an inch below the top of the tub. With jangled nerves she returned to the living room. She wanted to get this apology thing over with, see Robert out, and then have that relaxing bath she had planned.

She sat in the recliner opposite Robert and glanced at him pointedly.

He shifted in his seat, his forehead glistening with beads of perspiration. "Look, Justine, it was never my intention to hurt you. I—I was in a dark place emotionally with my wife, and you were like a ray of sunshine." He smiled at her crookedly. "Sorry, I know that's an overused cliché But after spending my evenings arguing with Katie, and my nights on a couch, I came to appreciate your positive, funny and charming personality…and I *wanted* that. I—I wanted *you*."

He paused, waiting for her to reply, but she had nothing to say—*yet*.

"I was all mixed up. I admit it." He looked away and gazed at the view of the bay. "It was exciting to be with you, and yet once I'd tasted some freedom I started wanting even more. More freedom, more fun, more adventure."

Justine felt a jab in the pit of her stomach. "And that's when you decided to break up with me?" she said, as steadily as she could. "You said the whole divorce thing had depleted you and that you didn't have the energy to carry on with a serious relationship. Only I found out the *real* reason you were 'depleted' when I came to the office early the next morning to pack my things and leave my letter of resignation on your desk… That's when I spotted your lover's panty hose on the couch in your office."

He cringed again. "I'm sorry, Justine. I was screwed up. I know I crossed the line." He gazed at her helplessly. "I hope you can find it in your heart to forgive me. I was so mixed up. Afraid of another commitment but hungry for love. I played with fire and you were the one that got burned." His eyes glistened. "I was the loser, letting you go." His voice broke. "I'll do *anything* to have you back."

Justine let out a deep breath. She hadn't expected *this*.

"I've rented the cottage on the property next to yours for a few days, hoping I can eventually convince you to forgive me and give me another chance."

He stood up and began walking toward her. When he was a foot away, he got down on one knee.

"I—I'm not seeing that other woman, Justine. I swear it didn't mean anything." He placed a hand over hers. "Tell me what I can do to get you to come back to me."

Justine's heart began to hammer. But not because she was overcome with joy at Robert's words, she realized. And his touch left her cold. She tried to slide her hand out from under his but he tightened his grip. She frowned and, meeting his gaze, saw his dilated pupils. She caught the unmistakable smell of alcohol.

"Robert, please let go of my hand." She said it quietly, trying to keep the alarm out of her voice.

He swayed a bit and moved closer, ignoring her request. And then she saw it over his shoulder—the bottle cap he had left on the base of the fireplace.

He had brought a bottle with him.

She had never seen him in this state, and tried not to think about what might happen if he was not in his right mind. She had to think of something to get him out of her house.

"Look, Robert, I forgive you."

To her relief, he loosened his hold.

"You do?"

He gazed at her wonderingly, and Justine knew then that the alcohol he had consumed had started to take effect. While he still had that dazed expression Justine managed to get up and start ambling away from him. Her gaze fell on the bottle that peeked out of his back pocket.

"Yes, Robert." She gestured toward the door. "But now you need to get back to your cottage."

He scrambled to his feet. Justine bit her lip. His senses might be dulled, but otherwise—

"*Please* let me stay, Just—Justine."

In a flash, he had reached her, encircled her waist with both arms and was brushing his cheek against hers.

Justine inhaled the heavy scent of alcohol on his breath.

Her stomach twisted, but before she could even think of breaking free he had pushed her back onto the couch and pinned her arms down. She tried to lift a knee but he flattened it with his own. She stared at his foggy eyes, and at the mouth that was looming over hers. She was strong, but he was a dead weight.

She closed her eyes, cringing at those lips about to touch hers…

"Luna—tackle!"

Sharp barks filled the room.

"Go get him!"

Robert Morrell backed away from Justine, only to be tackled by Luna. He was soon sprawled on the carpet, with Luna's paws and body over him, his face a mask of terror as she emitted low growls.

Casson strode over to help Justine up. Her eyes were wide as she took in the scene before her, her face blanched, her hair messed up. He gave her a tight hug, then with one hand swept her hair away from her face, something inside him melting as she met his gaze, her eyes glistening with relief and gratitude.

He turned away and, taking his phone out, proceeded to take several photos of Robert with Luna. "These are all I need to prove that you were trespassing." His jaw clenched. He shot an icy glare at Robert. "I hope you have a good lawyer. I'm calling the police."

"No, *pl-please.*" Robert attempted to sit up, but promptly lay back as Luna growled and pushed her face into his. "I wasn't going to— Justine, I'm really sorry." Tears glazed his eyes. "I'll be ruined…" he moaned.

"You should have thought about the consequences of your actions," Casson ground out. "Luna—sit back."

In the pathetic state Robert was in, it was unlikely he

would attempt anything. Luna obeyed, but stayed close to Robert, eyeing him warily.

Robert sat up, his head slumping in his hands. "Please…" He lifted his head and looked at Justine and then at Casson. "I promise I'll leave and never come back."

He had a resigned look in his eyes as his gaze returned to Justine, and Casson caught Justine's ambivalent expression. He started to dial for the police, but she placed a hand on his arm.

It took everything he had to put his phone back in his pocket. His eyes bored into Robert's. "You're one lucky snake," he rasped. "I won't call the police, but if you ever try to come near Justine again I'll file charges immediately. Not only for trespassing, but for attempted sexual assault. And, trust me, I'm on the best of terms with Attorney Joseph Brandis." He saw Robert's eyes widen. "Yes, *the* Joseph Brandis."

He watched as Robert slowly got to his feet.

"I don't expect you to drive, in your condition, but I want you out of the cottage first thing in the morning. Give me your car keys. You can walk back; it'll clear your head. Tomorrow you can walk over to my place and get your car—understand?"

Robert nodded.

"I didn't hear you." Casson took a step toward him.

Robert flinched. "Yes, sir." He dug his keys out of his pocket and handed them to Casson.

"Luna, follow him out."

Luna gave a short bark and leapt up to obey.

Robert stopped at the door to look back at Justine. "I'm s-sorry." Shoulders slumped, he left, with Luna and Casson close behind.

Casson waited until Robert was out of sight. He gave a whistle and Luna came racing back, her tail wagging furiously. Casson crouched down and scratched behind her ears. "Good girl," he said, emotion catching in his voice. He reached in his pocket and gave her a treat before opening the door.

Justine was sitting down on the couch. Luna bounded toward her and nuzzled into her hands. She seemed to snap out of her stupor and leaned forward to caress her.

"Thank you, Luna Lu," she murmured.

Casson's heart constricted at her use of Luna's nickname. He watched Justine plant a kiss on Luna's forehead, then bury her face in the soft fur around Luna's neck. When he saw Justine's shoulders shaking, and Luna attempting to lick her cheeks, Casson realized Justine was crying.

In two strides he was crouched next to her and had her in his arms. He let her sob on his shoulder, her chest heaving against him.

"It's over," he said huskily, caressing the back of Justine's head. Then, slowly, his hand slipped to her cheek and he turned her face toward him. "You're safe now."

Justine's breath caught on a sob. "But what if you hadn't shown up with Luna?"

He took her chin in his hand and with his other hand stroked away her tears. "We showed up. That's all that counts."

He looked into her eyes, more gray than blue now. Her lashes were laced with teardrops, and he was overcome with a feeling of tenderness.

"Come and sit here," he murmured, leading her to the love seat. "I'll make you a hot drink."

He took the soft throw that was on the arm of the love seat and draped it around her shoulders. Luna jumped up beside her, but before he could reprimand her, Justine smiled weakly at him.

"Let her," she said. "I don't mind."

Casson strode to the kitchen. He needed a drink himself.

Justine's words played over in his head. *What if you hadn't shown up with Luna?* He didn't want to think of what might have happened. If Robert had— No! He wasn't going there. It would just torment him. It was bad enough that he still had a picture in his mind of Robert bending over Justine, restraining her, about to put his mouth on hers.

Casson felt his stomach turn. He needed something stronger than milk. Brandy, maybe. He found a bottle, poured himself a shot, and put a lesser amount in Justine's milk.

"Okay, Luna—skedaddle." Casson sat next to Justine and handed her the cup of milk.

She took a tentative sip, then wrinkled her nose.

"Drink it all up," he ordered. "It'll help you sleep."

"Casson?" She looked at him with eyes that were starting to flutter in exhaustion. "Can you and Luna stay tonight?" She shuddered. "What if he comes back?"

Casson set down his glass, his heart jolting. He saw the fear in her eyes. "He won't come back," he assured her, squeezing her hand. "But, yes…we'll stay."

CHAPTER SEVEN

JUSTINE COULD BARELY keep her eyes open. She peered at Casson drowsily. "Thank you for staying. You can take the spare room…"

She stood up and headed for the stairs. Luna followed her with Casson close behind. At her doorway, she turned and pointed to the room across from hers. Casson nodded but didn't move.

"Goodnight," she murmured. "Oh, just a minute…"

She entered her room and grabbed the robe that hung behind her door. The one she had given him earlier.

Casson's mouth lifted at one corner. "Thanks. Goodnight, Justine." His hand brushed hers as he took the robe.

She saw something flicker in his eyes and wished she could tell him how much she yearned for his protective arms around her again, but she didn't trust herself in the hazy state she was in. Inviting his embrace could only complicate things.

She needed to sleep. Put the traumatic encounter with Robert out of her mind. She'd have a clearer head in the morning, and maybe then she might be able to make sense of her feelings about Casson. *For* Casson.

She realized he was waiting for her to turn in before heading to his room.

"You might want to close your door, Justine, or you

could find yourself sharing your bed tonight," he said huskily.

Justine felt something electric swirl inside her at the thought of him—

"With Luna."

Justine felt her cheeks burn. She lowered her gaze.

Of course. How ridiculous to think that he would—

"And then I would have to come in and get her off…"

Her head snapped up. There *was* something in his expression. She swayed suddenly and in a moment Casson was there, supporting her. She breathed in his pine scent, felt the strength of his bare arms. Her lips brushed against his neck, and she gasped when he suddenly scooped her up and carried her to her bed.

For timeless moments she felt she was suspended in paradise, with Casson's expression of concern spreading heat to every inch of her body. His eyes were fathomless, heady, and she wished the fog in her head would dissipate so she could—

"You've had a shock tonight, Justine. You need to sleep," he murmured against her ear as he set her down softly on top of the flowered quilt.

Luna nudged her way past him to place her head on the bed and he gave a soft chuckle.

"Don't even think about it, Luna Lu. You're sleeping with *me*, remember? Come on—let's go…"

Justine watched them disappear, and when she heard the click of the door she sighed and turned down the bedcovers. She undressed and slid into bed, too exhausted to find her nightie.

Within moments she felt herself drifting into sleep.

Leaving his door open a crack, Casson switched on a lamp on the night table and Luna settled down on the rug. He undressed and put on the robe, before stretching out on the bed.

He couldn't deny that Justine ignited something within him. Seeing her so vulnerable, unable to defend herself against Robert, had aroused something primeval in him. Maybe if Luna hadn't been there Casson might have given in to his baser instincts and pounded the guy. With no hesitation. But he had to admit he was glad that *that* scenario hadn't taken place. It wouldn't have been pretty.

Tonight had been an ordeal Justine wouldn't soon forget. He found himself wondering what exactly had happened in her relationship with Robert…how long they had been together…if she had enjoyed Robert's touch before their breakup…

Why did it bother him so much?

He hardly knew Justine. Yet when he had held her tight against him it had felt…*timeless.* Things had shifted, whether he liked it or not. She had managed to throw him off course. Made him question his motives. He had to regroup and think of a strategy that would give them both what they wanted. Surely they could find common ground and come to a compromise?

Somehow he didn't think it would be as easy as it sounded.

Listening to the raindrops batting softly against the window, he closed his eyes—although he wasn't sure how much sleep he'd get tonight, listening in case Justine called out…

Justine was awakened by a moan, and then realized it was coming from *her.* For a moment she felt confused, not sure where she was. Her head throbbed. She opened her eyes and instinctively squinted at the clock radio on her night table. *Almost five a.m.* She must have been dreaming, but she had no recollection of any details—and then she remembered the events of the night before. How Robert had come to ask for forgiveness, and how he had lost control. She felt her stomach constrict at the memory of how helpless she had felt, and how Casson and Luna had arrived just in time...

Why had they come to her house anyway?

She had been too shaken even to formulate this question last night, let alone ask Casson.

A warm rush permeated her body as she recalled how he had hugged her so tightly, prepared her a hot drink, scooped her up so effortlessly when she'd felt her knees give out... She had felt as safe as if she were snuggled within a silky cocoon. Even the effects of the brandy hadn't stifled the desire that had overcome her while suspended within those muscled arms. Nor the stab of disappointment when he'd set her down and left moments later.

Don't be silly, she chided herself. What had she *expected* him to do? She didn't know much about Casson Forrester, but one thing she instinctively knew was that he wasn't the type to take advantage of someone in such a compromised state.

And, despite her disappointment that he hadn't gone any further, she was relieved that he hadn't. If Casson took her in his arms again—and she had no reason to believe that he would even do such a thing—she wanted to have all her senses functioning at an optimal level, not depressed by alcohol or trauma...or a headache like the one she was experiencing now. She needed to take something quickly, before it escalated into a migraine.

She slipped out of bed and padded to the door. She started to turn the handle and suddenly froze.

She was naked, and Casson was in the room across from hers.

She shivered and retraced her steps to get her nightie from the plush chair by her bed. She stepped out of her room, glanced toward the room where Casson was sleeping, and tiptoed to the washroom, cringing when she heard the maple floor creaking on the way.

She closed the bathroom door gently and her gaze fell on the tub, still full of water. So much for her plans for a relaxing bath… She was about to drain it, then decided against it. It was still too early to make so much noise.

She found the bottle of pills and took two with water. She needed to have this headache gone before heading into the office. It was still too early to stay up, though. She'd be a wreck if she didn't catch a few more hours of sleep. She paused for a moment.

What day is this? Relief flooded her. *Friday. Her day off this week.*

But what if Robert came back?

She froze, and then reminded herself that Casson was with her. He would make sure Robert didn't come near her…

As she stepped gingerly into the hallway she heard a snuffle and looked across to see Luna's nose edging the door open. Before Justine could even think of dashing into her room Luna had bounded toward her.

Casson soon appeared, his hair disheveled, his robe obviously thrown on without thinking. It was inside out and he had tied the sash loosely. Justine felt her gaze settle on his muscled chest, the fine line of hair swooping downwards, and then she started to shiver…and giggle.

Casson's brow creased. "Do I look that funny?" He looked down at his robe.

Justine shifted. "No, it's your dog; she's tickling my feet."

She tried to back away from Luna, who was intent on giving her feet and calves a thorough licking. And then she realized how skimpy her nightie was. It was barely mid-thigh, with spaghetti straps and an eyelet trim around the sweetheart neckline. It wasn't transparent, but the fine cotton draped over her breasts accentuated their peaks.

Mortified, she started to edge toward her room, all too aware of Casson's gaze. Luna began to follow her.

"Luna—*stay.* Are you okay, Justine?"

His husky tone made her quiver inside, and she prayed her legs wouldn't buckle under her again. Although Casson was trying not to make it obvious, his eyes were flickering over her body, from her neck and shoulders all the way down to her thighs and calves. And then back to her eyes.

It couldn't have taken more than a couple of seconds, but to Justine it had felt like an eternity.

"Oh… Other than a dull headache, I'm okay." She crossed her arms over her chest. *"Stop, Luna."*

The dog had inched forward to start licking her feet again. Her tone had no effect on Luna, but in a flash, Casson was striding toward them both.

"Luna—stop." His voice was deep, authoritative, and he didn't have to put a hand on his dog. Luna snapped to attention and immediately assumed a sitting position, her chocolate-colored eyes never wavering from her master.

"You have to show who's Alpha," he said in a soft tone to Justine, his tawny eyes blazing, and she felt like melting on the spot.

CHAPTER EIGHT

IF JUSTINE DIDN'T soon go into her room he didn't think he could continue to maintain his composure. Standing there in that…that kerchief-sized nightie, she had *no* idea how she was affecting him.

His heartbeat had accelerated with every shift of his gaze. It had started with her tousled hair, sleep-flushed face and the graceful curve of her neck, then revved up as it descended to the compact but curvy areas covered by her nightie. Areas that he could only imagine cupping, squeezing, *kissing*. And the sight of those shapely tanned legs, and the way Justine had wriggled them away from Luna's attempts to lick them, had almost done him in.

Casson had had several relationships—all short-term, since he was determined to focus on building his business— but none of them had caused him the inner commotion he was feeling right now. He practically vibrated with the primeval impulse to gather his woman in his arms, lay her down and make her yield to him. *Willingly.*

But she was not his woman.

He felt a jab in his gut. He had to put a stop to this.

"I don't know about you, but I doubt I'll be able to fall back to sleep." He tried to keep his gaze fixed on her eyes and not her body. "How about I make some coffee?"

"Sure," she said lightly, letting her arms drop to her side. "I'll just have a quick shower."

She pivoted slightly and rushed into her room—but not before Casson had caught a glimpse of her bareness under the nightie. He let out a long, long breath and went to get dressed.

His mission was getting harder by the minute.

When Casson went downstairs, he turned on the light switch in the kitchen and put on the coffee maker. While the coffee was brewing he took Luna outside. It was still dusky, and the grass was wet. He scowled when he saw Robert's car. Robert would no doubt be sleeping for a while yet.

Out of the corner of his eye he saw Justine's turquoise retro-style bicycle. An idea popped into his head and he grinned. In less than a minute he had the bike and Luna in Robert's car and was on his way to giving the creep his early-morning wake-up call.

No point making Robert walk back to his place. No, *he* would take his car to him, and personally see Robert off his property. The bike-ride back to Justine's would take no time at all, and Luna would enjoy the run.

Justine towel-dried her hair and went downstairs. Casson was pouring coffee into two mugs. He looked up and smiled. Justine's pulse quickened. He looked so at home, standing behind the island...

"Let's take our coffee into the living room," he suggested. "We can catch the sun rise over the bay."

Justine's heart thrummed. The way he said it made it sound so *intimate*. She felt her cheeks burn as she started to follow him, and then, remembering Robert, walked tentatively toward the window and glanced out.

"He's gone," Casson said gruffly, "and he won't be back. I promise you."

Justine nodded, picked up her mug, and headed to the living room. She didn't need the details.

She started as Luna bounded in front of her and leapt onto the couch next to Casson. Seeing that he was about to order her off, Justine quickly said, "She's fine. She deserves special treatment after saving me last night."

She sat down on the love seat and bit her lip, the memory of Robert's face looming over hers making her stomach twinge.

Casson picked up his mug and strode to the fireplace. He stared at the painting while drinking his coffee. "I love this one," he murmured. *"Mirror Lake."*

"Oh? You're familiar with Franklin Carmichael's work?"

Casson smiled at her as if what she'd asked were amusing. "His and his buddy A. J.'s—and the rest of the Group of Seven."

Justine's eyes widened. "A. J. *Casson*," she said slowly. "So, what *is* the connection between your name and his?"

"My grandparents lived on the same street as the Cassons in north Toronto. They became friends. They loved his work, and by the time they passed away, they had quite a collection. My mother inherited it. She *loved* the Group of Seven. Casson and Carmichael were her favorites. And I inherited everything when she died."

Something flickered in his eyes and his brows furrowed. Justine wondered if it was sadness at his mother's passing, but she didn't have the courage to ask.

"Which is why," he said lightly, "she named me and my brother after them."

"Casson and Carmichael?"

"Yes and no. Casson and Franklin." He set down his mug on the mantel. He turned away to face the painting squarely. "Franklin was my little brother."

Justine caught the slight waver in Casson's voice. *Was*, he'd said. She felt her heart sinking.

"My father bought a limited edition print of *Mirror Lake* for my mom when Franklin was born. After he died they donated it to the Hospital for Sick Children in Toronto."

CHAPTER NINE

CASSON TOOK A deep breath and turned to face Justine. She had a stricken look, and her eyes had misted.

"I'm sorry," he said, returning to sit at one corner of the couch—the corner nearest the love seat where Justine was sitting. "It wasn't my intention to bring up my past." He set down his mug and glanced back at the painting. "It's just that that particular painting brings back so many memories."

And pain.

"Please, don't apologize," Justine said, her voice husky. "I'm very sorry for your loss. I—I can't even imagine…"

Casson felt a warm rush shoot through him as he met Justine's gaze. Her blue-gray eyes had cleared and were as luminous as the lake in the painting. He didn't make a habit of bringing up the death of his brother, but something in her expression made him willing to talk about it.

"It happened a long time ago," he said, patting Luna absentmindedly. "I was ten. Frankie was seven." He paused, his mind racing back to his childhood. "They found out he had a rare form of leukemia when he was six. He was rushed to SickKids and they started treatment immediately. Mom stayed with him there, and Dad stayed home with me."

Casson looked out beyond the bay window. The sky was

beginning to lighten, with intersecting bands of pink and pale blue. His stomach contracted at the memories of that year: his father becoming increasingly moody and agitated; the empty house when he got home from school; no welcoming hug and snacks from his mother; no little brother to play hockey or baseball with; his bad dreams and the nagging worry that Franklin would die...

"That must have been so tough..."

Casson's gaze shifted back to Justine. He breathed deeply. "What was really tough was visiting him at Sick-Kids. Seeing him with no hair, covered with bruises. Seeing him attached to tubes and hooked up to machines." His jaw clenched. "He was so small." Casson shook his head and averted his gaze. "Sorry. Didn't mean to put a damper on things..."

"No worries," Justine said, placing a hand on his arm.

His head jerked at the unexpected touch and his heart did a flip at the genuine caring in her voice. And in her gaze. She looked so sweet and natural, with her hair in that ponytail. Cheeks that looked as soft and rosy as a peach. Eyes that he could swim in.

He found himself drawing closer. She blinked but didn't move away.

He wanted nothing more than to kiss her. And, he could be wrong, but he thought she looked like she wouldn't have a problem with it. But he had a feeling that kissing Justine Winter now would not be wise. He had tasted those lips before, and he knew that once their lips touched it would be sheer torture to break away.

"I have to go," he murmured, looking deep into her eyes.

He wished he didn't, but he had a few things to do before his guests arrived. He saw the warmth in her eyes fading, and she withdrew her hand from his arm. He stood up and Luna, who had fallen asleep, stirred and jumped off the couch. Casson went back into the kitchen to get his hoodie and his keys, and then, nodding to Justine, headed for the door.

"Casson…"

He stopped and turned around. She was steps away, the fingers of both hands tucked into the front pockets of her Capri pants. "Thank you for…for staying the night."

He smiled. "My pleasure."

He opened the door and Luna bounded off.

Justine watched Casson and Luna get into Casson's truck, then returned to the kitchen, her thoughts turning to Robert. She had been such a bleeding heart, letting him in. But he had looked so tormented…and his apology *had* seemed genuine.

It was now obvious that in the time since she had resigned Robert had come apart. She had never known him to drink to excess, but last night he had revealed a different side to him. His alcohol-tinged breath, his unrelenting hold on her… She felt a shudder go through her again at the thought of what might have happened.

His divorce must have been harder for him to deal with than she had realized. Perhaps losing his wife and trying to adjust to all the changes afterward had been too much, inducing him to seek solace in the bottle.

Justine sighed. Robert was a fine lawyer, but even the finest lawyers were not immune to emotional collapse.

She inhaled and exhaled deeply. Could she believe he meant what he had said? He would leave and never come back? Justine had caught so many emotions in that look he'd given her at the door: regret, shame, embarrassment, despair. And fear. Most likely fear that Casson would press charges. Which meant that Robert wasn't so far gone that he no longer cared about his work, his livelihood.

Maybe what had happened last night would be his

wake-up call and he'd get help before his life spun completely out of control.

Justine bit on her lower lip. Countless times after she had resigned she'd wished she had explained to Robert how devastated she had felt at his infidelity. Betrayed. *Used.* How she had cried herself to sleep for days. How she'd half hoped he'd come after her and beg for forgiveness. And how, in her darkest moments, she'd thought that when he did she'd forgive him and they would start fresh…

But a month had passed, and then two more after her return to Winter's Haven, and Robert had never once attempted to call, let alone ask for forgiveness.

Seeing him last night had been *her* wake-up call, and she realized that deep down she had never known the true Robert. How could she ever put her trust in him again? No, she had no illusions about starting over with him, or of him being any part of her 'happy-ever-after.' And after the merry-go-round of emotions she had been through she wasn't ready to trust anyone else…

Justine started as she heard a knock on the door. Her stomach gave a lurch, and then she saw that it was Casson. Relieved, she opened the door.

"Luna sent me back," he said, a twinkle in his eye. "She'd like you to join us."

Her eyebrows lifted and she just blinked at him wordlessly.

"I need to drive to Huntsville to pick up a couple of things. Why don't you join me? *Us.* Luna says she's getting bored with my company. And with Spanish guitar music," he added with a deep chuckle. "Besides…you might just discover I'm not the man you think I am."

Justine's pulse had quickened at Casson's very first words. She was tempted to accept his offer, to let a fresh country drive distract her from what had happened with Robert, but… But was it wise to spend time with Casson, given the reason why he was here at Winter's Haven in the first place?

And given her undeniable attraction to him?

Luna barked from the open window and she couldn't help her mouth quirking into a smile.

Although she was well aware that her heart and mind were battling over her decision, she threw caution to the wind. "Tell Luna I'm in," she said, wondering why she sounded so breathless. "I'll just grab my handbag."

Casson had his window partially rolled down. Every once in a while he snuck a glance in Justine's direction. Luna had graciously given up her spot for her and was now in the back seat, head uplifted to enjoy the breeze. Justine alternated between looking out at the scenery and resting back against the leather headrest, her eyes closed and her lips curved in a relaxed smile.

His intuition had been right. She needed to get away from Winter's Haven—even if only for a few hours.

He was all too aware of her proximity: the curve of her peachy cheekbones tapering to her glossy lips, her fitted pink T-shirt rising and falling with her every breath, and her shapely legs so tantalizingly close to his own that every time he manipulated the stick-shift his hand came close to skimming her thigh. He didn't know what was louder: the thrum of the engine or the thrum in his chest.

Casson had to force himself to concentrate on the road several times, and after a stretch on the main highway southbound to Toronto, took Exit Ramp 213 toward Highway 141 to Huntsville. He felt a sense of contentedness with Justine sitting so close to him, even without music or conversation.

This highway had far less traffic, and Casson maneuvered the truck deftly through the winding turns and up and down the hillsides.

"I'll get us some breakfast when we get to my place."

"Your place?" Justine turned her head sharply to stare at him.

"We won't be long," he said casually. "I just have to pick up a couple of things."

He turned on a radio channel of classic rock tunes.

"Are you okay with this?"

At her nod, he cranked it up a bit and, grinning, pressed on the gas pedal.

CHAPTER TEN

JUSTINE'S PULSE POUNDED along with the bass of the stereo. She had enjoyed the quiet, but now welcomed the distraction of music and the kind of songs that she would ordinarily sing to while driving. Her feet and fingers tapped along automatically, and she had to consciously restrain herself from swaying to the music.

She stole a glance at him. The sun beaming down through the windshield and into his truck highlighted the soft golden-brown fuzz on Casson's forearms. His fingers tapped a beat on the steering wheel, and as the muscles in his arms flexed Justine's pulse quickened at the memory of those strong hands and arms carrying her to bed...

Justine was familiar with this route from when she had business in Huntsville, and always loved the views of the myriad sparkling lakes in the Muskokas, but somehow on this trip she barely noticed Lake Rosseau, Horseshoe Lake and Skeleton Lake, among others, and was surprised when Casson turned off the radio to announce that they were coming to Fairy Lake.

Soon Casson was driving through a winding stretch of woodland, with pinpoints of light sparkling through crowns of maple, birch, and pine. Eventually he turned into a long, paved driveway that she thought would never end. But when it finally did Justine couldn't help letting out a gasp. The house—no, *the estate*—was massive, with four dormer windows on the upper level, a wrap-around deck that seemed to equal the circumference of a football field, a four-car garage, and a view that could only be described as heaven, with Fairy Lake a brilliant blue reflecting millions of sun specks.

Justine was still gawking when Casson held the door open for her, and she climbed out, with Luna bounding after her. Two vehicles were sparkling in the sun: the silver-green Mustang convertible she had first seen Casson drive, and a heart-stopping red Ferrari Testarossa.

So Casson Forrester liked his toys. And flaunting his success... But did anyone really need four vehicles? She wondered what luxury model was behind the fourth door...

"Welcome to my place," he said.

Justine's eyes widened as she entered the marble foyer that was connected to a massive living area with gleaming maple hardwood floors and floor-to-ceiling windows. The Muskoka stone fireplace was the focal point, around which several luxurious leather couches were arranged. Hanging on the wall above the polished mantel were two paintings, and as Justine approached she saw that she had guessed correctly: one was a Casson and the other a Carmichael. Both depicted stunning Georgian Bay views. On the mantel itself there was a small baseball cap and a miniature red racing car.

So he was sentimental, too.

"Things from your childhood that you couldn't bear to part with?" she said casually.

She turned to see something flicker across Casson's face.

He stared at her wordlessly for a moment. "Those belonged to Franklin," he said finally, his voice breaking at the end.

He picked up the car and Justine bit her lip as she watched him.

"I came back to get his cap; I always take it with me when I return to Georgian Bay—especially when I go fishing… As for the car…" He picked it up and made the wheels spin. "Frankie loved his toy cars, and this was his favorite. Said he was going to get one when he grew up." His jaw muscles flicked. "Well, I got one for him…"

Justine felt something deflate inside her and her heart felt heavy. He hadn't bought the Ferrari as a status symbol, but as a way of honoring his brother's dream. Guilt washed over her. She wanted to apologize to Casson for being so judgmental, and then she remembered she hadn't voiced her feelings about him flaunting his success.

She gulped. Maybe she shouldn't let her feelings about Robert cloud her judgment about Casson. Maybe she should stop lumping them into the same box…

"Okay…" Casson pressed his lips together. "Let's lighten things up. How about I make you a light and fluffy omelet?"

His mouth curved into a smile and he motioned for her to continue into the kitchen at the other end of the room.

Justine nodded, and was instantly wowed by the chef's kitchen with its stunning curved granite island the color of sapphire, plush stools, and at least double the amount of cupboards she had, with a sturdy harvest table in the dining area that she was sure could comfortably sit twenty.

She sat on a stool and watched Casson in T-shirt and jeans, the muscles in his arms flexing with his every movement. Her heartbeat did an erratic dance…

Had he just said something to her? She stared at him blankly.

His mouth quirked, an eyebrow lifted, and he waved the spatula in his hand. "Wanna get the toast?"

"Sure."

Avoiding his gaze, she slid off the stool and put the toast on. *He must lift weights*, she thought, edging a glance at his arms as he flipped the omelets. *Or else he regularly lifts two-by-fours at his hardware stores.*

The sudden image of him wearing nothing but jeans and steel-toed boots, pumping a stack of wood, made her insides blaze.

Casson slid the omelets onto two plates, and Justine buttered the toast. He poured coffee into two mugs and sat down next to her.

"Bon appétit," he said, his eyes crinkling at her as he tasted the omelet. "Not bad."

"Delicious," she agreed.

"I'll believe it after you've had a bite." He looked pointedly at her untouched portion.

Justine could have kicked herself. *Good one.*

"I mean it *looks* delicious," she said lightly, gazing down at her plate.

His leg was almost touching hers, and she tried not to think about it, or about the way his jeans fit, and the way his arms looked, so smooth and bronzed.

Like a sculpture that you just wanted to stroke...

"More coffee?" His voice melded with her thoughts.

She turned her head, her stomach tightening at how close his face was to hers. His eyes were like shiny chestnuts, with flecks of gold around his dark pupils.

"Yes...please..." she managed, and then concentrated on eating her omelet.

Casson waited until Justine was finished and then offered to take her on a tour of the rest of the house. He started with his study on the main floor, and he could see that she loved it, unconsciously stroking the gleaming surface of his mahogany desk and pausing to peruse the volumes in his floor-to-ceiling bookshelves.

She turned to fix him with a crooked smile. "Is this a lending library?" she said, a teasing glint in her eye.

"Only for—"

"Oh!"

She had caught sight of the mahogany spiral staircase in one corner.

"That leads up to my bedroom," he said, as casually as he could. "When I can't sleep I like to spend time down here with my literary friends." He gestured toward the bookshelves.

Casson had a sudden vision of Justine in a silk robe, reading a book in his Italian leather recliner and then gliding up the staircase…

He gave himself a mental shake and suggested they go to the upper level. He ordered Luna to stay, and then walked out of the room and up another flight of stairs. He led Justine through two luxurious guest bedrooms, and then the guest bathroom, repressing his desire to smile as her eyes popped at the sight of the transparent walls of his shower stall, with its back wall designed to be the center part of a larger window overlooking the lake and hills. The enormous claw-foot bathtub looked out at the same view.

He proceeded toward the huge double doors leading to his bedroom. "Don't worry," he said in a conspiratorial tone, "I don't have any nefarious intentions. It's just that this room has one of the best views of the lake."

If Justine had been impressed by his study and bathroom, he could tell she was blown away by his bedroom, with its rustic four-poster king-sized bed, cottage-style dressers, pine-green and forest-themed linens, the huge walk-in closet, massive custom-built windows and a set of sliding doors. They opened on to a semi-circular deck that spanned from one end of the house to the other, with a hot tub in one corner and a screened-in sunroom with lounging chairs and a bar. And a pull-out couch.

"For those summer nights when I'd rather sleep outside," he murmured.

"Oh…my…" Justine looked out at the sparkling waters of Fairy Lake. "I… I have never seen anything like this. You must hate to leave this place," she said, glancing back at him.

He gave her a measured look. "It serves its purpose…" He hesitated, and wondered if he should tell Justine that, much as he loved his home, he felt that something was missing. Or maybe a special *someone*. But, no, there was no reason for him to go there.

He had learned to keep his thoughts and feelings in check since his childhood. Maybe he even shied away from serious relationships, from love, because of the trauma of losing his brother, and in some ways his parents as well.

Why would he do anything differently now and suddenly open up to Justine? Reveal all his thoughts, hopes and dreams to her? Share the real reason for his resort venture? Although he may have cracked a bit, telling her about Franklin's cap and toy car, he had no intention of ending up like Humpty Dumpty.

She walked to the edge of the deck and, looking over, gasped again.

He caught up to her and followed her gaze to the ground level, beyond the salmon-colored interlocking patio to a huge kidney-shaped swimming pool. Around it the lush landscaped lawns and gardens featured flowering bushes, working fountains and lounging areas. A white gazebo stood close to the waterfront, along with a half-dozen Muskoka chairs around a fire-pit.

A man trimming the hedges by the gazebo looked up at them and waved before leaving the grounds.

"That's Phillip, my gardener, groundskeeper, car maintenance man and all-around good guy," he said, waving back. "I lucked out when I found him. And his wife Sue.

She does the housekeeping and provides me with an occasional dinner when I don't want to batch it," he said, grinning at Justine.

"With a place like this, I'm surprised you have to *batch it* at all…"

The words were out before Justine could stop them. She felt her face igniting at her implication that women would seek his company only for his material possessions.

"I'm sorry. I didn't mean to imply—"

"That the ladies are all over me just for my hot tub and my pool?" He laughed. "I generally don't have time to do a lot of *that kind* of entertaining. My business ventures keep my hands tied. Although…" he raised his eyebrows and his tawny eyes pierced hers "… I occasionally *un*tie my hands…"

Justine's heart began to palpitate and she looked away. How could she even begin to respond? And what was this sharp twist in her stomach at the thought of his hands on another woman? In the hot tub and sharing his bed?

She felt pinned under Casson's gaze. Sensed he had moved closer. She couldn't help but breathe in his fresh pine scent, and when she tentatively looked back at him his lips were suddenly on hers, his arms bracing her against him. She gasped, and felt all her muscles slacken. Closing her eyes, she surrendered to the desire pumping through her. Pressing her hand against the back of his head, she responded hungrily as he deepened his kiss.

And then she felt him break away from her, so suddenly that she almost lost her balance.

"I'm sorry," he said gruffly. "I didn't intend to—"

"Neither did I," she said in a rush. "We should go in…"

When they were back on the main floor, Casson strode over to the fireplace and took Franklin's cap.

"This is what I came for," he said lightly. "And the Mustang. I won't be needing my truck for a while."

Justine was glad Casson had slipped in a Spanish guitar CD. Luna didn't seem to mind it at all, and had fallen asleep in the back seat. Justine closed her eyes, wishing she could fall asleep herself. It was so awkward now… especially in the more intimate confines of his Mustang.

She looked out her window, forcing herself not to steal glances at Casson. When he swerved slightly to avoid a porcupine she found herself pinned against him for a moment, and her heart flipped at the proximity of his firm lips…

Her thoughts tumbled about during the rest of the drive. And when Casson switched the music to Pachelbel's *Canon in D*, Justine felt herself swept up by the sensual strains of the violins and *basso continuo*, closing her eyes as the wind ruffled her hair.

As the Mustang started to slow down before turning in to Winter's Haven, Justine realized she must have dozed off. She asked Casson to drop her off by the office, and when he did, scrambled out of the car before he could get the door for her. He shrugged and got back into his seat.

"Thanks for the drive and breakfast." She managed a weak smile.

Two teenagers from one of the cottages rode by on their bikes and waved.

"Hey, mister," one called out, coming to a stop not far from the Mustang, its silver-green exterior and chrome sparkling in the sun. "She's a beauty!"

Casson removed his sunglasses and met Justine's gaze. "She sure is," he said softly. And then he turned and gave a thumbs-up to the boy.

Something swirled inside of Justine and spiraled up to her chest.

Had he just paid her a compliment? Or was the sunlight addling her brain?

Casson's car thrummed as he started the ignition, made a sleek turn and drove away. When he was out of sight Justine walked back to her place, needing the time to replay the events of the morning with Casson. She caught sight of the coffee mugs, and as she filled the sink with soapy water Justine felt herself burning with curiosity about his guests.

Well, she'd find out soon enough.

She dried her hands and walked over to look at *Mirror Lake*. She had always loved it, with its undulating hills, their stunning colors reflected in the glassy surface of the lake. Hues of green, purple, gold, red and blue, blending in sensuous curves and prismatic streaks across the hilly landscape. A feast for the eyes.

Looking at it now, she felt a lump in her throat, thinking of Casson's brother Franklin suffering at such a young age, and of his family, suffering along with him, all in their different ways. *Poor Casson.* He had been nine when Franklin was diagnosed and ten when Franklin died. *Ten!* Her heart ached when she thought of how Franklin's passing must have changed their lives. And how Casson was still honoring his brother's memory all these years later.

She had witnessed a hint of Casson's vulnerability when he'd told her about Franklin's cap and toy car, and she felt renewed remorse at her earlier thought that he had bought the Ferrari as a status symbol. Maybe Casson had been right… *He wasn't the man she'd thought he was.*

Justine had sensed that Casson was unwilling to open up any further and share more details of his past to her. *And why should he?* She didn't trust his motives when it came to Winter's Haven—and Casson was well aware of this—so why should *he* trust *her?*

She tore her gaze away from the painting and went upstairs.

By the time she'd got out of the shower and let her hair dry naturally outside on the deck, it was almost noon. She biked over to the office and while she waited for Mandy to finish a call, quickly checked the register and saw the names "Ronnie and Andy Walsh" listed as Casson's guests.

Mandy got off the phone, and Justine briefly told her what had happened with Robert.

Mandy's mouth dropped. "Thank goodness Casson came to your rescue," she said, her eyes wide. "And Luna! Talk about great timing!" She gave Justine a tight hug. "I'm so glad you're okay."

Mandy shot a glance toward the diner entrance.

"Your hero is in there," she said in a conspiratorial tone. "Having lunch with his guests. Oh, here they come!"

Justine looked casually over her shoulder. Casson was laughing, with a guest on either side of him. Not two brothers, as she had expected. A good-looking woman and a boy of no more than five or six. *'Ronnie' was a woman.* And the boy—it had to be her son—must be Andy.

The three of them looked like a family. As they approached, Justine tried to ignore the sinking sensation in the pit of her stomach, and she hoped her smile didn't appear as fake as it felt.

CHAPTER ELEVEN

CASSON HAD HIS arm around Ronnie's shoulder and was holding Andy's hand. Ronnie was a petite brunette, with a perky haircut that emphasized the fine bone structure of her face. She wore faded jeans and a retro-style cotton top with short gathered sleeves and a splashy flower print. Her running shoes were lime-green.

Tiny but not afraid to roar, Justine couldn't help thinking, unable to prevent a blistering sensation from coursing through her. *Was it jealousy?* She wished she could hide, but it was too late.

The little boy—Andy—was small, too. He wore a Toronto Blue Jays cap and a red and white T-shirt and jean shorts, and his skinny little legs moved quickly to keep up with the adults. He kept smiling up at Casson, and occasionally tugged at his hand.

Justine couldn't make out their conversation, but as they approached heard Andy saying something about catching a big fish. Casson threw back his head and let out a deep laugh, and Justine felt her stomach twist at the intimate scene the trio presented.

Mandy went back to her desk to accept a delivery, and Justine stood there awkwardly, knowing how strange it would look if she suddenly left.

She wished she had never decided to come to the diner for lunch. Somehow, her appetite was gone.

Casson was still smiling when they reached Justine, but his arm was no longer encircling Ronnie's waist. "Let me introduce my guests," he said. "Justine Winter, this is Veronica Walsh and her little fisherman Andy." He grinned down at the boy. "He says he wants to catch a *big* one while he's here."

Although he was pale, with dark shadows under his green eyes, Andy's elfin grin made his freckled face light up.

"Nice to meet you, Andy." She held out her hand and was pleased when he shook it and nodded.

"Nice to meet you too, Miss Winter," he said, looking up directly at her.

Justine smiled, impressed at his communication skills. She turned to Veronica. "I hope you enjoy Winter's Haven, Veronica."

What else could she say?

Veronica held out her hand, and for a tiny person her handshake was surprisingly strong.

"Please call me Ronnie." She smiled, her eyes crinkling warmly. "Everyone does—except for Casson, when he wants to be formal. Or when he's scolding me." She laughed. "You have a lovely place, Justine," she said, waving her arm in an arc. "Casson was right. He told me it was enchanting."

Justine avoided looking at Casson.

Of course he finds it enchanting; that's why he wants to take it off my hands.

Justine hoped her cynicism didn't show through in her smile, which was starting to waver.

"Hey, Cass," Andy pulled at Casson's hand. "When can we go fishing?"

Cass? It was obvious this was no ordinary relationship

for Andy to be using this nickname. Justine watched as Casson's eyes lit up again as he looked down on the boy.

"You've just barely arrived and you're hounding me already!" He chuckled. "Speaking of hounds—there's one waiting for you in Cottage Number One."

"Luna!" Andy tugged at Casson's hand. "Let's go, Cass. I can't wait to play tag with her! We can go fishing after that!"

"Bossy little thing, eh?" Casson's smile took in Ronnie and Justine. "I have a feeling I won't have a moment's peace while this munchkin is here. Hey, there, Andrew Michael Walsh." He feigned a stern glance at Andy. "If you pull my hand any harder it'll fall off—and I won't be able to fish with one hand."

Andy giggled. "Then we'll have to take *her* with us, since Mommy doesn't like to fish."

Justine flushed, not knowing what to say.

Ronnie burst out laughing. "Andy's right. All I want to catch while I'm here are some rays." She looked up at Casson and winked. "We'll settle into the cottage while you go and get Luna's food at the vet's." She turned to Justine. "Nice meeting you!"

As Ronnie's car turned the bend and disappeared Justine's mind launched a battle inside her brain's hemispheres of reason and judgment. Casson obviously had no scruples— kissing *her* during the storm, and again at his house, when all along he had a significant other.

How uncouth of him! Despicable, really, when the relationship involved a child.

A child who obviously adored him.

The more she thought about it, the more her stomach twisted at the thought of Casson deceiving Ronnie and continuing to allow Andy to become attached to him. If he and Ronnie broke up Andy would undoubtedly be heartbroken. Casson's underhandedness, his toying with the emotions of both Ronnie and Andy, was reprehensible.

He was toying with you, too…

She cringed.

And you enjoyed his charms…

"Are you all right?" Casson had turned to face her. "You looked like you were in pain…"

Justine caught a whiff of his cologne, its now familiar woodsy scent. She so wanted to give him a blast for being a cad, but the concern in his voice made her hesitate. And then she recalled the look of trust in Andy's eyes, the hero-worship…

"I'm fine," she heard herself reply coldly as his hand cupped her under one elbow.

She stepped away from him, trying not to make it obvious that she didn't welcome his touch. She swayed slightly and he reached out again. The pressure of both his hands on her bare arms sent a shiver rippling through her.

"Maybe the heat is getting to you," he murmured. "I'll grab you a bottle of water from the diner—"

"I can get it myself," she said curtly, and then, more politely, "Thanks."

Casson let go of her, gazed at her for what seemed longer than necessary, and then strode to his car. Afraid that he would turn around and see the conflicting emotions on her face, she fled into the office.

Mandy was preoccupied with a jam in the printer, and Justine was glad she had a few moments to compose herself.

She glanced out the window and watched Casson drive off, an ache blooming in her chest. Ronnie and Andy were only here for the weekend, but it sounded like they were going to have a great time with Casson.

"I'm not surprised he's taken," Mandy murmured. "But they're not engaged; I didn't notice any ring on her finger." She came around from the printer to look at Justine thoughtfully. "Hey, girl, this is your day off. Get thee to a beach. I hear there's a great one right here at Winter's Haven. And after all you've been through you need some serious relaxation."

Justine avoided looking directly at Mandy. The last thing she wanted was to show how emotional she felt, especially with some of the other cottagers now coming out of the diner.

"Yeah, I think I'll do just that," she said lightly.

Leaving the office, Justine got on her bike and pedaled furiously back to her place. Sweating, she peeled off her clothes in the upstairs washroom and got into a one-piece coral swimsuit. After slapping on some sunscreen, she grabbed a beach bag and threw in a book, an oversized beach towel, a small cushion and a bottle of water. With sunglasses and a floppy beach hat, she headed to the beach.

With any luck the cool waters of the bay would extinguish the blaze consuming her, body and soul.

On his drive to and from the town, Casson couldn't stop thinking about Justine's aloofness. And the way she had recoiled from his touch. If he had imagined it the first time he had extended his hand to her elbow, her reaction the second time around had left no doubt in his mind about her feelings. Yet she hadn't resisted his touch during the storm and after he'd kicked Robert out of her house last night…or this morning at his place…

Something twisted in his gut. Maybe Justine was only just beginning to process the traumatic impact of Robert's intrusion and attempted sexual assault. And was transferring her feelings of fear and distrust to *him*.

He had felt his own stomach muscles tighten when he'd gone to return Robert's car to him earlier. Robert had come to the door, his face pale and his eyes puffy, with dark shadows. After ascertaining that he was sober, Casson had handed him his car keys with a terse reminder of the promise he had made to Justine. Robert had apologized for the trouble he had caused, and with a look of resignation driven away.

Casson frowned. Justine hadn't trusted him to begin with. How on earth could he make that change now?

He strode into the cottage and plunked Luna's bag of dog kibble in a corner of the entrance. He couldn't help grinning at the sight of Andy and Luna in the living room, Andy giggling every time Luna licked his cheek. He ducked and feigned trying to escape, Luna skittering around him.

While Ronnie got Andy settled upstairs in the loft Casson prepared a couple of wine spritzers and brought them into the living room. His thoughts turned to Justine again. The feel of her in his arms... The look of her in her nightie...and in the turquoise swimsuit he had first seen her in.

He felt a swirl of heat radiate throughout his body and took a long gulp of his spritzer. He wanted her property, yes—but, like it or not, his body was telling him that he wanted *her*, too. There was absolutely no chance of *that* happening, though. He couldn't imagine that Justine would allow herself to trust him enough to share his bed.

Despite his attraction to Justine—no, he had to be honest with himself and call it what it was: his almost constant torturous desire that was aching for release—he had business to take care of. Contractors waiting. Timelines and deadlines. He had to find the opportune moment to bring up the property issue, and to convince Justine to sell.

If things went his way, he anticipated sealing the deal by the end of his "holiday" at Winter's Haven. But for now his plan would have to wait, until after Ronnie and Andy left.

While he waited for Ronnie to join him he tried to justify to himself why he couldn't tell Justine the real reason he wanted the Russell properties and Winter's Haven.

Maybe because that would make him vulnerable... And maybe he wasn't quite ready to reveal that side of himself to her...yet.

CHAPTER TWELVE

JUSTINE COULDN'T STOP thinking about Casson's guests. They were obviously very good friends, judging from his use of their nicknames. Veronica—Justine couldn't bring herself to call her Ronnie—was very pretty, confident, and seemed the type to say what she wanted to say. And from what she could see Andy was a polite little boy who had been taught good social skills.

It was obvious he loved "Cass." And for him to have developed a relationship with Casson they must have spent a lot of time together. Which meant Casson had spent even *more* time with his mother.

Justine felt something jab at her insides. She stopped and brushed the remnants of beach sand from her legs. *What did she expect?* That a gorgeous, successful entrepreneur like Casson Forrester would be unattached? *And why should she care?*

His intentions were not on par with hers when it came to Winter's Haven. She shouldn't even be trusting him, given his manipulative way of getting himself onto her property. And after Robert's infidelity she'd vowed she wouldn't offer her trust to any other man so easily in the future.

But you trusted Casson to stay over in case Robert came back...

Yes, she had. And he had comforted her too. Made her

breakfast at his place. *Kissed her.* And while he had been doing all those things Justine had forgotten what Casson was really here for.

Justine reached the house and went up to shower. She had spent more time than she'd originally planned on the beach. After a refreshing swim in the bay she had dried off on the chaise lounge and drifted to sleep, listening to the waves lap against the shore.

Now she towel-dried her hair and slipped into a pair of white denim shorts and a flowered halter top. She went down to the kitchen and grabbed a lemon-lime soda, and decided to make herself a tuna and tomato sandwich on walnut bread.

She checked the clock. She had a feeling it was going to be a long evening and night.

After finishing her sandwich, she went out to water her vegetable and flower gardens with the hose that was connected to a pump in the bay. Ordinarily she loved doing this—it was part of her morning and evening routine—but tonight she did it perfunctorily, lost in her thoughts.

A sudden bark startled her and she turned. Casson jumped back and Luna skittered away, barking at the offending spray of water. Justine dropped the hose and stared at Casson helplessly as he pinched his drenched shirt and pulled it away from his chest.

"I'm *so* sorry," she told him.

Luna came bounding toward her, now that she had relinquished her water weapon, and Justine patted her and glanced edgewise at Casson.

"I can get you a towel…" she offered contritely.

"If you insist," he drawled. "The funny thing is, I was coming to see you about getting a couple of extra towels for Ronnie and Andy. I was supposed to go back to the office earlier for some, but Ronnie and I got to talking, and then once Andy had a rest we spent the rest of the afternoon on the beach. It wasn't until after supper that I realized I had forgotten. By that time the office was closed."

His eyes narrowed as he spoke, and Justine could feel his gaze lowering over her body.

"I see that you were out on the beach as well," he said, starting to undo the top buttons of his shirt.

Justine frowned. *How would he know that?*

"You're more tanned than the last time I saw you," he said dryly.

He finished undoing all his buttons and flapped the wet panels of his shirt away from his body. Justine's gaze slid down and she caught a glimpse of his chest and sculpted abs. She felt her pulse accelerating, sparking an invigorating trail along her nerve-endings. When her glance moved upward she was mortified to find that Casson was well aware of her visual exploration.

"Yes, it was a perfect day to relax on the beach," she said, a little too brightly. "I hope your guests enjoyed it also?"

"Oh, they did. Andy and Luna had fun kicking a ball around before splashing about in the bay, and Ronnie enjoyed lying in the sun before her swim."

Justine wished he hadn't gone into detail. She didn't *want* to picture Veronica lying there in a bikini while Casson spread sunscreen all over her. But her mind had a will of its own, and she began to think of what he and Veronica might have been doing while Andy and Luna were playing...

Kissing, maybe. She'd have run her hands over the soft fuzz on his chest...

"I'd appreciate you lending us some extra towels."

His voice nudged her back to the present, and she nodded. "I'll only be a minute. You can wait in the porch if you'd like."

"Oh, by the way," Casson added as she opened the inner door. "I had another reason for coming by…"

Justine turned, and there was something in his voice that made her wonder if it had to do with Robert's departure. Or selling Winter's Haven.

She looked at him suspiciously, her guard up.

"If you haven't made other plans, you're welcome to join us for a campfire. I picked up a bag of marshmallows for Andy." He grinned and his gaze swept over her. "But you might want to change into something more substantial," he said, his gaze lingering on her exposed shoulders. "I don't want the mosquitoes to attack you when it gets dark."

Justine first thought was to decline. She couldn't imagine being the fourth wheel around the campfire.

What would they talk about? And did Veronica know that he was inviting her?

And then she heard her own traitorous voice murmuring casually, "Sure, why not?" before she flew in to get some towels, her heart a jackhammer.

Justine's acceptance took Casson by complete surprise. He'd been sure Justine was going to turn down his invitation. Earlier, she had been courteous enough to Ronnie and Andy, but Casson had detected a slight resistance on her part to over-extend herself.

He'd thought about it on the beach this afternoon while Ronnie had sunbathed and Andy had played with Luna. He'd tried to put himself in her shoes, having to put up with someone who had manipulated—though he would say *masterminded*—his way into Winter's Haven.

Of course Justine would be on the defensive—not only with *him*, but maybe even with his guests. Or rather *guest*. He wasn't an expert on female psychology, but he had sensed a bit of tension from Justine. Maybe it was the way she had glanced edgewise at Ronnie and stood there a little awkwardly, her cheeks like pink blossoms.

Luna flopped down on Justine's entrance mat. "Make yourself at home." Casson chuckled. "Although I might as well do the same."

He made himself comfortable on a padded wicker chair—or as comfortable as he could be with a wet shirt that kept sticking to him—and a minute later Justine re-emerged. She had changed into a red T-shirt and a navy hoodie and sweat pants. Her lipstick was the same shade as her top—a cherry-red that activated his pulse. She handed him a towel and placed a big nautical-style beach bag on the wicker chair next to him before bending down to put on her running shoes.

Luna ambled over to lick her face, making Justine lose her balance. Casson dropped his towel and leaped forward to help her straighten up. He heard her quick intake of breath and wanted nothing more than to lean forward and seal those lips with his own.

Taste their fruity nectar.

Unable to stop himself, he began to move his face toward hers...

Justine pulled away as if she had been jolted by an electric current. Something shifted in his expression and he gave her a curt smile.

"We'd better be going. Andy gets tired quickly, and usually has an early bedtime, but he won't leave me in peace until I make him a campfire and we have a marsh-mallow roast."

Justine nodded and saw his gaze drop to her beach bag. "A flashlight for when I walk back home," she said. "And the extra towels you asked for."

As they started walking Justine diverted her thoughts to what Casson had said about Andy getting tired and having a rest earlier. Most little boys his age had boundless energy. Many of the cottagers at Winter's Haven had kids staying, and they tore around like little hellions—often to the consternation of their parents.

"I noticed that Andy seems a little…fragile," she said, trying to break the awkward silence. "He must have had a late night before the drive here this morning; he has such dark shadows under his eyes."

Casson didn't respond. Justine bit her lip, wondering if she had sounded judgmental.

They continued to walk in silence along the road, Luna beside Casson. Justine kept her eyes on the sun-dappled shadows of the pines.

Suddenly Casson slowed his steps and turned to look at her. "It wasn't because he had a late night," he said, an edge creeping into his voice. "It's because he has cancer."

Justine felt waves of shock rippling through her body. For a few moments she couldn't move. Or speak. She stared up at Casson and knew her face must reveal the questions she wanted to ask but couldn't bring herself to for fear of sounding insensitive.

"He's in remission and undergoing maintenance chemo," Casson said. "His treatment has taken a lot out of him—*and* Ronnie—but he's a tough little guy, despite the impression he may give with those skinny little legs and body. He's got a lot of spirit…"

His voice wavered and Justine felt her heart breaking.

Casson looked away and continued walking. "He had some dizzy spells and nosebleeds when he was four," he said as Justine caught up to him. "And he was getting headaches. When he had a seizure with a high fever they did some tests and he was brought immediately to Toronto's Hospital for Sick Children, where they started chemotherapy—which took months. Once Andy was in remission they started maintenance chemo. He's now in his second year of that."

"Poor child…" Jasmine squeezed her eyes so she wouldn't cry, but felt a teardrop trickle down anyway. "And his poor parents." She shook her head. "I can't even imagine what they must have been going through…"

Casson didn't offer any further details, and Justine didn't feel it was appropriate to ply him with questions, so they walked in silence again.

No wonder Andy looked so gaunt beneath his baseball cap.

She didn't remember seeing any hair around his temples, but had just assumed that he had gotten a summer buzz cut.

Justine felt sorry for Veronica. How heart-wrenching it must have been for her to hear that her only child was afflicted with a disease that could take his life.

And what about Andy's father? Where was he? And what exactly was the relationship between Veronica and Casson?

It must have been devastating for Casson to learn of Andy's diagnosis as well—especially after having lost his brother to leukemia.

These thoughts and more kept swirling in her mind. She had been able to tell from that first meeting this morning that Casson had a special relationship with Andy. And with Andy's mother. They looked like a happy family, vacationing together and doing all the things that families did.

So why was *she* being invited to take part in their evening? If Casson and Veronica were more than just friends, wouldn't he want to spend the evening alone with her? Okay, Andy was with them, but he'd eventually go to bed…

Justine had no intention of asking Casson to enlighten her about any of these questions. They had arrived at the cottage and Andy was opening the screen door in excitement, holding the bag of marshmallows.

Casson's face lit up immediately. Seeing him like that

made Justine choke up. She hoped she could keep it to-gether now that she knew about Andy's condition. She smiled at Andy and he smiled back and waved before at-tempting to open up the bag.

"Hey, hold on a minute, kid!" Casson chuckled. "Let me get the fire going. If you open the bag now there won't be any left to roast."

"Aw, Cass, I promise I'll just have one…" Andy grinned.

"And I'll be watching him like a hawk to make sure," his mother said, emerging from the cottage. She greeted Justine with a smile. "So nice you could join us, Justine."

"Hi, Veronica." Justine returned the smile, not wanting to reveal how uncomfortable she was.

"Please." Veronica grinned at her as she came down the cottage steps. "It's Ronnie, remember? Only my mother calls me by my full name."

Justine laughed. "Okay—Ronnie. By the way, here are the towels." She pulled them out of her beach bag.

"Great—thank you." Ronnie took them and before opening the door said, "Can I get you a drink before we head down to the beach? I'm having white wine, but I can mix you a margarita, if you like, or a martini. I make a wicked chocolate martini!"

"Oh…um…a little white wine would be fine…"

"Great. How about you, Cass? A margarita?" she said teasingly.

Casson made a face. "I'll have a nice cold beer, thank you. A good Canadian lager for a good Canadian boy."

Ronnie let out a belly laugh. *"Andy's* a good Canadian boy. *You*—I'm not so sure." She turned to her son. "What can I get you, sweetie? How about some lemonade?"

"Sure, Mom," Andy replied distractedly, busy helping Casson gather twigs from the bushes nearby and putting them in a large canvas bag.

"Hey, Ronnie!" Casson grinned. "Would you mind

grabbing me a T-shirt and my hoodie? I don't want to get eaten alive by mosquitoes down by the water."

"Is there anything *I* can do?" Justine said after Ronnie had gone to get the drinks.

Casson turned and looked at her. *For a little too long.*

"You can help Ronnie bring down the drinks," he said finally, a gleam in his eyes. "Andy and I will head down to the beach and get the fire started. Ready, partner?" he asked the boy.

"Ready!" Andy nodded excitedly.

His baseball cap fell off, and Justine felt a twinge in her heart at the sight of Andy's shaved head. She watched them walking away, Casson's muscular frame next to Andy's little body, Luna bounding ahead of them. She could see that Casson was deliberately walking slowly so Andy could keep up with him.

He's a good guy, an inner voice whispered.

Justine shivered, even though the night air was balmy. She remembered how upset she had been after their first meeting in the office, and how rattled when he'd let himself into her house with Luna. And when she'd stumbled and fallen into his lap...

But she couldn't deny that he had some good qualities. He had stayed the night in case Robert came back, hadn't he? And the way he interacted with Andy, you'd swear he was the boy's father. *That's how a father should be,* she mused.

Another thought occurred to her. Could it be that Ronnie was divorced and Casson was potentially her next husband?

"Hey, Justine, can you give me a hand with this wine and the glasses? I'll bring the beer and the pitcher of lemonade. And Casson's clothes."

"Sure."

Justine stepped up to the door. She took the tray and held the door open for Ronnie.

As they walked down the path to the beach Ronnie said softly, "Isn't Casson something? He goes above and beyond when it comes to Andy… He's told you about Andy's condition?" She glanced at Justine.

"Yes." Justine felt Ronnie's gaze and turned to meet it. "I was so sorry to hear about that," she said simply. "I can't imagine what you and Andy have been through."

Ronnie's pace slowed. "I couldn't have done it without Cass. He's not only a great cousin, but an even greater godfather to Andy." Her voice quivered. "We're so blessed to have him in our lives."

Justine's heart was racing. *Cousin? Godfather?*

"He's like a brother—the brother I never had." Ronnie's eyes welled up. "Here I go, getting all weepy again." She blinked the tears away. "Casson's going to be a great dad someday. And an awesome husband for one lucky lady…"

Casson had the fire started by the time Ronnie and Justine got down to the beach. The dry kindling was crackling over crumpled up newspaper. He looked up briefly and nodded at them before arranging thicker branches in a spoke-like configuration. Andy threw in some small twigs occasionally, watching in fascination as the fire crackled and sent out sparks.

There were four Muskoka chairs arranged in a semi-circle behind the fire-pit, and in the middle a huge tree stump served as a tabletop. Justine set down the wine and glasses, and Ronnie followed suit with the beer and lemonade.

Casson took off his damp shirt and tossed it onto one of the chairs, before reaching for the T-shirt and hoodie that Ronnie had hooked over her arm and was now holding out to him. Justine was just steps away, and he could tell that she was trying not to glance at his bare torso.

Feeling a rush suffuse his body, he turned away to check the fire.

When the fire was robust, Casson stacked half-logs over the branches and in no time at all the fire was roaring. Feeling the sweat trickling down his face, Casson thanked Ronnie for the beer, and helped himself to a long swig. Ronnie poured Andy a glass of lemonade before filling the wine glasses.

"Here's to summer fun." Ronnie lifted her glass. "Cheers, guys."

Casson tipped his beer bottle to clink with Ronnie's glass. They laughed when Andy clinked his glass with them. When Casson turned to do the same with Justine their gazes locked. Something swirled in the pit of his stomach. Justine's face was mesmerizing in the light and shadows cast by the fire. Her eyes looked like blue ice, and standing so close to her beside the spiraling flames he felt desire flicking through his body.

He wanted her.

With a yearning that stunned him.

Out of the corner of his eye he saw Ronnie and Andy putting marshmallows on the branches Casson had collected and sharpened earlier. He was glad their attention was diverted, and even more glad that Justine's eyes seemed to be reflecting something he hadn't seen before. In her or in any other woman he had dated.

Maybe it was the romance of a campfire on a starry night, with the dark, silky waters of Georgian Bay just steps away, the soft gushing of their ebb and flow joining with the crackling of the fire. Maybe it was just the fact that Justine was one helluva beautiful woman, and that having already kissed those lips once, he felt the urge to kiss them again.

And again.

It was a good thing, perhaps, that Ronnie and Andy were there, or right now he'd be—

"Hey, Cass!" Andy called. "Come and roast some marshmallows. You too, Justine. Mom went to get me my hoodie."

Casson watched the expression in Justine's eyes change instantly. She gave Andy a bright smile and strode over to pick up a stick and a marshmallow. She laughed at the sight of Andy's sticky face.

A warm feeling came over Casson at the picture they made. Justine seemed so comfortable around Andy. *Natural.* Not stiff, like some of his past dates when he'd introduced them to his godson. Justine was chatting with Andy as if she had always known him. And he was responding in a spirited fashion, bursting into giggles at one point.

She would make a great mother.

A sudden mental image of Justine pregnant, her hands resting gently over her belly, followed almost immediately by a picture of him feeling the mound as well, startled him.

Where were these thoughts coming from?

Casson felt his heartbeat quicken and the sweat start to slide down his temples. He wiped his face with his sleeve and had another gulp of beer before rising.

As the four of them twirled their sticks over the flames Casson stole a glance at Justine. She was the first to be done. She stepped back and, after waving her stick to cool off her perfectly roasted marshmallow, bit into its golden-brown exterior and got to the warm, gooey white center.

"Mmm…heaven…" she said between bites.

She'd got some of the caramel center stuck around her mouth, and Casson found himself wishing he could lick the stickiness off…

"Hey, Cass, you need to concentrate a little better than that!"

Ronnie's laughing voice reached his ears and, looking away from Justine, he groaned when he realized that his marshmallow had blackened. Shrugging, he set down his stick.

"Here, let me show you how it's done." Justine grinned.

She prepared a new stick and twirled it slowly, until the marshmallow reached a toffee-like color, and then handed it to him. He bit into it, savoring its caramel sweetness, his eyes never leaving her face.

"That," he said, after finishing it off, "was the best marshmallow I've ever had. What do you say, Andy? Should we give Justine the prize for Best Marshmallow?"

Andy nodded vigorously. "But what do we *give* her, Cass?" He cocked his head in puzzlement.

Casson stroked his chin, pretending to look thoughtful. "How about we take her fishing tomorrow?"

"Yeah! Can you come, Justine?" Andy's face lit up. "You won the prize!"

Justine gazed from Andy to Casson and then to Ronnie, who was nodding approvingly.

"Yes—go! I don't fish." Ronnie chuckled. "I just eat."

Casson met Justine's gaze. "You can take us to the hot spots…"

He watched Justine's eyes flicker and her mouth twitch ever so slightly. Her gaze shifted to Andy, who had his little hands in a prayer position and was looking up at her beseechingly.

Her face broke into a big grin. "I guess I can't turn down first prize," she said, reaching down to give Andy a hug.

After they'd feasted on another round of marshmallows Casson walked to the water's edge and filled a couple of large pails. While he extinguished the fire Ronnie and Justine finished what was left of their wine and started gathering up the glasses, bottles and the pitcher of lemonade.

They returned to the cottage, and Andy said goodnight to Justine before going inside.

"Well, I'll say goodnight too," Justine said brightly, slinging her beach bag over her arm. "Thank you for a nice evening. It's been a long time since I roasted marsh-mallows."

"Goodnight, Justine," Ronnie said, waving. "Andy had fun with you."

"I won't say goodnight just yet," Casson said to Justine when they were alone. "I'm walking you home after I read Andy a story. *And it'll be a short one,*" he added huskily.

CHAPTER THIRTEEN

CASSON HAD INVITED her to wait inside the cottage, but Justine had said she'd be fine outside. The night air was warm and the half-moon provided some illumination. She sat on a lawn chair by the front door of the cottage with Luna at her feet. The screen on the door was partially up, and she could faintly hear Casson's voice.

Barely a few minutes had passed when Casson re-emerged. "The little guy was wiped," he said. "Couldn't keep his eyes open. By the third page he was out." Casson shrugged. "Come on, Luna." He ruffled her fur briskly. "Time to take Miss *Wintry* home." He flashed Justine a grin.

Justine rose and put up her hand in protest. "I'm a big girl and I can take myself home. Really." She looked at him pointedly. "I won't get lost; it *is* my property." She made herself smile in case she had sounded abrupt. "But, thank you; I appreciate your offer."

Casson's eyes glinted. "I'm not offering. You may know your way around, but I won't be able to sleep wondering if a big, bad wolf is following you. Or the three little bears."

Justine couldn't help laughing. "You've been reading too many kids' books, Mr. *Forrest*. Your imagination is running wild."

"Indeed."

The way Casson was looking at her made her heart do a flip. Taking a deep breath, she started walking.

If he wanted to walk with her she couldn't very well stop him. And, to be honest, she didn't really want to.

But having him walk so closely beside her was unnerving.

Why did he have to look so gorgeous, even in the moonlight?

Justine shivered, and before she knew it Casson had zipped down his hoodie and taken it off to put it around her shoulders.

Even though she had her own hoodie on, Justine could feel the warmth from his. She couldn't very well take it off and tell him the *real* cause of her shivering.

The fact that her attraction to him was alarming her, especially since the only reason he was at Winter's Haven in the first place was to find a way to convince her to sell.

But, although she might dislike Casson's intentions when it came to her property, she had to admit that there were things about him that she did like. *A lot.* The way he looked, for one. And the way he sounded. The way he cared for Andy.

The way he had come to her rescue and made her feel safe...

Her acknowledgement of liking Casson worried her. How could she even *think* of encouraging any of those feelings? What possible outcome could come from acting on them? After all, Casson would be leaving after his little holiday at Winter's Haven. And she'd still be holding the keys.

"If you're not doing anything tomorrow night..." Casson slackened his pace and waited until she turned to glance at him. "I'd really like to talk to you about my proposal."

Justine's heart plummeted. For a moment it had sounded like he was going to ask her for a date.

Get with it, an inner voice ridiculed. *He wants Winter's Haven, not you. And don't forget it.*

She gave a tired sigh. "I don't really see the purpose of a meeting. There's nothing that would make me contemplate selling. To you or to anyone else."

She picked up her pace, anxious to get home and away from any further discussion around Winter's Haven.

He stepped into place with her. "There are...things I haven't told you," he said softly. "Things that might just change your perspective."

Could he be anymore cryptic?

"If it has to do with offering more money, I'll save you the energy of making the offer." She smiled cynically and tossed her head back. "Not *everyone* can be bought."

"I realize that." He nodded. "I can see how much this place means to you." He reached over as they walked and shifted the hoodie on Justine's shoulders to prevent it from slipping off.

She felt his fingers pause momentarily, and her pulse drummed wildly. And then his hand was off her shoulder. He slowed his pace, and Justine felt like the path leading to her house was an eternity away.

Other than the tread of their footsteps, the chirping of the crickets was the only sound breaking the silence. Justine inhaled the sweet scent of a nearby linden tree.

This is all too much, she thought.

Having Casson walk her home was doing things to her that confused her. She was prepared to battle him verbally, whatever he proposed, and yet her body seemed to want to surrender to him...

Justine stopped walking and frowned. "Why can't you tell me *now*?"

Casson's mouth twisted. "There are things I need to show you as well, and I don't have them with me. Tomorrow we're fishing during the day, so I thought the evening would be a perfect time to—"

Justine practically jumped as Casson's cell phone rang. He reached into his back pocket and a frown appeared on his face.

"Hey, Ronnie, what's up?"

Ronnie's voice came loud and clear. "It's Andy, Cass. His temperature is way up and I'm worried he's going to have a seizure. I need to take him to the hospital…"

"I'm on my way," Casson told her, and stuck his phone back in his pocket. "We'll talk tomorrow," he said to Justine, his hand reaching out to squeeze her arm.

He whistled to Luna, who was investigating a scuttling sound in some bushes. Luna bounded after him and Justine watched with a sick feeling in her stomach as they ran down the driveway and disappeared around the bend.

Casson raced back to the cottage, every footstep matching the beat of his heart. Andy's face and arms were flaming hot. He was moaning, and couldn't keep his eyes open. Ronnie had placed a cool cloth over his forehead and pulled back his top blanket. Casson's heart twisted at the sight of him, and of Ronnie's pale face and wide eyes.

Casson picked Andy up and carefully made his way down the stairs. He set him down gently in the back seat of Ronnie's car while Ronnie sat next to him and fastened his seatbelt before placing a light shawl over him. After a dash inside to make sure there was water in Luna's bowl, Casson drove to the hospital in Parry Sound, hoping he wouldn't get stopped for speeding.

Andy was checked in and seen by midnight. But by the time the doctors had inserted an IV, run some standard tests, and the Emergency Room doctor had examined the results, it was close to four a.m.

Andy was transferred to a room. Although his fever had

dropped, the doctors wanted to continue to monitor him, given his condition and recent treatment.

Casson and Ronnie kept vigil by his bedside, taking turns to shut their eyes, and at seven a.m. a doctor came to explain that, although Andy was unlikely to have a seizure, he recommended that a follow-up appointment be made with Andy's specialist at SickKids.

Ronnie decided it was best to take Andy back home and make the appointment.

Casson wanted to drive them home to Gravenhurst, but Ronnie reassured him that she had caught enough sleep to handle the drive alone.

With her reassurance that she would call him if she needed him, Casson brushed a kiss on Andy's forehead and they left the hospital.

By the time he drove her car back to the cottage, and she returned to the hospital they would be ready to discharge Andy.

When Casson got out of Ronnie's car and she switched to the driver's seat he reached down to give her a hug. "Drive safely, Ronnie. And call me when you get home."

Casson watched her drive away, then entered the cottage to Luna's welcome. He opened the door to let her run out, and when they were both inside again took off his shoes and, without bothering to undress, fell on top of his bed and crashed.

Casson woke up three hours later. He felt pretty ragged, and could only imagine how Ronnie felt. He checked his phone and saw that Ronnie had texted to say they were home and she would let him know of any developments with Andy. He sent her a quick message, apologizing for sleeping through the text and sending them hugs.

He not only felt rough, he looked it, too, he thought a few moments later, staring at his reflection in the bathroom mirror. He stroked his jaw and chin. He had let his usual five o'clock shadow grow for over two weeks, and now he decided the scruff had to go.

After shaving he had a hot shower, letting the pulsating jets ease the tension in his muscles. He lathered himself with the shower gel provided, his nose wrinkling at the scent. It reminded him of something...of *Justine,* he realized.

He glanced at the label. Rose Rapture. Wonderful, he thought wryly, rinsing off, he'd always wanted to come out smelling like a rose. Stepping out of the shower, he grabbed a towel and briskly dried himself. Wrapping it around his hips, and stepping into flip-flops, he padded into the kitchen and put the coffee on.

Casson reached into the cupboard to get a mug, and then a movement at the screen door caught his eye. He stood there, mug in hand, towel around his hips, and met Justine's embarrassed gaze through the glass of the door.

CHAPTER FOURTEEN

JUSTINE HAD BEEN on the verge of turning away, but now it was too late. Casson had already seen her. She let her hand drop, wishing she had thought to call first. He didn't seem too perturbed over the fact that he was wearing nothing but a towel, though, and she tried to keep her eyes from wandering as he walked to the door. She focused on his face, now clean-shaven, and couldn't help but gulp.

Shadow or no shadow, Casson was gorgeous. Drop-dead gorgeous.

He opened the door and she blurted, "Is Andy okay? Is he back from the hospital? I made some chicken soup for him and some lemon blueberry muffins…" She stopped, and looked down at the stainless steel pot she was holding on to for dear life, aware that she was blabbering.

"That's very kind of you, Justine." Casson smiled. "His fever dropped, thank goodness. They checked him out… did some tests. He might just have been overtired, and with his compromised immune system it doesn't take much to knock him down. The doctor suggested Ronnie do a follow-up at SickKids. They're home now. Come in," he added, taking the pot and container.

The sight of his sculpted torso sent a ripple of pure desire through her body. As he set the items down on the kitchen counter she felt her cheeks burning. She patted

Luna and then turned around slowly, hoping Casson had gone to change, but he was still standing across from her, one hand on the back of a chair and the other on his hip.

"I suppose I should go and get decent," he said, the corners of his mouth lifting. "I'll be right back."

"Um…well, since Ronnie and Andy aren't here you can have the soup and muffins yourself…" Justine said, trying hard to keep her eyes on his face.

"I don't think so," he drawled, his eyes crinkling at the corners. "We can have the muffins with coffee. As for the soup—we can share it later. If you haven't already made supper plans."

He started to walk away, and then paused to look back at her.

"Since you're here now, we might as well have that meeting I was talking about yesterday. But I think you'll be much more receptive to what I have to tell you if I put some clothes on." He grinned. "It's so much more professional than just wearing a towel and Rose Rapture."

Justine felt her cheeks flaming. She couldn't tear her gaze away from him as he strode away, and her eyes took in every detail from his damp, curling dark hair to his muscled neck and sculpted arms and shoulders. And the firm slope to the small of his back…

As the door clicked shut Justine snapped out of her stupor and took a deep breath. She wiped her brow. It was a hot one today, but she felt even hotter inside—especially after seeing Casson half naked. Again, she wished she had thought to phone him instead of just showing up at his door…

She wondered what exactly he had to show her. He seemed to think it could sway her in some way. She couldn't help feeling apprehensive. Too much had happened since Casson had set foot at Winter's Haven, and somehow she had an uneasy feeling that he had something up his sleeve. Something that might tip the scales in his favor.

Justine braced herself. She had no intention of letting him weaken her resolve. No matter what he presented her with, she would turn it down.

"Hey, make yourself at home." Casson chuckled, coming out of his room with a large brown envelope in his hand. He had changed into a black T-shirt and a pair of faded jeans with a couple of worn-through spots above the knees.

Justine wished he didn't have to look so damned sexy. She pulled out a chair at the kitchen table and sat down while Casson poured coffee into two mugs. He set out the milk and then, sitting down across from her, helped himself to a muffin.

"Mmm." He nodded. "Thanks for breakfast." He pushed the container toward her.

"I had one earlier, thanks."

She stared pointedly at the envelope beside him. Casson had tried to hand her this very envelope before, when he had first come to her house. He had said it was a development proposal drafted by an architect friend of his, and had suggested that she at least give the plan and drawings a glance. He obviously thought that whatever was in the envelope might dispel her doubts about his venture.

Well, she still had doubts. Only she supposed she could let him at least show her his plans.

Casson set his mug down. "Look, Justine, do you have plans this afternoon?"

"Wh-why?" Justine shifted uncomfortably.

"It might take some time to go over the details."

"I can't imagine there will be much to discuss," she said, "so don't get your hopes up." She didn't want Casson to think that there was even the *slightest* chance she would change her mind about selling.

His eyes blazed into hers and his mouth curved slightly. "A man can always hope," he drawled. "Well?"

"Well, what?" She tossed her head.

"*Are* you free this afternoon?"

"I will be after you show me what's in the envelope. I'll have a few minutes. But then I have to run a quick errand before relieving Mandy. She's off early today to go to a wedding."

"Mmm…" Casson rubbed his chin. "I need more than a few minutes." He tapped his fingers on the table top. "Why don't we leave the envelope till later this evening? Do you have time to go out for lunch? My treat." He smiled crookedly. "To thank you for your kindness to Andy."

Justine felt a slow flush creep over her cheeks. "That's not necessary."

"Look, Justine…" He set his elbows on the table and leaned closer, his gaze becoming serious. "A lot has happened for both of us in the last couple of days. Let's forget about the sale and everything else for a while and just enjoy an hour. Away from work, away from worry. What do you say?" His eyebrows lifted.

Justine examined his face for the slightest sign of insincerity and couldn't find one. She glanced at the time on her phone. "I'm sorry. I don't even have an hour."

Darn, if only she had brought the soup over earlier…

"Thanks for the offer, though."

Flushing, Justine averted her gaze and patted Luna before leaving. She resisted the temptation of looking back as she walked toward her car.

As she pulled out of the driveway she glanced in her rearview mirror. Casson was in the doorway, watching her…

Casson rubbed his chin as Justine drove off. He was disappointed that his impromptu offer hadn't worked out, but there was still tonight to look forward to.

Justine's expression when she'd told him not to get his hopes up had been so different from when she'd had first arrived at the door, when she'd tried not to show that she was glancing at his body... He had caught a spark of *something* in those blue-gray depths then. Something that made him wonder if there was a current below the surface, a fuse that just needed to be lit.

No matter how much Justine tried to show otherwise, Casson felt deep in his gut that she wasn't immune to him. Maybe at first, when she'd fallen into his lap and they'd kissed, it might have been just physical for both of them, but after their evening around the campfire he'd sensed there was something *deeper*. He had *felt* it. It had been as if she were seeing him with new eyes.

He had caught her expression when he was with Andy, too; it had seemed softer, relaxed, approving. But of course there was a limit to her approval. She was far from approving of his intentions regarding Winter's Haven.

But maybe that would change tonight.

His initial plan was to show her the architect's drawings and then suggest she sell him Winter's Haven with the proviso that she would manage his new resort. If she accepted his offer he would agree to delay renovations or construction until he had a deeper understanding of the unique features of the huge parcel of land that comprised both the Russell properties and Winter's Haven.

Justine would be a great asset, and he was sure that eventually she would see that what he was planning would not be to the detriment of the landscape, but an enhancement— with the most important consequence being its benefit to kids like Andy, and their parent or parents, who deserved some pampering after dealing with the heartbreak of a cancer diagnosis and treatment for their child.

And then he would show her the deed.

She would be shocked, perhaps even angry, but it had

to be done. Justine had the right to know. And maybe the knowledge that he owned part of Winter's Haven already might just sway her into considering selling…

If Justine still balked after that he would pull out his ace: a considerable increase in his initial price offer and, if she agreed to it, an offer for her to continue to live in the house rent-free for as long as she was managing Franklin's Resort.

Casson closed the door. It was too bad their fishing trip today was a bust. Andy would have loved it. He checked the time on his cell phone and wondered how Andy was doing. His stomach twisted at the memory of Andy moaning, his face contorted and pale.

Grabbing his phone, he sent Ronnie a text.

Ronnie responded quickly, saying that Andy was resting and his temperature had stabilized. She thanked him for everything and promised to visit him again when Andy got the go-ahead from his specialist in Toronto.

The pot sitting on the counter caught his eye. The chicken soup Justine had made for a sick little boy she hardly knew.

His heart swelled.

She's a keeper, an inner voice told him as he placed the pot in the fridge.

"Time for a swim," he called out to Luna, and she bounded after him.

He could do with a splash in the bay.

Afterwards, Casson stretched out on a chaise lounge, and Luna plunked herself down next to him. He reached out and stroked her back. Much as he loved his dog, he thought about how nice it would be to have Justine lying next to him…

He propped himself on his side and looked out at the bay, a blue sheet twinkling with diamonds under the sunny sky. He could hardly believe that in two days his Franklin & Casson on the Bay exhibition would open.

Before he'd left home to take possession of the Russells' properties he had checked with all his contacts to ensure that everything was in place for the event. The paintings would be kept in a secure depository until the day before the opening. Lighting was adjusted. Security was arranged. Responses from the invited patrons verified. Media presence confirmed. An adjoining room had been prepared for the silent auction. The banquet courses were finalized.

All this had been delegated to a committee he had carefully chosen almost a year earlier. They were all prepared, as was he.

There was only one thing he hadn't planned or even considered up to now...and that was bringing a date.

CHAPTER FIFTEEN

JUSTINE LOOKED UP to see Mandy walking toward her. She hadn't even heard her car in the driveway.

"Nice cut and style," she said. "But what are you doing back here?"

"I left the wedding card on the desk. Here it is." Mandy peered at her with a slight frown. "Hey, why did you look so glum when I first walked in? Like you lost your best friend…"

Justine sighed and told her about Andy and his illness, and how Casson and Ronnie had rushed him to the hospital…

"Poor little fellow," Mandy said. "I hope it turns out to be nothing serious…" She sat on a corner of the desk. "My goodness, there seems to be a lot of drama around Casson Forrester. And not only at Winter's Haven."

"What do you mean?" Justine frowned.

"While I was waiting for my hairdresser to call me over I checked out the public bulletin board. There was a poster about an event that Casson's putting on at the Stockey Centre. It's being sponsored by his company, Forrest Hardware. I can't believe neither of us heard about it before."

"What kind of event? A home show?"

Mandy chuckled. "No, it has nothing to do with lumber or building. It's an art exhibition—two of the Group of Seven artists. Some of their most famous works will be on display for a week, and there's also a silent auction for one of the paintings on opening night, and an invitation-only fund-raising banquet."

Justine's mind raced.

Casson had never mentioned an exhibition when he was telling her about the Franklin painting...or had she forgotten?

No, she wouldn't have forgotten something like that.

And why hadn't he mentioned it at all today?

"When is this happening?" Justine tried to keep her voice steady, thinking about Casson's brother and his con-nection with *Mirror Lake*.

"All next week. Why? Do you want to go?" Mandy raised her eyebrows. "It starts on Monday night. Two days from now." She sighed dramatically. "I can't believe this guy. Not only is he gorgeous and successful—oh, and did I mention gorgeous?" She laughed. "He's also a devoted godfather *and* a patron of the arts. I've checked all the boxes under 'Man of Your Dreams.'" She glanced slyly at Justine. "Except maybe the categories of 'great cook' and 'even better lover.'"

Justine's mouth dropped open. "Are you *kidding* me?"

"I'm serious. He's single, you're single, and now that you've found out that Ronnie's his cousin you should grab your chance while he's on your property, for heaven's sakes." She gave Justine's shoulder a gentle punch. "I think you'd make a great couple."

"I think it takes a little more than *that* to make a cou-ple, Mandy," she scoffed, returning the soft punch. "And, besides, he wants my property—not *me.*"

Mandy walked away, shrugging.

Before the door closed behind her Justine called out sheepishly, "What did you say the name of the event was?"

"Franklin & Casson on the Bay."

* * *

Later, after closing the office, Justine went home and changed into a sky blue bikini. It was too humid to do anything but go for a refreshing swim.

Walking down to the beach, Justine couldn't stop thinking about Casson. About his exhibition and what he had told her about his brother Franklin, and what he *hadn't* told her. The fact that he was a patron of the arts just added to the data she had been unconsciously accumulating about him from the time he had stepped foot on her property.

There was quite an accumulation of physical data. She had to admit that when she wasn't involved with desk matters or the cottagers at Winter's Haven her brain kept summoning up images of Casson. They flicked through her memory as if she were looking through a photo gallery online: Casson in a tailored suit, his dark chestnut eyes glinting at her; Casson sitting in his Mustang convertible; Casson by the campfire and Casson walking through the door with a towel around his hips. Images that circulated constantly in her head.

The emotional data took up just as much space. The knowledge of his relationship with his brother. His congenial manner with Mandy and Melody and the cottagers in the diner. His kindness and caring toward Andy and Ronnie. His love for his dog. His appreciation for art. His entrepreneurial drive and success in building the Forrest Hardware chain.

But there was so much more that she wanted to know…

What had she filled her thoughts with before Casson walked into her life?

Whoa, there, she chided herself. He had walked onto her property, not into her *life*.

That realization sobered her. Besides his showing a typical male physical reaction to her on occasion, she couldn't delude herself into thinking that Casson Forrester had any emotional intentions or feelings toward her. Sure, he had shown some consideration, even kindness and concern, but…

But what? an inner voice prompted.

But she wanted more.

Justine bit her lip. Yes, she couldn't deny it to herself any longer. Casson had sparked something within her, and she couldn't control what it was igniting throughout her entire being—not only physically, but emotionally as well. She wanted *him.* Despite all her conflicting feelings about his ploys to get her to sell, she wanted Casson to want *her* more than he wanted Winter's Haven.

But it wasn't that simple.

Or was it?

The sudden urge to go and see Casson stopped Justine in her tracks. He *had* mentioned something about sharing the chicken soup…

She ran back up to the house, slipped on a pair of yellow cotton shorts and a shirt patterned with yellow daisies over her bikini.

Maybe she needed to *show* Casson Forrester that she was interested. Besides throwing herself into his arms—which was what she wished she could do—she had to come up with *something* to see if he was interested too.

And then maybe eventually she'd have the nerve to reveal the fact that she was falling in love with him.

Casson thought about going to the diner before supper. The swim in the bay had revitalized him, and he wanted to chat with the other cottagers and get a feel for what they liked about Winter's Haven and the area. This was his opportunity to discover what features to keep and what could be changed or added in future.

If Justine sold to him.

This last thought jolted him. Before, he had always thought in terms of *when* Justine sold to him.

Why the sudden uncertainty?

He brushed off any remaining beach sand from his feet and Luna's fur, hung his towel to dry on the outside line and entered the cottage. His gaze settled on the pot on the counter. Maybe he should scrap his idea about going to the diner now in case Justine decided to come over a little early…

While Luna was happily devouring her supper Casson went to his room and changed into a white T-shirt and khaki shorts. Whistling, he returned to the kitchen to check the soup, the aroma making his mouth water. He heard his phone ring from his bedroom and sprinted to get it, expecting it to be Ronnie.

His stomach twisted with the thought that Andy's condition might have worsened. But his phone didn't show any caller ID. He frowned.

"Hello?"

"Hello, this is Justine…"

Casson's stomach did a flip. "Hi."

"I—I thought I'd give you a call before coming to knock at your door," she said. "I have some time if you want to show me whatever it is you have to show me…"

Yes!

"Oh, well, a call wasn't necessary. You could have just come to the door."

He heard her clearing her throat. "Well… I just wanted to make sure you were…you weren't…"

He suddenly got it. She didn't want to come unannounced to the door and find him half-undressed again. The thought made him want to laugh, but he restrained himself.

"I'm fully clothed and I'm just heating up your soup," he said. "I was hoping you'd join me."

"Okay… I wouldn't want it to go to waste. And then we can talk."

"Are you at the office? When can you get away?"

"I'm at the end of your driveway," Justine said, and Casson detected a note of sheepishness in her voice. "I'll be there in a minute."

Casson looked out the kitchen window and there she was, straddling her bike as she paused to phone him. He saw her putting her phone in her pocket and start to pedal toward the cottage.

His smile turned into a grin before he burst out laughing.

Casson was holding the door open for her. Justine smiled her thanks and started to walk by him, but Luna's rush to the door stopped her in her tracks. She was penned in between Luna and Casson, who had now shut the door and was standing directly behind her.

"Hey, girl." Justine bent to pat Luna and then immediately regretted it, when her backside brushed against Casson's body. She straightened instantly, her face flaming, and was glad she couldn't see Casson's expression.

"Luna,—couch," Casson's amused voice drawled behind her, and Luna gave a plaintive howl but proceeded to obey.

Justine wiped her brow with her forearm. The humidity outside was high, but it was stifling in the cottage. She wished she could just strip off her clothes and remain in her bikini, like she did in her own house.

She glanced at him edgewise as he set the table. If he'd looked gorgeous in a black T-shirt, he looked magnificent in the white one he was wearing now. It emphasized his broad shoulders, and the firm contours of his chest and stomach. And his khaki shorts fit him oh, so well…

Justine couldn't help thinking that he looked like a hunky model out of a magazine.

Casson put a bottle of white wine in the fridge and then set the platter of cheese and crackers on the table.

"I suppose I should have thought of bringing something a little cooler," Justine said as Casson filled two bowls with soup, "but I thought if Andy was sick chicken soup would do him good."

"Your intentions were honorable," Casson said, and smiled, "and that's what counts."

Justine felt her insides quiver as she met his warm gaze.

They ate in silence for a few minutes and then Casson suddenly rose from his chair. "What am I thinking?" His eyes glinted. "There's cheese, but no wine on the table. Forgive me, my lady."

He gave a mock bow. A spiral of pleasure danced through Justine's body at his words. If only he knew how much she wanted to be *his lady*.

He poured white wine into two glasses and offered her one. "Let's toast our little Andy's health."

They clinked glasses and Justine's gaze locked with Casson's as she tasted the wine—a Pinot Grigio from Niagara-on-the-Lake. With its peachy bouquet and hint of vanilla, it complemented the Oka and the other cheeses Casson had selected.

"Let's take it down to the beach," he said suddenly, when they had each finished their first glass. "It's too hot in the cottage. I'll bring the wine and the glasses, and you can bring the cheese tray." He laughed. "Luna can bring herself."

Justine couldn't quite believe what was happening. Earlier she had decided to show Casson that she was interested. Now here she was, following this gorgeous man to a private beach where they would be sharing wine and cheese on the most sultry night of the summer.

She shivered in anticipation, the wine in her system already starting to loosen her up.

They sat side by side in the Muskoka chairs, nibbling on cheese and crackers and cooling themselves with wine. There was no breeze whatsoever, and the surface of the bay was mirror-still. In minutes it would be dusk, and Justine's pulse quickened at the thought of being with Casson in the darkness.

The sky was a magnificent palette in the twilight, with streaks of vermillion, orange, magenta and gold. She turned to Casson, exclaiming at the beauty of it, and met his intense gaze.

He held out his glass. "Here's to another beauty," he said huskily, and leaned over so that his face was close to hers.

Their glasses clinked but neither of them drank. Casson moved closer, and with a pulsating in her chest that spread down her body Justine felt herself tilting her face so his lips could meet hers. When they made contact, ever so lightly, Justine closed her eyes with the wonder of it. And when Casson's lips pressed against hers, and then moved over her bottom lip, she thought her limbs would melt.

She let out a small gasp, giving Casson the opportunity to deepen the kiss. She was sure her heart would explode as she reciprocated, tasting the wine on his tongue.

Justine lost all sense of time and space, and when he finally released her the glorious colors of the sky had faded to dusky gray and indigo. He took her hand and helped her stand up. Pulling her to him, he lifted his hands to cup the back of her head and kissed her again.

Justine wrapped her arms around his waist, then slid them up his back and around his neck. She trembled when his hands began their descent down her back and around her waist, before finding the edge of her cotton top. And then his hands were on her bare waist, searing her already heated skin.

"Let's go for a dip," he said, his breath ragged.

He pulled off his shirt and tossed it on a chair. He left his khaki shorts on. She let him help her pull off her top and shorts, and was thrilled at the way his eyes blazed when his fingers brushed against her bikini top and bottom.

Somewhere in the distance a loon gave its haunting call, and as they splashed their way into the still but bracingly cold depths of the bay, with Luna following, Justine felt freer than she had ever felt in her life.

After the initial shock of the water on their heated skin they automatically came together. The water was up to Justine's chest. Justine tilted her head back as Casson's lips traced a path up her neck to her mouth. He pulled her in even closer, and their bodies fit together in a way that sent a series of jolts through her.

As Casson's hands began to wander over the thin material of her bikini Justine gasped in pleasure at the sensation under water. She let her hands wander as well, sliding over the firm expanse of his back, exploring his contours. She kissed the base of his neck and his mouth, giving in to the desires that had been simmering within her and needing release for days.

Casson was in another world, with Justine pressed against him in the water, his senses filled with the sight and feel of her. He wanted to stroke every part of her with his hands and his lips, to make her gasp with pleasure. She looked like a sea nymph, with those smoldering blue eyes and silky skin. She was looking up at him now, their bodies locked together, their arms encircling each other.

The dark sky was suddenly lit up with a flash of lightning and the effect was surreal, the light reflecting in each other's eyes.

Luna started barking. She had already dashed out of

the water after a quick dip, and had been waiting for them on the beach, but now she was running about in a panic from the electricity in the air. When the rolls of thunder followed she started yelping even more, and ran frantically in and out of the water.

The rain started seconds later.

Casson took Justine's hand, and by the time they got out of the water and onto the beach the rain was pelting down on them. It was warm rain, but heavy, falling down in sheets. They quickly gathered their clothes, and the items they had left by the Muskoka chairs and table, and dashed to the cottage.

Once inside, they stood in the entrance, the rain dripping off their bodies onto the linoleum floor.

"Luna—stay." Casson patted her, trying to calm her. "Lie down, girl."

He turned to Justine and his heart thumped at the sight of her standing there, barefoot in her bikini, her drenched hair clinging to her cheeks, her dusky blue eyes wide and fluttering, her eyelashes beaded with raindrops. Despite the warmth inside the cottage, she had started to shiver.

He put his hands on her shoulders. "Don't move," he murmured. "I'm going to grab some towels."

He leaned over and planted a kiss on her lips. He had to tear himself away then, before his prehistoric instincts took over and he picked her up, dripping and all, and carried her straight into his man cave.

He brought back three bath towels. He placed one over Justine's shoulders and set one aside while he ran the third towel over Luna and wiped the beach sand from her paws.

"Okay, Luna, go on your mat."

He turned to Justine. She was towel-drying her hair. Gently he took the towel out of her hands and continued to pat her hair dry. Then he proceeded to dry her neck, her shoulders and back, before moving to the front of her body.

He held her gaze with his as he patted her chest and moved downward. By the time he reached her thighs and calves he could feel shivers running through him—although he suspected it had nothing to do with being cold.

"Here…" Justine took the towel from him and hung it on a hook behind the door. She reached for the remaining dry towel and wrapped it around his head. "My turn." She smiled shyly and started drying his hair. And then she followed his lead, slowly patting him dry, lingering in some areas more than others…

She made him catch his breath, and her eyes seemed to flash in delight at his reaction to her touch. When she was done they stood there, staring into each other's eyes, and he suddenly knew, without a doubt, that Justine had completely snagged him.

Hook, line and sinker.

CHAPTER SIXTEEN

JUSTINE PRACTICALLY JUMPED into Casson's arms at the next crack of thunder. Luna gave a howl and started to tear around the cottage, panting and giving low growls.

"You can't go home in this weather," Casson said, drawing Justine closer.

"You could drive me," she murmured, sounding unconvincing even to herself.

"I couldn't leave Luna alone; she'd be terrified," Casson said, sounding relieved that he had come up with an excuse. "You can have my room. I'll sleep on the couch. Luna will want me near her tonight."

Justine stopped herself from blurting out, *So will I.*

She took a deep breath. Things were spinning away too fast for her. *She* was spinning. She needed some space, some distance to make sense of what was happening between her and Casson. And spending the night in the same cottage with him, even if they were in separate rooms, would provide her with neither enough space nor distance.

"You should get out of your wet bikini," Casson said "I'll go get you some of my clothes." He chuckled. "I'll see what I can find in your size."

While he went to his room Justine went to comfort Luna. It felt so strange, walking around barefoot in a bikini *here*. Her stomach fluttered with the prospect of sleeping in Casson's bed. Could she trust him to stay on the couch?

Could she trust herself...?

Casson came out of the bedroom with a navy T-shirt. "This will have to do," he said, and held it out to Justine. "You can change in here."

Justine felt herself flushing. The T-shirt was large, and would probably reach her knees. *But she wouldn't be wearing anything underneath.* And of course it wouldn't cross Casson's mind to offer her a pair of his shorts.

She took the T-shirt from him and went into his room, shutting the door firmly behind her. She took deep breaths to slow down the beating of her heart. Scanning the room, she wasn't surprised to see how neat and orderly it was. Bed made, clothes hung up in the partially open wardrobe, and a suitcase in one corner of the room. Her eyes fell on the open laptop on the desk, and she saw the brown envelope he had brought out earlier.

She walked over to the bed and set the T-shirt on it while she took off her bikini. She caught sight of herself in the dresser mirror and felt her pulse leaping at the thought of Casson seeing her this way. She shivered and slipped the T-shirt on. It came to just above her knees, and it was baggy, but at least it was dry.

She still felt vulnerable, though, and had the crazy thought of searching through the drawers in the night table for a pair of his underwear. She sat on the bed, considering it, and saw a bottle of Casson's cologne on the night table.

Unable to resist, she picked it up. She uncapped it and inhaled the scent she had come to recognize: a blend of bamboo, pine and musk. An expensive Italian brand she had seen advertised in magazines.

A sudden thumping noise at the bedroom door startled her, and she fumbled with the bottle. She caught it before it could fall and break on the plank floor, but in grabbing it she accidentally sprayed herself.

Cursing inwardly, she set the bottle back on the night table. *Explain that to Casson...*

"Luna, get away from that door," she heard Casson say, chuckling. "Your friend is coming out any minute."

When Justine opened the door she saw Casson's eyes scanning over her appreciatively. He walked toward her and stopped, his nose wrinkling.

Justine smiled sheepishly. "Accident," she murmured, shrugging.

He leaned over and sniffed deeply, his nose and lips grazing her neck. She couldn't help shivering as he released his breath, and the sensation on her skin made her heart begin to pound.

"I guess I won't have to put any cologne on, then," he said huskily. "I'll go and change, too." He gazed at the bikini top and bottom in her hand, and then back at her. "You can hang those and your other clothes in the washroom."

When Justine returned to the living room she sat on the edge of the couch, her stomach in knots as she waited for Casson to come. She would tell him she was exhausted and would be going to bed right away, she decided.

A moment later he emerged, wearing blue-striped pajama bottoms and a beige T-shirt, holding a pillow in one hand and a change of clothes in the other. Justine's heart flipped. She stood up, knowing she'd better get to his room before...before her resolve started to weaken.

"I'm beat," she said. "I'll say goodnight."

She gave him a half-smile and quickly averted her gaze. She patted Luna, then gingerly stepped past Casson. To her relief he didn't stop her, and as she closed the bedroom door with a click she let out her breath.

She left the wooden shutters in his room partially open, so the morning light would wake her, and then turned off the light switch. As she slipped into bed she began to have second doubts.

Was she crazy? Passing up an opportunity to spend the night with Casson in this bed?

He would be beside her right now had she given him the slightest indication of wanting that.

Justine bit her lip. She had come to his cottage with the intention of showing him that she was interested and seeing if he felt the same. Well, she had no doubts that he was interested in her body—neither of them could deny the chemistry between them. But she wanted—no, *needed*—more than that. She needed to know that Casson Forrester wanted her heart and soul as well. When she knew that for sure, *then* she would be his.

She snuggled under the covers, savoring the feeling of intimacy in just lying on the sheet Casson slept on. She breathed in his scent on the pillow, and let it and the rhythm of the rain, and the muted grumbling of thunder, soothe her to sleep.

Casson stared at the door for a few moments after Justine had closed it. Tonight was going to be sweet torture, lying on the couch. How could he possibly sleep, knowing that Justine was only steps away? Especially after the intimacy they had shared?

He groaned softly and, turning off the kitchen light, made his way to the couch. He plunked down his pillow and stretched out. It was too humid in the cottage to cover up. And too hot for pajamas. He pulled them off impatiently, leaving his boxers on. With any luck he'd get a breeze coming through the screened-in windows during the night.

Good luck falling asleep.

Casson felt so frustrated. And deflated. Justine had relayed her intentions loud and clear after he had given her his T-shirt. *I'm beat. I'll say goodnight.* He couldn't deny it: if he had seen even a spark in Justine's eye to invite him to follow her into the bedroom he wouldn't have thought twice. But she had deliberately avoided looking at him.

Although he had seen her blue eyes darken with desire in the bay, and when they were drying each other, something had caused Justine to pull back. Could she still have feelings for Robert? *No!* He didn't want to believe that. His jaw tensed. Or maybe Justine's suspicions about his intentions had resurfaced, making her keep any attraction she felt for him in check, especially after her experience with Robert. Maybe she believed he was using her, trying to use sex to influence her decision not to sell.

She didn't trust him.

Casson felt as if someone had kicked him in the gut. He breathed in deeply and exhaled slowly. He wanted Justine to trust him, to believe that he wasn't using her.

But how could he convince her of that? Convince her that it wasn't just her body he had fallen in love with, but her gentle spirit?

Yes, he thought in wonder, *he had fallen in love with her.*

She was kind and considerate...making soup for a little boy she hardly knew. And it wasn't because she had some ulterior motive to get Casson to like her. No, it was simply a thoughtful and sensitive gesture. And she was kind to Luna. Casson had seen a flash of real sorrow in her eyes when he'd told her about how Luna had been abandoned and left at the side of the road. And what about her concern that Robert would be ruined if they'd called the police? It was only because of her that Casson hadn't gone down that route. *He* would have been much harder on Robert. And he really hadn't expected Justine to demonstrate that kind of compassion after Robert's behavior.

But Justine was soft. *Softer.* And that was what he loved about her. She had a gentleness and a generosity that his previous dates had lacked. He might have been too focused on building his business to spend time searching for the right person in his life, but now Casson realized that a search was not necessary.

He closed his eyes and turned onto one side. He felt drained. So much had happened since that first meeting with Justine. He let some of the memories play in his mind for a while, but then, remembering that tomorrow evening was the opening of the Franklin & Casson on the Bay exhibition, he pushed those thoughts back.

He had checked his email earlier, and everything was ready to go at the Stockey Centre. The banner stands were in place, the paintings were arranged, the lighting adjusted. And the A. J. Casson painting was sitting regally on an antique brass easel next to the mahogany desk in the silent auction room.

The media would arrive at five-thirty p.m. to interview Casson and local dignitaries. The doors would open to the public at six. Casson would make a formal address at six-thirty, sharing his vision of Franklin's Resort before unveiling the A. J. Casson painting.

He had arranged the hiring of two notable gallery owners, who were experts on the Group of Seven—especially the two featured artists—to interact with the public and enlighten them about the individual paintings on display. Casson would also mingle with the invited patrons and the public.

At seven, the invited guests would make their way to the banquet room, where they would enjoy a fabulous five-course meal. The event would close at nine o'clock.

Casson felt a twinge in his heart. The three banner stands he had ordered showed an enlarged photo of him and Franklin at their parents' friends' cottage in Georgian Bay. The title was at the top: Franklin & Casson on the Bay. One would be placed in the entrance of the Stockey Centre, another would be in the exhibition room, and the third would be in the room displaying the A. J. Casson painting for the silent auction.

The photo had been taken by his mother, in the summer two months before Franklin's diagnosis. He and Franklin were standing on the dock, the bay a brilliant blue behind them, and he was helping Franklin hold up his fishing rod. The fish—a pickerel—wasn't big, but it was a keeper.

The backs of Casson's eyes started to sting. He squeezed them shut and turned his pillow over.

Okay, Franklin, tomorrow evening's the big event. Get some sleep up there in heaven, buddy, 'cause you're coming with me, and it'll be past your bedtime when we're done.

CHAPTER SEVENTEEN

JUSTINE SCREAMED, AND seconds later her eyes fluttered open. She sat up, her back against the headboard, and then, her heart thudding, she heard the door clicking open. The light came on to reveal that it was Casson.

He turned the dimmer switch on low and closed the door behind him. He strode to the foot of the bed. "Are you okay? Did you have a bad dream?"

Justine felt her lip quivering.

The nightmare had seemed so real.

Casson had been walking her home, and they had arrived at the edge of her property when she'd caught sight of a wrecking ball, advancing toward her house. She'd started to scream, and Casson had tried to silence her with a kiss. She'd managed to pull away and had screamed again as one side of her house had caved in.

And then she'd woken up.

Justine blinked. The genuine concern in Casson's eyes pushed her emotions over the edge. She felt her eyes filling up and, biting her lip, nodded. "I—I was dreaming that—that you were starting to have my house torn down so you could build your resort…"

She shivered and burst into tears, covering her face with her hands. Then sucked in her breath when she felt a shift in the mattress and Casson's arms around her. She didn't have the strength to move away from the warmth of his embrace. She felt herself sinking against his chest, and as he held her tightly she let the tears flow.

How could she have such conflicting feelings about Casson? Her wariness about his motives concerning Winter's Haven was manifesting itself even in her dreams, and yet she couldn't deny or resist his magnetic pull.

"It's okay, Justine," he murmured, gently stroking the back of her head. "I would never have your home demolished; I can promise you that."

His heartbeat seemed to leap up to her ear, and for a few seconds she just concentrated on its rhythm while inhaling the heady pine scent of his cologne.

"I'm sorry," she whispered, moving her face away from the wet spot on his T-shirt. "I—I didn't mean to slobber all over you."

She looked up and met his gaze tremulously. His expression made her heart flip.

Slowly his hand slid from the back of her head to cup her chin. He held it there, and with his other hand slowly wiped the tears from her cheeks. His fingers fanned her face gently, and she felt an exquisite swirling in her stomach at his tenderness. When he leaned closer she stopped breathing, and when his lips kissed her forehead she blew out a long, slow breath and closed her eyes.

"Oh, Cass..."

His lips continued to trace a path over each eye, the bridge of her nose and her cheeks, before finding the lobe of her ear. There his mouth lingered, opening to catch the tip in his mouth. She drew in her breath sharply and a flame of arousal shot through her like the fuse on an explosive. By the time his lips made their way to her mouth her lips were parted and her whole body was trembling in anticipation.

His lips closed over her upper lip and then her lower

one, pressing, tasting, before exploring deeper. Justine let out a small moan and felt herself surrendering, her senses flooded with the taste, smell and feel of him. Her body and his seemed to move in synchronicity, and in seconds the bedcovers were off and they were entwined on the mattress.

Casson pressed her against him and she wrapped her arms around his back, reveling in the heat and hardness of his body.

Justine knew there was no going back when Casson's lips started tracing a path from her neck downward. She shivered when he lifted her T-shirt off, wanting to squirm as his gaze devoured her. Casson shifted to one side and in two quick movements his own clothes were off.

With a searing desire she had never felt before Justine extended her arms and Casson gave himself to her.

At the first light of dawn Casson woke up. He stretched languorously before easing himself off the couch. His body tingled with the memory of his lovemaking with Justine. After they had both been sated they had dozed off. Hours later, when Luna had started pawing at the door and whimpering, Casson had returned to the couch, not wanting to disturb Justine. Besides, he'd needed to be up early to prepare for opening night.

If he hadn't had the exhibition to host this evening he would have been happy to nestle in Justine's arms all day… but the reality was he had to drive back home to Huntsville, get his suit and shoes for the event, and exchange his Mustang for the Ferrari.

There was no way he'd be going to the opening gala without it. and with Franklin's ball cap on the seat next to him. Then he'd go back to the cottage, and hopefully he'd see Justine before heading to the Stockey Centre.

He decided it would be better to leave Luna there, for

when Justine woke up. He glanced at his bedroom door. He had left his laptop in his room but, much as he wanted to, he couldn't bring himself to go in. He checked for new messages on his phone instead and then, satisfied that his committee had everything in place, changed into jeans and a shirt.

Casson started as Luna pawed at the front door. He opened the door as quietly as he could and when they'd returned prepared Luna's dish and set it down.

"Now, you be a good girl until I get back, Luna. Shh... no noise."

He gave her an affectionate scratch behind the ears and then started to walk to the door. Suddenly his footsteps slowed and he abruptly turned around.

What am I doing? I need to let Justine know about the event...

Casson had thought about telling Justine about it a few times before, but had always changed his mind, waiting for the right time to enlighten her as to the real reason for his resort venture.

Well, it was now or never...

Taking a strip of paper off a notepad, Casson scribbled a note to Justine and left it on the table. She might be furious with him for arranging such an event before even securing Winter's Haven, but he was willing to risk her wrath by having her come to the Stockey Centre and learn the real reason behind his actions.

Maybe then she would have a change of heart.

And if she was still absolutely against selling Winter's Haven he would go ahead and make her a new offer.

She could keep Winter's Haven and he would develop only the Russell properties for his venture, with her as manager.

It would be on a much smaller scale than he had originally planned, but he was willing to make some changes if that would keep Justine happy. And *he* would be happy having Justine as manager.

Who was he kidding?

It wasn't just that he wanted a manager. He wanted the love of a woman.

One woman... Justine.

He finished the note, turned the coffee maker on, and then slipped quietly out the door.

CHAPTER EIGHTEEN

THE AROMA OF coffee tingled Justine's nostrils and she opened her eyes, disoriented. It took her a few seconds to realize that she wasn't in her own room. Turning her head to look around, she felt it all come flooding back to her.

She was in Casson's bed.

She had gone to bed in here and he had gone to sleep on the couch.

Her eyes widened at the onrush of memories…

She had screamed, and Casson had come to her immediately. She had been dreaming about her home being demolished… Casson had comforted her, making her forget her dream completely…

She caught her breath as she recalled the way he had ignited her with the gentle exploration of his lips and hands, the way her responses had made him bolder.

And she had done nothing to stop him.

She hadn't wanted to; she had luxuriated in every masterful move he'd made, driving her to reciprocate just as passionately.

She retrieved his T-shirt and put it on, her limbs weak at the thought of Casson being in the kitchen. She wondered if he would be returning to the bedroom…

"Cass?" she said out loud, and then waited, her heartbeat accelerating.

A scuffle at the door seconds later along with a whimper made her smile.

"Good morning, Luna," she called out.

She waited for Casson's good morning, but all she heard was Luna pawing at the door. Justine opened it and Luna barged in, wagging her tail, and promptly jumped on the bed.

"I hope your master gave you permission to do that," Justine said, wagging her finger at Luna.

She peeked out the door, expecting to see Casson, but he wasn't there. She didn't hear the shower, or water running in the washroom, so where *was* he?

Justine walked to the door and looked out. His Mustang was gone. And she hadn't even heard it. Mystified, she walked into the kitchen. He must have only just left; the coffee was still dripping. *But why?*

Had last night meant so little to him that he could just take off like that? Or had something come up with Andy? Had Ronnie called with an emergency?

Her heart began to thud. And then she caught sight of her name on the piece of paper taped on the side of the coffee maker. She peeled it off, and praying it wasn't bad news, began to read…

Good morning, Justine.

I hope you had a good sleep. I'm sorry I couldn't stay, but I have some business to take care of. I'm heading to my home in Huntsville to pick up some things, and then I'll be in and out of the cottage before an event I need to attend tonight.

I meant to tell you about it, and you may have heard about it anyway. The Stockey Centre is holding an exhibition this week of the work of two of the Group of Seven artists. It's called Franklin & Casson on the Bay. It opens this evening. Please come.

I've already taken Luna out this morning, and she's had her breakfast —don't let her tell you otherwise!

Please make yourself at home—I know; it is your home!—and help yourself to coffee and the fabulous lemon blueberry muffins on the counter. A special friend made them.
Casson
P.S. I would have really liked to have had breakfast with you, Justine...

He had added a happy face, and relief flooded her that Casson's leaving had nothing to do with Andy. But she couldn't help feeling disappointed at how impersonal the letter seemed. Until she got to the part where Casson called her "a special friend." Her heart skipped a beat at that. And his last line lifted her spirits tenfold.

It wasn't exactly a declaration of love, or passion, and he had made no reference to the time they had spent together— or *how* they had spent the time—but it told Justine one thing for sure: Casson would have remained at the cottage this morning if he could.

Which meant that he wasn't running away from her, and that the previous evening must have meant *something* to him. That maybe he might be wanting to continue spending time with her...

Feeling a little giddy with happiness, Justine poured herself a cup of coffee. She had already made up her mind; she was definitely going to see Franklin & Casson on the Bay!"

And the man she loved.

Casson rolled down the windows of his Mustang, enjoying the feel of the morning breeze as he exited the main highway and turned on to the country road leading to Huntsville. He smiled at the thought of Justine reading his note in the kitchen. He pictured her in his T-shirt, relaxing with a mug of coffee.

When had he realized that he loved her company, loved everything about her?

Falling in love had not been on his agenda. It hadn't even been on his wish list. But, despite their awkward start, he and Justine had more than made up for it.

His abdomen tightened at the memory of her body, soft and hard in all the right places. It would be sweet torture to be away from her for the entire day. He hoped she would be free to spend some time with him when he drove back to the cottage. And he hoped she would accept his invitation to come to the opening night of the exhibition. It was time she saw for herself what his resort venture was *really* about.

He'd wait until after the event to break the news about the deed, though. He couldn't predict her reaction, but if she felt the same about him as he felt about her—and he was sure that she did—he was confident that they could come up with a solution.

After tonight there would be no more secrets between them. Not that he had kept any information from her with the intention of gaining the upper hand. No, he had simply tried to assess what would be the appropriate time to reveal his real motive in wanting Winter's Haven. And when she would be most receptive to hearing the news about the deed.

It was time for Justine to know the truth. He had seen passion in her eyes, and his body had been rocked with the passion they had shared, but he was certain that what they had experienced was more than just physical. He was confident he had gained her trust.

Realizing that he had increased his speed in anticipation of seeing Justine, he eased his foot on the pedal. Getting a ticket now would just delay his return.

Patience, he told himself. *You're minutes away...*

He had been successful on one count. Now all he needed was Winter's Haven.

And Justine Winter.

Justine finished her muffin and coffee, gave a lazy stretch, and padded back to the bedroom. Luna followed, and Justine ruffled her fur affectionately. She sauntered to the window and opened the blinds fully, letting in the early-morning sun. Turning, she let her eye fall on the brown envelope on the dresser.

She pressed her lips together and picked it up. Casson had wanted to show her the documents inside it from the very beginning. And yesterday as well... She didn't suppose it would bother him if she went ahead and looked through it without him.

She brought the envelope into the living room and curled up on the couch. She took out the contents: a number of files separated by clips. She riffled through them quickly, her eyes registering survey documents and reports, a deed, architectural designs, and a typed letter.

Seeing her name in the salutation startled her, and she pulled the letter from the pile and started to read.

Dear Ms. Winter,

As you know, I have recently purchased the properties on either side of Winter's Haven from Mr. and Mrs. Russell. In perusing the documents I discovered that their ancestors—the pioneers who first owned the acreage that comprises both their and your properties—had partitioned the land and eventually sold the parcel that years later became Winter's Haven.

Well, a few generations have come and gone, and

it seems that the original papers were misplaced. After the Russells sold to me, and started packing, the original deed turned up and they passed it on to me. I looked it over the other night and compared it to the surveyor's report I received when my trans-action was finalized.

To make a long story short, it seems that a sec-tion of Winter's Haven is actually on the Russells' property.

"That's insane!" Justine blurted, letting out a hollow laugh before continuing to read.

I have verification that a section of your house and some of your property is actually sitting on what is now my property. You are welcome to check with your lawyer. I already have with mine.

The properties passed hands years ago, between neighbors and friends, and in one of those subse-quent transactions a new survey report had to be drawn up when the original deed couldn't be located.

Justine clenched her jaw as she rifled through all the documents and reports. Her cheeks burned. She bit her lip. *This couldn't be true.*

After poring over them a second time she sank back against the couch, the truth turning her body cold.

I am willing to discuss the ramifications of this finding with you, and anticipate our working to-gether to discuss options that will result in a mutu-ally satisfying solution.

I am prepared to make a substantial offer for Win-ter's Haven, and would like to meet with you at your

*earliest convenience to present you with my plans for
a resort development on the properties.*

*My contact information follows. I look forward
to hearing from you.*
Cordially yours,
Casson Forrester

Justine tossed the papers on the coffee table. The ice
that had filled her veins as she read every word of Casson's letter was now changing to a flow of red-hot lava.
She could still feel the burning in her cheeks, the roiling in
her stomach. Her breaths were shallow and her chest was
heaving, her lungs heavy with Casson's deceit.

How could he?

Why hadn't he shown it to her before? Or even mailed
it instead of playing games with her? Instead of manipulating his way into Winter's Haven after weaseling a deal
with the Russells...

The Russells sold willingly.

Justine put her hands over her ears in an attempt to
block that inner voice. Okay, so Casson had been proactive, jumping on an opportunity. The Russells had come
over to her office to say their goodbyes, and had expressed
their excitement at moving south to be with their daughter.
Casson had made a decision that they had been waffling
over very easy. His timing—and his offer—couldn't have
been better, they'd said.

But keeping the deed a secret from her was despicable.

So what exactly did she plan to do about this? Justine
tried to digest the fact that Casson had a claim on part of
Winter's Haven. No wonder he was always so relaxed,
even when she appeared unexpectedly at his door. It was
as if he owned the place already...

Had she known this right from the beginning she
wouldn't have ended up in his bed—that much she knew.

Her stomach tightened as if she had been pummeled. Hot tears slid onto her cheeks and she bit her lip.

Casson had used her—manipulating her to get her under his control, working to soften her up so she would sell...

Her fists clenched. Robert had controlled her in one way—slowly building up their relationship while his marriage withered, and then dropping her when she no longer served his purpose. Justine had vowed never to let another man control her. And yet here she was, caught in the web that Casson had woven so meticulously. She had allowed herself to be manipulated yet again.

She could kick herself for being such a fool. How could she have let her guard down?

And how could she face Casson? He must be gloating inwardly. And what would he be expecting of her now? To give in and turn over the property, seeing how she'd so readily turned herself over to him?

Not a chance in hell.

Wiping the tears from her face, Justine stared blindly out the window. She took no pleasure from the view, her stomach twisting at memories of her and Casson in the bay. And of how thoroughly he had seduced her after her nightmare...

He had been just as bad, if not worse than Robert.

Holding her hand over her mouth, Justine fled to the washroom.

When Casson arrived at his house in Huntsville he wasted no time in gathering what he needed for opening night: suit, shirt, cufflinks, tie and shoes. He had already taken the A. J. Casson painting from his collection to the Stockey Centre when he had taken possession of the Russell properties.

He was anxious to get back to the cottage in time to look

over his opening speech and have a few hours to himself before heading to the center. Well, not really to himself. He smiled. He wanted to see Justine. Invite her properly to the exhibition opening and the banquet.

He had goofed by not mentioning the banquet in his letter, but he hoped she would understand and accept. A surge of excitement shot through his body. He was already feeling high because his dream of a resort for children with cancer was about to kick off, and if Justine accompanied him to the opening event he'd be over the moon.

Casson pulled into a gas station and called the office at Winter's Haven. With any luck Justine would answer, and he'd ask her to meet him at his cottage…

"Hi, Mandy." He tried not to let his disappointment show in his voice. "Would Justine be in the office?"

There was silence, and Casson wondered if there was a problem with the connection.

"Oh…hi, Casson. She…she was in here earlier, but she went back home."

Casson frowned. Mandy's voice wasn't as cheery as usual. "Would you mind giving her a message? I'm on my way back and should be there in half an hour. I'd appreciate it if she could meet me at my cottage when she gets a chance…"

Another pause. Then, "Will do."

"Thanks." Casson turned off his phone.

He shrugged. Mandy must be having a bad day. Oh, well, in a very short time *his* day would be getting even better.

With a roar of his engine, he headed toward Parry Sound.

Justine bit her lip and tried not to cry as Mandy put the phone down. She had already spent an hour crying at home, before splashing cold water on her face and going to the office. She had said nothing to Mandy about spending the night with Casson; she felt too humiliated. The only thing she had shared was the information in Casson's letter about the property.

When Casson had called she had waved her arms frantically, so that Mandy wouldn't reveal that she was in the office. Now Mandy was looking at her worriedly.

"Justine, maybe you *should* go and meet him. He might have come up with a solution…"

Justine gave a bitter laugh. "If I didn't trust him before, I trust him even less now."

"But he said in the letter he wanted to discuss options. Just hear him out. At the very least you can tell him how you feel. I can understand that you're royally ticked off, Justine. But nothing will be resolved without talking to him."

Justine pursed her lips. Maybe she *did* need to tell Casson how she felt. She took a deep breath. Yes, she decided, she would be meeting him at his cottage.

Prepared and ready to do battle.

Casson had let Luna out and was giving her a snack inside when he heard the sharp rap at the door. His heart did a flip when he saw it was Justine, but his smile froze on his way to get the door. There was no returning smile from her. In fact her eyes were puffy and red, her expression cold. She held her arms stiffly behind her back.

He opened the door. "Justine? Has something happened? What's wrong?"

Justine smirked. "Really?" She held up the envelope she had taken with her. "*This* is what's wrong." Her hand trembled. "You deliberately led me on in your scheme to get me to sell Winter's Haven, knowing the whole time that you already owned part of it." She clenched her jaw.

"You could have given me the letter—or mailed it to me—*before*."

Casson glanced at the envelope and then back at her, temporarily stunned. "How…?"

He didn't need to finish.

He had left it on the desk.

"Look, Justine—"

"No, *you* look. What you did was despicable. You and Robert can shake hands. At least he was drunk and not in his right mind. But you knew what you were doing. You *knew*."

Casson's heart twisted.

How could he convince her she had it wrong?

"Justine, I swear I didn't plan it to work out this way—"

"You can't deny you had a plan." Her narrowed eyes shot ice daggers at him.

"Yes, I had a plan—but not the one you think. I planned to come to Winter's Haven, meet you in person, and try to sell you my idea for a resort. I found out about the deed *after* making arrangements to stay at this cottage. I was waiting for the right time to tell you about it."

Justine cringed. "And when *was* that? After getting me to sleep with you?"

A fist in the gut would have been easier to take than the disgust in her voice.

"Justine, I did not sleep with you because I had an ulterior motive. It was not in my 'plan.' What happened between us was not premeditated. I'm not that kind of a guy."

She opened her mouth as if she were ready to fire back a retort, then closed it.

"I never tried to take advantage of you, Justine. My feelings are genuine." He sighed. "But I know now that I should have told you about the deed right from the start."

Justine crossed her arms, her expression grim. "So what exactly are you prepared to do about it?"

"I'm prepared to have a discussion with you about options—"

"*What* options?" Justine said hotly. "I will need to consult a lawyer as to how the deed can be adjusted and... and..." Her jaw clenched, as if she'd realized it wasn't going to be a simple matter to rectify. Especially with part of a structure—her *home*—on his property. "I need to call my parents," she said, throwing her hands up in the air and staring up at the ceiling. "Maybe they'll know what to do."

Something shifted inside of Casson when he heard the hint of despair in her voice.

He didn't want to hurt her; he had never wanted to hurt her.

For the first time he realized how vulnerable she felt when it came to Winter's Haven.

"Look, Justine," he said softly, hoping to reassure her, "I'm not taking or claiming even a corner of your house or your land. Right now, I think the only option is to leave things the way they are." He leaned closer, forcing her to meet his gaze. "When we can come up with a satisfying solution for the both of us, *then* we'll do something about it. And update the deed."

"The only satisfying solution for *you* is to get me to sell you the business." Justine's voice was tinged with bitterness.

"There could be other solutions...and they may come to light before my holiday here comes to an end."

"And what if they don't?" Justine's voice held a challenge.

"We'll figure something out," Casson insisted. "Even if it means locking ourselves in a room together until we do."

Justine shot him a *you're out of your mind* look before handing him the envelope. "I've made a copy of everything to give to my lawyer," she said curtly. "And I've left another copy in the office with Mandy."

She turned to leave.

"Justine." He waited until she'd turned around. "I know you're still upset, and you have every right to be, but I meant every word I said. I'm really sorry I hurt you." His voice wavered. "You might think I'm crazy to even ask... but I'd really like you to come to the exhibition tonight."

Justine's jaw dropped and her eyes narrowed into two beams of fury. "You've *got* to be kidding."

She walked stiffly out the door, letting it slam shut behind her.

CHAPTER NINETEEN

IN THE OFFICE, after giving Mandy a condensed version of the meeting she had had with Casson, Mandy asked if Justine would be going to the opening of the art show. Justine became flustered, and Mandy gave her a comforting hug.

"Just go," she urged. "Give the guy a chance. Let him talk to you when the shock has worn off…"

Back at home, Justine debated for two hours over whether or not she should go. She was still angry and hurt, not to mention bewildered as to what purpose Casson had in asking her to attend the opening.

She wanted to punish him by not accepting, but a tiny voice inside her told her she'd just be punishing herself. She remembered how happy she had been when Casson had suggested she go in his note… Besides, she was not going *with* him; she could stay as little or as long as she wanted. And she had to admit she *was* curious…

So she'd brace her broken heart and show Casson that she hadn't come undone as a result of his deception—that she was strong and capable of standing up to him. *That she wasn't under his control.*

Her mind was too clouded now to think of a solution to the deed issue, but she would contact her parents' lawyer in the morning and book an appointment as soon as possible. There *had* to be a way of voiding Casson's claim to Winter's Haven.

With a defiant toss of her head Justine went upstairs to look through her closet. The warrior in her was *not* defeated, she realized, her jaw clenching. She *would* go to Casson's event.

Dressed to kill.

Justine decided on a sleeveless black dress with a diagonal neckline, accented with filigree silver buttons. After styling her dark hair in soft flowing curls, she put on the dress. It hugged her curves and stopped above her knees. She chose a pair of silver dangling earrings with diamonds and sapphires—her parents' graduation gift. And finally she picked out a black shawl that shimmered with silver threads.

She was pleased when she saw her reflection, liking the way the sapphire stones matched her eyes.

She applied the barest amount of make-up—some delicate touches of blue and silver-gray eyeshadow, and a frosty pink lipstick. Blush wasn't necessary; her cheeks were already flushed.

She stepped into black pumps with silver stiletto heels and, grabbing her silver clutch purse, walked gingerly out to her car.

When Justine arrived at the parking lot of the Stockey Centre many spots were already filled. As she circled around her heart skipped a beat at the sight of a gleaming red car in a far corner.

Casson's Ferrari.

She sat for a moment after turning off the ignition, her hands gripping the wheel.

Did she really want to do this?

People were streaming into the building, being welcomed by a smiling doorman. Women with elegant dresses and glittering shawls, and bling that sparkled in the late-afternoon sun. Men sporting expensive suits and ties, their shoes gleaming.

Justine took a deep breath and climbed out of her car.

The huge foyer was buzzing with chatter. Justine had only taken a few steps when the people in front of her moved on to join their friends. It was then that Justine caught sight of the words Franklin & Casson on the Bay at the top of a huge banner stand. Her gaze dropped to the life-size image of two boys, grinning and holding up a fishing pole with their catch.

And then she froze when she realized that she was eye to eye with Casson. Not Casson the man, but Casson the boy. Her pulse quickened and her eyes flew to the boy next to him, with his two front teeth missing. *Franklin*. Her eyes began to well up. Squeezing them to clear her vision, she stared at the little boy who had passed away a year after this photo was taken.

Justine gulped. She had come to see paintings by Franklin Carmichael and A. J. Casson. The last thing she had expected to see was a huge image of Casson with his brother. It was heartbreaking. *But why had Casson done it?* She knew the connection between the brothers and the artists, but she'd had no idea that Casson would reveal something so personal to the public.

"Mr. Forrester couldn't have picked a better photo for this exhibition."

A guide with the name 'Charlotte' on her tag stood next to Justine. "The brothers on Georgian Bay. And what a beautiful tribute to Franklin—to plan a resort in his name."

"Resort?" Justine said, dazed.

"Yes. You must have heard about it in the news? Franklin's Resort. Mr. Forrester has purchased property in the area and is planning a luxury resort for children with cancer and their families to enjoy for a week after their final chemotherapy and radiation treatments. There will be no charge for them—which is why he is seeking support to augment his very generous contribution and to help keep the project viable."

She pointed to the registration table.

"There's a donation box on the table, and in the adjoining room Mr. Forrester has unveiled an A. J. Casson painting from his own private collection to be auctioned off tonight." She smiled at Justine. "Please sign your name in the guest book—and if you would like to receive information about future fund-raising events for the resort, please include your email address."

"Thank you," Justine managed to reply.

She glanced again at the faces of the brothers and thought of Andy. Feeling her eyes prickling, she quickly signed the guest book, put a few bills in the donation box and then, stifling a sob, turned away and started making her way through the throng to find the washroom, where she could get control of her emotions in private.

Halfway there, the tears started spilling out of her eyes. And then she bumped hard into someone and almost lost her balance, teetering on her stiletto heels.

"Justine."

Two arms came out to stop her from falling.

"I'm so glad you could come."

She recognized the deep voice even before looking up at tiger eyes.

Trembling, she fell against his chest and looked up at him with blurred eyes. *"Why didn't you tell me?"*

"It's complicated," Casson murmured in Justine's ear while helping her regain her balance. "I know where there's a quiet place to talk. *Please,*" he added, seeing her hesitate. "We need to talk."

"Mr. Forrester!" a voice called. "May we have a moment of your time?"

Casson turned and recognized a reporter from the local paper, striding toward him. Jake Ross. Beside him was the paper's photographer—Ken—who had already taken some photos of him next to the banner stand.

Casson smiled and nodded, before turning to Justine to tell her she didn't have to leave while they interviewed him. But she had already walked away and the crowd had closed in around her.

Damn!

Hiding his frustration, he checked his watch and led Jake and Ken to a quieter corner. He'd try his best to hurry things along. He wanted to clear things up with Justine before the banquet and auction.

While Jake interviewed him, asking all the questions Casson had expected to be asked, Casson kept glancing toward the crowd. He couldn't see Justine at first, and then a small group shifted to gather around a series of Casson paintings in order to hear the gallery owner's description of the pieces and he glimpsed her there, her lustrous hair framing her beautiful face.

Casson could hardly concentrate after that, taking in her little black dress from its slanted neckline to where it ended above her knees. Her legs were stunning in silky hose, and those shoes... His pulse couldn't help but race.

He heard Jake ask him a question twice, and forced himself to focus. Casson thanked Jake when the interview was over, and then the photographer asked to take some photos of Casson with the paintings.

"We want Casson next to the Cassons," he joked.

The gallery owner paused as they reached the group, and thanked the guests in advance for graciously waiting while the media did their job. Casson tried to catch Justine's eye, but she was deliberately keeping her gaze on one of the paintings. He stood in the center of the display, with paintings on either side of him, and patiently did what the photographer suggested.

"How about one with some of the guests?" Casson suggested, and placed himself impulsively next to Justine.

She looked up from the painting and raised her eyebrows at him with a *what do you think you're doing?* expression. Just then the photographer began to snap some pictures. Justine turned toward Ken at the first click, and Casson took the split-second opportunity to place his hand around Justine's waist and press her closer to him.

Another *snap* and Ken gave him a wink and a thumbs-up before sauntering off with Jake toward a large group at the Franklin Carmichael display.

Justine strode off in the opposite direction.

Casson quickly caught up.

"Why did you do that?" Justine muttered, glancing from him to all the people who were looking their way, and then back at him.

Even with a frown she was gorgeous. "Because I wanted my photo taken next to a beautiful woman," he said. "You look amazing, Justine." His eyes swept over her and he couldn't help smiling. "I was hoping you would come."

"Why?" Justine stared at him accusingly. "So you could make me feel guilty for not wanting to sell Winter's Haven when it's for such a good cause?"

Casson's smile faded. "I had no intention of making you feel guilty," he said quietly.

"Well, I *do*," Justine said, her voice wavering. "I—I wish you had told me from the beginning that your resort was to be a non-profit venture to help kids with cancer, and not for your own personal gain."

"You were dead-set against my proposal from the beginning," Casson reminded her. "I *wanted* to show you the plans, remember? I drove over to your place, but you weren't ready to see them or to hear me out…"

He moved to let someone go by.

"So I decided I needed to wait for the right time. I wasn't sure how long it would take, but I knew I had to try to find the opportunity to do so. And that's why I booked myself into Winter's Haven."

Casson looked over Justine's head at the crowd.

"Look, we can't talk here. Let's go outside. I know where there's a private exit."

He led Justine through a series of hallways to a door that he made sure stayed open a crack using his car keys. They walked out into a private courtyard with a view of the bay. The water was lapping gently against the rocky shore and a couple of seagulls swooped high above.

Casson stopped and gently took hold of Justine's elbow. "I wanted to tell you I don't know how many times," he said gruffly. "But the idea of talking about Franklin to you made me feel…too vulnerable."

He looked into Justine's eyes and knew he owed her complete honesty.

"I grew up suppressing the truth that my parents—my mother especially—were so devastated with losing Franklin that they forgot…forgot they had another son who was still alive."

He took a deep breath.

"They forgot that *I* was devastated too. I didn't show it, I guess. I tried to be the perfect son for them, so as not to cause them anymore grief, but being perfect wasn't enough to get them to really notice me. Don't get me wrong. I had a nice home, plenty of food, a great education. I didn't want for anything like that. What I wanted most was something that died inside of them when Franklin died."

Casson felt the backs of his eyes prickling.

"And maybe because of that I never knew if I had the capacity to really love somebody other than Franklin."

"You love Andy and Ronnie."

"Yes, I do. And this resort is for Andy's sake, too." He heard his voice waver. "I wasn't able to do anything for Franklin, but I *can* help Andy and other children like him…"

He took Justine's hands and covered them with his.

"I came to Winter's Haven with one thought in mind, and then I found myself falling in love."

"It's not hard to fall in love with Winter's Haven."

"I meant with *you*, Miss Winter."

Casson realized that Justine's eyes were welling up too.

"I was waiting until I felt I could trust you with my feelings, Justine. Until I felt that you wouldn't be indifferent."

"Oh, Cass…" Justine wrapped her arms around him, pressing her head against his chest.

Casson felt something let go inside him. Those two words she had uttered told him everything.

He lifted her chin so she would meet his gaze. "When I found out about the property issue I intended to offer you some options—whether you wanted to sell or not. But something made me hold back. I eventually realized that the better option was to forget about trying to get you to sell, and focus instead on starting with a smaller resort on the Russells' main property. I planned to offer you a position as manager of Franklin's Resort, and then you could still manage Winter's Haven. At least I wouldn't lose *you*."

He gazed at Justine, and what he saw in her eyes made his heart leap.

"You won't lose me, Casson," she replied breathlessly.

Her eyes were shimmering as he pressed her closer to him. He kissed her gently, and as her lips moved to respond he deepened the kiss until they were both enflamed.

With ragged breathing, he pulled away reluctantly. "The

banquet will be starting any minute," he said ruefully. "And I have to get myself under control." He took Justine's hand. "Come and join me. I'll have them add another place setting at my table."

Justine looked at him tenderly and shook her head. "No; this is *your* night, Casson. You need to focus on what you need to say. For Franklin's sake…and for kids like Andy." She planted a soft kiss on his lips. "I'll be waiting for you back home, Cass. With Luna-Lu."

He watched her walk away, his heart bursting, and then, with a lightness he couldn't remember feeling in a long time, he headed to the banquet room.

CHAPTER TWENTY

JUSTINE LEFT THE Stockey Centre with a sensation of wonder that made her whole body feel buoyant. She replayed Casson's words constantly in her head while driving home.

I found myself falling in love... With you, *Miss Winter.*
He loved her.

And his honesty tonight had made her anger and hurt disappear. Her humiliation at being used—gone! Casson loved her, body and soul, and she loved him the same way. And trusted him.

But maybe she hadn't told him in so many words.

Well, she would make up for it tonight.

Her heart had broken when he'd told her about his parents. She could only imagine how lonely he must have felt. Growing up in the shadow of his brother's death. Craving the attention and love of his parents, whose grief had stunted any relationship they could have had with their remaining son.

Thank goodness Casson hadn't taken the dark path to get noticed. Fallen in with the wrong crowd. Justine's heart swelled with pride, thinking of how Casson had studied and worked hard to make something of himself. And if he had gone unnoticed in his youth, he was certainly making up for it now.

How could she have ever lumped Casson and Robert

into the same category? Who they were at their core was as different as dawn from dusk. Robert had acted in ways to satisfy his own ego, to benefit himself. Casson had been driven only by a selfless desire to use the resources he had to help children with cancer and to support their parents as well. And it wasn't a fleeting desire, but a lifelong intention. To honor his brother's memory.

Maybe she would have realized all this earlier, been open to Casson's vulnerability, if Robert's deception and her resulting distrust of him and other men hadn't influenced her judgment…

After leaving Casson, Justine had gone to take a peek at the A. J. Casson painting in the silent auction room. She'd been curious to see what Casson had so generously donated to help boost his venture.

A security guard had stood at the entrance, and Justine had passed him in order to get to the center of the room, where the painting was being displayed. A few other people had been standing around, gazing at the large oil painting on canvas and murmuring to themselves. The other invited patrons must have already left to attend the banquet, she'd thought.

Storm on the Bay was breathtaking. A dark sky was streaked with indigo, gold and red, and the swirling waters reflected the colors like cut glass. On the hilltops, pines swayed in every direction, their distinctive Muskoka shape instantly recognizable.

Justine had almost gasped when she'd read that bidding was set to begin at three hundred and fifty thousand dollars. But this was a prime piece of work by a member of the Group of Seven.

As the guests had bustled about, Justine had heard an elderly woman saying to her husband, "Imagine Casson Forrester doing all this to help children with cancer, in honor of his little brother. Now, *that's* my idea of a true Canadian hero!"

Smiling, Justine had taken her leave. And now here she was, in the driveway of Cottage Number One. With her master key, she let herself in.

Luna's affectionate welcome almost brought her to tears. She took Luna out for a break, made sure she had enough fresh water, and gave her a treat.

"Just for being my BFF," she said, and laughed, giving her a pat.

Justine went into the bedroom. The T-shirt was still on the bed, but it wasn't folded the way she had left it. A flash of electricity surged through her as she imagined Casson picking it up when he got back earlier. Justine shivered as she slipped the T-shirt over her body and breathed in the lingering scent of Casson's cologne. Desire coiled throughout her as she thought about how Casson looked tonight, in a tailored black suit and maroon tie...

With a contentedness and anticipation she had never felt before, Justine snuggled into the bed. She started when Luna suddenly nudged the door open and bounded on top of the bed.

"Okay...for a little while, Luna-Lu." She chuckled, rubbing Luna behind the ears. "Until your papa comes home."

She dimmed the lamp on the night table and closed her eyes, happily imagining everything that might happen after Casson walked in the door...

Justine felt the bed vibrating and blinked in confusion. Luna had jumped off the bed and Justine turned over to see Casson framed in the doorway, gorgeous and grinning, his black suit jacket draped over one arm and his maroon tie loosened.

She positioned herself on her elbows and flashed him a wide smile. "How did it go, Mr. *Forrest?*"

As Casson strode toward her he took off his tie and flung his jacket on top of her clothes on the chair. And then he was sitting next to her, his eyes gleaming.

"A resounding success, Miss *Wintry*. The final bid for *Storm on the Bay* was a whopping nine hundred and fifty thousand dollars."

Justine felt like crying and shouting with joy at the same time. She started to speak, but stopped when she felt her lips tremble. Her brow crinkled and a tear slid down her cheek.

"What's this?" Casson leaned forward and gently wiped her cheek.

He gazed at her so tenderly that Justine wanted to melt in his arms. She shifted to a sitting position and put her hands on his chest.

"I'm just happy for you," she said, fiddling idly with his cufflinks. "And for all the kids who are going to be able to stay at the resort one day. I… I thought about what you said before, Cass, and…and I will gladly accept your offer to manage Franklin's Resort."

Casson took her hand and slipped it underneath his shirt. The feel of his chest muscles and the beating of his heart made her pulse leap. She gazed into his eyes while he undid the rest of his buttons. And then, with a groan, he removed his shirt and wrapped his arms around her, kissing her with a passion that matched hers.

They fell back onto the bed, and Justine savored the firmness of his lips on hers. She ran her fingers through his hair and cupped the back of his head as his kiss deepened. She shivered as he kissed a path down her neck, sending flickers of heat through her. He stopped suddenly, and Justine's eyes flew open.

She watched in bewilderment as he got off the bed and began to kneel down on the rug beside the bed.

"Skedaddle, Luna," he ordered, and with a low grumble Luna got up and padded out of the room.

And there he was, on one knee, bare-chested, hair tousled from her touch, looking at her with those sexy, intense tiger eyes.

"What about my other offer?" he said huskily.

Justine frowned. *What other offer had he made?*

"I don't understand…"

Casson's eyes glinted. "The offer to be my wife."

He brought her hands up to kiss them, his gaze locking with hers.

"I love you, Miss Winter, and I would be honored if you'd accept my proposal to spend the rest of your life with me. I promise I won't pressure you about selling. Winter's Haven is yours, and I respect that. I'd be happy to develop only the Russell properties—*my* properties—for Franklin's Resort."

Justine breathed deeply, her heart ready to burst. "I rather think Winter and Forrester go hand in hand, don't you? Maybe we could change Winter's Haven to Winter's Forrest Haven. As for the offer to be your wife…" Her voice softened. "I accept, Mr. Forrester. And I love *you*."

She pulled at his hands and a smile spread across her face.

"Now, get up here, Cass, and let's seal the deal!"

EPILOGUE

CASSON LEANED BACK on the love seat with his arm around Justine. *His wife.* They had dimmed the lights and were gazing at the twinkling colored lights on the Christmas tree. Tinsel glittered from every tip, and the vintage Christmas ornaments that Justine had bought added to the brilliance.

He sniffed the air appreciatively. Justine had stuffed a turkey, and the aroma of it roasting, along with root vegetables and stuffing, was making his mouth water.

Ronnie and Andy would be arriving soon, to share their Christmas Eve dinner and to stay for a few days. Andy had been given a clean bill of health five months earlier, and had started to look more robust. His hair had grown in nice and thick, too.

Casson smiled. He couldn't wait to take him snowshoeing and ice-fishing. And skating on the bay. He had had a section cleared off for Andy to enjoy, with the new skates and helmet he would be giving him for Christmas, among the other things Ronnie had said Andy was wishing for.

Mandy and her fiancé were also on their way. They had set their wedding date for September, and were happily making plans. Justine's mom and dad were currently enjoying the heat in Australia, but had promised they would return to Winter's Haven in time for the baby's birth.

Casson put one hand on Justine's tummy and suddenly had a feeling of *déjà-vu*.

He had visualized this moment before…

His eyes sought Justine's—as blue-gray as the sky—and he gave a soft laugh.

"What's so funny, Cass?"

"I just remembered that I imagined a moment like this some time ago—when you were roasting marshmallows with Andy…"

She pursed her lips and he couldn't resist leaning forward to kiss her. *Thoroughly.*

When they drew apart, he saw that her eyes had misted.

"You and knowing we are going to have this baby are the best Christmas presents I could have ever hoped for or dreamed of," he murmured, stroking her head. "And when he or she is born in the summer, before the grand opening of Franklin's Resort, I'll be the happiest dad and man alive."

"Whether it's a boy or a girl?" She flashed him a grin.

"Whether it's a boy or a girl," he said solemnly, bringing her hand to his lips.

"We'll have to think about some names…" She cuddled up against him, placing her hand over his heart.

"Look, Justine!" He suddenly pointed toward the bay window. "A blue jay in the closest spruce tree."

He took her hand and led her to the window.

Justine caught her breath. "It's like a snow globe," she murmured. "How magical."

The snowflakes had been drifting down gently since early morning, and the evergreens were now padded with a soft quilt. The blue jay flitted from bough to bough, emitting its shrill cry and scattering snow like fairy dust. Its color was even more brilliant than usual against the dazzling white backdrop.

"How about Jay?" Casson said suddenly.

Justine's brow wrinkled as she gazed up at him.

"Jay…if it's a boy?"

Justine cocked her head at him. "I had a favorite doll called Amy. I was going to suggest Amy if it's a girl…"

The blue jay flew directly past the bay window.

Casson took both her hands, his tawny eyes blazing into hers. "I've got it! How about Amy Jay if it's a girl?"

Justine's heart flipped as she realized what Casson was getting at. *"A. J.,"* she whispered. "Oh, Cass, what a perfect name. I think Franklin would have approved." She placed a hand on her belly. "I have a feeling it'll be a girl…"

"And I have a feeling I'm in heaven," he said, and pulled her into his arms.

* * * * *

THE LIEUTENANTS'
ONLINE LOVE

CARO CARSON

This book is dedicated to the women of West Point, the ones who came before me, especially the Class of '80, who first proved we belonged, the ones who lived it with me, especially Chriss, who dragged me off post to have fun in Alabama, Texas and Panama, and Gill, who can make me laugh even while we're doing push-ups in a sawdust pit at Airborne School, and the ones who continue the Long Gray Line after me, especially 1LT Bethany Leadbetter, who so patiently answered this Old Grad's questions about today's service—and who is proof that the US Army has the country's best and brightest in its ranks.

Beat Navy.

Chapter One

Today, I was desperate for tater tots.

Chloe stared at her blinking cursor, her finger hovering over the enter key on her laptop. One second, not even that, was all it would take for that sentence to be sent to him, no way to take it back. Would he think she was dumb or would he think she was funny?

It shouldn't matter. The man was no more than a series of words on a screen, a modern-day pen pal. She wrote to him with BallerinaBaby as her user name. He wrote back as DifferentDrummer. A freebie conversation app had matched them up months ago and they'd been writing back and forth ever since, but Chloe knew that wasn't the same as being real friends in real life.

It shouldn't matter, but it did. She wanted to make him laugh. Something about his notes lately made her think her anonymous correspondent had been having a hard week. He had talked to her through all the crazy months she'd been bouncing from one place to another. He'd listened to all her thoughts and worries and hopes. It was the least she could do to help him out if he was tired and overworked. Friends and lovers ought to take care of each other. Chloe believed emotional support was just as important as physical compatibility in a relationship, so—

Chloe snatched her finger away from the enter key. She was looking at nothing more than the basic white screen of an outdated app, yet she was worrying about emotional parity in a relationship. She needed to keep the proper perspective on this…this…whatever it was.

What should she call it when her digital pen pal felt like a better friend than the living human beings around her? Borderline insanity?

She didn't know any of the human beings around her, that was the problem. She didn't know anyone in the entire state of Texas. She was newly arrived in a new town for a new job. All her stuff was still in boxes. The only constant was her pen pal. She didn't want him to think she was dumb, because if she lost him, too…well, she'd lose the most reliable presence in her life for these last five months.

Her cursor was still blinking. *Tots*.

Tater tots. Was that what she was going to talk about? She was going to talk about tots when what she was honestly feeling was lonely?

"Roger that," she said out loud, and hit Enter.

The alarm on her wristwatch went off. Time to get ready for work.

Chloe carried her laptop with her and set it by her bathroom sink so she could keep an eye on the screen. If Different Drummer was online, he would answer immediately. It was one of the things she loved about him. She smoothed her hair back and twisted it into the low, tight bun that she was required to wear every day.

Her cursor blinked in silence.

Tots!

Men didn't really joke about food cravings, at least not the men in her world, and there were plenty of men in her world. They talked about women, especially their breasts, and they talked about drinking, especially beer, but they didn't joke about food cravings.

The cursor kept blinking.

Food cravings. What had she been thinking?

She'd probably, finally scared off Different Drummer. There were so many jokes about women and food cravings, he might think she was confessing some kind of hormonal thing, a craving like pregnant women were supposed to get. Worse, maybe he thought it was a monthly craving. Guys were so squeamish about things like that. A definite turnoff.

She hadn't been trying to turn him off. She hadn't been

trying to turn him on, either. It wasn't like anyone could seduce a man with a line about tater tots.

She jabbed a few extra bobby pins into her bun. Seduce
him. Ha. She didn't even know what he looked like. The
simple little app didn't have the capacity to send photos.
She scowled at her reflection in the mirror. With her hair
pulled back tightly, her face devoid of any makeup—she'd
just sweat it off at work, anyway—she didn't look like any
kind of seductress.

She pulled a sports bra over her bun carefully, then wrestled the rest of the way into it. Good thing she was flexible. It
was the kind of bra that didn't let anything show, even when
she was soaked in sweat, the kind of bra that kept a girl as
flat as possible, because bouncy curves were frowned on in
her profession.

She pulled on her comfy, baggy pants and zipped up her
matching jacket, checking her laptop's screen between each
article of clothing.

He had to be offline. If he was online, he would have answered her...unless he was turned off by a ballerina who
was obsessed with tater tots. Which she wasn't.

She yanked on her best broken-in boots. If there was
anything she needed to stop obsessing over, it was him, the
mystery man who always seemed to get her sense of humor,
who always seemed as happy to chat with her all night as
she was to chat with him. It was too easy to forget it was all
an illusion. She wasn't really Ballerina Baby; he wasn't really a unique man who marched to the beat of a Different
Drummer, a mystery man who sent her long notes and found
himself hopelessly charmed by her words.

Was he?

Today, I was desperate for tater tots.

Blink, blink.

Nope. He wasn't hopelessly charmed. It was time for Ballerina Baby to join the real world.

Her fingertips had just touched the laptop screen, ready to close it before leaving her new apartment, when a sentence in blue magically appeared.

You crack me up.

He got it. She'd made him laugh. Mission accomplished.

The next blue sentence appeared: Or am I not supposed to laugh? The word desperate sounds rather...

Desperate? she typed one-handed. Then she stuffed her wallet in her pocket, but not her car keys. She knew from experience that if she started chatting to Different Drummer, she'd lose track of time and forget that she had to be somewhere. She bit down on the metal ring of her key fob, holding it in her teeth to leave two hands free for typing. She wouldn't forget about work as long as she had her car keys in her teeth.

Another blue line appeared on-screen. They say most men lead lives of quiet desperation.

Chloe raised one eyebrow. They slipped in famous quotes now and then, just to see if the other person would identify the quote, their own little nerdy game. This one was no challenge. How very Thoreau of you. (Too easy.)

He replied, You, however, are not like most men. (I knew it was easy.)

For starters, I'm a woman. Her words showed up in hot pink as she typed—the app's choice for female users, not hers.

He sent her a laughing-face emoji. I was thinking more along the lines that you don't seem to lead a quiet life. You also never sound desperate. I don't think you'd be quiet about it if you were.

She was typing while holding car keys in her teeth. Quietly desperate? He didn't know the half of it.

Were you able to procure the tots? Tell me you did it noisily.

Shamelessly. I bought a big bag of frozen tots at the grocery store a couple of hours ago. They didn't survive long.

You killed them already? All of them?

All of them. A one-pound bag.

Blink, blink.

For a moment, just one tiny, insecure moment, she worried again that she'd turned him off. Ballerina Baby didn't sound like the kind of woman who would eat a whole bag of tater tots at one sitting, did she? The next second, impatient with all these self-doubts, she sucked in a faintly metallic breath around her key ring and shoved aside all the insecurity. This was her friend—yes, her friend—and sometimes a pause was just a pause.

I've shocked you into silence with my brutal killing of a bag of tots, haven't I?

Not at all. I'm deciding how best to advise you so that you won't be tried for murder. I don't think they'd let you write to me from jail. I'd miss you.

Chloe's fingers fell silent. He'd miss her, and he wasn't afraid to say it. He was so different from all the other men she knew. So much better. Would he find it weird if she suddenly switched gears and wrote that?

Instead, she wrote: If I hadn't killed them all, they would have sat in my freezer, taunting me, testing my willpower. No, they needed to die. 'twere best to be done quickly.

Very Lady Macbeth of you. (Too easy.)

Yes, well, unlike Lady McB, I ate all the evidence. I guess I shouldn't feel too superior. In order to eat her evidence, she would have had to eat the king's guards. Rather filling, I'd imagine.

He had a quick comeback. If Macbeth had been about cannibalism, English class would have been much more interesting.

Ha. She smiled around the car keys in her mouth. At any rate, 'tis done. Half with mustard, half with ketchup, all with salt.

Then you're safe. We can keep talking. How was the rest of your day?

If only the last guy she'd seriously dated had been so open about saying he liked her. If only any guy she'd ever dated had been like Different Drummer.

But the car keys in her teeth did their job. They were getting heavy; she had to go.

I wish I could stay and chat, but I gotta run. And then, just in case he thought she was an unhealthy glutton, she added, Time to go burn off a whole bagful of tater calories. Talk to you tomorrow.

There. That didn't sound desperate or obsessed or…in love. She couldn't fall in love with a man she'd never met.

Looking forward to it, Baby.

But if they broke their unwritten rule and arranged to meet in real life…

The alarm on her wristwatch sounded again.

If they met in real life, he'd find out she was no ballerina—not that she'd ever said she was, but she'd never made it clear she wasn't. She certainly wasn't the kind of woman who was any guy's baby. Most guys were a little intimidated by her, something it had taken her a few years to realize.

But with him? She could show so many more sides of herself. The soft side, the insecure side, the side that worried about making friends, and yes, the side that adored the ballet. A lot of pop psychology criticized the digital age for enabling everyone to pretend to be someone they were not while they were online, but Chloe felt like this situation was the opposite. The anonymity let her be her whole self with Drummer, not only her work self. She'd be crazy to mess with a good thing. She'd follow the rules, and not try to figure out who he really was.

She picked up the last item she always wore for work, her patrol cap. The way she slid the camouflage cap over her hair, the way she pulled the brim down just so, were second nature to her. The cap was well broken-in; she'd been wearing this exact one throughout her four years as a cadet at West Point, the United States Military Academy.

Although she was so familiar with her uniform that she could dress in the dark in a matter of seconds when required, Chloe checked the mirror to be sure her uniform would pass inspection, as she'd been trained to do. The American flag on her shoulder and the name *Michaels* embroidered over her pocket were the same as they'd been since she'd first raised her right hand as a new cadet at the military academy and sworn to defend the Constitution.

The embroidered gold bar on the front of her hat was new. She'd graduated in May, so now she owed the US Army five years of service in return for her bachelor's degree. She was going to serve those years in her first choice of branch, the Military Police Corps. She was a second lieutenant now, the lowest rank of commissioned officers, but she was a commissioned officer with all the responsibility and authority that entailed. After four years of West Point in New York, three weeks of Airborne School in Georgia and four months of military police training at Fort Leonard Wood, Missouri, she was ready to lead her first platoon of MP soldiers here in Texas. So ready.

Tonight, she'd be riding along in a patrol car with the officer on duty, the first of a few mandatory nights familiarizing herself with the post she'd call home for the next three or four years. Once she knew her way around the streets of Fort Hood, she'd take shifts as the officer on duty herself, the highest-ranking MP during the midnight hours, the one who had to make the final decisions—and the one who had to accept the blame if anything went wrong.

First impressions were important. After West Point, Air Assault School, Airborne School and Military Police Basic Officer Leadership Course, Chloe knew exactly what was expected of her. She looked at the officer in the mirror and wiped the smile from her face. She could be Ballerina Baby tomorrow, cozying up to her Different Drummer and being as soft and girly as she liked.

In private.

Tonight, it was time for Second Lieutenant Chloe Michaels to go be a badass.

First Lieutenant Thane Carter was done being a badass—at least for the next twelve hours.

He was almost home. His apartment building was visible through his windshield. He kept moving on autopilot, parking his Mustang, getting out, grabbing his long-empty coffee mug and locking the car. He put on his patrol cap, an automatic habit whenever he was outdoors in uniform, pulling the brim down just so, and headed for his building, a three-story, plain beige building, identical to the five other buildings clustered around the apartment complex's outdoor swimming pool.

His primary objective for the next twelve hours was to get sleep, and a lot of it, ASAP—as soon as possible. Perhaps he'd wake up after a few hours and have a pizza delivered to his door later tonight, but then he'd go right back to sleep until dawn.

At dawn, he'd get up, put on a fresh uniform and return to duty at Fort Hood, where he was both the senior platoon leader and the acting executive officer in a military police company. That MP company, the 584th MP Company to be exact, was currently short one platoon leader, and Thane was feeling the pain.

There were normally four platoon leaders in the company, each officer in charge of roughly thirty enlisted personnel. Most of the year, MPs trained for their wartime missions, the same as every other kind of unit stationed stateside, rehearsing likely scenarios, keeping up their qualifications on their weapons. But MPs were unique: roughly one month out of every three, they pulled garrison duty.

Fort Hood was a sizable town, a military installation where sixty thousand soldiers and civilians worked and where tens of thousands lived with their families. Garrison duty required MPs to perform the functions of a regular civilian police department, patrolling Fort Hood in police cruisers as they did everything from traffic control to answering 911 calls. During that month, one of the four platoon leaders was always on duty as the officer in charge of law enforcement.

Except there weren't four platoon leaders at the moment, only three. Covering the night and weekend shifts among just three lieutenants meant that each of them was pulling a thirty-six-hour shift every third day. Officers didn't get the next day off after working all night. Thane had worked Monday, then Monday night straight on through until Tuesday evening. That thirty-six hours had been followed by twelve hours off to sleep, hit the grocery store, get his uniform ready for the next day. Wednesday would be a straightforward twelve-hour day, but getting sleep Wednesday night was critical, because Thursday morning would start another thirty-six-hour shift straight through to Friday evening.

The schedule was taking its toll. Law enforcement was important work. Necessary work. But after living the MP motto, Assist-Protect-Defend, for thirty-six hours straight, Thane was ready to assist himself right into the sack.

Alone.

To sleep.

He was single. Never married, no current girlfriend, not even dating. No surprise there. He'd worked—what? Thane counted it up in his head as he trudged from his parking space toward his mailbox, each step heavy with exhaustion. Twelve, twelve, thirty-six, twelve…hell, he'd only had twenty-four consecutive hours off one time in the past week, and it had been that way for weeks now. They really needed to fill that fourth platoon leader slot.

More downtime would help his sleep, but it wouldn't help his love life. Having no time to date was only half the reason he didn't have a woman in his life.

The other half was the scarcity of women with whom he could spend that precious downtime. The US Army was an overwhelmingly male space. Maybe 15 percent of all soldiers were women, but even so, the female MPs in his unit were off-limits. Whether he outranked them or they outranked him, dating someone within the same unit was a military offense, damaging to good order, discipline and authority, according to regulations, and grounds for a court-martial. Thane didn't need a regulation to keep him from temptation there, anyway. In the Brotherhood of Arms, the women he trained and served with were brothers-in-arms, too. Teammates, not dates. Half of them were married, anyway, which put them off-limits by Thane's personal code.

Of course, there were other servicewomen, single servicewomen, stationed at Fort Hood who were in units and positions that were completely unrelated to his, but there were roadblocks there, as well. Dating between an enlisted soldier and an officer was forbidden. Period. That knocked a couple of thousand women at Fort Hood right out of the dating pool. Since Thane was a commissioned officer, he could only date another commissioned officer who was not in his unit, but he rarely had a chance to meet female officers who worked in different branches of the army—that whole working thirty-six hours every third day had a lot to do with that. The police worked Saturdays and Sundays. And nights. And holidays.

Thane's brother, still living back home in South Carolina, was head over heels for a woman he'd met at work, one of his clients. But Thane's only "clients" were women who called 911 for help. Victims. Or they were women on the other side of that coin—not victims, but perpetrators. Two of the soldiers in his platoon had served a warrant on a woman suspected of check forgery today. Or was that yesterday? The days were all becoming one blur.

The odds of him meeting a datable woman at work were pretty much zero out of a million. Thane would've shaken his head in disgust, but that would've taken too much energy. One foot in front of the other, trudging past the apartment complex's swimming pool, that was all he had the energy for.

Building Six's mailboxes were grouped together in the stairwell. So were several of his male neighbors, all checking their mail at the same time, all in the same uniform Thane wore. At least one person in every apartment here was in the service. Everyone left Fort Hood after the American flag had been lowered for the day and everyone arrived home around the same time, an army rush hour. Everyone checked their mail before disappearing behind their apartment doors. They were all living off post in a civilian apartment complex, but the military influence of Fort Hood was impossible to escape in the surrounding town of Killeen.

As Thane used a key to open his little cubby full of two days' worth of junk mail, he exchanged greetings with the other men. To be more accurate, Thane exchanged silent lifts of the chin, the same acknowledgment he'd been exchanging with guys since the hallowed halls of high school. That had been eight years ago, but still, that was the level of close-ness the average guy reached with the average guy. A lift of the chin. A comment on a sports team, perhaps, during the NFL playoffs or Game Five of the World Series. Maybe, if he saw someone at the mailboxes whom he hadn't seen in a while, they might acknowledge each other with a lift of the chin and actually speak. "You back from deployment?"

The answer was usually a shrug and a *yeah*, to which the answer was a nod and a *yeah, thought so, hadn't seen you around in a while*, followed by each guy retreating to his apartment, shutting a door to seal himself off from the hundreds of others in the complex, hundreds of people roughly Thane's age and profession, all living in the same place.

He had no one to talk to.

Thane started up the concrete stairs to his apartment, each boot landing as heavily as if it were made of concrete, too.

He lived on the third floor, a decision he regretted on evenings like this one. Thane hit the second-story landing. One more flight, and he could fall in bed. As he rounded the iron banister, an apartment door opened. A woman his age appeared in the door, her smile directed down the stairs he'd just come up. Another man in uniform was coming up them now, a man who wouldn't be sleeping alone.

"Hi, baby," the man said.

"You're home early," the woman said, sounding like that was a wonderful gift for her. "How was your day?"

"You won't believe this, but the commander decided—" The door closed.

Thane slogged his way up to his floor.

Bed. All he wanted was his own bed, yet now he couldn't help but think it would be nice not to hit the sheets alone. He had an instant mental image of a woman in bed with him. He couldn't see her face, not with her head nestled into his shoulder, but he could imagine warm skin and a happy, in-terested voice, asking *How was your day?* They'd talk, two heads on one pillow.

Pitiful. What kind of fantasy was that for a twenty-six-year-old man to have? He was heading to bed without a woman, but it wasn't sex he was lonely for. Not much, anyway. He wanted someone to talk to, someone waiting to talk to him, someone who cared what he thought after days full of people who broke laws, people who were hurt, people who were angry.

Better yet, he wanted someone to share a laugh with.

He scrubbed a hand over the razor stubble that he'd be shaving in less than twelve hours to go back to work. Yeah, he needed a laugh. There was nothing to laugh at around here.

His phone buzzed in his pocket—two shorts and a long, which meant he had a message waiting in his favorite app. The message had to be from his digital pen pal. The app had paired him up months ago with someone going by Ballerina Baby. He didn't know anything about her, not even her real name, and yet, she was someone with whom he did more than nod, someone to whom he said something meaningful once in a while. He could put his thoughts into words, written words in blue on a white screen. He got words back from her, hot pink and unpredictable, making him feel more connected to the woman behind them than he felt to anyone else around here.

Thane took the last few stairs two at a time. He wanted to get home. He had twelve hours ahead to sleep—but not alone. There was someone waiting to talk to him, after all.

He unlocked the door and walked into his apartment, tossing his patrol cap onto the coffee table with one hand as he jerked down the zipper of his uniform jacket with the other. He tossed that over a chair, impatient to pull out his phone from his pocket the moment his hand was free. A real friend, real feelings, conversation, communion—

Today, I was desperate for tater tots.

He stared at the sentence for a long moment. What the hell…?

And then, all of a sudden, life wasn't so heavy. He didn't have to take himself so seriously. Thane read the hot-pink silliness, and he started to laugh.

The rest of his clothes came off easily. Off with the tan T-shirt that clung after a day of Texas heat. Thane had to sit to unlace the combat boots, but he typed a quick line to let Ballerina know he was online. You crack me up.

And thank God for that.

He brushed his teeth. He pulled back the sheets and fell into bed, phone in one hand. He bunched his pillow up under his neck, and he realized he was smiling at his phone fondly as he typed, I'd miss you. It was crazy, but it was true.

The little cursor on his phone screen blinked. He waited, eyes drifting idly over the blue and pink words they'd already exchanged. You killed them? he'd written, followed by words like *murder. Jail.*

He was going to scare her away. She'd think he was a freak the way his mind went immediately to crime and punishment. Did normal guys—civilian guys—zing their conversations right to felony death?

She must think he was a civilian. His screen name was Different Drummer, after all, nothing that implied he was either military or in law enforcement. They weren't supposed to reveal what Ballerina called their "real, boring surface facts," things like name, address, job. During one of those marathon chat sessions where they'd spilled their guts out, they'd agreed that anonymity was part of the reason they could write to each other so freely.

He hoped the way he used so many law enforcement references didn't give away his real profession. It wasn't like he was dropping clues subconsciously. Really.

He read her words. She made him smile with *ketchup, mustard* and *salt.* He wondered if she'd kept a straight face when she wrote that, or had she giggled at her own silliness? Did she have a shy smile or a wide-open laugh?

Then she told him she had to go. He had to act like that was perfectly okay. They'd talk some other time. But before closing the app he remembered the couple downstairs—*Hi, baby, how was your day?*

Ballerina Baby was the woman who'd greeted him after a long day of work.

Looking forward to it, Baby.

A subconscious slip? He'd never called Ballerina Baby just Baby before.

She didn't reply. All his exhaustion returned with a vengeance. If Ballerina couldn't talk, what good would it do to go out to exchange nods and grunts with everyone else?

He tossed his phone onto his nightstand and rolled onto his side, ready for the sleep that would overtake him in moments. But just before it did, he thought what he could never type: You mean more to me than you should, Baby.

Chapter Two

"Friday night. Almost quitting time, Boss."

At his platoon sergeant's booming voice, Thane tossed his cell phone onto his desk, facedown. He should have known that if he decided to check his personal messages for the first time in twelve hours, someone would walk in.

Thane could have stayed on his phone, of course. This was his office, and he didn't have to stop what he was doing and stand when a noncommissioned officer, an NCO, walked in. But he didn't want his platoon sergeant to see any hot-pink words that would encourage him to start giving Thane hell about women. As a commissioned officer, Thane outranked sergeants and other noncommissioned officers, but Sergeant First Class Lloyd had been in the army more than twice as many years as Thane. A platoon sergeant was a platoon leader's right arm. The platoon didn't run well without either one of them—and no NCO let his lieutenant forget it, either.

Sergeant First Class Lloyd was older, more experienced—and married, too. In other words, he'd enjoy razzing his bachelor platoon leader about his love life. Thane wasn't going to give him a pink-fonted excuse to do it.

Thane kicked back in his government-issued desk chair and put his booted feet up on the gray desk that had probably served all the platoon leaders who'd come before him since Vietnam. Maybe even further back. The battleship-gray metal desk was old but indestructible. He liked it.

"I take it you didn't come here to tell me the CO went home." Retreat had sounded, the flag had been lowered, all the enlisted soldiers dismissed, but the lieutenants were still here because the company commander—the CO—was still here. It wasn't a written rule, but Thane was old enough to know that it wasn't wise for platoon leaders to leave before the company commander did.

"It's Friday, sir. I wouldn't still be here if the CO had left." Just as the platoon leaders didn't leave before the company commander, the platoon sergeants didn't leave before the first sergeant did. Since the first sergeant didn't leave before the company commander did, here they all were, waiting for Friday night to begin.

Thane watched his platoon sergeant head for the empty desk next to his own. Was the man going to take a seat and settle in for a chat? It wasn't like him. Sergeant First Class Lloyd was a man of few words.

"Do you have any big plans for the weekend, sir?" asked the noncommissioned officer of few words.

"Just the usual."

"Kicking ass and taking names?"

"Not tonight. Lieutenant Salvatore has duty."

The man started pulling out desk drawers, then slamming them shut. "Whiskey and women then, sir?"

"Also not happening tonight." Thane leaned back a little more in his chair and tucked his hands behind his head. "Sleep. Nothing but sweet sleep."

His platoon sergeant spared him a quick glance. "You pulled another thirty-six hours, sir?"

An affirmative grunt was enough of an answer.

Without further comment, Sergeant First Class Lloyd sat in the desk chair and started testing its tilt and the height of its armrests.

"What are you doing?" Thane finally asked. "You planning on buying that chair after this test ride?"

"No, sir. Just seeing if I should permanently borrow it before the new platoon leader arrives."

Thane sat up, boots hitting the floor. "Don't get my hopes up, Sergeant First Class. Is there a new platoon leader coming in?"

"Yes, sir. In-processing on post."

"About damn time." Thane didn't like the look on the

sergeant's face, though. "Let's hear it. I can tell you got more intel."

"Brand-new second lieutenant, fresh out of Leonard Wood."

Fort Leonard Wood, Missouri, was the home of the Military Police Corps. All new second lieutenants had to go through the four months of BOLC, Basic Officer Leadership Course, there. If that was all his platoon sergeant had on the new guy, it hardly counted as intel.

Thane leaned back and laced his fingers behind his head once more. "It's that time of year. The college boys all graduate in May and complete BOLC in the fall. It would be too much to hope for to get someone with experience. It's butter bar season."

The term *butter bar* referred to the yellow color of the single bar that denoted the rank of second lieutenant. As a first lieutenant, Thane's rank insignia was a black bar on the camouflaged ACUs he wore almost every day, or a silver bar on the dress uniform.

"Sergeant First Class Ernesto has broken in his fair share of lieutenants," Thane said. "I'm sure he'll handle this one. I just want someone to throw into the duty officer rotation. A butter bar will work."

Sergeant First Class Ernesto was the platoon sergeant for fourth platoon. He'd been running fourth platoon without a platoon leader for three months, attending all the first sergeant's meetings for NCOs and then the commander's meetings for the platoon leaders, as well. Thane would bet money that fourth platoon's sergeant felt the same way he did. Even a wet-behind-the-ears butter bar would be better than nothing.

"Well, sir, you'll get to update that duty roster soon enough. The new LT already had one ride-along. A couple more ride-alongs this weekend, and you can add that name to your schedule."

"Do you have a name yet?"

"Second Lieutenant Michaels. I'll be right back." Lloyd rolled the office chair out the door. Each office in the head-quarters building held two desks. While fourth platoon had no lieutenant, Lloyd had been using the desk next to Er-nesto, two NCOs doing their NCO thing, but the new pla-toon leader would be in Ernesto's office now. Thane would have to get used to having his own platoon sergeant sharing this room again.

He picked up his cell phone and unlocked the screen. Pink words awaited him. *Something came up, and I won't be able to be by the phone tonight. There goes our Star Trek marathon. I'm sorry. The best-laid plans of mice and men...*

They'd planned to write each other while watching the same channel tonight—so he knew Ballerina Baby lived in the United States somewhere and got the sci-fi channel on cable—but it looked like his evening was suddenly free. And more boring. The disappointment was sharp, but he had to play it cool. He wasn't her boyfriend. He couldn't demand to know why she was changing her plans, and he shouldn't demand it. If Ballerina said she couldn't make it, he believed her. Thane frowned. He also wasn't sure who'd said the mice and men line.

Shakespeare? That was right nine times out of ten.

Gotcha. Robbie Burns. You're not a fan of Scottish poetry?

Damn. She'd gotten him last week with Burns, raving about how she loved her new sofa that was the color of a red, red rose. *No, but I'm a fan of Star Trek and I'm a fan of you. Now I only get one of those two things tonight.*

His platoon sergeant came back in, pushing a chair with squeaky wheels ahead of himself. Thane turned his phone screen off. With all the pink and blue letters, it practically looked like a baby announcement. Lloyd would have a field day with that.

Thane stood up. "I'll help you move the rest of your stuff. You prefer the squeaky wheels, huh?"

"No, sir. That's why I just upgraded. I'm going to leave this chair here."

"You're not moving back in?"

Lloyd had that grin on his face again, the one Thane didn't trust. "Well, sir, maybe an experienced lieutenant like yourself ought to show the new lieutenant the ropes. Maybe we should keep one office NCOs, one office lieutenants."

"No. No way. You're not sticking me with some fresh college kid. He's Ernesto's problem to deal with, not mine. That's what a platoon sergeant is for, to keep the rookie LT out of trouble."

Lloyd only grinned wider. "It's not my idea. Seems like the CO thinks you'd be the best man for the job. He told the first sergeant who he wants in each office. He wants you to babysit Lieutenant Michaels. I mean, train Lieutenant Michaels."

Thane cursed and rubbed his hand over his jaw and its five o'clock shadow, suddenly feeling each one of the thirty-six hours he'd been working. He'd wanted a fourth platoon leader to come in to lighten his work routine, but he hadn't wanted that new platoon leader to impact his daily routine this much. "That explains the grin on your face. I don't suppose there's any chance this lieutenant is OCS?"

OCS stood for Officer Candidate School. It was the quickest way for an enlisted soldier who already had a college degree to become an officer. Thane had only had a high school diploma when he'd enlisted, so he'd applied for an ROTC scholarship. After he'd served two years as an enlisted man, the army had changed his rank from corporal to ROTC cadet and sent him to four years of college on the army's dime. His prior two years as an infantry grunt made him a little older than most first lieutenants. He thought it made him a little wiser as well, since most ROTC grads were entering the army for the first time. If this butter bar was coming to them from OCS instead of ROTC, then he'd have some prior service, and he wouldn't be as much of a rookie. But Lloyd was still smiling. Not good.

"No, sir. Not OCS. Not ROTC, either. The word is that Lieutenant Michaels is fresh out of West Point."

"Are you kidding me?" The third way to become an officer was by attending the United States Military Academy at West Point, one of the country's oldest and most elite schools. *Elite* meant there weren't very many West Pointers in the army in general. Thane had worked with several, of course, and he couldn't honestly say he'd ever had a problem with a West Point graduate, but anything elite was automatically met with suspicion by everyone else, including him.

"Monday morning, sir, you get to share all your special secret lieutenant-y wisdom with a brand-new West Pointer. I'll be over in Ernesto's office if you need me."

"You're so helpful."

"You've been up since yesterday morning, sir. The CO hasn't. You should go home now." But as Lloyd left the office, he stopped and turned around. "Oh, and one more thing. Your new butter bar West Pointer office buddy? Word is that Lieutenant Michaels is a girl. See you Monday, Boss."

I wish I could sleep another four hours, but I'm burning too much daylight as is.

Thane glanced at the pink words as he poured raw scrambled eggs into a cast-iron skillet. Ballerina was going to have to dig deeper than that if she was going to stump him today. He'd slept until noon. The duty schedule had finally coincided with the right days on the calendar, and Thane had a whopping forty-eight hours off. He'd left the office Friday evening and didn't have to be anywhere until he took over at the police station on Sunday evening.

He typed on his phone with one finger while he kept his

Saturday morning eggs moving around with the spatula in his other hand. John Wayne. (Too easy. Really.) Why so tired?

Late night.

His flash of jealousy wasn't easy to laugh off. A single woman out late on a Friday night? Thane knew, somehow, that Ballerina would have no shortage of interested men around her. He had no idea what she looked like, but she was so full of life, so fun and quirky, men must find her as attractive in real life as he found her online. She must laugh and smile a lot with her real friends; there was nothing more attractive. Or maybe she was shy, making intelligent wise-cracks under her breath only to the one friend standing next to her. Also attractive.

This old app had no photo features. It didn't matter what she looked like, anyway. She was attractive to him in a way that went beyond blonde, brunette or redhead. Not only did it not matter, it would never matter. Other men would compete to get her smiles and hugs. He had no chance of being one of those men, the one who would pursue her until he was her favorite out of them all, until he was the only man she wanted to be with.

He should be satisfied that he was the man who got her thoughts and words, at least for now. When she found someone to love, he wouldn't even have that. Thane grabbed a fork and started eating from the skillet, standing up. Jealousy over a pen pal was stupid and he knew it. But…

She hadn't been able to chat with him last night, because she'd gone out somewhere.

He stabbed the eggs a little viciously. All right, so Ballerina had a life. He could keep this in perspective. She'd said something last night about working off that bag of tater tots she'd eaten. Maybe she'd had a rehearsal or even a performance. If she wasn't a ballerina, he still suspected she was involved with dance, maybe a dance instructor, or a choreographer. Like him, she often mentioned going to work out or being tired from a vaguely described workout.

He shoveled in more eggs and began to type. Out late for work or play?

There was a bit of a pause before she answered. Is this a trick question to see if I'll give you a clue about what I do for a living? Do I work at night?

Busted. Of course it was.

Of course not. How about this—did you enjoy your late night or were you gutting it out?

I loved it. I'm a natural night owl. I wish more of the world was. Even as a little kid, I hated going to bed for school. Kindergarten is misery for night owlets. Owlings. Whatever the term is. Why couldn't school have been from 8pm to 2am, instead of 8am to 2pm?

He put down the fork to type with two thumbs. You should've been a vampire. Do they have school-aged vampires? A kindergarten full of little ankle biters—literally, biters—who want school to start at 8 at night.

That doesn't seem right, she answered. I think you have to be a grown-up and choose to become a vampire. I don't think I would, though. I feel isolated enough already. If I became a vampire, I'd be so sad, watching everyone I know going to bed and knowing by the time they woke up, I'd be done for the day. I'll just have to stay a human night owl. (Is that an oxymoron? A human owl?) I don't have many night owl friends, though. In fact, you're the only one I can chat with at 3 in the morning. And because I know how to follow the ground rules, I'm not going to ask why you're sometimes awake at 3.

I'm a vampire.

Ha ha. I'm just glad that you're a night owl, too. You really are the perfect pen pal for me.

Thane finished his eggs and left the iron skillet to cool. At least one woman out there thought he was perfect because of his crazy military schedule, not despite it. His last girlfriend, a civilian he still ran into too often in the small world of an army town, had pouted every night and weekend that he had to work. Pouting wasn't as cute as it sounded.

Do you know the longest amount of time I've gone without talking to you? Ten days. And by talking, I mean writing to you in hot-pink letters, of course. Stupid app. It's so cliché, pink ink for girls and blue ink for boys.

I know. I'm so used to it now, I get startled when I type anywhere else and the words are black instead of blue.

I love this app, though, because it made us pen pals. I enjoy talking with you as much as with any friend I've ever had.

Thane smiled down at the phone screen. After a long pause, more pink appeared.

Do you think that's normal?

He stopped smiling. The answer, of course, was no. It wasn't normal. He took the phone out to his balcony, all four feet by two feet of concrete perch, three stories above the earth, and looked down to the complex's central swimming pool. Management had posted signs by the mailboxes that there would be a party today with free food. That party had started without him.

He didn't care. There was no one down there he'd rather be talking with. If it isn't normal, then we're both abnormal. It's easy to talk to you.

Agreed. Real people are hard.

I'm real, he wanted to write. But he didn't.
Do you have a close friend in real life? she asked.

Define friend.

I think that means no. If you had a close friend, you'd just say yes. You wouldn't ask me what a close friend is.

She had him there.

But I think you're normal...for a blue ink person. I read somewhere that the majority of married women will say their female friends are their best friends, when asked. But the majority of men will say their wife is their best friend. I remember that because I thought it was sad that there are apparently a lot of husbands out there who think their wife is their best friend, but she prefers a female buddy. Are you really best friends with someone if that person doesn't think you are their best friend, too? It's too much like unrequited love.

Who was his closest friend? His platoon sergeant came to mind immediately. They worked together every day, aiming for the same goals. They relied on one another. But Sergeant First Class Lloyd was not someone who would catch a famous quote in conversation—or who would laugh about it if he did. Heck, the platoon sergeant couldn't even call Thane by his first name. Thane was addressed as Lieutenant Carter or Sir. Sometimes LT, the abbreviation of lieutenant, or, if they were being really casual, Boss. That was it.

His company commander was another good man. More than a boss in the civilian sense of the word, but not a buddy. They shared some laughs, they were on the same page when it came to training and discipline, and they'd spent one Sunday in the field huddled over the same radio to get the play-off scores, because they cheered for the same NFL team. But the company commander was always the commander, with all the legal authority and responsibility that the position entailed. Thane was always Lieutenant Carter, no matter how many whiskeys they'd downed during officer-only dining-in events in the brigade.

Thane was pretty sure Ballerina Baby would expect him to call a close friend by his first name, at a minimum.

The only people at work who didn't call him Lieutenant Carter were the other two platoon leaders. They were good guys. One was married, one was not. The married guy's wife was named… Cecilia? Serena? Something with an *s* sound. If you couldn't name a friend's wife, he probably wouldn't qualify as a close friend in Ballerina's book. The other platoon leader was from Phoenix. Thane felt like he should get points for knowing that…okay, not a close friend. A friend, though. More than an acquaintance.

Laughter from the pool floated up to his balcony. Maybe he ought to care more that he didn't have a friend at his own apartment complex.

He tried to put the ball back in Ballerina's court. Do you have a real friend in real life?

Then he waited. She'd probably say yes. Jealousy reared its ugly green head again, and in that moment, he realized how selfish that was. His life didn't allow him to make friends in a normal way. Military rules didn't allow him to date any woman who interested him. Military schedules were demanding. Did he wish the same for Ballerina Baby? Just because he felt isolated, just because he felt lonely among the very same people whom he would willingly fight beside, that was no reason for him to wish the same for her. He wanted her to have it better.

Her reply was a question. You're real, aren't you, Drummer?

Poor Ballerina. She was the same as he, sharing all her

emotions with a stranger through an app. It filled a need, for certain, but even she didn't call him by his first name. No one called him by name.

Whose fault was that?

Thane looked at the pool party with new eyes. If he wanted someone in real life who would call him by name, then he should do something about it. He could start by putting on his board shorts and flip-flops, going down there and telling people his real name. "Hello, I'm Thane." And that would be followed by...

What? Awkward small talk. He and Ballerina had moved past that quickly, months ago. He wasn't the kind of guy who told jokes, but Ballerina answered his attempts at humor with her little pink *Ha*. That wouldn't be happening in the group down there, people who were laughing between the barbecue grill and the keg of beer.

Thane Carter in apartment 601 left his balcony and shut the door against the Texas heat and the party noise.

I'm real, Baby, and I'm here for you.

Chloe Michaels in apartment 401 wriggled into a sitting position on the floor of her new living room, sitting up with her back against a moving box. She never took her eyes off her laptop screen.

I'm real, Baby, and I'm here for you.

She slid right down to the carpet again. Jeez. The most romantic words she ever heard weren't spoken, but typed.

Drummer was the perfect man, and she was so glad to have him in her life. Normal or abnormal, she couldn't help but spin fantasies about a man who was so open with her. Her latest was that he might be a billionaire, for example, so determined to find out who she was and where she lived that he'd buy the company that ran this pen pal app. Then he'd find her when she wasn't expecting it. He'd stride up to her and say, "Hello, I'm Drummer. I wanted to meet you, touch you, kiss you and take you away from all this."

Of course, even a billionaire couldn't tell the US Army they didn't own her for the next five years. She would stay a lieutenant no matter whom she met and fell in love with. Frankly, she wouldn't want to go anywhere. She'd been sworn into the army as a new cadet just two weeks after she'd graduated from high school, and she'd been training ever since to be an officer. She wanted to do what she'd been trained to do.

She looked up from her laptop. Through her sliding glass door, past the edge of her little concrete balcony, she could see the swimming pool in the center of the complex. It was crowded. There'd been a flyer posted by the mailboxes about free burgers at the pool today. It looked like a full-on party to her.

This was where she lived now, and even if a billionaire named Different Drummer went to extremes to find her and then declared his undying love for her, she would not only stay a lieutenant, she would continue to be stationed right here in Texas. For years.

She ought to make friends here.

Drummer's icon flashed, indicating he was typing. Her heart did a little happy flip. They could type back and forth like this for an hour or two or more. They'd done just that many times.

Ok, Miss John Wayne, you said you were burning daylight. Big plans?

Chloe looked out to the pool. She had no doubt she was typing to a real person, but he wasn't a billionaire and he couldn't come sweep her off her feet.

I've been invited to a party. I want to take a nap, but I think I should go.

Why?

We just established that we don't have any close friends except each other. I love

Chloe stopped typing. She deleted the word *love*. They'd agreed that they were either normal or abnormal together. She didn't want to cross that line from abnormal to freaky-girl-with-fantasies. She typed *like*.

I like our long chats. I would miss you, too, if we couldn't write one another. But it wouldn't hurt to have friends around here. I might need a ride to the airport, you know, or need to call someone to jump-start my car battery. I know you'd reach through the clutter of all these pink and blue letters to lend a hand if you could, but since you can't, I ought to go to this party just to meet the people in my neighborhood. Could be a fireman or a postman in my neighborhood, you know? Right here on my very own street.

She hit Send. Good grief, she felt like she was cheating on the man, or at the very least suggesting to a boyfriend that they start seeing other people. She'd paraphrased what she could remember from an old song from Sesame Street, as if sounding like a cute child would soften her words. *Abnormal* was a mild term for her.

You should go. You'll make friends fast, I know it.

Oh. Chloe blinked at her screen in surprise. He wanted her to sign off and go to the party. What had she expected? That he would beg her to stay by her computer and talk to him and only him this weekend? He hadn't caught the reference to the children's show, either. She felt lonelier than ever. She couldn't exactly tell Drummer that she'd rather type to him than meet real people, even though it was true.

She wrote a different truth. I appreciate your vote of confidence in my ability to make friends, but I don't go to many parties. I doubt I'll make friends fast. I'm not really a "life of the party" kind of girl.

That was an understatement. While it seemed everyone else was pulling keggers at their civilian colleges, alcohol was forbidden in the barracks at West Point, and cadets weren't free to come and go as they pleased on or off post. Cadets who were caught breaking those rules faced serious punishment, even expulsion. Ergo, her party experience was about four years behind the average twenty-two-year-old's.

Drummer's answer was kind. Anyone who quotes Sesame Street is sure to make friends. How could anyone not like a person like you?

She felt a pang in her chest. He'd gotten it. He got *her*. If only...

I wish I knew you'd be there. It would be so much easier to put myself out there and say hello to strangers if I knew, at some point as I worked my way through the room, I'd eventually end up next to you. I'd be so glad to see your friendly face, and we'd kind of huddle together in a corner and ignore everyone as we updated each other on who was who at the party. I'd tell you not to leave me alone with the guy who just spent ten minutes lecturing me on the virtues of colon cleanses, and you'd say "What? That wasn't the start of a beautiful friendship?"

One swift, blue word: Casablanca.

LOL. Yes, and we'd spend the rest of the party hanging out

together and talking only to each other, nonstop, and I'd be so glad I came.

Chloe looked at her little pink scenario fondly. A little sadly. This was an even better fantasy than the silly billionaire one, but neither one could come true.

If that's what you want, Ballerina, then let's do that. There's an event I could go to today, too. We'll find each other afterward, and tell each other who was who at our respective outings. I want you to have a friend to call if your car battery dies. I could use one, too, for that ride to the airport. Let's do this together. Deal?

Chloe looked at the friendly blue words, happiness and sadness warring within her. He was the perfect guy and he'd come up with a perfect solution, but the bottom line was that they both needed to find someone perfect outside of this app.

If she went out, he'd go out. So, for his sake as well as her own, she started looking around her apartment for the box most likely to be hiding her bathing suit.

It's a deal. Talk to you later.

Looking forward to it, Baby.

Chapter Three

Life was better than she'd expected it to be.

The realization hit Chloe as she stood on her third-story balcony, performing a recon on the party down below. The Central Texas landscape was brown and sparse when she looked in between the identical buildings toward the horizon, but if she looked down, she saw a sparkling blue swimming pool. It was fall, but this was Texas, and there was plenty of warmth and sun to be had. Maybe Central Texas was more desert than tropical, but the whole apartment complex felt like a resort hotel to her.

Life had been pretty Spartan for the past four years. Room assignments at West Point had changed every semester; she'd had no choice but to move from one end of the same barracks hallway to the other, again and again and again. She'd always had a roommate, and they'd always slept in their assigned twin beds in alphabetical order. When she roomed with Schweitzer, Chloe Michaels slept on the left side of the room, because Michaels outranked Schweitzer alphabetically. When she roomed with Chavez, she slept on the right, but always, no matter which semester and no matter what her rank, she slept on a twin bed made up with a gray wool blanket that was stretched taut and tucked tightly into hospital corners, every single day for four years.

After graduation, the Basic Officer Leadership Course had housed her in the BOQ, the Bachelor Officer Quarters, at Fort Leonard Wood. The mini-apartment had seemed like a luxury despite being furnished in institutional army style with a vinyl couch and a chunky, square coffee table that had survived a whole lot of boots resting on it. Once more, she'd had an assigned roommate, but they'd had an actual kitchen. No more eating whatever was served in the mess hall three times a day. Even better, she'd had a bedroom with only one twin bed in it and a door that closed for privacy. That was a real luxury.

But now...

Chloe surveyed her new world. The complex had been built fairly recently, so everything was current, from the fresh paint on the buildings to the fresh carpet in her apartment. It wasn't a long drive to post, and while there were cheaper places to live, this apartment was still in her budget. She didn't need a roommate to split costs. She had the whole place to herself.

But the biggest luxury of all was this: the army hadn't told her to live here. She could live anywhere she wanted to, as long as she showed up for duty. She'd visited five different apartment complexes. She'd chosen this place, Two Rivers Apartments. That was more than a luxury. That was freedom.

How strange—how intoxicating—to realize she'd never have to stand at attention during a room inspection again. She'd crossed a finish line in a race she'd been running since the day she'd graduated from high school. This was it. This was the view from the winner's circle, a blue pool that she could swim in if she wanted to, or ignore altogether. Freedom.

She went inside, making a beeline for her laptop, an automatic reflex to share her joy with Drummer, before she remembered that he wasn't online. He was at an event. She was supposed to go to a pool party and make a friend, someone who was not him. Someone who was not whom she really wanted to be talking to. Her pleasure dimmed a little bit, but she was going to keep her word and go, and then she was going to cozy up with Drummer later and tell him all about it.

She closed her laptop and headed down the stairs. The flip-flops that left her toes bare and the sundress that left her shoulders bare felt exotic. Her hair swished over her shoulders with each step and tickled her cheek. As a cadet, she'd only had an hour or two each night before taps when, if she stayed in her barracks room to study, she could let her hair down. At BOLC, she'd been able to wear it down when she was in civilian clothes, which had been most weekends. Now, she intended to pin it up only when she was at work. Luxury. Freedom. Control over her own hair.

There was music coming from the pool. She could smell burgers on the grill. Those were things she'd be able to put into words when she wrote to Drummer tonight. But she didn't know how to describe the change in her life, this pay-off for years of hard work, for years of voluntarily subjecting herself to strict rules and a demanding regimen, all with the hope that someday, she would be done and it would all have been worth it.

Someday was today.

Today is the first day of the rest of my life. That quote would do, but she didn't know who'd said it or in which book or movie.

I'm saying it.

Yes, she was. She'd arrived at the party—figuratively and literally. Chloe opened the gate to walk onto the white concrete pool decking. Life was good and it was only going to get better.

And that was when she saw…him.

Their eyes met across a crowded pool deck.

Thane had never seen her before. He would have remembered if she'd gotten out of a car in the parking lot or checked her mail in the stairwell. Her hair was long but not too long. Brown but not very dark, almost blond in the sunlight. She was tall-ish. And since they were staring at each other a moment too long, he could tell from this side of the pool that her eyes were as dark as his were light. She'd come through that gate smiling, like she was eager to be here, and that smile never dimmed as their gazes met and held.

He liked the way she looked.

Then the moment was over because she turned away to

claim a chair, kicking off her flip-flops underneath it. She shook off a small case that dangled from her wrist by a strap and let it drop on the seat of the chair. It looked like a wallet. Thane's law enforcement training automatically calculated the odds for a theft. She shouldn't leave it sitting on a chair in plain view, even though this was hardly a high-crime area.

The apartment rent was just a little more than his monthly military housing allowance, an amount that increased as a soldier's rank increased. Everyone here could afford about the same apartment, which meant everyone here was about the same rank, first or second lieutenants, a few bachelor captains, and a handful of mid-career sergeants whose allowances were equal to a new lieutenant's. Not a hotbed of thieves, in Thane's professional police opinion, but still, she shouldn't leave a wallet out in plain sight like that.

She kept her back to him as she pulled off her sundress over her head. She wore a bikini underneath, but it was the sport kind like the female competitors wore on TV in beach volleyball or Ironman competitions. The suit suited her, so to speak. She wasn't just slender, she was toned, the muscles in her arms and legs tight—nicely firm backside, too. He fully appreciated the sight of a physically fit woman baring an acre of smooth skin to the sun. Whoever had come up with the idea for a pool party was a genius.

She rolled her wallet up in the dress and tucked it in with her shoes underneath the chair, out of sight. Beauty, athleticism, common sense—he'd definitely never seen her around here before. Which meant the odds were that she was someone's guest, which sucked, because the apartment residents were mostly male, so the odds were that she was here as some other man's guest.

Or maybe not. She peeked to see if he was still there, a millisecond of a glance, before she pretended she wasn't aware of him and studiously looked toward the barbecue crowd instead. The smile still lingered on her lips.

I'm still here, beautiful. It's okay to be interested in me. I'm interested in you.

Thane tore his eyes away from that smile to look where she was looking. None of the men around the grill seemed to be searching for his girlfriend. *Be single, be single. This could be the start of a beautiful friendship.*

Casablanca—in a flash, Thane thought of Ballerina and felt…guilty. Like he was cheating on her, which was ridiculous. They'd agreed they needed real-life friends and were both going out today to try to meet some. Instead, in had walked this beautiful woman, and his mind had chucked the friend quest far away and pulled the idea of a girlfriend close. That was fine, though. There was no reason in the world why he couldn't find a real-life girlfriend. After all, a girlfriend could jump-start a car or give him a lift to the airport and do all those things a pen pal couldn't do.

The woman—the very real woman—slid her hand under her hair and lifted it from the back of her neck for a moment. Then she let it go again, all that feminine hair falling over all that bare skin.

Thane looked away and took a deeper breath, a little extra oxygen to keep his thoughts from going haywire. But there was no doubt his thoughts were heading toward a whole new category of things that a pen pal couldn't do.

"How about those Cowboys?"

One of the mailbox guys called the question to him while working the tap of a keg, filling a red Solo cup with beer. He held up one that was already full and nodded toward Thane with that look that said, *Do you want one?*

Thane took it from him with a nod of thanks. "I think the Cowboys will take the Packers tomorrow. You back from a deployment?"

"Yeah." His neighbor shrugged.

"Thought so," Thane answered. "Hadn't seen you around in a while."

His neighbor lifted his now-full beer in a bit of a toast,

then sauntered away from the keg as Thane took a step in the other direction.

That was it, the complete guy conversation. Same as always.

It reminded Thane why he was here. He headed around the edge of the pool, walking with a purpose to get to the other side. He wanted someone to call him by his first name, and he knew exactly which person he wanted that to be.

"Chloe!"

And…damn it. There was the man she must have been looking for. Thane slowed his steps and took in the scene. The beautiful woman, Chloe, hugged the shirtless man who'd just run up to her with all the eagerness of a golden retriever.

Okay, so Thane wasn't feeling too kind. The man slobbering for her attention was probably just a couple of years younger than Thane, and probably an officer, too. But that man had something Thane didn't. He apparently had the affection of one woman named Chloe, whose smile for him was open, unrestrained. Dazzling.

Thane walked around the edge of the pool to her side. He was at the farthest corner from her, but even from this distance, that smile was everything. Some guys were breast men and some were into legs, and while Thane was all in favor of all of that, it was Chloe's smile that really knocked his socks off. It was happiness. Who could resist happiness?

Apparently not the men around this pool. Two more men left the grill and hugged Chloe. She was surrounded. The guys all looked the same. Everyone had a military haircut, everyone was physically fit, no one was younger than twenty-one and no one had reached thirty yet. Only Chloe was special. Thane couldn't take his eyes off her.

He didn't think she was in the military. She had the fitness thing going on, but there was something about her bearing…

She was too relaxed. In the eight years since he'd first enlisted, he'd come to realize that military life tended to make soldiers feel like they were stealing moments of fun or relaxation between deployments or missions or shifts, which was how he felt because it was indeed what he was doing. This woman looked like she had time, like she was where she wanted to be and enjoying it.

Maybe she was a local. She could be a yoga instructor, all smooth muscle and Zen contentment, the polar opposite of him and his career.

The guys around her talked over one another, laughing and gesturing. Chloe was laughing with them, but this didn't look like a boyfriend introducing his girlfriend to his pals. This looked like a reunion of people who were surprised to find each other here. Long-lost college buddies, maybe. That kind of thing happened in an army town all the time. Paths crossed unexpectedly with so many people coming and going as assignments began and ended.

She glanced his way and did a subtle double take when she saw that he was walking directly toward her. She didn't look away. Neither did he.

Another man came running up behind her, full speed. She started to turn with an elbow raised in a defensive move but the man plowed into her, wrapped his arms around her in a bear hug and let his momentum carry them off the edge of the pool to plunge into the water.

Idiot.

Thane didn't know a woman alive who appreciated getting thrown into a pool without warning. That fabulous smile of hers was going to be gone.

They popped up a couple of feet apart.

"Idiot," Chloe said.

Exactly.

But then Chloe broke into laughter. "You are so, so lucky you still have all your teeth, Keith. I was about to clock you with my elbow when I realized it was you. You better be grateful I've got ninja-like mastery of my ninja-like reflexes." They exchanged trash-talking banter until Chloe hoisted herself out of the pool.

Okay, she didn't sound like a Zen yogini. She'd gotten in some good zingers, though. Now she sat on the edge, her hair a waterfall down her back, her feet still in the pool. "I don't suppose any of you guys brought a towel? I don't have one. I wasn't planning on going in."

"Me, neither," said one of the dry guys. "Sorry."

"The sun's out," said another dry guy. "You'll be fine."

"Hey, the keg's been tapped." The tackling guy hauled himself out of the pool and headed over to the keg, dripping wet.

College buddies, for sure. If any one of them wanted to try to become more, he'd best get his act together. Thane wasn't going to hang back and wait for the pack of golden retrievers to grow up and man up.

Thane detoured a few steps to the chair where he'd thrown his things earlier and snagged his oversize towel with one hand. Then he walked up to the pool's edge and crouched down beside Chloe. "I've got an untouched beer here and a clean towel. You're welcome to one or the other or both."

"I'll take the towel, please."

They were strangers, so her smile for him was polite, pleasant, still beautiful. Thane set down the beer so he could shake out the towel and let it fall around her shoulders, keeping the action quick and casual. "There you go."

"Thanks."

He picked up the beer and sat next to her, putting his feet in the water, too.

She beat him to the introductions, holding out her wet hand for a shake. "And hi, by the way. My name is Chloe."

"My name is Thane. I wanted to meet you."

They smiled at one another.

This feels like the start of a beautiful friendship.

Chapter Four

They'd arrived late to the party, so the burgers were all gone.

Thane didn't care. Nothing could ruin this day. He'd met a girl, and now the sun was warmer, the trees were greener, the food smelled better. He could keep talking to her forever. He wanted to learn more about her, where she came from, how she felt about everything, where she was going. He wanted to keep looking at her beautiful face. There would be a first date, a first kiss. He couldn't wait for time to speed toward that moment; he was enjoying every second right now and didn't want this afternoon to end.

"It looks like our choice is hot dogs or hot dogs," she said to him. To the complex's maintenance man who was manning the grill, she said, "I'd like a hot dog, please."

Thane got two for himself and they headed over to the condiment table, where, unfortunately, two of the four golden retrievers were hovering. Chloe made the introductions. Marcus shook his hand. Bill had a beer in one hand and a plate in the other, so he did the lift of the chin. Of course.

"We went to school together," Chloe offered. Her hair was still wet but not dripping. She'd tied Thane's towel around herself, high under her arms. It made her look like she'd just stepped out of a shower. It was a very, very good look.

Judging from the way their gazes kept straying to the knot in the towel that rested just above her breasts, Bill and Marcus thought so, too. Bill turned away pretty quickly to set down his beer and pick up the mustard for his hot dog. If he cared more about mustard than hanging on to Chloe's every word, then he probably had something else going on with a different woman.

"Hey, are you still serious with that girl from Mount Saint Mary's?" Chloe asked Bill.

Thane wondered if she'd read his mind. Nah—Chloe

wasn't vain enough to assume every single man ought to be interested in her. Except every single man around here was—just not Bill.

Chloe pointed to Bill's plate. "You only put mustard on your hot dog. That reminded me about her."

"Mustard made you think of Susie?" Bill asked.

"Don't you remember the hot dog test? Mustard means a man wants to settle down."

"Oh, that dorky thing. I remember." He looked at his hot dog and started to laugh. "You aren't going to believe this, but Susie and I got engaged when I finished Airborne School."

The other dude dropped the mustard like it had burned him. "Which topping was for the good-looking men who like to show women a good time?"

"Marcus the man-whore," Bill muttered under his breath.

"I can't tell you," Chloe said. "That would invalidate the whole hot dog test."

Thane listened with one ear as he covered one hot dog with relish. Across the pool deck, he spotted one little table left in the shade. He'd ask Chloe if she wanted to go over there. Hopefully, the pack wouldn't follow. They weren't bad guys; they just weren't a beautiful woman wrapped in his towel, which was the only person Thane cared to talk to. He picked up the ketchup bottle and squeezed a hearty red line over the relish dog.

"The opposite of married is bachelor, which is what I am," Marcus said. "Suave and devastating bachelor. The opposite of mustard is ketchup, so it must be ketchup."

"That's right," Chloe said, and then a little silence followed as everyone looked at Thane.

He held the ketchup bottle in the air a second longer, then set it down.

"So, you're a playboy bachelor?" Chloe asked with a tilt of her head and a teasing voice.

He looked her in the eye as he silently picked up the mustard and squeezed that on his second hot dog.

Her friends loved it. Marcus nudged her with his arm. "So, what's that mean, Chloe?"

"I'm not done yet." Thane picked up a forkful of sauerkraut and plopped that on the mustard dog. The men hammed it up, their *whoa* and *watch out* sounding like they were watching a cage match.

Chloe didn't say a word. She just looked at him with that tilt of her head and a raised eyebrow, a smile threatening to break through her mock-serious expression.

Thane held up his plate. One dog with ketchup and relish, one dog with mustard and sauerkraut. That was genuinely how he liked them, so he raised an eyebrow, too. "Well? What does this mean?"

"It means," she said, her smile breaking through as her voice dropped into a quiet purr, "that you are a very interesting man."

"Watch out, everybody." Bill held up his beer and plate and took a step back. "Get out of Chloe's way."

Thane kept his focus on Chloe. "Let's see how you dress your hot dog."

"Can't do that." She held up her plate with her still-plain hot dog. "You see, I prefer mine...naked."

Marcus took a step back. "That's it, I'm outta here. Retreat."

Thane let Chloe lead the way to the little iron-lattice patio table in the shade. When they'd been sitting on the edge of the pool, feet swishing the water and accidentally touching now and then, she'd asked most of the questions. He'd lived at Two Rivers since it opened two years ago, he was from South Carolina, yeah, still a touch of the accent, and no, he hadn't been home since last Thanksgiving, a little less than a year now. It was a fifteen-, sixteen-hour drive so you really needed to fly and flying sucked lately, and yes, Austin was less than an hour's drive from here. Great city.

It was his turn. "Do you live here at Two Rivers or did your friends invite you over?"

"I live here."

"You must have just moved in."

"One whole week ago. What made you guess that?"

Thane polished off his first hot dog. "There's no way I wouldn't have noticed you already if you'd been living here for more than a week."

She went a little still at that. He hadn't said it like a cheesy pick-up line. He'd stated it as the fact that it was. Maybe that had been too direct. Maybe he was too accustomed to speaking bluntly during military operations. It was the truth, though, and she seemed like the kind of person who could handle a straightforward comment. She dealt with a pack of lieutenants like they were her brothers, when he suspected they were really angling for more. Surely, she could handle him.

"You're just flattering me now." She popped the last bite of her naked hot dog into her mouth. "I like it."

Yep. She could handle him.

"You're in the army, aren't you?" he guessed.

She nodded her head as she chewed, but for the first time, her expression dimmed a little. She was watching him closely for his reaction.

Were there men out there dumb enough to pass up a chance to spend time with her because she was in the military? Yeah, he knew a few guys like that. Old-school chauvinists. Insecure cavemen. Their loss.

She swallowed her last bite. "Is that a bad thing?"

"I hope not, since I'm in the army, too." He winked at her. She laughed.

She was too young to be one of the NCOs who lived here, but just to be safe, he pointed to the center of his chest, where his rank would be if he wore ACUs. "First lieutenant."

She tapped the knot of the towel. "Second lieutenant."

Perfect.

Thane pushed his plate out of the way and leaned forward, resting his forearms on the table. "It's not a bad thing that we're both in the service. It just makes it a little more challenging to coordinate our schedules if we wanted to do something like go to a movie. I'm willing to try it, though, if you'd like to go see a movie." Maybe he was holding his breath, maybe he was praying she wouldn't turn him down.

She leaned forward, too, and put her arms on the table. "That sounds like fun. Since you've been here a few years, you can show me which theaters are the nicest."

"I'll take you to the best one." He meant it. The pickings were generally slim in army towns, but Fort Hood was the largest post in America, so Killeen had become a good-sized city with it. Dinner, movie, drinks—he'd take her to only the best places. He had the crazy thought that he'd be doing those places a favor, letting them be graced by a woman who radiated such happiness. Dinner and a movie in Killeen would be just the start. He'd love to take her into Austin.

"What made you guess that I was in the army?" she asked. "I thought I was being a pretty normal civilian. I haven't been speaking in acronyms, have I?"

He chuckled and leaned back in his chair. "You asked how far it was to Austin, so you're obviously new to the area. The main reason new people pour into Killeen is because the army sent them here." He nodded toward the apartment buildings. "And the main reason people live here is because it's conveniently priced for a junior officer's housing allowance."

She chuckled, too, and leaned back in her chair.

This couldn't be going better. God, I'm glad I came.

"I thought my friends gave it away with their regulation haircuts. I didn't even know they were going to be stationed at Hood. I just ran into Keith at the PX yesterday, so I knew he was at Hood, but I didn't know he lived here in Two Rivers. Keith's the one who went swimming."

"It's a small world, five of you here from one college."

As soon as he said it, he knew. She had to be from West Point. They all were.

The vast majority of officers came from ROTC programs, but even if there were sixteen ROTC officers in a unit, they would most likely be from sixteen different universities. There might be only three West Point officers in comparison, but they always seemed to know each other. For her to have found four college friends in this one apartment complex? Yeah. They had to be ring-knockers.

"We all went to West Point," she offered, oblivious to what was obvious.

Thane had checked her left hand earlier. No engagement ring. No wedding band. Now he looked at her right hand. No West Point ring.

She caught his look and held up her right hand, wiggling her bare fingers. "I don't wear the ring all the time. It's not a requirement, you know. You're not wearing your class ring today, either. I'll have to guess where you went to college. Let's see, South Carolina...maybe Clemson? Wait—not the Citadel? Tell me you're from anywhere but the Citadel." She made a horrified face.

She did it so comically, it made him laugh. The Citadel was a private college that ran itself like a military academy. Thane had never had the money to go to a private college, which was one of the reasons he'd enlisted in the army at eighteen. "Nothing that bad."

"I know. I was joking." She dropped her horrified face and beamed at him, looking relaxed in his towel and ready for a long chat. "You'd definitely be wearing a big, honking ring if you were. Everyone calls *us* ring-knockers, but have you seen a Citadel ring? You'd think they won the Super Bowl or something. So, where did you go to school?"

"Duke University." He'd been able to start there at age twenty, after two years of enlisted service had helped him win an ROTC scholarship.

"*North* Carolina. Tricky of you. And your ring?"

"I don't ever wear a college ring. I didn't buy one."

"Why not? Duke's such a prestigious school."

"Now you're just flattering me. I like it."

She laughed, but she was still looking at him expectantly.

"I don't know why I didn't buy one. It's not really a big deal there."

She studied him. "That's interesting, that rings aren't a big deal at a big school like Duke. I try to imagine what life would have been like if I'd gone to regular college. Is it really like *Animal House*?"

"Not even close."

"Ever been to a toga party?"

He started to say no, but caught himself. "Actually, I have."

She wanted to know all about it. They talked, they told each other the little stories that made up their college lives. She was so enthusiastic about everything he told her, not like a standoffish, elite academy snob at all. It was surprising, the amount of college experiences she *hadn't* had. No fraternities or sororities. No weekend jobs at a local pizza place. No one already so drunk at two in the afternoon that they fell asleep in a dorm elevator. Hell—she hadn't lived in a dorm. She told him stories about daring Friday nights spent cleaning the barracks after taps in absolute darkness, so they'd pass Saturday Morning Inspections.

But she was so damned happy. Her buddies were really enjoying themselves, too, as if free beer and an apartment pool party were a vacation in the Bahamas. As usual, every West Pointer here seemed to know each other automatically, something that was at least mildly annoying to the rest of the army's officer corps. But talking to Chloe, Thane could see that there wasn't any mysterious network of ring-knockers. The West Pointers always seemed to already know each other because they *did* already know each other. They'd had no one else to get to know for four solid years.

Now that four years of a rather stringent life was over,

it sounded like Chloe was ready to do and see everything there was to do and see here in Killeen and Austin—and life. Thane was going to love being the man who did and saw everything with her.

There was no doubt in his mind that this was a woman who was worth dating, worth spending all his time with— hell, a woman worth *courting.* An hour talking with her in the shade felt like they were catching each other up on their lives before this day. From this day on, they would go out and experience things together. Chloe was terrific, all of her, inside and out, body and sharp mind and outgoing personality, this charming lieutenant from West Point.

It gave him hope for the new fourth platoon leader at work. Maybe the rookie West Pointer they were getting at the 584th wouldn't be so bad, either, the new female lieutenant his platoon sergeant had told him was…

Thane kept smiling as Chloe talked, but he took a long drink of his beer. Swallowed.

How many women went to West Point? Not many. If the army was roughly 15 percent female, then he'd bet West Point was about the same. Chloe would probably know the new platoon leader. So would Bill and Marcus and the other two guys. Right?

Another sip of beer. Another hard swallow.

For the first time, he wondered which branch Chloe was in. Somehow, he'd been thinking she must be in the same branch as her friends. A cluster of five new Signal Corps officers, or a new slate of field artillery officers, all reporting to duty at Fort Hood at the same time. Right?

Not likely. They didn't know each other from going to one branch's Basic Officer Leadership Course. They knew each other from earlier than that. They'd probably been surprised to see each other today because they'd graduated last May and then scattered to five different courses in five different branches of the army.

He pushed it to the back of his mind. Chloe's branch and

his branch would come up in conversation. There was no rush. They weren't doing anything wrong. There were no regulations against eating a hot dog at an apartment pool with anybody.

"Here, I'm dry enough. Let me spread out your towel so it will dry." Chloe stood up and untucked the towel knot. In one easy move, she peeled off the damp towel and swirled it like a cape to lay across the back of the chair.

Thane stopped thinking. She was all but nude on the other side of the table, not two feet away from him, flat stomach and sexy belly button at his eye level. He must look like a cartoon character, eyes bugging out of his head, mouth hanging open, tongue hanging out. Or else he looked like a stoic army officer, face devoid of expression. He hoped the latter. Cartoon on the inside, stoic on the outside. Overwhelmed.

Had she dropped that towel to overwhelm him intentionally? He managed to look up to her face, but no. She was oblivious, bending over in those bikini bottoms—holy hell, what a body—to grab her chair by its arms and drag it out from under the shade, chatting away the whole time. "It'll dry faster in the sun." She looked up to the sky to judge where the sun was and turned the chair so that it was sideways to his, then she flopped back into it.

"Ahh," she sighed, as she stretched out shapely legs and leaned her head back, closing her eyes as she tilted her face up to the sun. "I love this weather."

Was he supposed to speak? He cleared his throat. "You won't love it in July." She had her eyes closed; he could keep his eyes on her. "It hits one hundred and ten. Even higher."

She opened one eye to look at him. "Aren't you supposed to say, 'But it's a dry heat'?"

He grinned at her droll comment. "It's like living in an oven. Ovens don't have humidity, but they can roast a turkey."

She laughed. "I guess I'll find out myself in July. But today is perfect."

Yes, it is.

"It's so much better here than Leonard Wood."

He stayed perfectly still. He didn't even take a breath as the bottom dropped out of his world. Fort Leonard Wood. Home of the Military Police Corps. The one post that trained every damned MP in the whole damned army. Damn it, she was an MP.

She might be assigned to a different company. As long as we aren't in the same company...

They couldn't date if they were in the same *unit*. There were three MP companies in his battalion. As long as she wasn't in his battalion, then...

"It got below forty the night before I left Leonard Wood. I had enough of frozen winters at West Point. I picked Fort Hood because it wouldn't snow here. I didn't expect it to still be warm enough to sit by a pool, though. Life is good."

There was no other MP battalion here for her to belong to. The next level up was the 89th MP Brigade, headquartered here at Hood. Maybe she was assigned to brigade headquarters, maybe...

Maybe he was kidding himself.

Fourth platoon was getting a female West Pointer on Monday. West Pointers were a small percentage of all army officers; women from West Point were even more rare. There would be no other female West Point officers leaving Fort Leonard Wood and arriving at Fort Hood this week. Not another one this year. The woman Thane wanted to take to the movies just for the pleasure of having her company, the woman he was staring at, lusting over right this second, had to be Second Lieutenant—

"Michaels!" A man barked out the name from the other side of the pool deck's fence like an angry drill sergeant.

Chloe jerked upright and whipped around in her chair, blinking in the sun, her face a solid mix of anger and bewilderment. Thane stood up, ready to step in. Who the hell did this guy think he was?

Then Chloe made a little happy yelp of a noise and jumped to her feet. She nearly ran the few feet to the chest-high fence, but when Thane expected her to throw her arms around the man she obviously knew and was obviously happy to see, she came to a stop just before him and clasped her hands behind her back.

"It's so good to see you, sir. I didn't know you were at Hood."

"Come here. You're not a cadet. You can call me Greg." The man reached over the fence and yanked Chloe into his arms.

Thane realized he was clenching his jaw. All these old friends sure didn't miss the chance to hug her in her bikini. How many old friends could a woman have who'd lived here only a week?

Apparently, a half dozen or more, when the woman had graduated from West Point.

West Point. *Michaels.*

Fraternization. Court-martials.

Thane hadn't hugged Chloe yet. He never would.

Chloe turned to him. She wanted him to meet her old friend. It hurt Thane's heart. She was opening up her life to him, welcoming him in, because she still thought he was an interesting man. She still thought they were new friends and on their way to being more, to dinners and movies and a first kiss good-night.

They weren't.

It was all he could do to keep going through the motions. This Greg guy had to be about his age, twenty-five or -six, yet Chloe acted as though Greg far outranked her. Thane shook hands. With his gut churning, he made polite conversation. "Another West Point classmate?"

"Oh—no, a classmate is someone in your graduating class. Greg was a firstie—a senior—when I was a plebe. Not even a plebe yet. He was my CO for Beast Barracks."

"Beast Barracks is basic training at West Point," Greg

explained, bending forward to brace his arms on the fence, settling in for a chat. Yeah. Who wouldn't stop and chat with Chloe?

"I've heard the term," Thane said neutrally. He felt trapped. He needed to break up with a woman the same day he'd met her. It was the last thing in the world he wanted to do.

"He was scarier than the drill sergeant in *Full Metal Jacket* during Beast," Chloe said, "but he watched out for us the rest of the year."

"Hazed her a little bit, but she was a stubborn little cuss. Couldn't break her." Greg smiled at Chloe. "Looks like you turned out just fine."

Thane didn't miss this Greg guy checking out the way his *plebe* looked now, four years later. Thane couldn't date Chloe, and it was going to kill him to watch her date anyone else.

"So, how do you two know each other?" Greg asked. At least Chloe's former cadet CO had the decency to see if the coast was clear before putting a move on her.

Chloe smiled at Thane, happiness that killed him, then did an adorable little duck of her chin, although she was the last person he'd expect to be shy. "We just met today. He's going to show me around town sometime."

No, I'm not. So sorry, Chloe. So very damned sorry.

He kept going through all the motions, listening to them reminisce for a polite amount of time before excusing himself to get a beer, and did anyone else want one? No?

Thane stood at the keg for a red plastic cup of beer he didn't even want, trying to brace himself against the hurt he was going to cause when he told Chloe this whole day had been a big mistake, when out of the corner of his eye, he saw a man in uniform heading toward the parking lot, carrying a black MP bulletproof vest. Thane snapped out of his pity party. He could mourn his disappointed heart later. Right now, he needed to avoid immediate trouble.

The man walking by the pool's fence was a platoon leader from one of the other MP companies in the battalion. He was in his ACUs and carrying a thermos in one hand, that black vest in the other, obviously on his way to take over as duty officer. He spotted Thane and raised the thermos in a brief wave. "Wish me luck. Saturday night and a full moon. Phillips owes me a case of beer for covering this shift for him."

Thane did the lift-of-the-chin greeting, all he could manage as dread filled his chest. That had been a close call. Too close. Five minutes sooner, and that lieutenant would have seen Thane smiling and laughing and sitting nice and close at a cozy table for two *with his fellow platoon leader*. And it was far too true that it didn't always matter what you were doing, it mattered what it *looked* like you were doing, and that would have looked bad. If Chloe arrived at the battalion Monday morning and that lieutenant had recognized her as the girl Thane had been cozying up to at the pool, the rumor mill would have exploded like a bomb detonating.

Legally, they'd done absolutely nothing wrong. Thane would be able to stand in front of the CO and honestly tell him he and Lieutenant Michaels had only talked. But the gossip surrounding that closed-door meeting would tarnish a reputation, and Thane already knew it would be her reputation that got tarnished far worse than his, as unfair as that would be. Women were just under greater scrutiny. She'd be toast before she even got to put her name on their office door. What made a man look like a stud would make a woman look like…

Yeah. She'd start out deep in a hole that she hadn't dug. He couldn't do that to her.

He needed to leave ASAP, before more people saw them together. This situation was like a hand grenade that had had its safety pin pulled and was now primed to explode. The second Thane could get Chloe alone, he'd tell her they were assigned to the same company. He could slide the safety pin back into place and set the hand grenade down safely. Nothing had to explode. He'd leave Chloe here where he'd found her, with her classmates and her former cadet CO, and he'd go back to his apartment, shut the door and resume his regular routine. Alone.

Alone, damn it, with no Chloe to wine and dine and talk to.

Ballerina Baby.

Not totally alone. Ballerina would be waiting to hear from him. The only safe person he'd had to talk to before this pool party was still the only safe person he had to talk to. How could he explain this whole debacle to her without explaining that he was in the military, with all the ins and outs of rank and fraternization? He couldn't. He was going to have to deal with the hope and grief of finding and losing a wonderful woman all on his own.

Thane turned to see if Chloe was back at their table, so he could get this conversation over with before they were busted. She wasn't at the table and she wasn't by the fence. She was probably near the grill, talking to one of the golden retrievers. Thane walked in the opposite direction, yanking his towel off the back of her chair as he passed it, heading toward the pool house with its restrooms and dinky outdoor shower. His chair was in the shade of the pool house, the chair he'd dropped his stuff on eons ago, before he'd ever seen Lieutenant Michaels and her happy smile. If he'd known then what he knew now…

He would've stayed in his apartment and talked to Ballerina.

He scuffed on his flip-flops. He needed to be ready to leave as soon as he filled Chloe in. The lieutenant they'd just missed by sheer luck wasn't the only MP living in the entire six-building complex.

"Hey, Lieutenant Carter."

And there was another. Thane turned around slowly. An MP, one of the NCOs from his own company, was being friendly. Specifically, it was Staff Sergeant Gevahr, who was a squad leader in fourth platoon. Chloe's platoon. Sergeant Gevahr would directly report to Chloe on Monday.

Thane needed to handle this grenade very carefully. He prayed Chloe wouldn't spot him and come over to stand by his side while he talked with her squad leader. If she didn't come over, if the sergeant had just arrived and if Thane could leave immediately, then there'd be nothing for the sergeant to see. *If* the sergeant hadn't seen them together yet. If he already had...

If he already had, then when Staff Sergeant Gevahr met his new platoon leader on Monday, he was going to recognize her and that grenade would explode.

Thane pulled his apartment keys out of the pocket of his board shorts, making it clear he was on his way out. "Hey, Staff Sergeant. What's up?"

Staff Sergeant Gevahr only started to laugh. "I was going to ask you that, sir. I was going to come over and say hi at least an hour ago, but it didn't look like you'd appreciate the interruption. Who's the new girlfriend, sir?"

The grenade was about to explode.

Chapter Five

Chloe felt like she just might explode with happiness.

As she washed her hands in the pool house bathroom, she looked at herself in the mirror over the sink. Who cared about the half-wet hair, drying without the benefit of a comb? Chloe couldn't stop smiling.

Thane. Thane, Thane, Thane...

She'd never been so crazy over a man so quickly. The endorphin rush was like a runner's high, but without the miles of exertion one had to go through first to reach that point. The burst of adrenaline was like the one a child felt on Christmas morning, not the kind a soldier felt during a dangerous live-fire exercise. She glanced in the mirror again. Still smiling. She couldn't stop—because Thane felt the same way about her. She knew that, because he wasn't afraid to say he liked her.

Just like Drummer.

Her heart pounded for a moment, a guilty beat.

What was she going to tell Drummer about their little experiment? That it was a smashing success? That she'd found more than a friend? She wouldn't have a chance to tell Drummer about it until much later, because Thane had made it plain that he wanted to keep spending his time with her *today*. He wasn't going to do that nonsense where a man asked for her number and then waited three days or a whole week before calling, all in an effort to not appear desperate.

Thane wasn't a desperate man. Just the opposite: he knew what he wanted, and he wasn't afraid to come and get it.

Her heart pounded again, from a better emotion this time. She'd been away from Thane for at least ten minutes. Seeing Cadet Towers—now Lieutenant Towers—*Greg*—had been nice, but Chloe wanted to be with Thane instead.

She finished drying her hands on a paper towel and went

to grasp the swinging door's handle just as someone else pushed it in toward her. A woman with an empty stroller struggled in the doorway, a baby on her hip and a toddler dragging behind. Chloe stepped back and held the door open as they crowded into the little two-stall space.

Outside, she heard a man's voice. "Girlfriend? Give me a break, Staff Sergeant."

It was Thane talking. He used a different tone of voice talking with a man than he did with her, but she recognized his voice, that barely there Southern drawl. She'd been listening to that voice all afternoon, and she was looking forward to listening to it for weeks to come. Months. Years. All right, it was too soon to be thinking in years, but this man was really something special.

She was smiling at the thought when Thane said, "I don't stick with one woman very long."

Oh.

That was before he'd met her, though, right? She was a new person, maybe a new chapter in his life...but still, he really didn't sound like himself. He sounded kind of arrogant.

Outside, a different male voice said, "Every man says that, sir, until he meets—"

Inside, the mother told her toddler to get up from the floor. "It's dirty. Yucky."

The same man sounded like he was laughing. "—change that real quick. I've been watching you talk to that girl all day. Just one girl, sir. Just one."

"Talking," Thane emphasized with a definite scoff in his tone. "When all I do is talk, there's your clue."

Ouch.

Chloe stayed where she was, wedged by the sink as she kept holding the door open with one hand. She felt like she'd missed something. Thane was talking about some other girl, surely.

"Now, sir, I was born at night, but it wasn't last night.

A man doesn't sit at a little tiny table with a woman for a whole afternoon—"

The mother's voice was an octave higher. "Get off the floor, Mattie. Now."

There was a moment of silence as the last of the *now* echoed off the tile.

Thane spoke. "Did you see her face?"

"Well…no, sir." The man sounded just a little bit hesitant at the question.

That had been kind of a weird question. *Did you see her face?* Chloe looked at her face in the mirror. Nothing weird to see there.

"She had her back to me, sir. But that's a fine-looking back, if you don't mind me saying so, and judging from your face, the front view must be at least as good as the back view."

Chloe held her breath.

Thane didn't say anything for the longest moment. "You've been here a while, then. Did I catch you on your way out?"

"Yes, sir, but—"

"Great. I'm leaving, too. Let's go."

"But, sir. What about your lady friend?"

Thane lowered his voice, but she could still hear him. "She's not a friend, and she's definitely not my lady. You didn't see her face. If you had, you'd fully appreciate why I'm making an escape with you."

It was a punch to Chloe's gut, a blow that did real damage because she hadn't been prepared for it at all.

"You sure were spending a lot of time with her—"

"Do you see any other single women around here? I had to take what I could get. Trust me, I can't take anymore, so do me a favor and let me walk out in front of you. Don't even look toward her. If she turns around, I don't want her to see anything except your back, hiding mine. I appreciate the cover…"

Their voices faded away.

How could she have been so wrong? How could she have so completely misjudged him?

The door slipped out of her hand and swung gently closed. She stood there, paralyzed, until she realized she was staring at herself in the mirror. There was nothing wrong with her face. There was nothing—it couldn't have been Thane. It wasn't Thane speaking.

She grabbed for the door handle and yanked it open. Among the mostly stationary folks mingling on the pool deck, two men were moving briskly, heading directly for the gate. One was a stranger. The other was Thane, head high, shoulders back, her towel—his towel—thrown over one shoulder. Leaving without saying goodbye. Leaving without a word of explanation.

If you'd seen her face... I'm making an escape.

She fell back against the wall with the pain of it. He'd liked her. He'd liked her as much as she'd liked him. Why would he say such a cruel thing?

Chloe knew, objectively, that she didn't have an ugly face, but his words tapped into years of insecurities. There was still plenty of simmering resentment out there against women in the military, too many "jokes" about how they must all be ugly gorillas, how they all must hate men, how they all must be whores. Women too ugly for any man to sleep with, yet who slept with numerous men—all contradictions, all cruel. And it didn't matter when Chloe told herself it was all false, not when she'd heard it, or hints of it, or felt it behind her back every week and month and year. Year after year, since the year she'd turned eighteen.

That seed of doubt could be consciously squashed, but it was still there, that tiny bit of herself that wondered not only if she was less than a woman, but if there was something wrong with her for wanting to serve her country.

The tiled wall hadn't held her up. She vaguely realized she'd slid down and was hunkered down on her haunches.

"Yucky." The toddler chewed on her fingers as she stood eye to eye with Chloe. "Yucky."

"Mattie, come here. Leave the nice lady alone." The mother's voice had turned gentler as she glanced sympathetically at Chloe while buckling her infant into the stroller.

"Oh—no, it's all right." Chloe rose up again, feeling the burn in her thighs from the squat. "Here, let me get the door for you."

She followed the woman and children out of the bathroom. She surveyed the pool scene, but she didn't want to stay here, not even with friends from West Point.

Friends. One of them had been her friend while they were cadets. Two of them were more like acquaintances whom she'd had in a class or two. Greg Towers had been too many years ahead of her to be a friend, and Keith had surprised her by being friendly to her today, because, frankly, he'd been an ass at school.

If she called being body-slammed into a pool "friendly," that is. She'd played it off because that's what one had to do. Deflect, act like you can handle anything, pretend they didn't upset you. She was a pro at that. She had to be to survive.

Chloe didn't run, but she didn't waste any time, either. She stalked over to her stuff, unrolled the yellow dress and caught her cell phone case, then started pulling the sundress over her head as she headed toward the gate. Anger was building inside her. Fury. All she wanted was to be alone. She couldn't wait to lock herself back in her apartment. She didn't want to talk to another human being for the rest of the weekend—no one except Drummer.

He was the only one who'd understand.

Thank God she had someone who'd understand, because she surely didn't have someone who would tell her about toga parties and smile at her stories and take her to see a movie.

She made it all the way to apartment 401 before the fury deserted her and left tears in its place.

* * *

What would you do if you were me?

Chloe hit the enter key and chomped down hard on an-other frozen grape, her twentieth, at least. Fresh fruit was her current favorite comfort food. Strawberries, blueberries, peaches—anything that she'd had to live without for the last four and a half years.

The dining facility at Leonard Wood had served bananas and oranges. So had the mess hall at West Point. Those fruits were kept in stock because they were hardy, and they came with their own thick skins. She was done with bananas and oranges. She was sick of having a thick skin.

Because right now, I'm just stress-eating grapes. Have you ever put grapes in the freezer? Amazing. They stop just short of turning into ice cubes.

She didn't care if dudes didn't talk about food cravings. She was talking to Drummer without a filter today. He was either her friend or he wasn't. If he couldn't handle her on-line, then it would be best if he just disappeared.

Like Thane had.

She popped another grape in her mouth.

Blue words came across her screen. I thought tater tots were your comfort food of choice.

Good. Drummer could handle her even when she didn't weigh every word.

The tots are all dead, remember? I've moved on. Grapes are my victims now.

Chloe looked at her laptop screen with its jaunty little lines of pink and blue type. She sounded so jaunty herself, didn't she? Tots and grapes, ha ha ha.

She was brokenhearted.

You're doing better than I am, **Drummer** wrote. I'm half-way through a cholesterol-filled pepperoni pizza. No one can fault you for grapes. No one can fault you for anything. What would I do if I were you? I'd look in the mirror and remind myself that I'm smart enough, I'm good enough, and gosh darn it, people like me.

She snorted. Saturday Night Live (too easy).

(Of course it was easy, but you've had a hard day.) Then I'd come up with a plan for what to do if I should run into friends who are not really friends again.

Chloe had chickened out. She'd told Drummer that she regretted going to her party, but when he'd asked why, she'd focused on Keith's friendliness-that-wasn't-really-friendliness. The more she thought about it, the more aggressive she realized Keith's poolside tackle had been. There was a time and a place for aggressiveness. Hand-to-hand combat training? Check. Slamming a woman into the water who'd just arrived at a party? Wrong.

But even there, she hadn't given Drummer the ugly truth. It made her sound so wimpy, that she'd been dunked—hard—and left to look like a drowned rat the rest of the party, yet she hadn't done anything to defend herself except laugh it off.

Instead, she'd told Drummer something vague, saying someone who wasn't really a friend had gotten in a cheap shot. So much for her determination to talk to Drummer without a filter. She couldn't imagine what Drummer would think if she told him it was an actual *physical* cheap shot, being tackled from behind.

It was a no-win situation, anyway. She tried to explain that much to Drummer. How do you come up with a plan? It's not like there are many options. You either complain or you laugh it off. I went with laugh it off this time, which made everyone around me happy and kept the party mood going.

If I'd complained…well, you get labeled as a complainer or a whiner and no one wants to be around that. They sure won't line up to volunteer to take you to the airport if they think they'll be stuck in a car with a whiner.

Give me a little more information on what went down today. I'll help you brainstorm some options.

No. No specifics, remember? This anonymity thing is working for us.

Drummer sent her an eye-roll emoji. Okay. So, you ran into someone you thought was a friend and then they were not. What is your goal in life?

You mean my goal with this not-a-friend? I don't have one. I'm fine with him—or her—not being my friend.

No, I mean your goal in life. All of life. Big life.

Big life? She stuffed the last two grapes into her mouth at once. They were so cold, they hurt.

Life goals she had, but they were all specific and clearly defined: to serve her nation as an officer in the MP Corps. To be a platoon leader, to take care of her troops and to set a good example for those she led. She couldn't tell Drummer any of those goals and still keep any anonymity.

All of her previous goals had been equally specific. As a cadet, she'd aimed for grades that would rank her high enough in her class to get her first choice of branch and then her first choice of post, somewhere snow-free. Even in high school, she'd had specific goals on the school track team—earning a varsity letter was a must for her academy dream. She'd had goals on the SAT test—she needed to at least match the average of new cadets to become one herself.

She looked around her mostly empty apartment, the one

that would never be inspected, as she sat on her new couch that was as red as a rose. She'd met her past goals. She felt trained and ready to accomplish her future military service goals. But what was her real goal in life? Big life?

I want to be happy. She hit Send before she could censor herself.

Good. The blue answer was immediate. Drummer thought something as vague as happiness was a good goal? That made her feel marginally better.

Let's measure your options by whether or not they'll make you happy. One option is to laugh it off. You tried that today, and it didn't make you happy, right?

Nope. It was a reflex at the time, but now I feel like a doormat.

Doormats are not happy. But Ballerina, listen. Don't be so hard on yourself for laughing it off. You tried a viable option to handling unwanted attention, one that must have worked in the past or it wouldn't have been your default, right?

Chloe stopped crunching her grapes for a moment. How did he do that? How did Drummer know everything about her?

But that option didn't sit well with you, so let's move on to option two. You could ignore this person, pretend you didn't see him/her, or pretend you didn't hear him/her. Next time you see this person, will ignoring her make you happy?

Maybe.

Maybe's not good enough, BB. This is your one and only life. Maybe means no, ignoring this person isn't going to make you happy. And you already tried laughing off her joke that was really an insult. That's a no. So, option three, you could confront this person. Will telling her off make you happy?

Maybe. It was a him, by the way, not a her. I couldn't really respond. He just got in his hit and walked away before I could answer.

Keith had jumped out of the pool and headed for the keg. Whatever.

Thane had gotten in his hit—*Did you see her face?*—and left, too.

The hurt of Thane's hit was so fresh, still shocking in its cruelty. Chloe let the fury come in to push the hurt away, typing with hard hits on the keys. I don't know if confrontation will make me happy, but it will keep me from feeling like I feel tonight, which is basically powerless. I've put up with a lot of crap so far in life, and I'm reaching a point of boiling over. She hit the send key so hard, her finger stung.

Let's come up with a plan, then. Your default next time, if there is a next time, will be to confront him. When you boil over, you don't want to be burned. You want to keep that steam directed to the correct target, right? The key will be confronting him in a way that won't make you look bad to anyone else. Wouldn't want you to hurt your reputation at your job, for example.

Keith was not her target. Chloe had dealt with him and his kind for years. But if she ran into Thane someday in the parking lot, she didn't want to pretend she didn't see him and skitter away.

Right. Plan C—controlled confrontation. I'm ready.

Chapter Six

"Good evening, ma'am."

"Good evening, Sergeant First Class." Chloe set her black bulletproof vest on the edge of the watch commander's desk. The police station was built for efficiency, not beauty, especially here in the back of the building, with the briefing rooms and holding cells. The decor was little more than metal lockers and functional, plain furniture.

There was something exciting about it, though, with its hot links to fire stations and its wall maps delineating all their areas of responsibility across three counties in Central Texas. Everything was plain and boring, yet everything was in a state of readiness. There was a palpable sense that all the calm and order could change in a moment, and the people in this building knew they would be the quickest to respond, the first to help. *Assist-Protect-Defend.*

Calm and order were very much the order of the day—or evening. Sunday evening at the police station was far quieter than Friday night had been. Chloe was ready to go, though. Tonight was her second ride-along with the duty officer, her chance to keep learning the post's layout—really, to keep learning the whole job. She knew all the official radio communication standards, for example, but on Friday night, she'd had a hard time following the sound of the dispatcher coming over the radio at real speed in the patrol car. The most important thing she'd caught was that the officer on duty was 310, or three-ten. When dispatch said the words *three-ten*, she needed to pay attention. When another MP requested that three-ten come by for support, that meant her.

Well, it meant the duty officer. Plus her, the ride-along. And their driver, of course. Friday night the driver had been a specialist from first platoon. A specialist was the next rank up from a private first class, making him an enlisted man with a couple of years of service under his belt. With the driver and the real duty officer in the front seats of the patrol car, she'd sat in the back, trying not to think about how many drunks or drug addicts had sat where she was sitting. It was hard to see exactly which streets the patrol car was taking and hard to hear the radio as well from the back seat, but that was the only option there was. She'd just suck it up and keep doing her best from the back seat tonight.

It was a relief to be working at a real-world task tonight. Memorizing the layout of an entire town would surely keep her mind busy. She'd had too much time to think since yesterday's pool party. Talking to Drummer hadn't even been a distraction, because whether Drummer knew it or not, Thane had been the subject of their conversation. There was nothing she could do alone in her apartment that kept her mind off Thane.

She'd tried. The army had provided shipping for her move to Texas, and her stuff had arrived. But unpacking boxes when she'd been looking forward to a date with a handsome man had been depressing. From school, she'd shipped to herself a footlocker of cadet uniforms that she'd never wear again and the world's heaviest boxes of textbooks that she'd never read again. The army had authorized one shipment from her "home of record," too, which was her parents' house. Her parents had given her the dresser and bed she'd had since childhood. It was another twin bed, of course, but one that didn't have to be made up with a gray blanket in hospital corners. She'd bought a new bedspread at the PX, a grown-up coverlet in soothing shades of blue and green, but still, her childhood bedroom furniture made her a little homesick.

Her mom had also given her some spare pots and pans, so Chloe had tried cooking to keep herself busy. She'd moved from healthy grapes to the ultimate comfort food, hot and rich macaroni and cheese, yet eating straight from the casserole dish as it sat on a footlocker was a poor substitute for dinner at a restaurant, sitting across a real table from a handsome man.

And, damn him, Thane was a handsome man. A jerk, but handsome. He had dark hair and light eyes, a mouth that she'd imagined kissing hers, plus shoulders and biceps and chest muscles all deliciously defined.

"Lieutenant Carter is the officer on duty tonight, ma'am." The watch commander was a senior NCO, the most senior one working tonight, the same man she'd met on Friday's ride-along. The watch commander stayed at the station to oversee everything from walk-ins to the holding cells to the dispatchers. "I told him you'd be riding along. He said he'd wait outside for you. Just through the briefing room and out that back door."

Chloe put on her protective vest, getting it situated above the thick black belt that held her sidearm in its holster. "No briefing today?"

"The NCOs handle that, ma'am. It's up to the lieutenant if he wants to be there or not."

Lieutenant Salvatore had stood in the back of the briefing room Friday. Chloe guessed this Lieutenant Carter did things differently. She nodded at the watch commander and headed through the empty briefing room, tugging the black vest down. The bright white letters spelling *Military Police* across her chest made it clear to good guys and bad guys alike exactly who she was on any scene, something that could otherwise be confusing when law enforcement and perpetrators were often all wearing the same camouflage uniforms. It gave her the odd sensation of wearing a half shirt, because the heavy part of the vest didn't cover the lower part of her stomach.

She pulled her patrol cap out of her pocket and slid it on so it sat properly, just above her low ballerina bun. Then she was out the door, into the twilight. A patrol car was parked off to the side, a male lieutenant leaning against it, arms crossed over his chest, studying the ground at his feet. She adjusted the brim of her hat just so with one hand and tugged down the black vest quickly with her other, still annoyed at that bare-belly sensation.

"You must be Lieutenant Carter," she said in a voice to carry over the several paces of asphalt between them.

He lifted his head and looked at her from under the brim of his patrol cap.

She stopped walking.

The silence between them went on too long as a thousand thoughts raced through her head.

Someone had to say something. She did. "Are you kidding me?"

He just kept his eyes on her, those light-colored eyes, his expression as grim as a man at a funeral. Grim, but not surprised.

Drummer's advice was fresh in her mind. Option one: she could be polite, say *gee, isn't this awkward*, laugh, and pretend everything was okay. *It didn't sit well with you, Ballerina.*

Option two: she could ignore him. Impossible, since he was an MP and on duty tonight. *It won't make you happy.*

Option three: controlled confrontation.

She didn't think happiness was really going to be the outcome, but Drummer had been right, the other two options would leave her seething with resentment toward Thane and disappointed with herself. She wasn't going to smile and pretend everything was okay.

Her heart was pounding underneath all the layers that were supposed to protect her: vest, armor plates, ACU jacket, tan T-shirt, sports bra. There was no protection against emotions. Her heart still took the hit of seeing his handsome face again, so unexpectedly, the face she'd smiled with, flirted with, trusted…all while he'd been finding her face not good enough. He'd made her hope for more. He'd made her want him.

Bastard.

She let fury squash the heartache and took a minute, gaze locked with his, to consider what to say. She'd been caught off guard, but Thane was not shocked to see her at all.

She started there. "You're not surprised to see me."

"Hi, Chloe."

"You knew? You knew we were both MPs? We're both— hang on. Are you in my company?" She was pretty certain Salvatore had said that just the lieutenants from the 584th were taking shifts this month.

He nodded solemnly. "I'm first platoon. You're fourth."

She saw red. But she also saw the white badge on his black vest, the white and green patrol car he leaned against, and her awareness of her situation kept her in control. That, and her four years of military training. She was standing outside a police station, in uniform. Soldiers, other MPs, were coming and going through the same side door she'd used. She could have happily gotten in Thane's face like she was hazing a plebe, but she wouldn't do anything to draw attention to the two of them. She wasn't going to boil over and burn herself.

She took those last steps to stand in front of him and crossed her arms over her chest as he uncrossed his. He stayed where he was, leaning against the driver's side door. In silence, she stared him down, using the same iron glare she would have used if he'd been a plebe, and she'd ordered him to stand at attention with his back against a barracks wall, braced as he struggled to recite a long passage of General MacArthur's words correctly to the last syllable.

Thane looked away. He took his patrol cap off, smoothed his hand up the back of his hair, put the cap back on. "I didn't know you were riding with me tonight. I'm just glad someone mentioned it in time for me to get out here before you arrived. I didn't want anyone in the station to see your shock."

"You sunovabitch."

He looked back at her.

She kept her voice low, just between the two of them.

"You know what would have prevented a lot of shock? If you'd introduced yourself properly at the pool."

"I didn't know who you were. Not right away."

"When did you know?" *Was it before or after you decided my face was too ugly for you?*

"You mentioned Leonard Wood while we were talking."

"And you kept talking to me?"

"I—" Whatever words he'd been about to say got stuck in his throat.

"You kept talking to me. You never bothered to say you'd been to Leonard Wood, too, or that you were an MP, too."

"I was going to."

"But you didn't. Didn't fraternization occur to you?"

"Yes."

"You were toying with my career." *And my heart.*

Thane pushed away from the patrol car and stood over her. She wasn't a short woman, but he still was taller by several inches. If he thought she was going to be unnerved by the way he looked down at her, if he thought she'd blink or back away even a half step, then he truly had no idea where she'd lived or what she'd been through to make second lieutenant.

"I can't toy with your career without toying with my own," he said.

"True. I don't know what makes a person take the kind of risk you took, but I didn't choose to take that risk. Maybe it gives you a thrill to push the envelope and not get caught, but I worked too hard to be standing right where I am today to risk it all like that. Your little game isn't fun when it can hurt someone else."

"There was no game. I didn't know the new LT's name was Chloe, only Michaels." He paused. "It was never a game."

She blinked. It was never a game? He spoke so sincerely, trying to soothe her feelings now, wanting her to think the only reason he'd dumped her stone-cold was because he'd figured out they were going to be in the same unit.

Oh, how she would have loved to have believed that. Her heart wouldn't hurt so much if she could fool herself into thinking his heart had been involved, as well. She would've been gullible enough to believe him right now, too, if she hadn't opened a bathroom door and heard the truth. *When all I do is talk to a woman, there's your clue. I had to take what I could get.*

He'd been playing games, all right. He'd left without a backward glance once she'd agreed to go out with him. He was the kind of man who was all about the chase. The hunt. The kind of guy who would win a woman's heart just to prove he could, then dump her. How many Monday mornings in the cadet mess hall had she spent listening to the guys describe their weekend conquests, bragging about how they'd charmed a woman, how they'd looked her in the eye and used the line *I really love you* just to get her into bed? Chloe knew that game.

Fool me once, shame on you. Fool me twice...

There'd be no second time. She was completely immune to Thane's nice-guy act. He'd made sure of that with the way he'd walked out.

"Yeah, look, Thane. *Carter.* Cut the crap. From this point on, it's got to be all work and no play. No more of your games. Don't bother testing out your charm on me. We work together, nothing else. Can you handle that?"

An NCO in a black MP vest called over them. "Lieutenant Carter, we're ready to go if you are, sir."

In icy silence, Thane stepped around her to head across the parking lot toward a formation of about twenty soldiers, lined up in two rows.

Chloe turned to follow.

Thane stayed a half step ahead of her as they walked, but after a few strides, he looked at her over his shoulder and spoke in a voice that was quiet but dripping with scorn. "Here's the thing, Michaels. I'm ahead of you in every way. You don't have the knowledge I do of this post, you don't know how the company operates and you have zero real-world experience in law enforcement. The question isn't can I handle you. The question is, can you keep up with me?"

The NCO-in-charge was addressing his two rows of MPs as Thane stood off to the side with Chloe—Lieutenant Michaels—standing at his shoulder like a shadow.

All work and no play. Can you handle that?

Definitely. He'd expected her to be shocked. He deserved a medal for making sure she wouldn't be shocked in front of the people she'd have to work with from now on. He'd been thoughtful, damn it, having her meet him outside. She'd used the privacy he'd given her to chew him out.

He'd expected her to be hurt. Instead, she'd zeroed right in on the specifics like a detective. When had he known and why hadn't he spoken up sooner?

He slid her a look as the NCO read off the list of vehicles for which alerts had been issued. Chloe was listening. There was no smile. She didn't radiate happiness. In fact, she looked fairly fierce, concentrating on descriptions of stolen cars and vehicles suspected of being involved in crimes. Thane had a feeling he could ask her to list all the vehicles' makes and models when the NCO was done, and she'd spit them right out.

Because she was sharp.

She was also beautiful.

Both were reasons why he hadn't leaned forward at that little patio table and said, "Leonard Wood? Are you an MP? So am I."

It should have been the easiest, most obvious thing to do. But he'd sat there, devastated. In denial. Mentally grasping at straws, looking for a way for the truth not to be true.

He'd felt the loss of a relationship that would never be, but, obviously, she hadn't. *Cut the crap.* All work and no play for Michaels and Carter was how she wanted it? It was exactly what she was going to get.

It was time to train the rookie. "Before every shift, we conduct PCCs just like we were leaving the wire downrange. PCC stands for pre-combat check."

"I know. You can inspect everyone while I stand here and watch, or it can take half as long if you take the front row and I take the back."

She wanted to conduct the inspection herself, with all the experience of a single ride-along under her belt? He almost had to admire that level of cockiness.

Fine. If she wanted to jump into the deep end of the pool, he'd let her.

Done with his briefing, the NCO called the two lines of waiting soldiers to attention, then turned to salute Thane.

Thane returned the salute and stood in front of the MPs. "I've got a ride-along tonight, Lieutenant Michaels. She'll be taking over fourth platoon, starting tomorrow."

That was enough of an explanation. He walked to the first soldier in the first line, and gestured for Michaels to start the second row.

Thane looked over each soldier from head to toe. He could tell in a glance if they had their uniforms on straight, if haircuts were in regulation, faces had been shaved, ACU trousers were properly bloused over their combat boots. Tonight, he was looking to make sure no one had tried to lighten their load by taking an armor plate out of its pocket on the black vest. He asked each soldier to turn on his flashlight, to show him they had latex gloves in a pocket, handcuff keys, their own military ID. All the while, he kept one eye on Michaels. She was doing the same.

Almost.

She was so damned sure of herself. She executed a sharp left face to step to the next soldier in line. He wanted to scoff at that level of drill and ceremony, one usually saved for formal events like changes of command in the regular army. It so clearly marked her as fresh out of West Point. He wanted to scoff, but she did it without any pretense, moving down her line as if proper military courtesies were as natural as breathing to her. On her, that strictly executed drill looked kind of cool.

Thane finished his row and waited off to the side of the formation for her to finish with her last soldier. "Everything good?" he asked her conversationally.

"Yes, s—" She caught herself almost calling him *sir*. She wasn't a cadet anymore, as her *friend* Greg had pointed out, but even the cocky Michaels forgot that now and then, apparently.

He managed not to smile at that little gaffe. He had a bigger mistake to point out. "You sure about that? Everyone has a working flashlight?"

"Of course everyone's got a flashlight. Do you require them to be on the belt or in a vest pocket?"

"Soldier's choice." Then he spoke so softly there was no way anyone in formation could hear him. "That's the kind of thing you should have asked before inspection, don't you think?"

He didn't give her a chance to respond. Instead, he took a step toward the formation and looked down her row. "Second row, take your flashlights out, turn them on and point them my way."

They did. One soldier, just one, had a flashlight that didn't light up.

These soldiers were from third platoon, but Thane knew them all by name. "Specialist Wesson, dead batteries? Come on, you know better."

The NCO was on it, dismissing Wesson to go inside and scrounge up either new batteries or borrow a working flashlight. With a quick exchange of salutes—proper but casual salutes, like real soldiers, not West Pointers—Thane turned over control of the personnel to the NCO, and headed to his patrol car. Michaels kept pace beside him, her chin still up despite the fact that he'd just taught her a lesson.

That was what he was here for. And if the lesson had been

taught in a way that she'd never forget, so much the better. He deserved a pat on the back for not rubbing it in her face with an *I told you so*. Little butter bar West Pointer, so sure she knew how to inspect the—

"You forgot to inspect one thing," she said.

"What's that?"

"Me."

"You're an officer. You have to police yourself."

"Fine. Then I have to tell you, since you didn't notice it, that I haven't drawn a radio yet."

Everyone else had one, a walkie-talkie style of radio with a cord that attached to a small, square speaker/microphone combination. Most MPs kept the speaker clipped on their shoulder, so they could hear and answer dispatch without having to take the bigger, clunkier radio off their belt.

Thane kept walking, but he glanced at her, trying not to look like he was inspecting her gear. The vest looked right. She had the standard sidearm, a nine-millimeter Beretta, in the same holster they all wore. Hers was on her right hip. She must be right-handed.

He had a fleeting memory of Saturday in the shade, of wanting to know every little detail about her. She was right-handed.

As if he cared.

"You don't need a radio." He sounded curt, even to himself.

"Yes, I do."

"You're either going to be in the car with its built-in radio, or you're going to be with me." Thane had a radio, of course. "Most of the initial dispatches are done through the computer. I'll angle it so you can see the screen."

"I need a radio so I can hear the *radio* traffic. If you haven't tried it before, let me tell you that it's hard to hear what's going on from the back seat. If I had a handheld unit, I'd be able to keep track better. It's easier to learn all the call signs and codes if you can hear all the call signs and codes."

Smart aleck. Thane kept walking toward the patrol car, away from the station where all the handheld radios were stored. "Not an issue. You won't be in the back seat tonight."

"You're going to take the back seat?" She seemed surprised, pleasantly surprised. "I appreciate that. It will be easier to get my bearings and see where we're going."

"I'm not sitting in the back." He was the officer on duty. He needed to see where the hell he was going more than she needed to be able to read street signs. "I'm driving."

"Lieutenant Salvatore had a driver. Specialist Baker, first platoon. He must be your soldier."

"During law enforcement rotations, the officers take different shifts than the enlisted. Our days are broken into twelve-hour shifts. Theirs are eight. They work three days on day shift, three on mids, three on nights, then get three days off. You won't be working with your own platoon most shifts."

"I know. I already got the basics. This isn't my first ride-along."

His first impression of her had been that she could be a Zen-master fitness and yoga instructor, happy with the world and her place in it. Now he watched her as she stalked away from him to head for the passenger door of the cruiser. Zen yoga? Not a chance.

Thane took his time walking up to his side of the car just to annoy her.

She kept talking. "I wasn't asking why you weren't working with a soldier from your own platoon. I was asking why you didn't have a driver. Is it up to each duty officer to decide if he wants a driver or not?"

"It's Sunday. Nothing happens on Sundays, so we don't put as many MPs on the road. When was your other ride-along?"

She opened her door and stood there, talking to him across the roof of the car, along the length of the blue-and-red light strip. "Friday night."

He opened his door. "On Fridays and Saturdays, everyone gets a partner."

Everyone got a partner at work, he meant. Thane's Saturday night after the pool party had been lonely as hell, but at least he'd had Ballerina to talk to about their wasted attempts to make real-life friends. Friday night, he hadn't even had that. Ballerina had made him laugh about tater tots and then run off for her late night, a late night she'd said she enjoyed. Without him.

"Tonight, Michaels, it's just you and me."

He got in the car and slammed his door.

Chapter Seven

Chloe got in the patrol car and slammed her door shut.

"What are you doing?" Thane demanded.

She had no patience for his high-handedness. "I'm getting in the car. What do you think I'm doing?"

"Getting in the car," he agreed. "Now you can get out of the car. In the real army, we don't go anywhere in any vehicle before we PMCS it. That's preventative maintenance checks and services. Since I'm the driver, I get to sit here while you walk around the vehicle and tell me if all the headlights and brake lights are working."

She jerked her car door open. "I know what the hell PMCS means." She got out and slammed the door. Jeez, the man thought it was her first day in the army. Everything about him irritated her.

I only have to work with him for two or three years. No big deal.

She stood in front of the car and held out her right arm to indicate that he should turn on that side's blinker. Then the left. She stalked around the back, consciously noting the tires looked inflated and didn't have worn treads, and repeated the exercise as Thane watched her in his rearview mirror. Right arm. Left arm. She'd never done this on a patrol car before, but over the years she'd done it on dozens of HUMM-Vs and a five-ton truck and—

She jumped a mile at an earsplitting burst of sirens. Blue and red lights flashed on top of the car, then stopped just as quickly. She swore, she swore, *she swore* that not only could she see Thane's shoulders shake with laughter, but she could hear the man laughing through the windows and over the sound of the car's engine.

She got back in and slammed the door. "Har-dee-har-har. You made the new guy jump."

"Yes, I did, Michaels."

They were going to use last names? Fine by her. She kept up her frosty pose as he powered up the laptop that was locked into place on a bracket between their seats. Thane hit a square on the touch screen to notify the dispatcher that 310 was now in service.

Chloe fastened her seat belt. Her handcuffs were situated on the back of her black belt in a bad spot. They were pressing into her spine, and the seatback pressed her weapon forward so that the muzzle end of the holster jabbed her in the thigh, but she'd be damned if she was going to wriggle all around to get comfy like a child. Like a new guy. A rookie.

Even if he was a first lieutenant and she only a second, lieutenants were generally considered one rank. They didn't salute each other. They called one another by their first names, but since Thane had just called her *Michaels*...

"It's going to be a long night, *Carter*." The last-name thing was good. Carter was whom she had to deal with. Thane could be a distant memory of a sucker's dream.

"Oh, it's going to be a long day, too, Michaels. A lot of long days." His smile was as mocking as his tone of voice as he put the car in Reverse and backed out of the parking lot. "In the morning, you're moving into my office."

Nothing happened on a Sunday, until it did.

It was nearly midnight, and Chloe and *Carter* were fixing themselves foam cups of coffee at the PX's Shoppette, a 24-hour convenience store on post. They stood on opposite sides of an island that held pots of hot coffee and all the accompaniments that went with them. They'd both chosen the brew labeled "Bold." Chloe was putting plain creamers in hers. On his side of the green Formica counter, Thane was adding all kinds of crazy crap to his cup. Cinnamon, vanilla powder, cocoa powder—every coffee garnish there was.

He had to be screwing with her, mocking her hot dog analysis. She pretended she wasn't watching.

They were the only two customers in the place, if they could be called customers. MPs got free coffee here all night long. Thane had turned down the volume on his radio, but the indistinct voice of the dispatcher rumbling from the little speaker clipped to his shoulder still overrode the overhead Muzak every few minutes.

Thane put one pump of vanilla syrup in his coffee. One pump of chocolate. One pump of caramel. One pump of sugar-free caramel—yep, he was screwing with her. She debated whether or not to tell him he was neither interesting nor amusing when he suddenly chucked the whole cup in the trash and started striding toward the door.

"Let's go, Michaels. That's us."

"What's us?"

Thane was already slamming the glass door open. This was not a drill. Chloe chucked her cup in the trash, too, and ran after him, calling a one-word apology to the store clerk as she burst out the door after Thane.

He was already in the car, engine on. She got in her side and had barely gotten her door closed before he backed out of the parking space. He hit the buttons for the lights and sirens—they weren't nearly as loud in the car as they were outside. Still, she reached for the two-way radio to turn up the volume just as he hit the street and floored the gas.

"Seat belt. Now. You check my right at intersections."

She complied with the seat belt. She guessed she was supposed to look right for oncoming traffic. Salvatore hadn't gone anywhere while using lights and sirens on Friday night, so she wasn't positive. So much for Sundays being slow.

"Where are we going?"

"Am I clear on the right?"

They'd already reached the next intersection. The light was red, but they were going through the intersection, anyway. "Yes. Clear."

But Thane had already bent forward to look around her head as he drove through the intersection.

She tried again. "What are we—"

"You call out 'clear on the right' or 'not clear.' Make sure that 'not clear' is loud."

"Roger. What's going on?"

"Officer down."

The radio chatter was nonstop now. Chloe picked out more words. "Domestic disturbance?"

"Shh." He shushed her angrily, listening to the radio and concentrating on the road as he sped toward whatever was causing nonstop radio chatter.

She shushed. A car ahead of them took an eternity to pull off the road and get out of their way. How could that driver not see red and blue lights flashing in the dark of the night?

The traffic light at the next intersection was red. "Clear on the right."

Thane slowed down, anyway.

"Clear on the right," she repeated. Did he not trust her? But no, out of the corner of her eye she saw he was concentrating on the left, wanting to be sure an oncoming car had seen their lights and was slowing down. He never even looked her way to see if the right was clear, since she'd said it was. He relied on her, as he should.

As they sped through the intersection, a male voice came on the radio, hard to understand because he was panting. "Hood, three-twenty, I'm up. I'm okay, suspect ran back in the house, blue shirt, basketball shorts."

Thane relaxed the tiniest bit.

Another radio voice said, "Three-thirty, out at three-twenty."

Thane turned off the main post road into one of the housing developments. He turned off the siren but left the emergency lights on. They were getting close, and Chloe needed to know what they were getting close to. The cuffs at her back and the holster on her thigh weren't toys. "You gotta clue me in."

"Domestic. That was three-twenty, the one out of breath.

He got into a wrestling match on the ground with a male. He's okay now, but the male got away and locked himself back in the house."

"With whomever called 911?"

"Gotta assume so. Three-thirty's there now for backup, but we're still going, too."

This was serious. The suspect had already attacked an MP. He could be in the house hurting his victim. He could be in the house arming himself with a personally owned weapon.

Thane killed the lights—not just the red and blue ones, but the headlights, as well.

Chloe had never felt more awake in her life, her brain and body both alert to real danger. "What's the address?"

"There." Thane rolled slowly past a street where another patrol car was parked with its emergency lights flashing in the night. He kept rolling along the side of the house on the corner, then braked. Waited.

Chloe looked where he was looking. The house on the corner was completely dark. Nobody home. "This corner house?"

"Yeah." He leaned forward a little farther. Without taking his eyes off the night, he put the car in Park, slowly. Undid his seat belt. Waited.

Chloe undid her seat belt.

"Look at the back porch," Thane said. "Do you see...?"

They'd gone dark and were on the side of the dark house. She couldn't see much of the back porch, only a corner of a patio awning and a few bushes.

A bush rustled.

"There he is." Thane exploded out of the car and started running.

Goddamn it, goddamn it—Chloe threw open her car door, feeling like she was moving in molasses, like one second was too long to take to get out of a car. She took off after Thane, but he shouted at her, "Call it in."

She didn't have a damned radio. She kept running after him. *"Go call it in."*

He was the ranking officer. She had to follow orders, even if it went against every instinct to let him go after the bad guy alone. She changed direction, ran back to the patrol car, yanked open the driver's door and ducked her head in, trying to keep an eye on her partner as she yanked the car radio's microphone out of its clip. She pressed its key.

"Three-ten." Now she was the one out of breath. She released the key. There was only silence on the other end of the radio. Damn it—she'd said three-ten first, as if she was trying to reach three-ten. She was trying to reach the Fort Hood dispatcher. *"Hood*, three-ten."

"Go ahead." The dispatcher sounded skeptical, since a woman was saying three-ten when everyone knew Lieutenant Carter was on duty.

"Three-ten is chasing down that domestic suspect. The male. On foot. They're headed down…the cross street."

Damn it again. She didn't know where they were. She looked at the computer screen and found the domestic disturbance dispatch in a second, but the address given wasn't this side street.

"Street name?" the dispatcher asked.

"Hold." She had to drop the mic and go halfway across the street to read the sign in the dark, run back and pick up the mic. "Bundy Street. Headed…" Crap. Was this street running north-south or east-west? She didn't know—but they'd been heading toward the airfield when they'd pulled off the main road, and they hadn't changed directions in the housing development. "Headed toward the airfield."

"Roger, three-ten. All units be advised, suspect is on foot—"

Chloe dropped the mic and backed out of the car, ready to run after Thane. As much as it was ingrained in her to obey lawful orders, it was also ingrained in her to never leave a team member to go it alone in combat. But she paused before slamming the door and joining the chase on foot. Logic ruled: minutes had passed since the chase had started. She'd never catch up.

She got back in the car and started the engine, then drove along the fence line. One of the other MPs, either 320 or 330, was running through the backyard now, too. He made a hard turn and headed down the backside of the block of houses, so the suspect must be running through yard after yard with Thane on his tail.

The suspect would have to come out at the end of the row of houses and cross another street. Chloe hit the gas. She could pass the MPs on foot and head the bad guy off the next street over. She looked in between every house, hoping for a glimpse of any of the three who were on foot. No luck—but just as she turned the corner, a man in a blue T-shirt and basketball shorts burst out of a backyard to cross the road.

She was right there in her marked police car, slamming on the brakes. The suspect stopped and changed direction to run from her car, but that sent him running right back toward Thane just as he burst out of the hedges and onto the street. Thane grabbed the suspect by one arm when he tried to dodge him, twisting it up behind the man as he resisted. Both men fell forward to the ground.

Chloe threw the car in Park and got out, running in the light of the headlights toward the two on the ground. Thane had the suspect down face-first and had control of one of the suspect's arms behind his back, but he couldn't get a handcuff on him because the suspect was flailing around with the other hand, awkwardly trying to reach behind himself blindly to hit at Thane.

Chloe started to grab for the suspect's flailing wrist, but saw the flash of a knife in the man's hand. She reared back from the blade and stepped on his forearm with her combat boot instead. "Drop the knife."

He didn't, but he was immobilized, so she knelt while keeping his forearm under her boot and started to pry his fingers from the knife, a kitchen knife by the looks of it. The guy was completely freaking out, using all his might to clutch the knife despite the fact that he was lying in the grass at the side of the road with two people pinning him down.

Thane was breathing hard and not talking. He closed one handcuff around the wrist he controlled. Chloe placed the palm of her hand on the suspect's shoulder. She spoke firmly. "This is over, soldier. This part is over. You know that. Let go of the knife so we can get you back on your feet and move on. This part is over."

The suspect was straining, holding his head up, but Chloe kept repeating herself. The suspect was under their control, his knife hand rendered useless. She didn't see a need to use any additional force. The suspect would tire on his own; he couldn't keep straining against them forever.

"Open your hand," she ordered, as calmly as she'd say *pass the ketchup*. "Let go of the knife. I can't hear your side of the story until we get these cuffs on."

With a wordless shout of despair and defeat, the suspect dropped his forehead into the scrubby grass and gave up, his muscles going slack, his hand opening and the knife falling out. Thane grabbed his wrist and jerked his arm out from under Chloe's boot before she could get off. She stood and kicked the knife to the middle of the road as Thane finished cuffing the suspect.

Another MP had come out from the backyards—either 320 or 330, Chloe assumed—and now bent forward to rest his hands on his knees and catch his breath. Thane stood up and dusted himself off. His breathing had nearly returned to normal. He lifted a hand to acknowledge the other MP, then wiped the side of his face on his jacket sleeve.

"Well, that was fun," he said.

Chloe knew that kind of army humor. When they were in the middle of an eight-hour road march that utterly sucked and the skies decided to open up and drench everyone, one soldier might conversationally say to the next, *Well, isn't that rain refreshing?* or *Great, I was hoping the road would turn to mud.*

So Chloe just shook her head. "Nothing happens on Sunday night, huh?"

"Didn't want you to get bored." Thane looked down at the suspect. "Let's get him to his feet."

They each took an arm and hauled him up, then walked him to the cruiser. As Thane patted him down, Chloe retrieved the knife, her first piece of evidence, ever. Once Thane had seated the suspect in the back seat and Chloe had popped the trunk to get out a proper plastic bag for the knife, they stood once more on opposite sides of the patrol car. Over the roof, Thane asked, "Are you ready for some more fun?"

"Like what?"

"Now you get to hear his side of the story."

Chapter Eight

It wasn't that fun.

The suspect's side of the story consisted mostly of four-letter words. He cursed Michaels almost exclusively, although Thane was the one who'd caught him.

Thane told himself that it was just part of the job. He told himself that Michaels needed to get a thick skin and get it fast if she was going to spend years as an MP. He told himself that he'd heard worse said about himself. He'd heard worse said to other female MPs. He'd heard—

"I thought you were going to tell us your side of the story?" Thane interrupted. "All we're getting is some piss-poor attempt to impress us with your vocabulary."

The suspect paused in his tirade to throw a few curses Thane's way, then resumed calling Michaels every name in the book. Thane guessed that she was a bigger threat to the loser's manhood than he was. The suspect could tell his buddies that a man had chased him down without losing face. Clearly, he had an issue with a woman rendering his arm immobile and his knife useless. After all, this particular suspect had been beating a helpless woman. He wouldn't want a woman to be able to fight back.

Fortunately, it took only a minute to get back to the suspect's house. An ambulance had arrived, contributing its emergency lights to the patrol cars of 320 and 330.

They left the suspect in the back seat with both his seat belt and handcuffs on and headed up the walkway toward the house. Thane caught Michaels squinting away from the flashing emergency lights. If one were prone to migraines or seizures, the lights would be crippling, really. He didn't have to worry about that with Michaels, however. He was certain Michaels was as healthy as all get-out, because…

He pushed away the memory of Chloe in a bikini.

Because Michaels wouldn't have been commissioned if she had epilepsy. *That* was why he was certain.

But the lights could be painful to anyone's eyes, so as they passed 320's patrol car, Thane opened the driver's door and reached in to shut off the emergency lights. Same with the next car. He didn't touch the ambulance. He wasn't responsible for that vehicle, and the paramedics were going to be running with lights to get the victim to the hospital, judging from the chatter on his radio…radio chatter that Michaels probably couldn't hear, standing an arm's distance away from him. He probably should have listened to her and let her draw a radio.

He placed his hand over the speaker clipped to his shoulder. "They're going to take the wife to the hospital."

"How do you know…?" She looked at his hand. "Never mind."

Thane hoped he was pulling off the stoic army officer face again. A trainee didn't need a radio. She'd said that Salvatore hadn't given her one on Friday, either. Thane wasn't going to feel guilty about it. "The other MPs are in the house with the paramedics. It gets crowded. I'm waiting out here, because there's no reason to wade in there and have the MPs feeling obliged to stop and report to us. Plus, we've got that bozo in our back seat."

Michaels had her arms crossed over her chest as she stood on the street beside him, facing the front door of the house. She had that fierce look on her face again, that one that meant she was concentrating on something critical.

Thane looked around. The situation was under control. There weren't even any nosy neighbors to herd away. He wondered what she was concentrating on. After hearing the suspect's F-word-laden side of the story, Thane could guess.

"Don't put too much stock into the suspect's ranting. You'll hear worse, you know. I've been called every name in the book by now."

Her gaze ricocheted from the house to him. "I'm a big girl. I can handle cursing."

Her dark eyes reflected the ambulance lights. Her voice was steady. She didn't seem to be shaken up at all by the chase or by facing her first armed suspect. He felt proud of her—no, that was ridiculous. He was just glad she seemed to be able to handle herself because she was going to be part of his company. He was relieved that he wouldn't have to coddle a thin-skinned butter bar, that was all. She was taking this in stride.

He approved.

Meanwhile, Michaels shrugged. "You can almost feel sorry for him. He's the most miserable human being I've ever seen, really, almost like a wild thing, lashing out at anyone he can see. He's lost everything, and he knows it. I'm sure he'll be court-martialed and kicked out of the service. There goes his salary. There goes his house. There goes his life. It's all his own fault. He's made himself powerless."

Thane was silent. Her level of understanding, even her sense of compassion, struck him as extraordinary for someone so new to it all. He looked at Chloe's profile, at beauty illuminated by flashes of red and white against a black night, and felt that kick in his chest again, that loss of knowing he'd never be able to have this woman in his life.

Keep it in check, Thane.

He did have her in his life, as a fellow platoon leader. It was good from a professional standpoint that she hadn't taken the suspect's ranting personally. It was interesting, nothing more, to hear her thoughts on the suspect and how he was lashing out because his life as he knew it was over.

How long would that compassion last? This was only her second night in the real world.

There was a commotion at the front door of the house. A paramedic, his back to them, pulled one end of a stretcher through the front door. A woman was propped up on the stretcher. Beside Thane, Michaels's expression remained neutral, as did his own, but the victim's expression was undeniably heartbreaking. There was all the sorrow, there was the misery that had been missing in the suspect's rant.

The paramedics had put one of the victim's arms in a sling. With the other, she clutched a towel to her head, a white towel soaked in red blood, vivid in the red and white ambulance lights.

Michaels took in a single deep breath, then turned around and walked back to the patrol car.

Maybe she was hiding her shock at the extent of the injuries. Maybe she was hiding tears. She'd handled the chase, the apprehension, even the suspect's insults just fine, but seeing a helpless victim, that must be Michaels's weakness.

Thane couldn't blame her. The injured woman looked so small on the stretcher, so much smaller than the man who was locked in his back seat. It infuriated Thane that a man could even think about using fists and knives against a person so defenseless.

"Carter," Michaels called. She didn't sound weak. She didn't sound shaken.

Thane turned around.

She was standing at their patrol car, directly in front of the window where the suspect sat. "Come here and help me block his view of her. He shouldn't get to gloat over his handiwork, the bastard. God knows she shouldn't have to see his face right now."

So maybe Michaels wasn't weak or tearful at the sight of the victim. Maybe she was pissed and protective. A good combo. She had great potential. Great instincts. His first impression of her, that she was something special…

Forget that first poolside impression.

Thane stood beside her and helped her block the victim's view of her attacker. Through the closed car, the suspect's voice was muffled as he ranted at the world some more. Thane paid as little attention to it as Michaels did.

She watched the paramedics loading their patient into the ambulance. "What's next?"

"Now, we get to enjoy the beauty of being three-ten." Thane crossed his arms over his black vest and leaned against the patrol car. He could feel the suspect kicking the door, a little thunk of vibration against Thane's back. "We're going to put this wonderful human being in three-twenty's car. This is his case. He gets to transport the suspect to the holding cell at the station and handle the paperwork. You and I will get back on the road and wait for the next call."

As the duty officer, he was required to go to all felonies and domestic disturbances. Other than that, 310 basically served as backup to the entire post, rolling by when they were near a call, checking on every MP who was out there at least once during the shift. They could go to any call that sounded interesting, a perk of being the duty officer instead of a regular patrol confined to one smaller area of post. There had to be some perk for these thirty-six-hour shifts.

"If there is another call, that is. Sundays really are boring."

Chloe could feel Thane staring at her as he sat behind the steering wheel, buckling his seat belt.

She glared back.

Thane put the car in gear and headed out of the housing development. "Let's go back to the Shoppette and get that coffee."

Chloe pushed her seat belt lower across her lap, under her belt full of equipment that she hadn't used. There was only one item she'd needed at the scene. "I don't need coffee. I need a damned radio."

"Look, you did really well. Using the car to cut off his route was a great idea. I don't know what all your pissed-off-ness is for. You did fine."

"The reason I had to drive the car was because you ordered me to stay behind to use a radio that was attached to the car. You ran after him alone and put yourself at risk. What if I hadn't gotten there?"

"Then I would have taken him on my own."

"He had a knife."

"I'm aware of that. You don't always get a partner, Michaels. If you weren't there, I would have dealt with it. You better be able to handle things solo, too."

"This isn't about me being solo on some future hypothetical call. It's about you failing to use your resources wisely. I am your resource tonight, but you wasted me on a radio call." She waited for him to tell her she had a lot of nerve, calling herself a resource when she was the new kid on the block.

He didn't say that. "I didn't waste the fact that I had an extra person with me. Someone had to call it in."

"*Someone* could have made the call as she ran, if she'd had a handheld radio. You set me up for failure, and in this case, that could have been deadly. For you."

"I set you up for failure? Failure?"

"You asked me to do something you knew I couldn't do. I didn't have a radio and I didn't know what to say. I told you I'm barely catching all the call signs, and you didn't even tell me which street we were on. I looked like an idiot. Or I sounded like an idiot."

"I doubt that."

"What is the code for 'officer running on foot after the suspect'? I didn't know. What if it had gone differently and you were the one who got tackled? What is the code for 'officer down'?"

"You can just say 'officer down.' We're discouraging codes. They don't mean the same thing from one town to the next. Use plain language."

"Really? And what was said on your radio that made you chuck your coffee and run?"

He hesitated. She saw his jaw clench. "Nine-nine-nine."

"Which means?"

"Officer down."

She threw up her hands. "Point proven. I wouldn't have known to say nine-nine-nine if I'd gone into those bushes and found that you were the one who was pinned down. While you were trying to teach me a little lesson on how unprepared I am for this job, you put yourself in danger."

"Teach you a little lesson? You think I was intentionally trying to make you look bad?"

"Yes."

There was a moment of silence on Thane's part as they sat at a red light. Then he started shaking his head slowly. "In the middle of witnessing a suspect fleeing the scene, I stopped and thought to myself, 'Hey, how can I make Michaels look bad? I know, I'll make her call it in to the station when she doesn't know how.'"

Her mistakes had been broadcast to every MP working tonight, to the dispatchers and to the watch commander. Chloe's first impression on the people she was required to lead wasn't going to be good, and she knew it would be hard to overcome. She had Carter to thank for it, as if he hadn't already gone low enough yesterday by pretending to be attracted to her when he didn't even like her face.

"Why *wouldn't* I think that? You've already—" She wasn't going to mention the pool. The flashlight incident would do. "You've already tried to make me look bad with your little flashlight stunt."

He shrugged, completely unconcerned. "I'm sure you did fine on the radio. I didn't give you a task I didn't think you could handle. You're the one who gave yourself the task with the flashlights."

She didn't want to go off on a tangent about flashlights. *Controlled confrontation.* "I need a radio before we do anything else tonight."

"I was already planning to stop at the station to get you one. I was going to get you a cup of coffee first. Forget it. We'll just go to the station."

"Good."

It was hard to believe that just yesterday afternoon she'd been eager to eat an entire dinner with this man. Now, even a cup of coffee would taste sour if he was around.

Chapter Nine

Second Lieutenant Chloe Michaels was done being a badass—at least for the next twelve hours.

She was almost home. Her apartment building was visible through her windshield. She parked her Charger and got out, putting on her patrol cap and pulling the brim down just so. She forced herself to put one foot in front of the other, trudging past the swimming pool without one glance toward the blue water…or the little table for two.

Man, she was tired. It hadn't even been thirty-six hours, just twenty-four since she'd reported for duty at the police station. She'd never admit it to a soul at the 584th, but twenty-four hours was a very long time to stay sharp and act her best among strangers in a strange place. She'd tried to make a positive first impression while mentally filing away her first impressions of everyone she met—which had seemed to be nearly every soldier out of the one hundred and twenty in her company. She was grateful that literally every soldier in the US Army wore a name tag.

Chloe passed the mailboxes without stopping, since she didn't care if there was a flyer posted for another poolside event coming up. She already had a close friend, thank you very much. As soon as she got to her apartment, she'd check in with Different Drummer. She'd been away from her laptop for so long, and she missed him. He already knew her; she already knew him. She could slouch on the couch and talk about *Star Trek* or Scottish poets, and Drummer wouldn't be shocked or appalled or even impressed by the new lieutenant in the unit. He'd just laugh with Ballerina Baby.

She started up the concrete stairs. At least she felt reasonably confident that she'd made it through the last twenty-four hours without shocking or appalling anyone, except maybe Lieutenant Carter. The night had been one long, unrelenting trial of having to deal with Carter, but the day had gone better.

For one thing, she had a platoon sergeant who seemed to know what he was doing. Sergeant First Class Ernesto had decided she needed a tour of her new world, and she'd been relieved to have him escort her to the barracks, to the motor pool, to the dining facility.

She'd needed that break from Tha—Carter. Except for the minutes she'd spent in the bathroom, she'd been with him for every single second of each of the twelve hours in the patrol car. Even the bathroom hadn't been much of a break; she couldn't help looking in the mirror and wondering what was wrong with her face.

Worse, Carter hadn't been kidding about sharing an office with him. Little wonder that she'd jumped at the chance to go to the motor pool with her new platoon sergeant.

The same office. *The same office.*

She'd get through it. She had no choice but to get through it. Chloe slogged her way to the second-story landing and paused for a deep breath. Why had she chosen an apartment on the third floor? One more flight. Then she could collapse.

At least her platoon sergeant had gotten a good impression of her before she'd even walked into the headquarters building. *Nice to meet you, ma'am,* had been followed immediately by *Word is, you had quite the night.*

She'd held her breath as her platoon sergeant had told her what he'd heard. She knew he hadn't heard anything from Carter, because she'd been with Carter. But whomever he'd heard it from, it was all good. Three-thirty must have seen her kneeling over the suspect, immobilizing his arm with her boot. He'd seen her kick the knife out of the way. She was particularly relieved to hear that, despite feeling like an idiot on the radio, she'd apparently come across as calm and collected when her voice had been broadcasted to every MP on post.

The accuracy of the platoon sergeant's intel impressed

her. "Is all of this gossip, or did this come out on an official report somewhere?"

"Gossip, ma'am?" Sergeant First Class Ernesto had pretended horror, making her smile as they walked down the line of their HUMM-Vs. "We're all members of the United States Army here. We don't have time to gossip."

"Sure, you don't."

"But word can travel around here at combat speed. When the word involved the new LT, that invisible hotline between our building and the station just about burned up."

"In that case, thank God that hotline had a good report on me. I'll take it."

Chloe reached the last step of her climb. The third-story landing could have been made of gold instead of concrete, she was so glad to see it. She unlocked her door, walked into the cold air-conditioning and stood there. She took her patrol cap off automatically, but she was too tired to remember what she was supposed to do next. In the dark apartment, the sky looked bright beyond the sliding glass doors to her balcony. The first colorful clouds of the approaching sunset were visible between the two buildings on the other side of the complex. Now she remembered: that balcony, that view, that was why she'd wanted the third floor.

She sank onto her new, red couch. She ought to pour herself a glass of wine and drink it on the balcony…but she made no move toward the kitchen. First, she unlaced her boots and hauled each one off with one hand. She looked toward the kitchen. She looked out the sliding glass door. And then she turned and did a face-plant on her couch, which felt as welcoming as a bed of red roses.

She slept.

Thane bunched the pillow under his head and tried not to be absurdly emotional about his pen pal.

Ballerina was gone.

Since the discussion they'd had after their failed friend-experiment on Saturday, she hadn't posted anything. Not one hello, not one silly sentence.

He missed her. He'd been looking forward to talking tonight with a woman who didn't annoy the hell out of him.

He'd been stuck for a solid twenty-four hours in the Chloe Michaels show. The entire company was buzzing with positive crap about everything she did. Soldiers were bound to like an officer who wasn't afraid to jump in during a physical altercation, but even the stupid stuff was working in her favor. The ludicrously formal way she'd conducted her inspection had somehow fulfilled everyone's expectations of how a West Pointer ought to render military courtesies, as if his soldiers had forgotten that there were other West Point officers of various ranks already in the battalion, including the commander of the 410th, the operations officer on battalion staff—hell, Thane didn't keep track of everyone's commissioning source, but there were more. The point was, Michaels was far from the first one anyone had ever met.

But she was the newest. And she was female, which shouldn't matter, but it did. Add in her good looks and the way she seemed equally comfortable talking to the most junior private or the battalion commander, and—well, she was a novelty, that was all. Thane just had to grit his teeth until the buzz died down.

Between that eternally long ride-along and the steady stream of curious folks who'd come by his office all day, he'd only had a couple minutes of privacy to check his phone. Each time, the app's white screen had been frustratingly blank. Nothing pink to pick him up.

Now that he was home, he'd spent the last two hours trying to reach Ballerina.

Nothing.

The last time they'd talked, he'd given her advice, encouraging her to confront her adversary, but now he realized he hadn't really had enough information. After the domestic he'd worked last night, he was worried. The image of the wife on the stretcher, bloody towel to her head, wouldn't go away. She'd looked so frail compared to the man Thane had apprehended.

Thane stared at the empty phone screen and wondered what Ballerina's physical appearance was like. Was she frail? She worked out, he knew that, but if she was a wisp of a ballet dancer, should she really be confronting adversaries?

She'd been upset by a man. She'd told him the friend-who-wasn't-a-friend was male. What if she got hurt?

The thought made his stomach turn, made every muscle in his body tense. Where was she?

Hey, Ballerina Baby.

His cursor blinked for long minutes.

He'd been at work for only twenty-four hours, not thirty-six, so he wasn't as tired as usual. Thane adjusted the pillow one more time and settled in to write her a letter.

It's been two days, but it feels like a week since I last talked to you. You are never far from my thoughts.

That had been true once he'd gotten rid of Michaels. The moment her platoon sergeant had taken her off to the motor pool, Thane had checked this app. Before that, it had been all Michaels, all of the time—not all of it bad. He could still see the look on her face when she'd stood in front of the patrol car window, so that a victim wouldn't have to see her abuser. Pissed off and protective, he'd thought at the time. Who would protect Ballerina like that, if Thane's poor advice had caused her to be hurt?

I hope you haven't had any more run-ins with your friend that isn't really a friend. I wish you could give me more details, because my imagination is running wild. When I suggested confrontation, I didn't take into account that confrontations can turn physical. I'd only been thinking about speaking your mind, but this guy could be more dangerous than you think. If you have the tiniest bit of an unsettled feeling about him and his potential for violence, stay in public whenever he's around. Has he ever tried to get you alone? I regret advising you to confront him without insisting on more details first. I forget sometimes that women are vulnerable.

Probably because the women he worked with were MPs who were armed and trained. They'd stand on a man's arm or kick away his knife. But Ballerina? Thane might have advised her to confront a man who could be twice her size, for all he knew.

I wish I had some way to check on you when you go silent on this app. I worry about you, Ballerina. I'm afraid this new advice is too late. Please drop me a line when you see this, even if you don't have time for a long conversation. Heck, a single word will let me breathe easier. So please, Baby, check in.

Thane stared at his blue words a moment. No ironic quotes or movie references came to mind—just real worries. He set his phone on his nightstand. Whether he'd been up twenty-four hours or thirty-six, he needed to sleep. Tomorrow would be another long day at work, and he'd have to spend it with Michaels taking up space in his own office.

Was it just Friday night that he'd been feeling isolated, a man who slept and worked and did little else? Suddenly, women had taken center stage in his life, women like Chloe Michaels. Hard to believe he'd ever spent an entire afternoon smiling at her in the shade. She was beautiful and smart and too confident for her own good. She was going to be a thorn in his side.

Women like Ballerina Baby. He craved a conversation

with her, but she was missing and there was nothing he could do about it. God, he hoped she was safe.

Then there was the woman on the stretcher, a tragic image etched in his brain by flashes of red and white lights...

Thane punched his pillow into shape. One good thing about working for twenty-four hours: he'd be able to sleep even with all these women on his mind.

Eventually.

Thane had to punch his pillow into shape a few more times before sleep would come.

Chloe woke to the sound of a car engine, and another. And another.

They were muted by the sliding glass door, but the fact that there were so many must have permeated her consciousness enough to wake her up. She forced her eyes open and blinked at the gloom of her apartment. The dim sunlight outside her sliding glass door hadn't changed. It was still sunset.

The engine sounds faded in the distance. Where was everyone going? It was like an evacuation order had been given, an order she'd totally missed.

Orders. The army.

"Oh, crap." It hit her all at once. It wasn't sunset; it was sunrise. Sunrise in the army meant it was time for PT, or physical training. That meant calisthenics, the daily dozen, followed by group runs with cadences being called to keep everyone in step.

Here at the Two Rivers apartment complex, that meant half the residents were all leaving at the same time to get onto post before 6:30 a.m.—and it meant Chloe was late.

She ignored every sore muscle in her body, every stiff joint from sleeping on a sofa rather than her bed. She'd slept on worse, on dirt, branches, rocks. She'd slept sitting up in trenches she'd dug. This discomfort was nothing.

She stripped out of her ACUs, all the way to the skin, on her way to her bedroom. She pulled out the top drawer of her childhood dresser and grabbed some fresh underwear. She wrestled her way past the strong elastic of a clean sports bra, yanked open the second drawer and pulled out the black T-shirt of the army's physical fitness uniform. Jeez, she hadn't had a chance to shower since reporting to duty Sunday afternoon. It was Tuesday morning. She ran into her bathroom, threw on some deodorant and then her shirt.

In shirt and underpants, she brushed her teeth, then looked in the mirror—*screw you, Thane*—and fished all the bobby pins out of the remains of her bun, tossing them onto the hard counter, where they skittered off in all directions. With the elastic ponytail holder clamped in her teeth, she started ripping a brush through her hair. Fast.

Move, move, move, to be late is to be dead...

They'd killed her for lateness at West Point, that was for sure. Each simple tardy to class had resulted in four hours of walking the area in Dress Gray—with a rifle, of course, just to make the suck more of a suck—back and forth over a paved square that was surrounded on all sides by barracks buildings, in silent monotony, hour after hour. What kind of punishment was there in the regular army? What would the commander do to her?

He couldn't do anything that would be worse than the way she was blowing the positive first impression she'd made yesterday. Twenty-four hours of good work would go down the toilet when she came rushing up, panting and late, to the PT formation. Her whole platoon would know she'd failed to make it on time.

Her stomach hurt.

She was starving. Lunch yesterday had been a long, long time ago. That was okay. She'd done worse, gone for days without food during survival training. How far did the company run on a typical Tuesday? Two miles? Three? She could handle that without any fuel in her body.

She used her hands to pull her hair back into a ponytail, a style allowed only during PT. *Pants.* She bolted back to her bedroom dresser, yanked open the second dresser drawer, then paused. Was she supposed to wear the PT uniform's pants or shorts on this post? They'd been in pants at Leonard Wood, but it was so much warmer here. What had this post's commander authorized as the uniform? She jogged to her bedroom window and peeked through the blinds, hoping to spot someone else on their way to PT.

Half the cars in the parking lot were gone. The ones that had woken her had probably been the last few, doors slamming and engines revving, peeling out of here because they were running late. Even though only a couple of minutes had passed since she'd woken, there was no way she'd make it downstairs, drive to Hood, park at the headquarters building, run to the PT field and be standing in front of her platoon by six thirty.

She still had to go. Better late than never, she supposed. But she returned to the bathroom at a walk, not a run. She was thirsty. She could run three miles hungry, but not dehydrated. PT wasn't a life-or-death situation, but that kind of foolishness could turn it into one, or at least into something serious. She'd seen people pass out in run formations, hitting the pavement and getting trampled by the next row. Chloe filled her cup with tap water and chugged it down while watching herself in the mirror.

"This isn't life or death." She said it out loud to her reflection, sternly, because her heart was pounding as hard as if her whole world was on the line. She still felt like a cadet, trying to meet impossible demands: memorize the menus for the day, the front-page stories from the newspaper and all the other daily knowledge upperclassmen required, polish her shoes, shine her brass, prepare her room for inspection, ping—walk briskly—to an academic building to pass a multivariable calculus exam, then run back to the barracks to get into full regalia for an afternoon parade.

Her heart must have beat this hard more days than not, especially during plebe year. Panic had become a normal emotional state, one she'd learned to function well in. If Drummer were here, he'd say it was understandable that she was defaulting into that mind-set now, because that's what had worked in the past.

Perhaps that hadn't been the best thing to learn at her alma mater.

Chloe was in trouble for missing PT, of that she had no doubt, but what good did it serve to rush about in panic now? This was a new life. An adult life. A better thing her alma mater had taught her was to take ownership of her failures. Cadets could not say anything except *No excuse, sir* when asked why something had gone wrong or something had been left undone. It had rankled as an eighteen-year-old, wanting to explain all the circumstances but being able to say only those three words. Now, it was second nature.

She'd missed PT this morning. No excuse. This situation wasn't ideal, especially not on her second day in the unit, but she'd report to the commander, apologize for being late, and take whatever butt-chewing he dished out. She would stand through it without flinching—and *that*, her alma mater had certainly taught her how to do.

Then she'd sit in her new office, five feet from Thane Carter, for twelve hours.

Chloe stared at her reflection a moment longer. She told herself her stomach hurt because of hunger, not dread. She pulled off her black shirt and turned on the shower. She was going to report to the commander showered, fed, hydrated, wearing her ACUs and looking like the calm—not panicked—professional military officer she was.

And *then* she'd deal with Thane Carter for twelve hours.

Chapter Ten

Chloe used her extra time to stop at the drive-through doughnut shop on her way to the post. She bought a dozen doughnuts, all different flavors, plus one extra for herself. The doughnuts were a shameless attempt at damage control, a small positive after the big negative of oversleeping.

The headquarters building was nearly empty. PT had finished, and everyone had gone to their quarters to shower and eat and return in ACUs for the rest of their day. Chloe had time to kill. She savored her doughnut, wiped the sugar off her lips, shot the balled-up napkin for two points into the basket that was Thane's trash can, then turned her chair over to figure out which wheel was making that god-awful squeaking noise.

As soon as she heard her platoon sergeant arrive down the hall, she picked up the doughnut box and headed to his office. Even though she was his boss, she owed him an apology. Maybe *because* she was his boss, she needed to apologize for letting their whole platoon down. At the very least, she owed him the first pick of the doughnuts.

She told him the truth. She'd overslept. No excuse.

Ernesto seemed surprised. "The platoon wasn't at PT this morning, ma'am. During garrison duty, the soldiers working shifts are excused. It's pretty much just headquarters at PT."

Only headquarters did the routine 6:30 a.m. PT during garrison months? It made sense. The supply sergeant, the motor pool mechanics and the rest kept regular hours, but the MPs performing law enforcement did not. Her platoon hadn't been out there in the predawn, running in formation without her.

She didn't even try to keep the relief out of her voice. "I'm so glad to hear that. I'll just go explain to the CO, then."

"Well, ma'am, you can do that if you want to, but I don't

think it's necessary. You officers usually write where you're going on that whiteboard in the orderly room. When you weren't at PT this morning, I took the liberty of writing 'in-processing' next to your name. No one's expecting you to be at any particular formation today."

Chloe was speechless. He'd covered for her, and he'd done it in a perfectly reasonable way. For four years, she'd heard that every new lieutenant needed to pray for a good platoon sergeant, because a good one could smooth the way. She'd assumed that meant the sergeant would know all the right paperwork forms to use or how to procure the right equipment, but this? She wasn't in trouble. At all.

Ernesto prompted her. "You do still have some in-processing to take care of, right? You're authorized five days, and they had you riding along on at least one of those. Gotta get a parking pass or drop your medical records at the clinic or something?"

"Yes, of course. I'll go take care of…something like that today." Forget Thane Carter, forget Different Drummer—Sergeant First Class Ernesto was her favorite man in the world right now.

She handed him the entire box of doughnuts. "Could you find a home for these, please?"

He took them with a smile. "Roger that, ma'am."

Chloe smiled, too, all the way back to her own office, practically dizzy with relief, until she saw that Carter had arrived. He was at his desk, typing something on his personal phone, scowling away, and he didn't even greet her with a grunt.

She sat in her chair. The wheels squeaked loudly. There was no way he didn't know she'd walked in.

"Good morning," she said, just because Carter didn't want to talk.

He tossed his phone onto his desk, but didn't stop scowling.

"Bad news?" she asked, nodding toward his phone.

"No news." His scowl didn't let up. "Why does it smell like doughnuts in here?"

"I don't know." She shrugged and did the first thing that would make her look busy—opening her government-issued laptop. Her personal laptop was still sitting in her apartment, as it should be, but she wished she could write to Drummer. She'd ask him if he'd ever dreaded something he'd been sure would be hell, but then it had turned out to be a piece of cake? Or a doughnut? That was it—she could make him laugh by telling him that she'd had nothing but a box of doughnuts with which to face a hellish morning, but a coworker had turned her morning into a piece of cake. She'd taken the cake and given away the doughnuts, and gotten the better end of the bargain.

She stared at the army laptop's unfunny home screen. It felt like a million years since she'd last talked to Drummer. It would be at least another ten hours before she got home. Meanwhile, she only had Carter to talk to, a handsome man who hated her, a man who was raising an eyebrow at her in question.

Oops—she'd been looking at him instead of her screen.

"You're riding along with me again tomorrow night." Carter looked about as thrilled as she felt.

"Great," she said with zero enthusiasm. The more he glared at her, the more she craved the warmth and approval she got from Drummer.

Tonight. She just had to wait until the flag was lowered tonight, and then she could leave Carter's hostile company and go spend the evening with Drummer.

He was such a better man.

Dear Drummer,

I just got home and read your letter. I'm so sorry you've been so worried. Nothing terrible happened to me. I was away from my laptop, and couldn't check our app. I've been missing you!

Chloe hit Send on that much and stopped to unlace her boots and take off her jacket. She was determined not to pass out tonight before doing the essential things, like eating dinner, and most of all, talking to Drummer.

Drummer came first, food could come second. The emotional blue words he'd written had tugged at her heartstrings. How wonderful it was to have someone really worry for her. How awful it was that she'd given him cause to worry.

The only terrible thing that happened was that I made you worry for no reason. I'm so sorry. I didn't forget you. I just wasn't physically near my laptop. You were always on my mind.

She pulled off her socks and wiggled her bare toes. She could feel Second Lieutenant Michaels giving way, relaxing, morphing into Chloe, lover of the ballet and pop culture and Scottish poetry, lover of Drummer's words and thoughts and friendship, just a girl in love with her boyfriend.

Just a virtual boyfriend—but he was a real person. But not a man she knew in real life.

Thane Carter was a man in real life. Annoyingly, an image of him popped into her mind. Not Carter the MP officer, sweating from a foot chase, cuffing a suspect. Not the fellow platoon leader kicking back in his desk chair, smirking at her. For just a brief moment, she remembered the Thane Carter who'd knelt beside her at the edge of the pool, offering her a beer and a towel and his company. The sun had been shining and the water had been blue…

Well, that had gone nowhere.

Drummer was so much better. He didn't insult her face, for starters. He hadn't ever seen her face, but if he did, she was sure he wouldn't hate it. He surely would never stand around with other guys in public and discuss her shortcomings.

She carried the laptop into the kitchen. Blue letters suddenly ripped across the screen. There you are!!!! Thank God. Where have you been? Who were you with? Not the jerk I told you to confront, I hope.

Oh, boy. Drummer was real, all right. Real and upset. She set the laptop down next to the fridge, but she didn't type immediately. If she decided the jerk he referred to was Keith from her cadet days, then she could say she hadn't run into him again yet. But really, the jerk they'd discussed Saturday night was Thane, whom she had confronted and now had to work with.

Drummer wrote into her silence. I'm sorry. I'm not trying to interrogate you. The only truly important question is this: Are you safe?

She'd already said that she was okay. What made Drummer suddenly afraid she might come to physical harm? She'd been obsessed with keeping her heart safe, not her actual body. Yet Drummer was worried enough that he'd missed her Willie Nelson quote, *You were always on my mind.*

She hadn't meant to scare him with her neglect. The guilt she felt for taking their virtual relationship for granted felt very real.

More blue words filled the silence. (Willie Nelson, by the way. Too easy.)

I'm physically safe, I promise. Safe and so relieved he was still teasing her with a *too easy.*

Chloe blew a kiss at her screen and opened the fridge. Yogurt and coffee creamer and some leftover macaroni and cheese huddled together on one shelf in the otherwise-empty fridge. She put the mac and cheese in the microwave and got a spoon to start on the yogurt. She could eat and type.

Emotionally, I'm doing all right, too, now that I'm getting to take a break and catch up with you. If my goal in Big Life is happiness, then I need to talk to you as often as possible. It makes me happy. (Could be Elvis, too, you know. He sang it first.)

Her pink words hadn't pushed all his blue words off the bottom of the screen yet. She reread them. He sounded so different. Something had happened to Drummer. She was almost certain.

What makes you think I could be in physical danger? she asked.

Bad things happen to good people.

She abandoned the spoon in the yogurt and ignored the beeping of the microwave. What happened to you? Are YOU safe?

I'm fine. Wasn't talking about myself. I just saw some things at work that

The words just ended. Chloe shifted from bare foot to bare foot on the cold linoleum as she waited.

This anonymity thing has its limitations, he wrote. I can't tell you about my job and you can't tell me about yours. But can you tell me if you are safe at work? Safe at home?

Chloe went still. At work, she carried a loaded Beretta and drove at high rates of speed through red lights. Was she safe?

She remembered Thane's drop-everything response to the nine-nine-nine code, the way 330 had arrived so quickly to assist. Two more patrols had been on their way before dispatch called them off once 320 had radioed that he was safe.

I stay very safe at work. I am never alone. I always have reliable colleagues around me.

Including Thane. He'd been so callous and careless with

her heart, but if she ever said nine-nine-nine into a radio, he'd do whatever it took to get to her.

She'd do the same for him.

It was an unquestionable commitment that was hard to explain to civilians. For Drummer, she tried. I honestly feel safer at work than I would if I were out on the town by myself.

I'm glad to hear it. You have no idea how glad. Maybe we should rethink that confrontation plan tonight, though. Even someone you think would never hurt you might.

Too late. I already had it out with him.

God. And you're ok. Good. How did he take it?

He took it like a man. Chloe deleted that as soon as she wrote it. It sounded too much like a positive trait. He didn't run away. That's something. She hit Send.

Did he apologize?

No. But he didn't try to gaslight me, either, and pretend I was remembering things wrong. He didn't play like it was no big deal or say he'd just been kidding and I was over-reacting. I hate when people do that.

Years of living with *No excuse, sir* had made her pretty intolerant of excuses, she supposed. She did have to work with Thane, so it was good to know he wasn't the kind to make up excuses. Too bad he was the kind who tried to charm a woman he wasn't really interested in, just for kicks, just for an ego boost.

If I'd done the usual avoid-conflict thing, then I would have been the one playing it off like it was no big deal, which would probably have already resulted in me giving myself an ulcer overnight. Laying everything out plainly was good. I wouldn't say it made me happy, but at least I don't feel like a doormat right now.

From there, Chloe and Drummer eased into their comfortable relationship and spent the evening cracking jokes about leftover food and the remains of a television series that should have ended at least one season earlier than they did.

She couldn't ignore her hunch, though, that some aspect of Drummer's life made him think women were vulnerable. She knew he wasn't a billionaire and there was no reason to assume he was a drummer any more than she was a ballerina, but with his knowledge of Thoreau and Shakespeare, she'd always pictured him in an erudite kind of profession. If he was a drummer, then he was a percussionist in a symphony, perhaps, or a man seeking a PhD in music studies.

She had to frame it a little differently now. He must be around a grittier way of life. Maybe he was the drummer in a rock band, a big star who'd seen too many women crushed by crowds or overdosing on drugs at wild backstage parties.

Okay, that was a bit far-fetched. More realistically, he'd be the drummer in a fledgling rock band that was playing gigs until closing time in bars that had back alleys. Dangerous back alleys. Had he seen a woman become the victim of a terrible crime?

She was so very tempted to suggest they reveal their professions. He might be reassured to know she was a soldier and an MP.

Or not.

He might worry even more. Most people thought of the military as a dangerous profession. Law enforcement was considered a dangerous profession. Put them both together…

He wouldn't feel better at all.

She couldn't change their relationship and make the man feel worse at the same time.

The best leftover in the world is fried chicken. She hit Send with a sigh.

No way. The coating gets all soggy in the microwave. If you can't nuke it, it's not a good leftover.

Chloe rolled her eyes. He was such a dude sometimes. You don't microwave it. You eat it ice-cold, preferably while standing in front of an open refrigerator door.

You're weird.

Do you know what else tastes great, no matter how long it's been left out?

I'm afraid of this answer.

Candy, candy canes, candy corn and syrup. Chloe hit Send, and waited. One second, two—

Elf—great Christmas movie. (And too easy.)

There. She'd made Drummer feel better. Telling him she was an MP in the US Army would only have made him feel worse.

It wouldn't have made her feel good, either, to be honest. Once people found out where she'd gone to school or that she was an officer, they expected her to act a certain way, all gung-ho and oo-rah. Her career was a huge part of her life, but it wasn't every minute of it. The last time she'd been home, she'd gone to her mother's book club's tea party. She'd been having fun, until she was asked what she did for a living. Once her profession was known, there'd been the inevitable questions, even requests for demonstrations, like could she do a man's push-up?

Duh. As if there were even such a thing as girl push-ups

in the army. There weren't. Of course she could do regular push-ups—she never referred to them as man push-ups—but she didn't want to put down her plate of pretty appetizers to prove it at a party.

She was relieved to have remained Ballerina Baby tonight. She bid Drummer a fond adieu.

His response was different than his usual "looking forward to it." Now that I know you are alive and safe, I'll be able to sleep tonight. Lock your doors and don't talk to strangers, ok?

She hadn't done such a good job making him feel better, after all.

Drummer wasn't worried that she'd get caught in a hurricane or a tornado, nor something as common and simple as a car accident. He was worried that she'd be a victim of an assault and battery. She was the least likely woman to be a victim of a crime—not impossible, but not probable.

You, too, she wrote. By the way...

Yes?

This concern for my safety has me thinking about women in general, and crime statistics in general. Are you worried about me just because I'm a woman?

She watched the cursor blink once. Twice. Three times.

No. I'm worried about you because you're important to me, Baby. If anything bad happened to you, it would be bad for me, too.

Chloe felt her heart beating, hard, in time with the blinking of the cursor.

After long seconds, she typed one word: Same.

Lame. She was so lame. She carried her laptop into her

bedroom, closed it and plugged it in to its docking station. The sound of its familiar click brought tears to her eyes.

Tears? She refused to cry as she pulled a nightgown out from the drawer below her PT uniforms. It was just a click. Nothing but a stupid click.

It was all she had.

Drummer was the perfect guy. He genuinely cared about her. She had a friend in him, a confidant, but every time she went to bed, she was alone.

She crawled into bed and lay silently in the dark, when what she wanted to do was rage at the universe that life was unfair. She couldn't take a laptop to dinner and a movie. She couldn't kiss a laptop. She was twenty-two years old. She wanted more. She wanted passion. She wanted *sex*, but it had to be with someone who meant something to her.

Not possible. The only man she was interested in was the one in her laptop.

She tried to imagine what it would be like if her virtual boyfriend became reality. She'd have a man to rest against. Maybe they'd fall asleep together while spooning, her back to his chest.

Chloe felt herself drifting off to sleep, lulled by her own fantasy. He'd have his arm around her waist, and she'd know when he was falling asleep because the weight of his arm would grow heavier.

She snuggled the side of her face into her pillow, almost smiling as she imagined snuggling with her nameless, face-less *him*. She would be warm when she spooned against him, maybe too warm, but she wouldn't move because she loved falling asleep like this, knowing that the last face she saw before she fell asleep would be the first face she'd see when she woke up.

He'd have a handsome face. Very handsome, with light-colored eyes that crinkled at the corners a bit because he was smiling at her, enjoying every word she said, laughing at every joke.

Chloe jerked awake.

That was Thane Carter's face. Wrong man. So very wrong, and she needed him to get out of her head. She punched her pillow once, twice, and tried to fall back asleep.

Damn it.

She wished that she'd never laid eyes on First Lieutenant Thane Carter. He already made her real life harder. Now he was ruining her imaginary one, too.

Chapter Eleven

Chloe sat at her desk and struggled not to fall asleep in front of Carter.

She'd only been here two weeks, but she'd fallen asleep in her office chair twice. Carter just loved to wake her up. The first time, he'd put his phone on her desk quietly, like a sneaky weasel, then set it off to play the reveille bugle call. The next time, he'd sailed a paper airplane right into her head while he stood in the hallway. Judging from the paper airplanes littering the floor around her desk, it had taken him at least four tries to land a plane on her head—or else he'd hit her four times but she'd been sleeping too hard to notice.

If the paperwork part of her job wasn't so boring, it wouldn't be so hard to stay awake. It would also help if she wasn't trying to stay awake for thirty-six hours at a stretch. She was part of the regular duty officer rotation now. She'd come to one conclusion: there had to be a better way.

A leader didn't bring a problem to his or her superior's attention without also presenting a possible solution. She knew what the sleep-deprivation problem was. She needed to come up with a solution.

"Yo, Carter. Where can I find the schedule for the duty officers?"

"Don't worry, you're done for the month. No more garrison duty. We'll go into training for our combat missions now. This is your last thirty-six hours for two months."

"I wasn't worried. I want to see the old schedule. Is it all laid out on a calendar somewhere?"

It was like pulling teeth to get him to do it, but Carter finally sent a file from his army laptop to hers with the dates and names going back a month. She read it over, mulled it over. When there'd been only three lieutenants, it must have been brutal. With four lieutenants, it was still exhausting.

They weren't at war. They weren't deployed in a vola-
tile part of the world. They weren't even training to handle
sleep deprivation in a future war zone. This was just actual
sleep deprivation, and she couldn't see a reason to punish
themselves physically like this. Instead, there was a very
good reason for them not to: they were performing a real
law enforcement mission, not rehearsing for one, and that
mission required them to make decisions with clear heads,
not exhausted ones.

"What are you frowning at?" Carter asked. The man sure
did watch her a lot, considering she was only worth talking
to if no other single women were around.

Ha—there were no other single women around. She was
it. Tough luck for him; she didn't feel like talking. "Nothing."

When Chloe wanted to see a problem, it worked better
when she could sketch it out with old-fashioned pencil and
paper. Chloe pushed her laptop out of her way and flipped the
least-important-looking document on her desk over. The back
was a plain white page, beckoning her to find a pencil and
make it come alive. She made columns and rows, sketching
out a calendar, then wrote in the days of the week. With one
eye on the computer screen, she started transferring names
and dates, turning them from a list of words on the screen
into something she could see as a picture, shading in work
with diagonal lines, shading in time off with crosshatches.

"What are you doing?" Carter asked, sounding irritated.

"I'm concentrating."

Out of the corner of her eye, she could see him looking
up at the ceiling as if he was praying for patience, but she
ignored that and the too-familiar pang in her heart. *Handsome man; hates me.*

It had only been a couple of weeks. She'd get used to it.

A half hour later, she had a new plan. It ought to work,
it could work, but she didn't know how to go about presenting it to the level at which it needed to be approved. She
looked over at Thane. It would be nice to ask his advice, but

he'd made his feelings toward her clear the first night they'd worked together. It was up to her to keep up with him, not for him to mentor her.

Maybe Salvatore would look it over for her. She took her paper and pencil and started out the door.

"Done for the day?" Carter asked.

"Are you done for the day?" she countered. "Then I'm not, either."

Like it or not, she was tied to Thane Carter. They worked together and they had to suffer together, but if her new plan could be implemented, at least they would both get more sleep. Maybe they wouldn't get on each other's nerves so badly if they were well rested.

It was worth a try.

Thane took his place at the conference room table in the battalion headquarters building.

The commanders of each of the companies that made up the battalion were here, as well as the command sergeant-major and the primary members of the battalion staff. Notebooks, pencils, inside jokes and barbs were all brought to the table as everyone waited for the battalion commander, Colonel Stephens, to arrive.

Thane wasn't normally a part of battalion-level meetings. He'd just returned to Fort Hood yesterday after a week with his parents for Thanksgiving. As soon as he'd signed back in, the CO had signed out, taking off for his own week's leave. As the most senior platoon leader in the 584th, Thane also served as the executive officer, or XO.

The XO took over the CO's duties in his absence, so Thane was sitting in his CO's place at the battalion commander's weekly meeting.

It wasn't his first. He enjoyed them. The senior members worked well together, and that attitude transferred all the way down to the newest private.

The operations officer, Major Nord, came in and dropped a notebook onto the table. Right behind him was...Chloe.

The pang in Thane's chest was instant and too familiar. *Pretty woman; hates me.*

Thane ignored that. He'd had no idea Michaels was coming to the meeting today. It made a commander look bad when he didn't know what his own people were up to.

She took a seat behind the major, in a chair against the wall rather than at the table. Why was a butter bar who'd only been in the battalion for three weeks here at a battalion staff meeting? Michaels should have briefed him on her purpose here. Hell, she ought to have given him a heads-up that she'd be here at all. Thane glared at her. She pretended she didn't see him.

"Staff. Atten—*tion.*" The major called the room to attention, and everyone stood, heels together, arms straight by their sides, as the colonel entered the conference room.

"At ease," Colonel Stephens said. He sat at the head of the table, then everyone took their seats. Colonel Stephens looked up one side of the table and down the other, no doubt doing a quick mental roll call of his own staff. He nodded Thane's way. "I see we've got Lieutenant Carter here today."

"Good morning, sir."

"All right, let's get out of here on time for once. S-1. Go."

The S-1 was the staff officer who handled administration for the battalion. As the captain went over his current challenges, Thane found his attention wandering...to Michaels. Why the ever-loving hell was she here? She wasn't taking notes, or else he'd assume she was a Goody Two-shoes who'd asked to sit in for her own professional development.

The S-2 began her report, covering intel and physical security of the property. Finally, thirty minutes into the meeting, the S-3 began his report. Major Nord sat forward in his chair. "As we discussed, sir, we're considering changing the current schedule for the MPDOs."

Thane glanced at Michaels. MPDO, the Military Police

Duty Officer, concerned them personally. Since they were lieutenants, they were the only two in the room who actually pulled that duty.

Major Nord turned and motioned to Michaels to come to the table. She stood to his left. "I've asked Lieutenant Michaels to be present to answer questions. She designed the new schedule."

Holy hell. She'd been here three weeks. *Three weeks.*

Michaels's plan was simple. The lieutenants of two companies would share MPDO duties, making at least eight lieutenants available. They'd be on call for two months instead of one, but they'd serve every eighth day instead of every fourth. This would be less disruptive to each company's training, and it would be less taxing on the individual lieutenants physically. It also meant that lieutenants from one company would be the officer in charge while another company had its usual month of garrison duty, but Michaels pointed out that lieutenants covered shifts for lieutenants from other companies on occasion already.

It took Michaels just minutes to present the idea. She stated her objective, outlined the current course of action and compared it to her alternate course of action, presenting her logic in the same order as a damned battalion-level MDMP, a formal and lengthy process to develop missions.

Total overkill.

Granted, she kept it brief and there was nothing wrong with following that MDMP sequence, but it was overkill for a platoon leader to use the format. It was overkill for a new lieutenant to be here at all.

Then again, this was the girl who'd held court at the grill, decreeing what ketchup and mustard represented while everyone listened. Why shouldn't she stand here and tell a roomful of company commanders that she could schedule their lieutenants more effectively?

The S-3 had already endorsed the plan, obviously, or he wouldn't have had Michaels present it. Thane had to admit that pulling those thirty-six hours less than once a week sounded a hell of a lot better than the way they'd been doing it. Honestly, he didn't know whether to love her or hate her.

Love was out of the question. Hate crept in.

It crept in, and it found a resentful place to stay when the battalion commander turned to Thane and put him on the spot. "You've been pulling these thirty-six-hour days for how long now? How long have you been in my battalion?"

"Two years, sir."

"For two years, you've been pulling these shifts?"

Everyone was looking at Thane as if these shifts were something unusual—or as if he shouldn't have been pulling them for two years.

Thane leaned forward. "That is the job, sir. I execute the mission as assigned. All the lieutenants in the battalion do, one month out of every three."

His battalion CO studied him for a moment. "That's good."

You're damned right, that's good. I didn't whine and complain about it like Michaels.

Colonel Stephens turned back to Major Nord. "I want the thirty-six hours cut down. After they work an overnight, I want the lieutenants to check in with their companies and handle any meetings or paperwork or whatever the hell the commanders want to do with them, but let's get them off duty by 1100 hours. I don't want a bunch of zombies behind the wheel after the flag goes down."

"Yes, sir." Major Nord jotted down the battalion commander's new orders. "Are we adopting the new schedule, as well?"

Colonel Stephens settled back in his chair. "What do you say, Carter? You're the one who's been pulling these thirty-six-hour shifts."

He didn't even glance Michaels's way. "I think it will work, sir."

"Sure it will. It's so simple it makes you wonder why nobody thought of it sooner."

Thane kept his expression neutral. Inside, he was seething at the subtle criticism that Thane hadn't brought this to his attention sooner.

"One company has to suck it down to get started. I know you just finished pulling rotation every fourth day, but are you LTs in the 584th volunteering to keep working another month with the 401st?"

Clearly the battalion commander thought Thane had seen the plan before this meeting. Maybe Thane's CO had. If so, he'd failed to let Thane know whether or not he wanted his lieutenants to commit to another month of shifts. Even if those shifts would be only every eighth day, it would still take each of his lieutenants out of training and keep them on the duty schedule through December. If anyone had planned to take leave over Christmas, they might be forced to change their plans.

Make a decision, Lieutenant. It was a stock phrase, one meant to remind new officers that it was better to make a decision, even if it turned out to be the wrong one, than it was to waffle and never decide. Thane decided. "It looks like a good plan in the long run, sir. We'll suck it down for the next month to put it in motion."

The meeting moved on. Thane listened and contributed appropriately, but his thoughts were still focused on Michaels. On one hand, he admired her ability to see a problem, come up with a solution and present it to the battalion commander. That took chutzpah. That took confidence. And for just one second, as Thane looked at her profile, he remembered walking toward her on that pool deck, drawn like a magnet to that confidence.

He hadn't realized he was staring at her, but she must have felt the weight of his stare, because she glanced at him.

He looked away. She'd gone around him to the S-3. Thane was right there in her office with her. As the senior platoon leader, he was the person she could have come to for input. As her acting XO, he was the person she should have come to before the commander. Hell, just as the guy whose desk was next to hers, he was the man to whom she should have casually mentioned her idea. Why hadn't she?

No reason, except she wanted to catch him off guard. Publicly.

Love her or hate her? She'd tried to make him look bad in front of the battalion commander.

Hate it is, then.

"Michaels!"

Chloe had had enough of that drill sergeant tone to last her for the rest of her life. She turned around to find the person who'd just addressed her as if she were the lowliest plebe. It had better be someone who outranked her, or she'd be pissed.

It was Carter. She was pissed.

He walked up to her. "I hope you're happy."

Big life. Happiness. Drummer respected those goals.

"I hope so, too. Why do you think I'm happy?"

"You succeeded in getting your revenge."

"I succeeded in getting us a more sane duty schedule."

"Never take your XO by surprise like that. You could have at least given me a warning order."

Warning orders were basic communications that alerted units to stand by for new orders. She didn't owe him any warning order. "What would I be getting revenge for?"

"For the flashlight episode. For the way you think I threw you on the radio that first night. Who knows what your beef is? You tell me."

As if she'd open a discussion on how he treated single women with ugly faces when there was nobody better to talk to. That colored her opinion of him, but that was personal. She hadn't let that motivate her to do anything positive or negative, professionally.

Chloe started walking. Carter did, too.

"So, you think I actually developed and presented a new duty officer schedule to the battalion commander *not* to solve a problem but just to get revenge on you for something about radios and flashlights? Let me put your mind at ease, Carter. I could give a rat's tail about those things."

"You should have told me you were attending the staff meeting today. Instead, you went behind my back to the battalion S-3. When does the most junior platoon leader in the whole battalion go hang out with the S-3?" Thane stopped short.

She stopped.

Darn it, she shouldn't have stopped. "What now?"

"You know him from West Point, don't you? The S-3 is a West Pointer."

"He's a major. He had to have graduated, like, when I was in fifth grade. I don't know him. You seriously are paranoid." She held up her right hand and flashed her class ring at him. "This really doesn't communicate directly with the Pentagon. I told you that ring-knocker thing was a myth."

She'd told him that during that long, cozy talk, the day she'd spent with a handsome man who, it turned out, hated her. In silence, she started walking again.

Carter was silent, too, keeping pace beside her.

Controlled confrontation. They had to work together. They had to rely on each other professionally, but right now, they were both seething in silence. This time, she was the one who stopped walking.

He stopped walking.

"I didn't go to the S-3. I went to Salvatore. He liked the plan. We went to the CO together. The CO picked up the phone and called the S-3, and that's when I met Major Nord." It was all on the up-and-up. There'd been no subterfuge involved.

"Why would you go to Salvatore when I'm sitting at the desk next to yours?"

"Because, Carter, you've made your position toward me

perfectly clear from the first ride-along. You say you're not here to be my mentor? Fine. The kindest thing I could say is that you at least set an example, but the truth is, your contempt came through loud and clear when you told me to try to keep up."

"You said all work and no play."

"I am working. You're just mad that I'm keeping up."

She turned on her heel and walked away.

Chapter Twelve

I wanted to talk to you today. Chloe hit Send.

Great. I'm here. Let's talk.

Something happened at work, like six hours ago, and I wished I could talk to you then and there.

You have a phone, Ballerina. I have a phone.

Chloe stared at those words in horror. He wanted to talk? Actually speak? With voices instead of fonts?

She couldn't do that. She just couldn't bare her soul on a telephone. When she saw her words written out in pink, she often had second thoughts before sending them. If they'd been live on the phone the other night, she probably would have blurted out that he didn't need to worry about her because she had an entire police department behind her, and that would have been the end of their relationship as they knew it. Ballerina Baby would never have been the same to Different Drummer.

I can't call you. Talking is not the same as writing. It would change everything. I need to keep you in my life just as we are. I rely on it. She typed fast and hit Send without pausing, rushing the words as if she were blurting them out loud. Pleading out loud.

Seconds ticked by without any blue words.

This was why, this was exactly why, she didn't want to speak to him on the phone. Without having a chance to think through each sentence, she would say the wrong thing.

But blue words appeared. I meant that I write to you from my phone app, and you could do the same. I know you use your laptop, but that's not as handy for you, obviously. If you downloaded the app on your phone, then you could write to me anytime—like six hours ago, when you needed me. If you wrote to me and I was anywhere I could possibly answer you immediately, I would. I don't want things to change, either. I rely on our conversations, too, and this would make it easier to have those conversations.

Chloe lifted her eyes from the laptop screen to the sunset. It was getting cooler now, past Thanksgiving and heading into December. Once the sun went down, she'd have to leave the plastic chair and table she'd bought for her concrete porch and go inside her apartment. The season was changing, and her evening routine had to change with it. Would it be so awful to change how she communicated with Drummer, too?

If she started using her phone, he would be writing to her throughout her day. She tried to imagine sitting at her desk and getting a quick note from him. It would be…warm. Something to offset the presence of—

Carter.

Chloe froze in her chair as she squinted across the parking lot. She'd been looking between two buildings to see the colorful sunset, but some movement on a balcony had drawn her eye to the building on the left. A man with dark hair in a military cut, with shoulders that looked buff even from here, had walked onto his balcony, head bowed, phone in his hand. Good God, that couldn't be Carter, could it?

It could be any military guy. She knew Carter lived in this complex, but she hadn't seen him around. She'd never gone back to the pool, and she'd never tried to find out which of the other five buildings was his.

She held very still, so she wouldn't draw attention to herself as she checked the man out. Whom was she kidding? That was Carter. She'd spent enough hours with him to recognize him anywhere.

He lived on the third floor of his building, just as she lived on the third floor of hers, directly across the parking lot. He stopped staring at his phone, letting his hand drop as if he didn't like what he saw on the screen, and then he looked up—or rather, straight across the parking lot. Toward her.

Goddamn it, goddamn it...

Chloe got up from her chair, carrying the laptop but leaving the wineglass, and ducked into her apartment, sliding the door shut. She pulled the string to close the vertical blinds. Maybe he couldn't tell it was her from a distance. After all, she had the advantage of being able to change her hair from a ballerina bun to loose, long hair. Maybe that was adequate camouflage.

Her heart was pounding. She sank onto her couch and set the laptop in her lap. Her phone was where she'd left it earlier, on her footlocker-turned-coffee-table. She stared at the phone a moment. It was an instrument that could change the best thing in her life to something different. Something better. Something worse.

Her routine was going to change, anyway. Her nightly glass of wine on the porch with Drummer had just gotten blown up. It would never be relaxing again, not when she'd have to keep an eye out for Carter. Why not download the app on her phone? It would be like having an ally in the office, someone with whom she could exchange sardonic observations whenever Carter was being especially Carter-like.

Okay, I'm going to download the app to my phone now.

Chloe hit Send.

Chloe.

That had to be Chloe on that balcony, with that long hair swishing over her shoulders as she disappeared into her apartment.

It's not Chloe, it's Michaels. But he'd forgotten how long her hair was when it was down. The door slid shut behind her, and the sunset's golden beams hit her apartment and reflected off the glass. Michaels had made another rookie mistake by choosing that apartment. In the summer, that direct sunlight was going to overpower her air-conditioning.

He looked down at the phone clenched in his hand. I'm going to download the app.

He tore his mind away from Chloe, happy to be distracted from the sight of long hair swishing in the sunset. This was great news; if Ballerina disappeared again, at least every message he sent would go to both her laptop and her phone, doubling his chances of reaching her.

More pink words demanded his attention. Have you ever gotten your dream job and then found out it's not so dreamy?

He glanced across the parking lot at the closed glass door with the annoyingly bright reflection. Isn't that pretty much every job in the world?

Uh-oh. I didn't realize you didn't like your job, either. Do you ever just want to go crazy and yell "Take this job and shove it"?

(Johnny Paycheck, at every karaoke night in every bar, everywhere. Too easy.) It's not the job. It's the coworkers. Coworker, singular. One lousy coworker is trying to sabotage me.

Are you okay? Is he succeeding?

Her questions brought Thane up short. Since the night he'd worked that domestic and then hadn't been able to reach Ballerina, she'd been repeatedly asking him if *he* was okay. He didn't like Ballerina assuming he was vulnerable. It didn't sit right.

Maybe she imagined him as some weakling. He wished he could tell her he was a soldier—for her own peace of mind, of course. Not for his own pride.

Of course I'm okay. Of course I am.

He was. Although he'd been angry with Chl—Michaels at the staff meeting, Thane was coming out of the whole episode with a much better work schedule.

This coworker won't succeed in making me look bad. It's just a pain in the neck to deal with. Thane refrained from using *she* or *her* to refer to the coworker. Ballerina didn't need to think that he was vulnerable to attacks from a girl. It had nothing to do with his pride.

Okay, it had everything to do with his pride.

Ballerina didn't seem to notice. I hope it's nothing more than a pain in the neck, I really do. This app is taking forever to load onto my phone, by the way. It says the most recent version is from 2014. I bet it's no longer being actively updated. I hate when developers just quit maintaining their apps. I had a yoga app I really loved, and one day, it just wasn't there. The phone had done one of those automatic upgrades overnight, and the old app hadn't been updated to handle it. Poof! It was gone.

Ballerina did yoga, did she? Thane smiled at the clue. He spared one second to glance down at the pool and only half a second to remember how he'd once wondered if Michaels was into yoga. Boy, he'd gotten that wrong. She probably kickboxed opponents for fun.

But Ballerina? She really did do yoga. It fit with what he knew of her. She always found something funny in their mundane conversations, because she wanted to make him laugh. And she wanted to make him laugh because she cared about him. She was the kind of nurturing person who wouldn't want to do anyone any harm. After a day in a patrol car dealing with angry and upset people, he appreciated that. He needed that. He needed Ballerina in his life.

If he told her so, it might sound a bit intense, coming out of the blue when the subject was entirely different. He kept it light. A yoga app? There are a million of them. You must have found another one to replace it.

Well, yes, but it was never the same. I liked things the way they were. It would REALLY never be the same if we had to download a new conversation app. What if we didn't have a chance to switch to a new app before this one went poof? I'd know you were out there somewhere, but I wouldn't be able to find you. I'd have to post one of those personal ads. You know the kind, the ones aimed at perfect strangers that say, "We talked in line at the coffee shop and I fell in love with your shark-tooth necklace." I bet those ads never work.

Thane turned his back on the reflected sunset and leaned against his balcony railing as he typed. The sun was sinking fast. It was turning colder. That one wouldn't work with me. I've never worn a shark-tooth necklace. I'm not sure where to buy a thing like that. Who makes them? Maybe the guy who answers the ad could tell you, and you could tell me.

What kind of necklace do you wear, then?

Dog tags.

The desire to tell her the truth hit him with almost brutal force. He wore dog tags. He was in the service, and he wanted to change the rules of their game. He wanted real names, real jobs, real contact. Ballerina was terrific, but lately, instead of filling the loneliness, talking to her only amplified it.

He knew what had changed. He'd met Chloe Michaels, and now he couldn't stop wanting everything that was missing in his long-distance friendship with Ballerina. A words-only relationship meant there was no smile, no sun-kissed skin, no swish of hair, no sharing of a silly hot dog test.

No sex.

Long-distance relationships were a big part of the military. Couples did stay together through deployments by texting and writing letters just as he and Ballerina did, but there was one important difference. Those couples knew their letter-writing months were temporary. Even if a whole year apart stretched before them, they still knew that they would be reunited.

Thane needed that. Ballerina was like a girlfriend, but she wasn't. He needed to know that someday, he would go on leave and fly across the country just to meet her. He wanted to walk off a plane and be greeted with a hug and a smile. He wanted to know their relationship would continue to grow, because it was the best thing he'd found, and he didn't want it to die a stagnant death.

I don't wear jewelry. Our ad would need to say something like, "My words were in blue and yours were in pink. We talked about everything and I could tell you anything, except my name. That was a mistake, because now I've lost you. If you don't respond to this ad, I'll be wondering where you are for the rest of my life."

A chill settled around him as he looked at the words he'd just sent. This app could stop working without warning. If he lost her, he probably would be crazy enough to try a personal ad, because he'd have nowhere else to even begin a search. Ballerina was right; those ads never worked. Where could he even place an ad aimed at the entire United States? If the app crashed, Ballerina might as well be wiped off the face of the earth.

Thane typed quickly against that cold future. My ad was a little too real, wasn't it? But it will happen. Sooner or later, this app will be obsolete. If we're not going to exchange names and numbers, we should at least give each other an email address. We can keep using this app exclusively, if that's what you want, but we should have a backup just in case. It would leave too big a hole in my life if a computer

glitch stole you from me. Can we bend our rules this once?
An email address so that we aren't vulnerable?

Thane hesitated before hitting Send. He didn't want her
to keep thinking of him as vulnerable. He hit the backspace
arrow with his thumb, back, back, back.

An email address so that we won't have our routine upset
by a computer glitch one day?

He hesitated again. A routine. He couldn't call a girl a
routine. That was no way to woo a woman. Back, back, back,
before he could fall back into his fantasy of having an actual
woman to woo. Woo? Sheesh.

An email address so that a programmer's laziness doesn't
tear us apart without warning?

He hit Send.
The cursor blinked in silence.
He hadn't been persuasive enough; she was taking too
long to think about it. She didn't want anything to change.
She'd been crystal clear about that, but exchanging email addresses really wouldn't have any effect at all. It was just extra
insurance that they'd be able to remain online friends. He
wanted more, true, but he also couldn't lose what they had.

Thane gave in to the evening chill and went back inside
his apartment to try again. Don't be afraid that I'll start spam-
ming your inbox. It's only to have in case the app crashes.
Trust me, an email address won't change a thing.

Pink letters spelled out an email address, highlander@
ctx.com.

Thane tapped the email address quickly, as if it were
going to disappear, and created a new contact for it in his
phone. First name: Ballerina. Last name: Baby.

There, she was safe in his phone. Adding her to the list
of people he interacted with every day made her more real

than ever. She was a contact he could reach with an email address that ended *@ctx.com*, the same as half the soldiers in his platoon.

Half his soldiers?

They had that same ending on their email addresses because *ctx* stood for Central Texas. The suffix *@ctx.com* was a popular internet provider's domain name, a company out of Austin.

Ballerina lived near him.

Thane slowly sat on his couch, keeping his eyes on his phone, not daring to adjust his grip on the device. It was like a grenade that was about to go off.

This changed everything. Thank God.

He hesitated, thumbs over the screen. She was afraid of change; he needed to break this to her gently.

Hey, BB, you know how we've wondered whether this app matched us up by design or by pure luck?

Yes?

I think it was by design.

Why?

Because I recognize the @ctx.com part of your email address. We both live in the Austin area.

Nothing, just a white screen.

He typed in his email address for her. It ended with @gmail.com. That domain name could be from anywhere in the world. If she'd had one of those email addresses, too, a gmail or even an old aol.com, they'd never know they lived in the same state.

But she'd used ctx.com, so she was either in Austin or somewhere reasonably close, like Temple or Waco.

Or here in Killeen.

Thane stood to pace. She was his closest friend, his favorite person to talk to, and now…she could be more. This was incredible. This was fantastic.

This is awful, she wrote.

Thane stopped pacing. It's a lot of things, but not awful.

She didn't reply. He ran one hand up the back of his neck as he waited.

Hey, Ballerina? You there? Don't go silent on me. Please. As soon as he hit Send, he regretted it. That had sounded too much like begging, like a vulnerable man begging. He needed to keep it light. If you disappear now, I'll have to take those personal ads out all over Austin.

Silence.

He tried again. The only quotes I can think of about silence are from Simon & Garfunkel. Please don't make me write out the lyrics to "Sound of Silence." Short version: silence sucks.

At last, she responded. I can't catch my breath. Don't you see? This feels like the app crashed, after all. Ballerina and Drummer as we knew it just changed. Forever.

Chapter Thirteen

Chloe chucked the live hand grenade as far as she could, then dived behind the dirt berm with the NCO in charge of this position on the firing line. The explosion vibrated the earth. Dirt sprinkled from the sky onto her Kevlar helmet.

For the first time in forty-eight hours, she smiled. Sometimes, when everything was going wrong, a girl just needed to blow crap up.

"Nice throw, ma'am."

"Thanks, Sergeant."

"Most women don't throw that well."

And…poof. There went her good mood. "Seriously, Sergeant? Should I give you the formal lecture on gender bias, or should I just point out that the only person who's failed to qualify so far today was a guy?"

The soldier to their right threw his grenade. Chloe and the sergeant stayed crouched behind their berm with their heads down, but they knew the grenade hadn't gone very far and hadn't gone very straight, because the explosion shook the earth hard and dirt rained down on them.

They cussed in unison.

"Make that two men who failed," the sergeant muttered.

Chloe almost laughed. "I'm going to be very fair and not say that most men don't throw well, even though those two suck."

The sergeant chuckled, maybe a little nervously, maybe a little relieved. "You've got a point there, ma'am."

The order to clear the firing line came from the loudspeakers on the tower.

Chloe stood up and dusted herself off. "All right. I'm outta here. Stay safe—especially when those two come back on the line to try again."

Chloe cleared the range and returned to the little set of

wood bleachers behind the firing line. As she took out her ear plugs, other members of the 584th took their places by the berms, waited for their commands from the tower—which was more like a lifeguard stand—and then threw their hand grenades, one at a time. Everyone on the bleachers booed and cheered the throws, acting more like fans at a baseball game than soldiers practicing the use of a deadly close-quarters-combat weapon.

Chloe's grenade-induced adrenaline buzz faded as she drank from her canteen. Explosions were all well and good, but it didn't change the fact that her relationship with Drummer had come to an abrupt end.

Drummer didn't get it. No, Ballerina. This is the opposite of a crash. Instead of disappearing, now we can actually appear. In person.

Night after night, she'd been going to bed lonely, angry that the only man she cared about was stuck in her laptop. Now, she was angry that he was so eager to jump out of that laptop and kill this friendship.

Don't you want to meet, Baby?

No.

His silence after that had been awful, which was why, exactly why, she was afraid to talk to him live. She could be too direct, something that was good in the military, but bad in every other aspect of life. She'd hurt Drummer with that curt *no*.

The only way to explain herself was to lay her insecure soul bare. What if we met and you decided you didn't like me?

Not possible.

That was very sweet, but very wrong. It was quite possible

that he wouldn't like her. It happened to her all the time, in situations where she least expected it. She'd just had a nice surprise insult from the sergeant on the firing line. The last time she'd gone to church with her parents, she'd worn her dress blue uniform, and a lovely little old lady had hissed at her that she was stealing a job from a man.

Drummer wouldn't be mad at her for being a girl...but he might not like the fact that she was a soldier.

He might not like that she was in law enforcement, either. Just this week, Chloe had stopped her patrol car behind a motorist with a flat tire. The driver had started ranting and raving at her before she'd even walked up to him, furious that she'd stopped to ticket him for blocking traffic. It hadn't even occurred to her to give him a ticket. She'd stopped because her red and blue flashing lights would keep him safer from oncoming traffic while he changed his tire.

Three more grenades were thrown. Each explosion vibrated the cold plank she sat on. The next three soldiers filed onto the firing line. Even in his helmet and combat gear, Carter was easy to recognize. Something about his height or the set of his shoulders...

Thane Carter. There was another person she'd thought liked her, but he'd decided she sucked. He was even pissed off that she'd developed a better work schedule for him.

It's always possible for someone not to like me, she'd written to Drummer last night.

His answer had been direct. Tell me what about you is unlikable. In six months of near-daily conversations, I haven't seen it yet.

She'd paused, hands poised over her laptop keys. He might not like her because she was...what? She wasn't a bad person. She wasn't a bad cop. She didn't even look bad in a mirror. She'd had another moment of clarity on her bright red couch: she liked herself.

She just could never predict when someone else wouldn't.

The range ended too soon. The NCO in charge hustled

the troops through a trash detail, then called them into formation and marched them out to the dirt parking lot. Chloe didn't need to look toward Carter for a clue about what to do. She already knew when a sergeant ordered troops to fall in line, he wasn't addressing commissioned officers. She walked behind the formation with Carter.

They didn't speak. They had nothing to talk about.

The parking lot was empty. The troops were here. The trucks were not. *Hurry up and wait* was the army way. Everyone sat on the ground in place to wait, helmets off, phones in more hands than not. Chloe didn't feel like sitting. It was nice, as an officer, to have the prerogative to stay on her feet and pace a little bit behind the troops.

Carter was doing the same. The frosty silence between them continued, until Carter pulled out his personal cell phone. Chloe pulled out hers. If Carter could do it, she could do it.

She checked her app. Drummer still thought meeting in person was a great idea—and his flashing icon indicated he was online right now.

She typed as quickly as she could on her phone. What if we meet and have nothing to talk about?

That won't happen. It can't. Star Trek can be endlessly dissected, if nothing else.

A laugh escaped her. The soldiers didn't seem to notice, but Carter looked at her sharply.

Jeez. She was allowed to laugh in uniform. She turned her back to Carter, and gave her attention to the man who didn't disapprove of her. Yet.

Thane was as hungry and tired as every other soldier by the time the trucks finally pulled into the parking lot.

Hungry, tired...and hopeful. Ballerina seemed to be adjusting to the idea that they lived too close not to meet. Not even a long, uncomfortable ride in the back of a troop transport could dampen his spirits now.

Ballerina was in the middle of doing something. She kept dropping quick BRBs, the acronym for *Be Right Back*. Thane imagined her at a dance rehearsal, stealing moments between scenes to check her phone, the way he was stealing moments to check his.

He pocketed his phone to vault into the back of the truck and take a place on a hard bench. He looked around at the soldiers and tried to imagine a dance troupe instead. A ballerina…her hair must be up in a bun, exposing a graceful neck. She'd be intent upon her work, physically strenuous work, so perhaps she'd have a fine sheen of sweat on a clean face. Really, not so different from a female soldier.

With a jolt, he realized his gaze had drifted to Chloe Michaels. She really was quite pretty and her hair was always tightly pulled back like a ballerina, and—

Michaels plopped her Kevlar helmet on her head and fastened the chin strap.

So much for that.

The truck took off. Thane checked his phone.

The ctx email address I gave you is new. It's not the one I had when I first signed up for this app. We weren't matched up because we both live in Austin.

But you live near Austin now? **Thane asked.**

Yes, but I'm not what you think I am.

Not human? Not female? Not in your 20s?

I'm all those things, but I'm not a native Texan.

I'm not, either.

I'm not a ballerina.

I'm not, either.

At the opposite end of the truck bed, he heard Michaels snort in amusement at something on her phone screen.

Thane returned to his phone, but he felt impatient. He was done with phone screens. He glanced at Michaels again, at her graceful neck and her elegant profile. He wanted a real woman, a real dinner, a real conversation, and he knew exactly whom he wanted to have it with.

Ballerina Baby.

Baby, doesn't it drive you crazy that the app knows something about us that we don't know? Let's get together and figure out why this app matched us up.

He waited. The brown scenery went by, uninteresting, flat. The diesel engine droned on. Then his phone vibrated in his hand, two shorts and a long.

I guess I'm just delaying the inevitable. How do you want to meet?

How? ASAP.

Thane kicked back on his couch. Thursday night in December meant an NFL game was on, same old routine.

December means the Nutcracker. I'm not a ballerina, but I do love the ballet.

But this Thursday, he was making plans to meet Ballerina, and that was most definitely something new.

He'd told her months ago that he'd never seen a live ballet, so now she suggested they meet in Austin at a ballet performance: I guarantee you'll recognize every single piece of music in the second half. I just hold my breath the whole time, one great dance after another. It's a celebration of the most luxurious foods from around the world.

Wait—the Nutcracker ballet is about food?

Ballerina was the only friend with whom he could learn something new about ballet while watching an NFL game. She had the game on, too, but she wasn't impressed with the lackluster offense. Neither was he. The ballet convo was more absorbing than watching another punt.

Coffee is represented by a sort of Flamenco ballet in Spanish costumes, for example.

Thane chuckled, alone in his apartment. I thought ballets were supposed to be romantic. It's about food? I can get behind coffee.

Well, it's supposed to be a kind of paradise, see? The nutcracker has become a prince, and he wants Clara to have the best of everything. Coffee is one of the best things in life, so it really is romantic.

I love a girl who thinks food is romantic. Is there a dance for steak and potatoes?

No—it's flowers. Sugar plums and mirlitons.

What's a mirliton? Never mind. I'm in.

Together, they logged on to the ticketing website. Together, they decided which seats to get. She insisted on paying for her own. Thane couldn't really stop her from buying Mezzanine D130 for herself, so he bought Mezzanine D131, and silently vowed that he'd be paying for dinner and drinks and anything else she wanted to do the rest of the night. The rest of the weekend.

The rest of their lives.

I'm looking forward to it, Baby.

"Friday night. Almost quitting time, Boss." Sergeant First Class Lloyd walked into Thane's office. "Do you have big plans for the weekend, sir?"

Thane could speak freely, because Michaels had left about fifteen minutes ago. "Yes, Sergeant First Class, as a matter of fact, I do."

"Kicking ass and taking names?"

"Not until next week." Again, since Michaels had left, Thane could speak freely. "That new duty officer schedule is a godsend. I have actual weekends."

"Whiskey and women then, sir?"

"Wom*an*. Singular. Just one."

Lloyd pulled Michaels's desk chair over with a squeak of wheels. "I didn't even know you were dating anyone. Is this exclusive?"

"After tomorrow night, it will be."

Lloyd cleared his throat before adopting a fatherly tone. "This sounds serious, Lieutenant Carter."

"It is."

It felt good, really good, to say he was serious about Ballerina. Thane had never been more serious about a girl in his life.

"My wife is going to want all the details, sir. How long have you known this woman?"

"Since June."

"But—" Lloyd sat back, incredulous. "You never—"

"We've been friends since June, just friends." Thane didn't bring up pen pals. He didn't want to have to defend an online-only relationship. It wouldn't be online-only for much longer, anyway. "But this weekend, we're taking it to the next level. I want to do this right, a big night out. I'm taking her to the *Nutcracker* in Austin, for starters."

Sergeant First Class Lloyd got one of those grins on his face, like he knew something that Thane didn't know. "When a man looks as excited as you do about going to the ballet, the woman must be something special. How special are we talking, sir?"

If she's even one-quarter as funny and smart and caring and happy as I think she is...who can resist happiness?

"If this weekend goes the way I think it will, I could be buying a diamond ring for someone as a Christmas gift."

Chapter Fourteen

Seat D130.

She'd be sitting in D130. Thane's heart pounded as he headed up the stairs to the mezzanine level. He could run this flight of stairs without breaking a sweat, but knowing each stair brought him closer to Ballerina Baby made his heart pound in a way exercise didn't.

He was stuck going at a snail's pace, moving with the crowd of folks dressed for the holidays, little girls with tinsel in their hair, little boys wearing their first neckties. Red and green, silver and gold were the colors of Christmas, but Ballerina had told him she'd wear something pink and blue, like the words that made up their friendship.

Thane scanned the crowd, looking for pink and blue in the holiday-colored sea that flowed steadily upward. He'd dressed for an Austin Saturday night at the theater, navy blazer and a dress shirt, no tie, with dark-washed jeans. Like most of the men, he wore polished cowboy boots, because he'd lived in Texas for years now, and he was taking a girl out on the town tonight.

He reached the top of the stairs. The mezzanine level's lobby was simple, a carpeted space between the theater doors to his right and a glass wall to his left. Beyond the glass, the view of Austin at night was the star of the show.

It couldn't hold his attention. Thane walked straight to the theater doors, waving off the program an usher held out. The house lights were still up. Conversation among those finding their seats provided a background hum of pleasant expectations. Individual instruments were being tuned in the orchestra pit, their random notes adding to that sense of building excitement.

Thane headed down the aisle toward the balcony railing. Row D would be only four rows from the front edge. Ballerina had preferred being in the center of row D rather than off to one side of row A. She'd written passionately about being able to see the entire scene and symmetry of the choreography from the center; she really loved this ballet.

Thane put his hand on the railing, feeling a sense of vertigo as he headed down the aisle at the crowd's pace, keeping an eye on the letters that designated the seating. Row I, row H, row G.

He hadn't felt this lightness or eagerness or whatever it was since…well, since that poolside afternoon with Chloe. He'd been so certain, so sure that person was going to be part of his life, a good part. The ground had dropped out from under him when he'd realized she was his fellow platoon leader. That onslaught of vertigo had been sickening.

This vertigo was intoxicating. This was pure anticipation. This was Ballerina. He'd known her for six months, not one afternoon. He knew her likes and dislikes, her sense of humor, her favorite shows and songs. He knew she cared for him. He knew her heart's desire was to have more friends, her goal in life was happiness.

This was it. The real it. The one woman who might end his bachelor days.

Row D, at last.

Thane started to sidestep his way toward the middle. D117, 118…

He lifted his eyes, his heart in his throat. The seats in the middle were still empty. Beyond them, people were coming down the aisle on the opposite side. A white-haired couple, a young family, a beautiful woman in black, eye-catchingly beautiful—

That woman in black.

Michaels?

It took him a second, but he recognized her. Her black dress reminded him of an ice-skater, with a pastel bow tied around her waist before the skirt flared out. As always, just the sight of her made his jaw clench and his muscles tense.

Her hair was pinned up, but not pulled back as tightly as usual. It was looser, softer, and a few pieces had come down and were sort of wavy. *Tendrils*, that was the word.

Thane stopped as she continued down the far aisle. For the love of—what the *hell* was Michaels doing here? This was worse, exponentially worse, than the way she'd shown up without warning at the battalion staff meeting. Not only was Michaels at the same performance, she was going to sit in the mezzanine, disrupting his night like she disrupted everything else. Now how was she going to attack him, undermine him, make him miserable? He didn't want to deal with Michaels and her damned perfect *tendrils* when he was dying to meet someone else.

"Are you going to pass me or not?" A man in the seat before him had twisted sideways to give him room.

"Sorry."

But Thane took only one more step before stopping, watching in horror as Michaels entered row D from the other side. Good God, what were the odds? This was insane. It was the biggest night of his life, the night when he was finally going to meet the woman of his dreams, and Michaels was here to make it all difficult.

He retreated. He backed out of the row and went back up a few steps, row E, row F, going upstream against the flow of people. He paused there. He'd let Michaels take her seat, then he'd go back in and be careful not to look toward her end of the row as he took his seat in the center. If he didn't make eye contact, he wouldn't have to acknowledge her existence at all.

He watched Michaels pass seat after seat after seat, smiling and nodding thanks as she worked her way into the row, his horror growing as she got closer and closer to the center of the row, right to where he and Ballerina were going to meet.

No.

Michaels was wearing black, not pink and blue. It was a

freak coincidence that she was standing in the center of the row. She'd probably entered from the wrong side and would keep moving to this end, to a seat near his aisle.

The house lights dimmed halfway. Patrons started hustling toward their seats in earnest. Michaels stayed where she was, right in the center, and sat down.

Thane didn't move as the world dropped out from under him.

Then anger propelled him. Thane turned to walk up a few more rows. He didn't want Michaels to see him. He'd wait, out of the way, until he saw Ballerina show up, because Michaels was not, could not be, Ballerina.

He stomped up to row G. Row H.

Not. Possible.

There'd been some mistake. Thane turned around and leaned his back against the wall, leaving room for others to continue past him. He focused fiercely on the row closest to the railing. That was A. The next one back was B, then C, and...D. No mistake. Michaels was sitting in D. In the center.

He glared daggers at the back of her head, hating all those tendrils and curls and *flowers*. His heart contracted hard in his chest; those flowers in her hair were pink and blue.

Ballerina was Michaels.

The house lights went dark. The chair to her left remained empty. The orchestra continued tuning up, the random, discordant notes from individual instruments screeching into his skull.

An usher with a flashlight asked Thane if he needed help finding his seat. Thane grabbed the program from the usher and sat in the closest seat that was open. He watched Michaels look down her row to her left, then to her right.

He refused to feel guilty. Michaels wouldn't exactly jump for joy if he came sidling through row D and took Drummer's seat. She'd have a heart attack. She hated him as much as he hated her.

The conductor raised his baton; the overture began. Thane

wasn't directly behind Michaels, but off to the side, so he could see a little bit of her profile. Her face was illuminated by the light of her cell phone as she typed something rapidly. Her earring sparkled as it reflected the phone's light, then she tucked a curl behind her ear. Her hair was disconcertingly feminine, a few little braids holding the flowers among those loose curls. It looked like something a bride would wear.

Total overkill.

Typical Michaels. He hoped she hadn't paid money to have her hair done like that. Tonight was just supposed to be a meet and greet. She'd placed way too much importance on the whole thing. She'd taken it too seriously.

The curtain rose, and she turned off the too-bright light of her phone screen. The audience applauded. Thane's phone buzzed in the inner pocket of his blazer. Two shorts and a long.

No way in hell was he going to check that. All those months of pink words, all that hope he'd placed on them, and she'd been lying to him the whole time. Her personality in real life was nothing like she'd been online. There was a word for that, for people who developed fake online personalities just to see if they could capture someone's devotion: *catfishing*. She'd catfished him, damn it.

He stewed, he steamed, he looked at her and then resolutely looked at the stage instead. Ten eternally long minutes later, the people onstage were still dancing at a stupid party. Not even dancing—it was just slow walking. There was no point to it, just a parade of historical gowns.

He wished he'd never come.

He wished the app had crashed.

I would have spent my whole life wondering where you are.

He was spared that much, at least. He knew exactly where she was—and he wished like hell he didn't.

Michaels looked to her left one more time. She looked to her right again. *Clear on the right.* She wasn't even watch-

ing the ballet she supposedly loved so much. She was looking for him, her little catfish victim.

She'd have to keep looking. Drummer was a definite no-
show.

The interminably long ballet kept going and going. Onstage, a rat with a crown on its head was tiptoeing around a
bed. Who thought of this stuff? It was as unfathomable as
everything else this night. A lame swordfight followed between the rat and the nutcracker. Thane watched the back
of Michaels's head as she dropped her chin to look down to
her lap. A quick flash of light followed. She'd checked the
phone, of course.

To see if I answered. Me, of all people.

The woman to the right of Michaels shifted angrily in her
seat and held her hand up in an exaggerated way to block
the light. The phone went dark immediately, but Michaels's
profile was lit now by the white light from the stage as fake
snow started to fall.

He could see her face clearly. It was easy to read her lips
as she said, "I'm sorry." She bowed her head. She didn't
even look at the stage.

Neither did Thane. He looked at her and all the sorrow
on her face, the—the *hurt.*

Thane scrubbed his hand over his jaw, so recently shaved
for a woman he'd thought he knew. He couldn't look at Michaels's bowed head, at the sad curve of her mouth. Instead,
he stubbornly looked at the stage, where, finally, what he
recognized as ballet was taking place. Dozens of women in
white tutus and white pointe shoes were striking ballet poses
in a snowstorm for some reason, jumping in a formation of
two rows so perfectly aligned, they put the military to shame.
For a second, one flash of a second, Drummer thought how
easy it was going to be to tell Ballerina something he could
genuinely appreciate about her beloved ballet.

One millisecond later, he remembered who Ballerina
was, and he couldn't take the flash of pain, not one more

time. He was on his feet without thinking, sidestepping out of the aisle, ignoring dirty looks from the usher and sneaking out the door.

Chapter Fifteen

Thane's phone buzzed in his pocket, two shorts and a long. He wasn't going to look at that app ever again.

The mezzanine lobby was mostly empty except for the bartenders at a bar set up at one end. The Austin city lights were bright, a view that would be romantic in other circumstances. Any other circumstance.

He knew he should leave, but he sank onto the only furniture in the place, a long bench covered in black leather. What a frigging disaster this night had turned out to be.

So why wasn't he leaving Michaels in the middle of her little row in the middle of her little ballet?

The theater doors to his left and right opened, and people began pouring out for intermission. Thane opened his program, prepared to duck behind it as he kept an eye out for Michaels. He needed to know where she was in order to avoid her.

There. She walked right past him in pair of high-heeled sandals, deadly-looking stiletto heels.

He didn't look away; he needed to keep track of her. Her skirt ended well above her knee. Between her hemline and her pink-polished toes, her nude legs drew his eye. She moved differently in high heels than she did in combat boots, that was for sure. He'd always thought she was pretty, but he hadn't seen her legs since that day by the pool, when she'd been barefoot in a sports bikini. Tonight, in high heels, she looked…elegant.

All right, she looked sexy. Then again, high heels made a woman's legs, any woman's legs, look sexy. The last thing Thane needed to see was a sexy Chloe Michaels. He resented her for looking so good, all dressed up for a night on the town with a man. With him.

If she'd known it was him, she wouldn't have come here at all.

He was leaving, damn it, but she was leaving first, heading straight for the stairs with quick steps. Her skirt swished around her thighs and she moved as lightly on those high heels as if she wore them all the time, when he knew for a fact she did not. She nearly ran down the stairs, disappearing from his view, her hand barely touching the rail.

He didn't care where she was going. For at least sixty seconds, he sat still, telling himself he didn't care. It would probably be safe for him to leave using the opposite stairs. But his phone felt heavy in his jacket pocket. Had she left him a message—had Ballerina left Drummer a message—telling him where she was going?

Thane stood up to leave.

And pulled his phone out. White screen, pink letters. I know cell reception in this building is spotty, but if you get this, stay in your seat. I just realized there is a D130 at orchestra level. I'm in D130 on the mezzanine level. I'll come down and find you. I'm so sorry for the confusion! I'm here, I promise.

He slid his phone back in his jacket. He had every intention of going down the stairs and out to the parking garage, but instead he went back into the theater. The house lights were up, bright. He stayed close to the wall, cursing his own curiosity with every row he passed, until he stood at the balcony railing.

Down below, to the right, were the doors closest to the stairs Michaels had just taken. Row D had to be close to the stage. Everyone who was going to leave for intermission had left at this point. Perhaps only a quarter of the audience remained in their seats, so it was easy to spot Michaels as she walked in.

The sorrow had been replaced by an expectant look. She smiled, radiant with hope, and Thane felt his heart contract again. This was wrong, all so wrong. She was going to be disappointed in just a minute. Whoever was sitting in Orchestra D131 was not him.

It was like watching an accident unfold in slow motion. She found the right row. She tugged her dress into place, fingertips grazing that pale pink ribbon around her waist as she looked down the mostly empty row. Thane glanced down it, too. There were a few elderly folks still seated. A middle-aged man, too, probably twice her age with the beginnings of a bald spot, easy to see from above. Chloe kept a determined smile on her face and scooted her way down the aisle. She made contact, polite conversation with a sweet smile. She touched the sleeve of the man with the bald spot, and from here, Thane would have sworn he saw the word *Drummer* on her lips.

No?

No, the man shook his head.

She nodded, she gave the group a little wave, and she turned around to walk out. Thane looked, really looked, and he saw Ballerina walking away, light on her feet, hair done up in feminine flowers, skirt swirling around her thighs. Ballerina.

His fantasy. If Drummer had been any other man in Central Texas, he would've been suckered into believing that this graceful Ballerina was authentic. She wasn't, and Thane knew it. He sat beside her in the office, rode beside her in troop transports and coordinated company exercises with her. He knew the sound of her voice over the radio in his HUMM-V and over the radio in his patrol car. He *knew* Michaels. That girl down there was a fake, deceiving a man who'd been nothing but kind and supportive to her since June.

The audience began filing in again. The orchestra started tuning up. Thane sidestepped the entire length of the balcony railing to the far side of the mezzanine, just to avoid the woman he'd come to see—the woman who'd come to see him, with hope and anticipation written all over her face. Her disappointment had been equally obvious.

So is mine.

Thane headed for the lobby, his feet feeling heavier with every step. There was no one to talk to, no one to see. The lobby was almost empty, except for the bar in the corner. Thane headed over.

The bartender nodded toward Thane. "What can I get you, sir?"

With a lift of his chin, Thane indicated the whiskey bottle on display. "Single. On the rocks."

So few words to sum up so much.

Chloe returned to the mezzanine level at a more sedate pace. She wasn't going to let her hopes rise too high, not again, but as she walked down the aisle to row D, she looked toward the center. Maybe, finally…

Her seat was empty. The one next to hers was empty, too.

"Are you coming in or not?" The man in the aisle seat had done the usual half twist to tuck his legs to one side.

Chloe mustered up a polite smile. "No, sorry. I'm not going to…no. Sorry."

She dragged herself back up the stairs, reached the lobby and checked her phone. Again.

She didn't have much of a signal, so she walked closer to the windows and held her phone out. Maybe her messages hadn't been sent yet. Maybe they were all piling up, waiting until she caught a better signal. Maybe Drummer's phone was being just as unreliable. Maybe the performing arts center's Wi-Fi had been overwhelmed by a thousand phones at intermission.

She turned off her phone's Wi-Fi and switched to cellular data, hope rising in her heart just one more time.

She stood there with her hand outstretched, staring at the white screen like it was a crystal ball, until her hand started to tremble.

She was a fool.

Behind her, a pair of long black leather benches ran parallel to the glass wall. She sank down on one and stared out at the city lights as the lobby emptied and the theater filled. At least the view of Austin didn't disappoint her. Everything else, every single other thing, did.

She didn't have the heart to go back in the theater and sit with that empty seat beside her for another hour. The last hour of her life had been miserable as she'd stared at the stage, trapped between the empty seat to her left and an angry woman to her right. Not that she could blame the woman. A bright cell phone screen was inexcusable in a dark theater, but Chloe had checked her phone because she'd felt so desperate. Quietly desperate.

They say most men lead lives of quiet desperation. But you're not like most men.

Yes, she was. She would have given anything for anyone, anyone at all to come fill that empty seat. Someone too old, too young, handsome or plain, too thin, too fat, someone who talked brashly or stuttered shyly—she didn't care. It would have been Drummer, and if she'd felt no romantic spark with him, she still would have had someone to talk to. She still would have connected with a human being who wanted to know her instead of waiting with that awful, achingly empty seat beside her.

"Michaels? Is that you?"

Good God. Thane Carter. She focused on the city view and pretended she hadn't heard him.

He walked right up to her, blocking the view. "It is you. Mind if I sit down?" He didn't wait for her answer, but sat on the bench with her. She scooted away a few inches, but she couldn't go far, because she was on the end of the bench. Jeez, he didn't have to sit right beside her on this one. Right next to her was an entire second bench.

"I'm—I'm waiting on someone, actually." She looked over her shoulder at the last few stragglers who hadn't gone back into the theater. Drummer could still show up. There might have been an accident on I-35, all lanes closed, traffic redirected, detoured through side streets. Drummer, of course, would have too much common sense to try to check his phone or type her a message while he was behind the wheel.

Carter looked over his shoulder, too. "Where is he? I assume it's a he?"

She sat up a little straighter and looked back out the window.

"Big secret?" he pressed. "Hot date? Must be a hot date. I've never seen you so…" He had the nerve to flap his hand in her general direction, from her head to her lap. "So…girly."

"Could you please leave?"

He held up a glass tumbler of ice and amber liquid. "As soon as I've finished my whiskey."

"Shouldn't you be in the theater with whatever woman you came here with?"

"You know, it's possible I came by myself, because I enjoy the ballet."

"No, it isn't."

"No, it isn't." He frowned and took a slow, deliberate taste of his drink.

She stopped watching his lips on the glass and folded her arms across her chest, her usual defensive posture around him. "Is she even here?"

"Oh, she's here, all right." Carter's gaze dropped to her folded arms for the barest of seconds, then back to the Austin view.

Chloe looked down. Crap. Folding her arms in uniform was no big deal. Maybe it even gave her a little tough swagger. But in a dress with a V-neck, it emphasized her cleavage. She dropped her hands to her lap, then the bench. She felt the pink satin ribbon under her fingers and smoothed it out. The ribbon was such a sign of how desperate she was not to miss Drummer. She'd been afraid the flowers in her hair weren't obvious enough, so she'd stopped at the flower stand in the lobby to buy a yard of satin ribbon to tie in a bow around her waist, so that her black dress wouldn't be so black. *Quiet desperation.*

"How about you?" Thane asked. "Don't you want to get back inside and see the rest of the show? I bet you love the second half."

She frowned at his mocking tone.

He kept it up. "I bet you think people interpreting the emotions of candy canes and gingerbread makes perfect sense. I bet you call it art when it's nothing more than holiday tripe."

She gasped at his attack. "Yes, it's art. Art doesn't have to be tragic."

"It does if art imitates life."

"*The Nutcracker Suite* is some of the most thrilling choreography set to some of the most stirring music ever written. It's a lighthearted subject and a joyful setting, but that doesn't negate the fact that it is a work of genius that millions of people have enjoyed for over a century."

Carter raised an eyebrow at her lecture, then raised his highball glass in a toast.

She relaxed the tiniest bit.

"There's no plot." He tossed back a swig, not a sip, of the whiskey. "It's a boring Christmas party followed by a snowstorm and dancing candy."

This was just what she needed, a horrible, emotional evening capped off by Carter insulting one of her favorite things in life. She could have cheerfully shoved his butt off the bench with her stilettoed foot, but instead she slid the last inch away from him and sat on the end of the bench in silence.

She debated whether or not Carter would consider it a victory if she moved to the second bench until the glass window reflected movement at the staircase. She looked toward the stairs and blocked out everything and everyone except the man coming up the steps. He was a little frumpy and rumpled, but harmless-looking. Could he be Drummer?

The man called out to one of the lobby stragglers, then walked over to shake hands with him.

She let out the breath she'd been holding.

"Who are you looking for?" Carter looked around her to the staircase. "Don't you know where your date is?"

"I'm not on a date."

"Really? This is how you dress when you go out by yourself?"

The man hated her. First her face, now her dress. She hardened her heart, or she tried to. It was difficult when her feelings were already so battered. "I'm not on a date, but I'm not by myself. I'm expecting someone, and I'd appreciate it if you didn't take his seat."

"I'll move when he shows up." Carter swirled his ice for a moment, then checked his watch. "He's really late."

Carter always wore a watch, but this wasn't his sturdy, shock-proof outdoorsman model. This one was sleek and sophisticated—a surprise. His whole appearance was a surprise, actually. She'd never seen him in civilian clothes. Board shorts and a bare chest by the pool didn't count.

He looked just right for Austin after dark. His jeans were so dark, she hadn't realized his pants were denim until just now, when she dropped her gaze to the ribbon in her hand and saw the contrast of his hard thigh against her dress's soft, black chiffon.

She jerked her skirt away. "He'll be here. And when he gets here, I don't want to be seen sitting all cozy with another man."

"This is cozy?" His mocking tone set her teeth on edge. "I'd hate to see your definition of cold."

She couldn't do this. The worry and the hurt were weighing her down. It took effort to keep them from crushing her. She had no energy left to parry Carter's disapproval.

She swallowed down the tears that were so close, too

close, to the surface. They made her voice sound a little rough, and too quiet. "Please. I'm begging you, sit anywhere else in this building, but not on this one bench. Anywhere else. Please."

He stared at her, or glared at her, for a moment. "Okay, fine." He stood.

She was surprised. Relieved. "Thank you. Good night."

Carter walked away to the far end of the long bench, then rounded it and started walking back toward her, toward the stairs. She felt him pass behind her and sighed in relief.

Then he sat down.

On the second bench.

A whole six inches away from her.

I cannot believe this. Controlled, direct communication didn't work with this man. Chloe fell back on the other option. *Ignore him.*

They sat shoulder to shoulder, she facing the window, he facing the theater, in silence. After a moment, she cautiously turned her phone over. Nothing. She looked toward the stairs, but now she had to look around Carter to see them. If Drummer came up those stairs, he'd see Carter first, not her. She wanted Drummer to see a woman with pink and blue flowers in her hair. She touched them lightly, to be sure they were still there, secured in the braided sort of twist she'd spent so much time on this afternoon.

Carter looked toward the stairs with her, then looked back at her and shrugged.

She shot him a dirty look as she felt a loose piece of baby's breath and tucked it back into a braid.

"What's that look for?" Carter asked. "Now what did I do?"

"It's just—if he comes up, I want him to see…" She started to point to her hair, but caught herself and let her hand plop back into her lap.

"You want him to see what? Flowers in your hair? Is that supposed to mean something?"

"Never mind."

"Since when do you wear flowers in your hair? I've never seen you do anything like that."

She rolled her eyes. "You can't wear flowers in uniform."

"Exactly. You don't wear flowers in your hair. Does this guy have any idea that you're an army officer?"

No, she hadn't told Drummer, and she'd been trying to justify that for weeks now, and damn Carter for poking at a sore point. "That is none of your business. Being an army officer has nothing to do with anything."

He snorted, and then he polished off the last of his drink. The ice clinked against the glass as he gestured toward her waist. "This whole pink-ribbon-and-flowers thing isn't the real you. If you present yourself as this sweet girly-girl, he might be a little disappointed when he finds out what you really do for a living. You're looking all sexy tonight, but what's he going to think when you have to leave his bed at dawn for a grenade range?"

And *that* poked at years of insecurity, at all the criticism that serving as a soldier meant she wasn't a normal woman. She hated to hear Carter sounding just like one of those people who made her feel like a freak.

She swept up the long end of the pink ribbon in her hand. "Maybe *this* is the real me, and the camouflage and combat boots are the deception. Maybe I've been deceiving *you*, not him. What if, this whole time, I've been tricking you into thinking I'm a serious army officer—your fellow MP who has your back—when what I really am is a soft 'girly-girl' who loves the ballet and puppies and kittens and sunsets?"

He'd gone very still, staring at her without blinking.

She wasn't going to blink first, that was for damned sure. "What if the real me is a girl who gets a little homesick at her new post, and who gets royally sick of always having to prove that she's qualified for her job despite her gender and her age and anything else that anyone else feels free to criticize, and so she chucks all that competitive crap for a chance to be her real self with a real friend? She wants to spend one evening, just one, with a friend who knows the real her and who likes the real her and who doesn't care what she does for a living or even what her *face* looks like." She leaned forward, leaning into all the hurt. "And that friend, Thane Carter, is definitely not you."

He didn't move. For a few intense seconds, they glared at one another, long enough for her to notice every shade of blue and gray in the irises of his eyes, long enough for her to breathe in an aftershave he didn't wear to work.

He dropped that icy-blue gaze to the pink ribbon in her hand. If she tried, she could imagine that a little sadness touched the angry set of his mouth.

"Yeah. It's not me. I'll see you Monday." He stood and walked away, carrying his glass to the bartender in the corner of the lobby.

Chloe stood, too. Drummer wasn't coming, and sitting alone on a bench wasn't going to change that. She didn't want to go back into the theater, because she didn't need to watch the final scene, where the little girl wakes up to find it was all a dream, and her brave and protective nutcracker prince is nothing more than a broken wooden toy.

Chloe headed for the exit, walking toward the staircase that no one had used to come and find her. The end of the ribbon was still in her hand, so she pulled it, untying the bow, pulling the ribbon free from her waist. As she passed the lobby's large trash can, she raised her hand high and dropped it in.

Chapter Sixteen

"What's that in your hand?"

Ernesto hadn't even made it to his desk, and his fellow platoon sergeant had already zeroed in on the plastic food container he was carrying. "It's a piece of cake. My wife made *tres leches* this weekend."

"Outstanding. Monday mornings need all the help they can get."

"It's not for you, Lloyd." Ernesto tossed his hat on his desk. "The LT was pretty down at PT this morning."

"Yours, too? Carter's all pissed off at the world today. He had high hopes about some girl he was going out with this weekend. I didn't even need to ask if it went bad."

"Michaels was supposed to have a big weekend, too. I did ask. Get this—the guy didn't show."

"He stood her up?" Lloyd whistled low. "Men can be such dumbasses. I know I was, but still—Lieutenant Michaels? I was never *that* dumb."

Ernesto glared at him as he sat.

"I mean, if I were a younger man. And not married. And not an NCO."

"And not in the same company."

"Don't give me your protective-father glare. She's not your teenaged daughter. I can't help it if it's obvious she's got a pretty face."

"She's more than a pretty face. She's smart. She's got her act together. She's the whole package."

"I know that, *Dad.*" Lloyd shook his head. "And still, some dumbass stood her up. Men."

"Men." The LT hadn't been in her office yet when he'd walked by. Ernesto kicked back in his chair. "Makes me glad I'm married. I wouldn't want to go through all that garbage again."

"Man, the things I used to do for the sake of a woman. Going to chick flicks. Paying *money* to see chick flicks. Hell, Carter went to a ballet this weekend, poor sucker, and got nothing for his trouble."

"A ballet?"

Lloyd laughed. "Can you believe it?"

Ernesto stopped lounging. "My LT was supposed to have her big date at a ballet this weekend, too. She said it wasn't a total loss, because at least she'd gotten to enjoy the *Nutcracker*."

She'd said it with a shrug and a smile, but Ernesto knew a brave lie when he heard it. His LT hadn't enjoyed anything. She'd been hurt. His wife's cake was the best Ernesto could do for a broken heart.

"Guess that goes to show you the ballet is a sucky place for a date. Hold on." Lloyd sat up. "They both went to a ballet this weekend? And now they're both…?"

They stared at each other. Neither one of them wanted to say it out loud.

"Just a coincidence," Lloyd said.

"Yeah." Ernesto tried to think of a single time the two LTs had shared a laugh or a joke or even a meal in the dining facility. Never, not that he'd seen. "They barely tolerate each other."

"Yeah." Lloyd tapped his desk idly. "But they're both single. Right age for each other. Same kind of attitude. You ever notice that he's got a Mustang and she's got a Charger? I mean, those are competitors but they're both muscle cars. They're both—"

"Stop." Ernesto didn't want his platoon leader anywhere near that kind of trouble. She was a good kid, a real good kid, the kind of LT he hoped would stay and make a career out of it. She wouldn't have much of a career if she got caught fraternizing.

"That would be one hell of a match." Lloyd lowered his voice. "It'd be a hell of a court-martial, too."

"No one's getting court-martialed."

"Letter of reprimand, then."

Ernesto stood and picked up the cake, ready to go find his LT before trouble could find her. "Think about it. Carter went on a date that went south. Michaels didn't go on a date at all. She got stood up." As soon as he said it, he could breathe a little easier.

"That's right, that's right." Lloyd clutched his chest. "Man, that got a little scary. For a minute there, I could kind of see the two of them together."

"They hate each other."

"Right."

"So there's no need to see anything."

"Right."

Ernesto left to go find his LT, anyway.

Dear Drummer,

The cursor blinked. Chloe stared at it, hands poised over her laptop keyboard, waiting for the right words to come to her.

Nothing.

She didn't know what she wanted to accomplish with this letter. She'd been stood up on Saturday and looked at a blank white screen all day Sunday. Today had been one of the hardest Mondays of her life.

I can't stop thinking about you.

She paused. Some cooler, more rational voice said he didn't deserve to know that he'd gotten to her so badly. He shouldn't get to gloat over hurting her feelings. If he was not going to write to her, then she shouldn't write to him, either. Right?

Chloe sighed. She couldn't muster up any anger or

indignation. She didn't have any sense of pride or self-preservation. She just felt empty.

I don't know what made you change your mind. At the theater, I spent the whole time trying to imagine where you could be, but in the end, it doesn't matter. You had your reasons, and they were important to you. I only know you weren't with me, and I missed you.

You must have your reasons for being silent now, too. A blank white screen says it all. This friendship has run its course for you.

"But not for me," she whispered.

You are gone as surely as if a computer glitch had taken you from me without warning. But since it didn't, I have a chance to tell you how much this friendship has meant to me. You've been my stability, my constancy, my anchor while I've been moving from one side of the country to the other. I never told you that, did I? From May to November, I was sent from New York to Georgia to Missouri to Texas. I felt like one of those cartoon hobos with a stick over my shoulder, carrying all my belongings tied up in a red handkerchief. Well, packed in the trunk of my car. My job changed, my coworkers changed, my roommates changed, even the clothes I wear every day changed. My whole life changed, but you were constant. For six months and 2,500 miles, I could stop and open our app and there you would be, friendly words in that friendly blue font, without fail.

Chloe stopped typing to wipe her cheeks. It was okay to shed a few tears. She was inside, not on the balcony where Carter might spot her. Nobody would know that the bold new MP officer in the 584th had spent her Monday night crying over the end of a silly online friendship.

Thank you for keeping me company all these months. Thank you for listening, and for offering good advice—and it was always good advice. I know this, because I didn't follow your advice Saturday night, and things turned out badly.

I couldn't sit next to your empty seat for the second act. I stayed in the lobby, waiting, because I still had the hope that you had only been delayed. I kept checking my phone, though, and that blank white screen was breaking my heart, so I was not ready at all when that friend-who-isn't-really-a-friend walked up to me.

The timing was awful. I should be used to his insults at this point, but when he made fun of my appearance, I kind of snapped. All your advice on controlled confrontations went out the window. I was hurting, and I lashed out at the only person there was to lash out against.

In the moment, it felt like he deserved it. But now, all I can think about is the way he'd walked up to me and said hello, and the way I told him to sit anywhere, anywhere, except next to me.

I want to delete that sentence so that you won't know how awful I can be, but maybe I should leave it in. It was awful of you to stand me up, but it was also awful of me to tell that man I didn't want him near me. I wish I could take it back. If you wish you could take it back, too, then please know that I would still love to talk to you as we always have.

If not, then I'm still glad that, out of all the gin joints in all the towns in all the world, this app sent you walking into mine. I loved being your—

Ballerina Baby.

* * *

Two shorts and a long.

Thane stood on his balcony in the cold December air and glared at Building Four's empty matching balcony. She was over there, just behind those sliding glass doors, and she was trying to reach him. Or rather, she was trying to reach Drummer. He'd promised her he'd be at the theater in D131, and she'd driven an hour to Austin to meet him, and he hadn't shown up. Why would she try to talk to him now? A woman like Michaels would kick a man's ass for standing her up—or at least write him off as a total loss, no longer worthy of her time.

She'd be fine.

She just hadn't been fine yet today. She'd been really quiet, actually. And sad. Her platoon sergeant had seen it. He'd brought her some cake. That was nice; she had someone who'd try to cheer her up in the future. Michaels wasn't friendless, for God's sake, no matter what she'd said so passionately with her pink ribbon in her hand.

She was going to be fine.

Thane looked at his phone. The app's icon indicated one message was waiting. It was probably *screw you and goodbye*. The way she'd walked into row D, down there at orchestra level, so full of hope—she must have been so pissed off when the man had said he wasn't Drummer.

But Thane couldn't fool himself. He'd been able to see her face. She hadn't been pissed off. She'd been sad.

He stared at her empty balcony a moment longer, then he opened the app on his phone. Dear Drummer—

By the time he got to all the gin joints in all the towns, he knew he had to write her at least one more time.

Casablanca. (Too easy.) I wish I had an easy explanation about Saturday. I do not. But I want you to know that you did nothing wrong. If I could have made everything turn out differently, I would have.

Thane did not hit Send.

He'd wanted everything to turn out differently, it was true, for every selfish reason. In his perfect scenario, he would have walked into row D and found a woman who was beautiful, easy to talk to, quick to smile, interesting to him, interested in him. He'd experienced that only once before in his life, with Chloe, stunning Chloe, with whom he'd damned near fallen in love at first sight.

He'd wanted a new woman to be as exciting as Chloe. He'd wanted lightning to strike twice.

Only now, on a miserable, lonely Monday evening, could he admit to himself how much he still missed Chloe and the dream of what might have been. The reality was that, from the first moment of that first ride-along, Chloe had never acted like a woman who'd missed the dream of being with him. In the parking lot of the MP station, rather than being shocked or hurt or sad when she'd seen him, she'd taken him to task. Chloe had turned into Michaels within a few sentences, and he'd been resenting her ever since.

Ah, hell. The truth hit him in the face. Michaels was Ballerina, so the friend-who-wasn't-a-friend was him. She'd confronted him in the parking lot because that's what *he* had advised her to do.

He looked once more at her sliding glass doors. All along, he'd been the coworker who made her professional life hell. As Drummer, he'd been so worried that the not-a-friend would hurt her...

And he had, a low blow when she'd least expected it, on a Saturday night when she'd been all dressed up for her favorite ballet. Thane closed his eyes against the memory of the hope on her face every time she'd turn to look at that mezzanine staircase.

He slunk back into his apartment, slid the door shut and leaned against his wall. He looked at his phone once more, and felt all the truth of his blue words. I want you to know that you did nothing wrong.

She wasn't going to believe him. Her letter was too full of apology, telling him she was sometimes a bad person, too, offering him an easy olive branch.

She should have told him to go to hell. She'd done nothing wrong at the theater, and he'd stood her up. One month ago, she'd done nothing wrong by the pool, and he'd left her without an explanation. She'd done nothing wrong by requesting a radio on their first ride-along. She'd done nothing wrong by developing a better duty officer schedule. She'd done nothing wrong.

But he had.

He slid down the wall, wishing he could start over. That was impossible, but if he could tell Chloe everything and ask for a second chance—but that would be fraternization. Lieutenant Thane Carter couldn't open his heart to her.

Drummer could. As long as Chloe never found out that Drummer was him, she would be safe from any fraternization charges. She would be completely innocent.

He wouldn't be, but it was a risk he needed to take. He needed to be Drummer for her, just for a little bit longer, so Ballerina wouldn't be left so abruptly alone.

At the same time, Thane Carter could start being a better friend to Chloe Michaels. He couldn't court her. He couldn't date her, but he could be her friend. Maybe, once she had that real-life friend she wanted so badly, she would say goodbye to Drummer on her own terms. She'd be free to find a new man to love.

It wouldn't be him. He could only be her friend.

If I could have made everything turn out differently, I would have.

Thane hit Send.

Chapter Seventeen

Christmas Eve at the brigade's dining facility was a come one, come all feast for the soldiers who stayed in the Fort Hood area during the holidays. Soldiers with their spouses and children, their parents and a few sets of grandparents, would shortly begin making their way through the cafeteria-style line of food stations for an old-fashioned turkey dinner with all the trimmings.

It was traditional for the officers to dress in the service uniform, the formal dark blue suit with rank and regalia displayed to precise standards. They showed up with medals on their chests and spit-shined shoes, and then were sent behind the food line like school cafeteria workers to serve the holiday meal to their troops.

Thane had always enjoyed it. As an eighteen-year-old private, he'd gotten a kick out of having a full-bird colonel scoop mashed potatoes onto his plate. As a twenty-six-year-old officer, he got a kick out of watching his soldiers interact with their children. It was priceless to hear the toughest, most battle-hardened sergeants say things like *It's not polite to put your fingers in your sister's nose at the table.*

Thane had already taken his holiday leave at Thanksgiving, weeks before the *Nutcracker* debacle. He'd driven to South Carolina, seen his folks, hit the old bars, and affirmed that the gulf between himself and the friends he'd left behind when he'd joined the army was still there.

Christmas would be spent here. Thane looked for the mess hall sergeant, ready for his assignment to scoop sweet potatoes or ladle gravy. The battalion commander would be carving the turkey. The CO of the 410th was already posted by the trays of green bean casserole, and standing over there, next to the pumpkin pies, was Michaels.

Chloe.

Thane devoured her for a hot second with his eyes. She wore the crossed pistols of the Military Police Corps on her lapels, the gold embroidery of her rank on her shoulder boards, silver wings on her chest for Airborne and Air Assault qualifications. Lieutenant Chloe Michaels in her dress blues should be on a recruitment poster. Young girls would aspire to be her. Parents would want their daughters to turn out like her. What man wouldn't admire her?

He did.

The mess sergeant saved Thane from his own thoughts by handing him a pair of tongs and sending him over to a giant basket of rolls. Bread was the last station before the dessert table. He'd have to stare at Michaels's back the whole time. Great.

Actually, it *was* great. Michaels's uniform was perfectly tailored to her trim waist. Her skirt was hemmed to fall precisely at the middle of her knee. Her legs weren't nude like last Saturday, but smooth with the polish of panty hose. Her black pumps weren't stilettos, but they were high-heeled. She wasn't dressing like a sexy girlfriend, but a professional officer in a uniform that carried both authority and history.

She looked sexy, anyway.

Music came on the loudspeakers, families came through the doors.

"Merry Christmas, sir."

"You, too, Sergeant First Class. You want the pretzel roll or the sourdough?"

Passing out rolls didn't stop him from thinking about Chloe. No wonder the girls in his hometown bars hadn't held any appeal for him at Thanksgiving. He'd looked. He'd wanted someone to knock him out. Plenty of pretty women had talked to him. Even the most distant acquaintance greeted him with a hug and a kiss on the cheek, soft hands on his chest, his neck, his biceps. Everyone had smiled, but no one had been intriguing enough to invite out to dinner, no one had made him want to go somewhere quieter to get to know her. Thane had given up looking for more, and had tried to enjoy the flirting for what it was.

It wasn't much. He'd left the bar and gone to his parents' house, so he could type on the phone with Ballerina instead. He'd wanted her to be that real-life friend more than ever, but she could've lived a thousand miles away, for all he'd known at Thanksgiving. Now, on Christmas Eve, he knew Ballerina was here.

For two hours, he watched her give children extra whipped cream. For two hours, he felt his heart break. The most he could hope for with that amazing woman was the friend zone. Hell, he needed to dig himself out of a hole just to *get* to the friend zone.

It was time to start digging.

When the dinner was over and only the cooks and a few officers were left, Thane filled a plate with everything except a roll and took a seat across from Michaels.

She nodded to acknowledge him, nothing like the girls at the bars back home. No smile. No words. No touch.

He wanted that touch. He couldn't have it, but the desire scrambled his brain. It was hard to speak casually to her. *Ballerina, it's me...*

It's me, the guy who stood you up.

"What are you doing tomorrow for Christmas, Chloe?"

She gave him an odd look. "I'm the duty officer, *Thane*."

Ah, he'd slipped and called her Chloe, thus the odd look.

"How did you get stuck with duty on Christmas Day?" Just two days ago, she'd left their office and gone home at 1100 hours after pulling duty. She shouldn't be the MPDO for another eight nights.

"I volunteered."

"For Christmas? You didn't take leave on Thanksgiving, either, right?"

"Right. I didn't." She was so formal in her formal uniform, but she was distant with him in combat boots, too.

They ought to be closer, like teammates. They ought to at least be on a first-name basis.

"Chloe."

"Thane."

He almost smiled as she imitated him. If she only knew how much he liked hearing her say his name...

"Chloe, you don't have to deprive yourself of a chance to see your family. There will be plenty of times in your career when you won't have any choice about working a holiday. You'll be working a flood or an ice storm or something else you can't control, or you'll be stationed halfway around the world in a hostile environment. When you're stateside, it's expected that you'll take at least one of the winter holidays off. It's not wimping out to go see your family."

She looked at him with a little wrinkle of concern between her eyebrows.

"Unless you aren't close to your family?" Thane asked. "Did I bring up a sore subject?"

"I get along fine with my family."

Of course she did. He'd never heard Ballerina complain about family drama.

"Then be sure to go home now and then. When you decide to go, let me know." Thane decided to be the first to smile. "I'll give you a ride to the airport."

Her eyes opened wide. Damn, was that something he'd talked about with Ballerina or with Chloe?

Sergeant Gevahr, the squad leader who lived at Two Rivers, passed their table, wishing them both a happy holiday with his civilian girlfriend. Chloe smiled and gave him a little wave goodbye. She returned her attention to Thane, and her smile faded away to that formal nothingness.

He needed to fix this relationship. It wasn't acceptable to him anymore that her smile died when he was around.

"Why did you volunteer to work Christmas?"

"I designed that schedule. You and Salvatore and Phillips

got stuck with extra shifts this month because of it. I wasn't going to let you miss Christmas, too."

"It was an extra three shifts for each of us in the whole month of December. Big deal. Don't sit there feeling guilty. Tomorrow should have fallen on one of the 410th guys, anyway. It was their month to pull duty before the new schedule, so they were already expecting it. You didn't need to take one for them."

She tilted her head and studied him. "What is this about, Carter? Are you giving me advice? Are you *mentoring* me now?"

"Believe it or not, I'm not always a jerk. Try me. What's going on?"

"Nothing."

"Something." He pushed the salt and pepper toward her when she reached for it.

"Nothing, and I want to keep it that way. I don't want anyone to have cause for complaint about a schedule that was my idea."

"It might have been your idea, but it was the battalion commander's decision. If anyone gripes about it, tell him to take it up with Colonel Stephens."

She only sighed and moved on to her dessert.

"Has someone said something to you?"

"Of course not." She cut through her pumpkin pie with the side of her fork, making a sharp little clink of sound on the sturdy plate. "No one will gripe about the new schedule to my face. That's too easy to deal with. I'm trying to make sure no one has a reason to sneer at me behind my back. How dare that new female officer come in here and change the way we've always done it?"

Thane said nothing. It was too close to what he'd thought himself.

"In every assignment, I walk in with two strikes against me, and I know it. I'm female and a West Pointer. I have to prove I'm... I don't know. Normal, for starters. Then worthy of the rank on my shoulders."

Again, it was too close to true. Before she'd even made it to the unit, Lloyd had taken great glee in announcing Thane's new office mate was going to be a West Pointer and a girl to boot. The comment had seemed harmless, even routine, but today, over a piece of pumpkin pie, Thane realized that he and everyone else had indeed been reserving judgment.

She'd proved herself to everyone during their first ridealong—everyone in the 584th. When she'd been the duty officer this month, she'd probably had to prove herself all over again to the soldiers of the 410th. They must have been judging her every move far more than they had with him or Phillips or Salvatore. When she joined a unit, she had to prove herself upon arrival. When Thane joined a new unit, he was assumed to be competent unless he proved otherwise. Subtle difference, but it was a real difference.

Chloe shrugged like they'd been talking about the weather as she ate her dessert. "Anyway, if I just take the Christmas shift myself, that removes one more thing someone might gripe about when I'm not around. So far, the dynamics in our battalion seem to be good, at least to my face. I'd like to keep it that way. Pulling duty is like a Christmas present from me, to me. I've given myself one less thing to worry about." She finished her pie and tossed her napkin onto her tray. "Well, you have a nice Christmas—"

"Chloe."

"Thane."

"The dynamics are going well behind your back, too, not just to your face. I'm in the boys' club by default. I would've heard any negative comments about you. There aren't any." Thane pushed his plate out of the way and leaned forward, resting his forearms on the table. "If anyone did something idiotic, like blame you when they pulled a bad duty officer shift, I'd set them straight right then and there."

After a long moment, she stood. With tray in hand, she nodded at Thane.

"Same."

Then she walked away.

How was your day?

Chloe stretched out on her sofa with her laptop on her stomach. It was noon on the twenty-sixth of December, and she'd just gotten home after being the Christmas MPDO. Drummer had left this question for her on the app, probably expecting her to read it after a normal workday at five or six o'clock. She'd leave him an answer and then go to sleep.

It was really slow and boring, since it was Christmas. I had a nice Christmas Eve dinner with my coworkers, though. It ended a little weirdly. Mr. Not-a-Friend made an appearance.

And?

Chloe lifted her hands from the keyboard in surprise at the blue And? She hadn't expected Drummer to be online. His icon hadn't been flashing when she'd logged on.

And he was mostly ok.

Mostly?

Thane had been more than okay. He'd looked far too handsome in dress blues, which had made her as uncomfortable as seeing him in civilian clothes at the *Nutcracker*. She preferred Thane in baggy camouflage. In dress blues or in denim, or definitely in a bathing suit with a bare chest, Thane was too attractive to ignore.

He never seemed to be attracted to her, but he had tried to share a meal and a conversation, which was weird in itself.

Mostly. I had to educate him a little on boys vs. girls. I get so tired of boys vs. girls in my job. He told me how I should act toward the other guys, but it's how he would act. It's a different minefield for girls, but not a lot of men get that. The boys always assume they are the standard. There's a certain arrogance in being sure your way will work.

He's arrogant? Could it be anything else? Is he older than you are? Is he more senior in your career field?

Chloe froze with her hands over the keyboard—again. How did Drummer do that? Since the very beginning of their relationship, he'd always been so insightful despite the limited details they gave each other.

Yes, he's both. He likes to lord that over me. But lately, he's actually been helpful on occasion. He's not hard to work with.

That's good. You're making progress with him, then.

Progress? Chloe hadn't been trying to do anything except avoid him.

This is the same guy that we had to come up with options for. Controlled confrontation and all that. I guess that was the right way to handle him, since he's being nicer now. That's good, because my job requires a lot of teamwork.

Teamwork. What do you do for a living again?

* * *

Across the parking lot, in Building Six, Thane waited for her reply.

If she'd just break the boundaries they'd set and say she was in the military, then he could say he was in the military, too. He could direct the conversation naturally from there. They were both in the military, both in the Austin area. It would be obvious to conclude they were both at Fort Hood.

They would agree to meet, and this time, he'd sit beside her, wherever it was. He would pretend that he was just as surprised as she was. Surprised, but not entirely shocked, because they would have already been expecting to meet a fellow army officer. Just not each other.

But once she realized he'd been her online love for more than half a year, he'd sweep her off her feet in real life. He'd wrap his arms around her, something more sensual than the hug that every other friend gave her. He'd savor the warmth and weight of her body in his arms. He'd pull all the pins out of that ballerina bun and let her hair cascade to her shoulders. He'd bury his hands in it, he'd look into her brown eyes as he traced the curves and lines of her face with his fingertips, and he'd finally, finally taste her lips, just like he did in his dreams.

The cursor blinked at him.

He willed her to answer him, just a few words: *I bet you'd never guess this, but I'm in the military.* That was all she had to say. He would take it from there.

His dreams were unrealistic—and against regulations—but meeting in real life would be a good start. The kiss would have to wait, but their fragile friendship would become solid. Someday, they would no longer serve in the same unit, and once that day came, he would woo her, court her, pursue her with all the emotion he currently had to keep tightly leashed. If she would just give him the opening, just tell him she was in the military…

That wasn't very subtle, Drummer. We've done pretty well by keeping our careers a secret since last June. I don't want to change that now.

"Damn it." He pushed to his feet and paced the width of his apartment. Chloe was so by the book. Such a little rule follower.

Her next words cooled his frustration before it could pick up steam: If we'd met at the theater last week, we would know each other's careers and a lot more right now. Maybe it would have been better, but then again, maybe not. Maybe we wouldn't even be friends anymore. But without having met and without knowing the details of our lives, we are definitely still friends. Let's not mess with what works.

He had blown it, not her. Thane had walked away from her at a pool party. Drummer had stood her up at a theater. Why should she trust him in either of his personas again?

Can we talk later, Drummer? I just got home from my job, and I really need to get some sleep. But I really need to have some fun after that. Will you be around?

He never wanted to hurt her again. He couldn't refuse to be there if she needed his company, so he kept up the charade. I'll be around. Get some rest. If you haven't got your health, you haven't got anything.

It took her less than a second. (The Princess Bride! You finally quoted the Princess Bride!) I'm only going to sleep for a couple of hours, because I don't want to get my days and nights mixed up. Let's do dinner and a movie. You pick the movie and tell me what channel, okay?

There was only one possible answer: As you wish, Baby. As you wish.

Chapter Eighteen

Six weeks.

It had been six weeks since Thane had found out who Ballerina really was. Six weeks since he'd started being a real-life friend to Chloe, so she wouldn't need her virtual friend, and she'd let Drummer go.

No luck.

Drummer still enjoyed talking to Ballerina too much. He meant to dial back his engagement with her as Drummer and let Thane fill in the gap, but then they'd start typing back and forth about which movie was the most quotable—he said *The Godfather*, she said *The Princess Bride*, but they used *Casablanca* the most—and next thing he knew, he'd spent another entire evening online with his best friend.

Six weeks. The clock was ticking. He'd gotten some firm dates through the S-1 today. He was going to be promoted to captain in May. Then he'd be sent to the captain's course at Fort Leonard Wood in June, a six-month school. That would be followed by an assignment as a company commander.

Unless he blew it before then. He'd have to do something really stupid, like drunk driving. Like disobeying a regulation—like fraternization.

Four months. He had four months before he could tell Chloe how he felt, legally. Four months until he could apologize for things she didn't know he'd done. Four months before he could try to turn friends into lovers while he lived in Missouri and she in Texas.

There would be no long-distance romance without having that friendship first. He needed to get rid of Drummer.

No time like the present.

They were at their desks. Thane sat back and typed a line to Ballerina on his phone, a casual blue hello. He hit Send.

Chloe's phone buzzed a second later. He watched her concentrating on her government-issued laptop, typing away diligently at some necessary bit of administrative work. She glanced at her phone. Kept typing.

Thane sent Ballerina another line. *Are you busy?*

Another buzz. Another quick glance.

Thane really shouldn't enjoy teasing her this much. One more message. This time he stood up as he hit Send.

Her phone buzzed.

"Yo, Chloe. Your phone is blowing up. Got a secret admirer?"

She glared at him, but she picked up her phone. Thane stepped around his desk as she opened a very familiar white screen with pink and blue writing.

"Who's bugging you?" he asked.

"None of your business."

"You're not still exchanging sweet nothings with the creep who stood you up at the *Nutcracker*, are you?"

She typed a word, maybe two on her phone, and hit Send.

His phone didn't buzz; he'd set it on silent. He crossed his arms over his chest and leaned against her desk, half sitting on the corner. "You are."

"I am not."

"You're almost blushing. Lieutenant Chloe Michaels isn't the blushing type. You wouldn't be lying, would you?"

She set her phone on her desk, screen side down, and sat back in her chair, crossing her arms like his. "I never type sweet nothings. He and I discuss things that matter. Conversations I wouldn't expect you to understand."

Thane bit his tongue. Hard. They conversed about vampire kindergartens and cold fried chicken. They rated the hotness factor of the 1960s aliens that appeared on the original *Star Trek*. "Why would you do that? Why should you discuss anything with him, sweet or not, when he stood you up?"

"He couldn't make it."

"That was December. It's February. It's been two months. Has he tried to set anything up that he *could* make?"

"It's February first. It's only been six weeks."

"I'll take that as a *no*. Aren't you bothered that he hasn't tried to see you again?" *Come on, Chloe, dump the guy.*

"We enjoy talking to each other. We talk for hours. We don't need to meet in person to do that."

He needed to try a new tactic. He'd been so frustrated when he'd wanted to meet Ballerina and she'd said no. Maybe if he could get her to want to meet Drummer and then Drummer said no…

"Why don't you take the first step? Maybe he's embarrassed about being a no-show last time. Maybe he'd be relieved if you gave him a second chance. Invite him to a movie or something."

"If he wanted to catch a movie, he's man enough to say so."

"I'm telling you, he's waiting for you to make the first move. I'm a guy. Guys know how guys think."

She tilted her head and studied him a moment. "How about your date at the ballet? Are you two still hot and heavy?"

"I never claimed we were hot and heavy, but I like how your imagination works."

"I'm not using my imagination. It's observation. You weren't dressed like a man who was expecting an intellectual date with his platonic friend."

Thane had to smile at that. Chloe had liked the way he looked that night, apparently. "Don't you think a woman would be pretty mad if I missed the second act to drink whiskey with you?"

"With me? You told her you were with me?" Her tone of voice made it sound like an utter impossibility. "Tell her not to worry."

"It's hard to tell a woman not to worry if I spend the evening enjoying a whiskey and conversation with a woman in a low-cut black dress."

She blinked—but she recovered quickly. "You were enjoying yourself? Hardly."

"Don't sell yourself short. It's not that hard to enjoy a conversation with you."

She looked at him like he was absolutely insane. Damn, they had a long way to go.

"Come on. I'll prove it to you. Let's go get lunch."

"Where?" She was always suspicious when he was nice to her.

"The dining facility's serving hot dogs and tater tots today. I remember that you like your dogs naked, but how do you dress your tots?"

She looked away from him. He'd noticed before that she didn't like to be reminded about their first day at the pool.

He didn't back off. "It's like your hot dog test. I'll learn all about your personality. Come on, Chloe. I'm starving."

"Fine."

Success. When she stood up and grabbed her patrol cap, he had to work to stay cool about it. They walked out of the headquarters building together. Like associates. Like fellow platoon leaders in the same unit. Like friends.

"Let me guess," he said, feeling jubilant that he had her by his side. "With everything I know about you, I predict that you'll put ketchup on half of your tots, mustard on the other half, and salt the heck out of everything."

"What—how—" She looked shocked at his guess.

"Not a hard guess. You're a pretty salty woman. Must come from somewhere."

They walked a little farther in silence—and in step. Thane wondered if that was just a military thing, or if he and Chloe were tuned in to each other.

"Tater tots don't reveal a thing about a person," she said stiffly, still in sync.

"Then you've got nothing to fear. We can safely enjoy lunch and still not accidentally like each other."

"No chance of that."

"Really?" He'd said that wrong. He sounded a little, just a little, wistful. But she hadn't sounded as convinced as she usually did, either. "Really, Chloe? There's no chance that we might like each other?"

"What do you mean?"

It wasn't time to reveal everything. It might never be time to reveal everything, but he could at least tell her part of the truth.

"Do you ever think—"

Two privates walked toward them on the sidewalk. They saluted. "Good afternoon, sir. Good afternoon, ma'am."

He and Chloe returned their salutes.

"Do I ever think what?" Chloe asked. At least he had her curious enough to continue the subject.

"Do you ever wonder how we would have gotten along if the first time we'd met had been at work instead of at that pool?"

"No." Chloe looked away, predictably. He'd mentioned the pool.

Another private came toward them on the sidewalk, a sergeant close behind her. The closer they got to the dining facility, the more salutes had to be given and returned.

Thane waited a moment for the soldiers to get a little distance away. "I wonder about it. If the first time I'd met you had been at the station, if the watch commander had introduced you as the new platoon leader, I would've been more open-minded. I would have given you a chance instead of arguing before we even got in the car."

"Oh." She wouldn't look at him.

He couldn't keep his eyes off her. "I would have been impressed with you by the end of that shift, Chloe. You've got the right attitude. You've got common sense. I would have felt like the 584th had won the lottery when it came to new lieutenants."

"As opposed to what? Since that didn't happen, you don't think I'm a lottery prize?"

"As opposed to the way I acted. I acted like I wasn't impressed, but I was. I should have been a better mentor from the very first night, instead of—"

Another soldier jogged toward them in a rush, slowed to a walk, saluted. "Afternoon, sir, afternoon, ma'am." Started jogging again.

"Better?" Chloe asked. "You haven't been any kind of mentor at all."

"I know." They were getting close to the dining facility, so they'd be running a gauntlet of military courtesy in a moment. He had to speak now or hold his peace. "I'm glad you've had Sergeant Ernesto. He won't steer you wrong. But I've given up being an ass, Chloe. It's too hard to sustain it around a person who doesn't deserve it. Who never deserved it. If Ernesto's not around and you need anything—"

They both greeted the major who came out of the dining facility and saluted him. Thane stopped just before the door. "Before we go in…"

"What?" She looked a little apprehensive.

He didn't want to freak her out. It was time to lighten up. "Before we go in, let's hear your guess on the tater tots. How do you think I take them?"

"You're weird."

He smiled. That was almost a term of affection between Drummer and Ballerina. "Take a guess."

"I think it's a trick question. I think you choose french fries."

He laughed, genuinely surprised. "You're right. You're one hundred percent right. How'd you guess that?"

"You take your hot dogs all fancy-schmanzy. You probably take your side item plain. For balance."

"Balance. You take your hot dog plain, and your tots fancy. Between the two of us, we've got all the bases covered. I told you, we might turn out to be friends."

"Heard you had quite the night, sir."

Chloe hung up her desk phone and looked at her platoon

sergeant. He'd come into her office, two steps behind Thane, but apparently not to talk to her.

Thane sat, slowly, heavily, like his body was weighing him down. The chair wheels squeaked loudly. He half-heartedly raised an eyebrow at her, but barely returned her grin.

They had a running joke about that squeaky chair. Last week, they'd sneaked it into Lloyd's office and taken his. Like a game of hot potato, Lloyd had traded it out for one in the orderly room. Yesterday, the chair had made its way back to Chloe, so she'd switched it with Thane's while he was on duty. He should have grinned at the squeak and started planning where to dump the chair next, but instead he was rubbing his forehead like a man who was even more exhausted than a twenty-four-hour shift normally made a person.

"You should go home now, sir."

Thane had no grin at all for Ernesto. "I'm fine, Sergeant First Class. I know Lloyd's out for the week, but you don't have to take over his mother-hen duties. I'll go home when my work is done."

Ernesto shook off his XO's words. "There's nothing critical on the schedule today, sir. No reason to not go home."

Thane pulled a clipboard out of a drawer and slapped it down on his desk. "This fire marshal thing is due. Today. Regulation requires an officer to do it. I appreciate your concern, Sergeant First Class, but if I say I'm fine, I'm fine. I'll go home when I'm ready."

For the last two weeks, ever since Thane had buried the hatchet over hot dogs and tater tots, they'd been conspiring together to come up with practical jokes and laughing nearly every day. This morning, Thane did not look like a man who had laughed in a year.

Chloe had no idea what was going on, but she trusted Ernesto. If he thought Thane should go home, then Thane should go. No one could make him go except the CO. She checked her watch. The CO wouldn't be out of his battalion staff meeting for a couple of hours.

Thane looked more than tired. More than angry. Something was wrong.

"I can do the fire marshal duty," she said.

"No."

"Why not? What's involved?"

He sighed as if she'd asked a difficult question. "You check the gauge of every fire extinguisher in every building and initial that each one is charged."

"I can certainly see why they need a commissioned officer for that." What a typical army thing, to require an officer's legal authority for such a simple task. She would have laughed if Thane didn't look so angry.

Concern and kindness from Ernesto were only making him bristle. She'd have to try something else.

She stood and picked up the clipboard. "Do you think I can't handle this? You're not that special, Thane. My initials are just as legal as your initials."

"It has to be at the S-3 by noon. The brigade S-3, not the battalion S-3."

"Ooh, scary." She wiggled the fingers of one hand like something was spooky—her right hand, just to annoy him with her ring. Then she smacked him lightly on the shoulder with the clipboard. "I can handle this, Thane. You look like hell. Go home."

She left before he could argue with her or try to take the clipboard back. On her way out, she exchanged a quick glance with Ernesto.

Make him go.

Chapter Nineteen

Assist-protect-defend.

Thane couldn't get the motto out of his damned head. It pounded in his brain as he pounded up the concrete steps toward his apartment.

He'd taken such pride in his profession. Assist, protect, defend—it sounded so selfless, so noble. He'd helped a lot of people in the past two years. Each one had made him more confident that he'd be able to help the next one. A kind of arrogance had built, unchecked, because he had always been able to help the next one.

Until now.

The accident scene had been a nightmare. A single car upside down on an empty country road, its deflated airbag hanging out a shattered window, headlights still on and beaming into the night, illuminating the unmistakable mass that was a human being in the middle of the road.

Thane had been calling it in on the radio as he'd driven closer, when his own headlights had shone on a second body in the road. He'd slammed on his brakes so that he wouldn't hit it. Her.

He'd thrown his car in Park and gotten out, but as he'd dropped to his knees by the woman in his headlights, he'd spotted the third body on the shoulder of the road.

Assist, protect, defend—which one?

For one hideous second, he'd knelt there, paralyzed. Where could he even begin? What help could he possibly be? He was insignificant in the face of real laws—of physics, of biology. Force and velocity defeated skin and bone, and the badge on his vest didn't mean he could change the laws for these three people. *Here we all are, gathered together in these headlights. Helpless.*

One frozen second—and then all his years of training had

kicked in, and he'd given all he had to the woman under his hands. There'd been no pulse. There'd been a lot of blood. He'd forced breath into her lungs, tied a tourniquet between exhales.

The woman on the shoulder had regained consciousness, moaning in pain for long moments, then gaining enough strength to cry out for help. As he'd worked on her friend, Thane had assisted her using the only thing he had left: his voice. *I'm here. Help's coming. Hold on. Hold on.* Short sentences were all he'd been able to manage as he'd kept breathing for the woman who'd lost so much blood.

She'd begun breathing on her own by the time they loaded her into the back of the ambulance. The conscious woman had been loaded into the next ambulance. Paramedics had clustered around the third woman, the one so far down the road, his headlights hadn't touched her. The medics had done their job while he'd done his, directing MPs to secure the scene until the traffic investigators could arrive with their tape measures and cameras.

The ambulances had screamed away, sirens fading as they took the broken bodies and left the broken car. Traffic would do their analysis and arrange the tow truck. Thane's part was over; 310 was free to go.

He'd gotten a lot of pats on the back, approving touches that told him he'd been a success. Success had been bloody. He'd needed to clean up, so he'd gotten into his patrol car and headed back to the station. When the watch commander had brought him a cup of coffee, Thane had known he looked as rough outside as he felt inside.

But soap and water and a cup of coffee did a lot for a man. The relief that the woman hadn't died under his hands had turned to a strange sense of euphoria, but it hadn't lasted long enough. Anger had set in by the time he'd left the station and gone to his office.

Anger that he still felt as he pounded up the stairs. Anger at himself for that second of paralysis. Anger that he'd had his blissfully ignorant arrogance stripped away from him in a frozen moment on the blacktop. He'd never again be able to take life for granted the way he had before he'd knelt on the road.

Life was vulnerable. Life could not defy physics, and yet, Thane passed door after door where full lives were lived. He was surrounded by life. He had a life.

It was so incredibly valuable. What should he spend it on? Happiness.

Ballerina's goal. He'd asked her what her goal in life was, big life, but he'd never stopped to ask himself the same thing.

Thane reached the top of the stairs. Before he pulled out his apartment key, he pulled out his phone. He wanted to talk through everything with Ballerina, but her real name was Chloe, and he knew she was currently counting fire extinguishers.

She was counting those fire extinguishers for him, because she cared about him. Somehow, by some miracle, she cared about him.

That was so incredibly valuable. Caring for another person, loving another person, that should be his priority in life. He loved her. He'd loved her since the first marathon typing session with Ballerina, eight months ago.

He put his phone away and walked into his apartment, alone.

Never delay happiness. He'd heard that before, but now he felt the urgency.

Never delay happiness—but he couldn't even try to find happiness with Chloe until June, when they would be a thousand miles apart.

The anger came back and choked him.

When Chloe got back to her office, Ernesto was waiting. "Word came from the hospital, ma'am."

"Who is in the hospital?" she asked calmly. Her gut

churned. Had Thane been more than tired? Had she walked out of here and left a critically ill man behind?

"Lieutenant Carter worked an accident scene last night. The LT was first on the scene. Word is that he was the only one on the scene for a while. It happened out on a range road, so it took the ambulance a little extra time to get there. Three victims. Single-car rollover. All of them were ejected from the vehicle."

Chloe crossed her arms over her chest, but no layers, not arms, not jackets, not shirts, could protect her heart from feeling pain. No wonder Thane had looked so rough.

"How many fatalities?" Times like these, she knew she wasn't normal. She was able to stand in the face of terrible news and function with a clear mind. Not a normal response, but a necessary one.

"Lieutenant Carter did CPR on one woman. She's in the ICU, but she's still alive. One was conscious when they brought her in. She's going to make it for sure, they say. The third one got thrown the farthest from the wreck. She passed away about half an hour ago. I thought maybe you or the CO would want to stop by Lieutenant Carter's this evening to update him."

The flag wouldn't go down for another six hours. Thane should be sound asleep right now, but she didn't like the idea of him being alone for the next six hours if he wasn't.

"I'll go now. Put me down as LOP on your way through the orderly room, please."

"You got it, ma'am."

LOP stood for *Lost on Post*. It meant that, while somebody was not quite skipping work, it was best not to track whatever they were doing too closely. If the CO wanted to know more, he would ask her. Everyone else would just accept that the LT was out on a task of personal importance.

Thane Carter was of personal importance to her. She just didn't want to analyze why. It was just true.

* * *

"Come on, Thane. I know you're not asleep. I saw you sitting on your balcony."

Thane looked through the peephole. Chloe was standing there in her ACUs, but she didn't look happy to be there.

He didn't want her to be there, either. This was not a good time for him to have to pretend that he saw her as just his teammate. Just a friend.

"Shouldn't you be at work?" he hollered through the door.

"Shouldn't you be asleep?" she hollered back.

He sighed and opened the door, but he left the chain in place, keeping her out as if she might be dangerous.

She was. Dangerous and terribly beautiful.

She held up a handful of napkin-wrapped circles. "I had to confiscate some cookies before the dining facility opened as part of my fire inspection. Chocolate chip today."

He stuck his arm through the gap, palm up. "Thanks."

She held them just out of his reach. "Come on. Invite me in. I've never seen your place." The smile on her face was hopeful.

He'd killed that hopeful smile at the *Nutcracker*. He probably couldn't live with himself if he killed it again.

Thane pulled his arm back in, shut the door to take off the chain, then stepped back and let her in. She took off her patrol cap and handed him the cookies. And crumbs. They spilled out of the napkins onto his floor. He brushed some off the plain T-shirt he'd put on after his shower. She walked right past him, looking at his place with blatant curiosity.

"Does it pass inspection?" he asked drily, still standing by the open door.

She turned around, smiling like she was pleased with herself for having gotten past his attempt to keep her out. "I think you could possibly get a larger TV in here, maybe an inch larger, if you really tried. What is it with guys and giant TVs?"

He shut the front door. "Out with it, Chloe. The cookies are nice. What's really going on?"

She sighed and sat on his couch. "I've got news. From the hospital."

"Go ahead."

She gave it to him straight, all facts, no speculation, no emotion. Any other way would have driven him crazy.

"At least the lady I worked on is hanging on."

Since Chloe seemed in no rush to leave, Thane sat down, too—in the recliner. He was not going to cozy up on the couch with Chloe.

"You did well," she said.

He just looked at her, a real-life friend, sharing his space. It was so unremarkable. It was the reason for living.

"So eat a cookie." She winked at him, then picked up his remote and flopped back on the couch cushions. She found the on button quickly. "Dang, look at the picture on this thing. It's like being in a movie theater."

"Aren't you supposed to be at work?" The cookie tasted like manna. She must have stolen it fresh out of the industrial oven.

"Aren't you supposed to be sleeping?"

"If you leave, I'll sleep."

She used the remote to gesture at the recliner. "If you fall asleep, I'll leave."

She started scrolling through one hundred channels, making him smile at her wisecracks about what made each show unwatchable. It was like having Ballerina on audio instead of in writing. Thane pushed his seatback back, letting the recliner do its recliner thing.

And then he woke up. The TV was still on, and when he turned his head, he saw Chloe was still on the couch. She'd taken off her ACU jacket and was lounging back in the plain brown uniform T-shirt, legs still hidden by camouflage, her booted feet resting on his coffee table.

"You didn't leave."

"It's one heck of a TV. Besides, I've got to see which of the three houses these yahoos choose—oh! I knew it. Idiots." She tore her eyes from the screen and looked at him. "Why would you pass on the French château with the mountain view that was *in budget*? Why? Who does that?"

"Watching TV is pretty stressful for you, isn't it?"

"Yeah. I'm going to go back to work, where life is easy." She stood and stretched, arms high over her head as she yawned.

Chloe in a bikini, standing less than an arm's length away, dropping the towel, moving her chair into the sun. The lust hit Thane hard. Lust for Chloe. Lust for life.

Never delay happiness. But he had four months until June. Four months until he'd be far, far away, trying to capture happiness by asking her to be more than a friend over the phone. Asking her to wait for him, for six months while he took the captain's course. A company command after that, anywhere the army wanted him to go, perhaps another hardship tour in Korea. Hardship tours meant no family members were stationed with the soldier. He gave the army credit for understanding what a hardship was.

Chloe deserved better.

She was oblivious to his thoughts as she put her ACU jacket back on and zipped it up. Thane stood, too, and moved to the door with her.

"This was fun. We should do it again sometime." She picked up her patrol cap. "I'll come over next time *Pride and Prejudice* is on. Mr. Darcy will be life-size on that screen."

He couldn't laugh with her. Her smiles were killing him. She was everything he wanted, and everything he couldn't have.

"Anytime," he said, anyway.

"Great. I gained a friend and a TV. Why didn't we become friends sooner?"

He slipped. He was tired, he was emotional, and as he looked her in the eye, he slipped right into honesty. "Because we both remember that afternoon by the pool, and how much we wanted to date each other. We didn't think friendship would be enough."

Damn, he could kill her smiles without even trying.

"You never wanted to date me, Thane. You should be honest about it." She tossed her patrol cap a few feet in the air, spinning it like a chef with pizza dough. Caught it, tossed it. "It's not a bad thing. It actually makes it easier to work with you, knowing that I'm not your type. You were just flirting with me…recreationally, shall we say? Trying to see if you could get the single girl to believe your lines."

He frowned. "I don't flirt recreationally. I don't flirt at all."

"Oh, but you do. And you were very convincing, but I know that's what you were doing. You said so."

He stepped closer. "Never. I said it was never a game."

She snorted in disbelief and spun her cap in the air, keeping the cap between them, giving herself something to look at instead of him. "You're talking about when we met in the parking lot for our ride-along."

"Yes. I said it was never a game then. I'm telling you the same thing now." He snatched her cap out of the air and leaned in close, so close he could feel the air move when she sucked in a breath. "Chloe Michaels, it was never a game."

"I'm talking about earlier than that. I heard you at the pool. You told a friend that you were just taking what you could get, because there wasn't any other single girl to talk to."

"You are nobody's idea of taking what they can get."

"I was in the bathroom, Thane. I could hear you with your friend. 'Did you see her face? Believe me, if you'd seen her face…' Sound familiar?"

The entire, desperate conversation with Gevahr came back to him in a single burst. He knew exactly what she was talking about.

"My God, Chloe. You heard that?" He shook his head

as he looked at her and remembered those critical minutes when he'd been trying not to get them caught. "I can't believe you ever spoke to me again."

"I wouldn't have. The army didn't give me a choice, did it?" She smiled, a sort of smart-aleck grin, all bravado. "Don't worry. I didn't get a complex over it. I know my face isn't hideous."

"Not even close. You're beautiful."

"Stop. Seriously. I'm just not your style, and I'm cool with that."

"You are exactly my style. Chloe, I was talking to Gevahr."

He knew when that sank in; her smile faded away.

"It was Sergeant Gevahr, and I'd just figured out you were going to be his platoon leader like five minutes earlier. He said he'd been watching us together, and I was so damned afraid I'd just blown your reputation—but you'd had your back to the pool most of the time. He hadn't seen your face. I made him leave before he could."

Her face. He was looking at her beautiful face now, her lips parted, her eyes wide, her attention riveted on him. He'd come closer to her with each word, until she was nearly backed against his wall. They stared at each other, emotions running high. Hot. God, he could kiss her.

He could not.

"I saw you walk away." She glanced upward, replaying the scene in her mind. "You had your towel over your shoulder, and…oh. It was Gevahr, wasn't it?"

He stepped back, because he had to step back. Her cap was crushed in his fist. He wanted to speak, but his throat felt tight, so he nodded.

She took in a shivery breath and dropped her gaze. "You should have told me."

"I didn't know you'd overheard anything."

"You should have told me," she whispered.

He had to touch her. Her cap was in his fist, but with his other hand he reached toward the curve of her cheek—

He forced himself to stop. Touching her face was too intimate. It was a line that couldn't be uncrossed. He touched her lapel instead, straightening it, his fingers touching fire-retardant industrial cloth instead of Chloe's skin.

"I'll tell you now. The truth was, you looked beautiful. Your smile slayed me. When I said I wanted to take you to dinner and a movie, I meant I wanted to spend every free moment I possibly could with you that day and the next day and the next, as far as I could see into the future."

She stayed perfectly still, eyes downcast.

He dropped his hand to his side. "But then I realized we were both MPs."

She burst into motion. She snatched her cap out of his fist and sidestepped him, turning on him so he was the one against the wall. "You walked out on me. Whether you had a good reason with Gevahr or not, you should have doubled back to the party to explain why you'd just walked out on me. I would have understood all the implications if you'd said you were in the 584th. I might even have thanked you for distracting Sergeant Gevahr. But you didn't. You left me there, and I had no idea why. It was—it was—"

"Heartbreaking," Thane said. That was how he'd felt.

"It was humiliating. There is no excuse for that."

He couldn't defend himself. She was right.

She was also waiting for him to say something. "At the time, I told myself there might be more MPs there, so I shouldn't go back. Another MP had already walked by the fence before I talked to Gevahr. But the truth was—"

The truth was, he'd gone back into his safe world with Ballerina, to try to squash his feelings for Chloe before Monday.

"The truth was, I knew we'd be meeting again on Monday. I tried to convince myself that would be enough time for both of us to shrug it off and move on. It wouldn't have been. Then you rode along on Sunday instead." After Drummer had advised her to choose a confrontation instead of a conversation. He shook his head at the memory. At himself. "I botched everything up, Chloe. I'm sorry."

"Well." She pulled herself together as he watched. She simply took in a deep breath and stood up straighter. By the time she breathed out, she was Michaels. Chin up. Gaze direct. Cool and calm. "This has been a very interesting lunch hour. Or three hours. I'm going back to the office. I'll see you tomorrow."

She reached for the doorknob. He placed his palm on the door to stop her. "I don't want to go back to being Carter and Michaels."

"Are you about to say, 'Can't we still be friends?' That's a breakup line, Thane. You can't use it. We never dated."

She was still hurt. He'd caused this woman too much pain, and yet she'd come here today with cookies and her company when he'd needed her most. Tonight, she would spend all night talking to him on their app if he needed her company, even though Drummer had caused her pain, as well. There had to be a limit to how much pain she was willing to take.

"No, we never dated. I was devastated at that pool party when I realized that this—" He looked at her flushed face, her angry eyes, her ballerina hair and her military uniform. God, how he loved her. "When I realized that this wasn't meant to be. I handled it badly. I'm sorry. I will always be sorry. And yes, I'm asking you to be my friend, anyway."

The sound of her angry, shallow breaths was worse than anything she could have said.

"I know it's asking a lot," he said. "I know you had to forgive your other friend, too, after the ballet. Maybe we can only be expected to tolerate a certain amount of offenses against us, and you've hit your limit. But, Chloe…"

He looked into her face with real regret. "But, Chloe, if you could only forgive one man, then I'm jealous that it was him."

She stopped breathing. "You and I are in the army, Thane." It came out as a whisper. "At least with him, there's a chance... But you and I? We could only be friends."

"That's a lot. That's more than I deserve. Can we make this the start of a beautiful friendship?"

Chloe bit her lip at his *Casablanca* quote, but after a long moment, she opened the door, and he watched her walk away.

She hadn't said yes.

Chapter Twenty

Dear Drummer,
I think we should meet.

Chloe hit Send. She refused to watch that blinking cursor, so she went into the kitchen and poured herself a glass of wine. Then she came back to her living room to peek through her vertical blinds. Thane's balcony was empty. The coast was clear.

She went outside to her little patio set and arranged her laptop and her wine on the table.

Why? Drummer asked.

Chloe's heart sank. Why would you ask why? You don't want to meet me any longer?

I do. I'm just wondering why you changed your mind.

She picked up her wine and sat back, trying to imagine what a confident, fun woman would give as her reason. She ignored Thane's balcony so deliberately that, of course, she noticed the second his glass door slid open and he stepped out, concentrating on the phone in his hand.

The thought came to her as an old reflex: *handsome man; hates me*.

Except he didn't.

Her heart tripped in her chest as she watched him—okay, as she devoured him with her eyes. He was still wearing that snug T-shirt, those loose track pants that had fallen so nicely over his perfect, muscular backside. She wondered if his feet were still bare. She wondered if he'd gone back to sleep after she'd left. Wouldn't it be something if he'd chosen to sleep on the couch because the pillows had kept her shape or her smell?

A silly fantasy. But when he'd said he wanted to be friends, he'd also said she was beautiful.

He lifted his hand and waved at her.

She set her wine down a little too abruptly and gave him a quick wave back, then she bent studiously over her laptop, like it held all the answers to the universe.

Perhaps it did.

Why? I want to meet you because I need a hug now and then. I'd like to hear you laugh when I laugh. I'd like to crash on a couch and do nothing with you.

She ran her fingers over the pink and blue words, a friendly blend, a comforting pattern. She said out loud what she could not write: "I want to meet you because you are the only man who could possibly save my heart from Thane Carter."

I don't know if I can, Baby. I'll get back to you on that.

"Oh." Her breath hitched on her disappointment. She looked in Thane's direction. He was looking in hers.

She wasn't going to cry in front of him. She picked up her laptop and her wine, and went back inside.

"You are out of your mind, Lieutenant Carter."

Thane stood at attention before the brigade commander's desk. This full-bird colonel, the highest-ranking military police officer on post, the provost marshal of Fort Hood, was the last man standing between Thane and his chance at happiness.

"You somehow got your CO to sign off on this. You got your battalion CO to sign off on this. But now it's on your brigade CO's desk, and the buck stops here. My answer is no."

Thane did not flinch outwardly. Inwardly, he did not flinch, either. He exploded—but his military bearing did not change.

"What do you have to say, Carter? How are you going to handle that?"

"There is nothing to say except 'yes, sir.' There is nothing to handle. I will continue to obey all lawful orders and execute the mission."

I will continue to delay happiness.

The colonel let the silence go on a good, long while. "Close the door, Carter. Have a seat."

That was a lawful order. Thane obeyed it. It was a rare occasion, a very rare occasion, when a brigade commander sat down for a one-on-one talk with a platoon leader. Rarer still to have the door closed.

"You are one of the sharpest lieutenants I've seen in my career, Carter. You are being sent to the captain's course at the earliest possible date. You have been recommended for company command by your entire chain of command, including me. I'm doing you a favor here. Never give up your life because some girl strikes your fancy. Nothing that goes on in a bedroom is as important as your career."

"I appreciate that, sir."

The colonel sat back in his leather wingback chair. "Good, good—"

"And I would never do something so foolish. That is not the situation here, sir."

The colonel only raised an eyebrow in question.

Thane took that as permission to speak. His best shot at happiness was in the brigade commander's hands, and every word counted.

"My time as a platoon leader will end the day I make captain. There's a five-week gap between that promotion in May and the start of the captain's course in June. Colonel Stephens told me he'd planned to assign me to the battalion

S-3 shop with Major Nord. I'm not derailing that career path, sir. I'm just asking to make that move twelve weeks earlier."

"That's what Colonel Stephens said to you, is it? Guess what he said to me. He asked me to clarify the definition of 'unit' as far as fraternization goes. Two officers in the same company are obviously in the same unit, but he asked if I thought there was enough of a degree of separation if one officer is in a company and the other is on battalion staff. I have a feeling you've brushed up on the details of fraternization, so you know that's decided at the brigade level. Right here, by the man sitting in my chair."

"Yes, sir."

"I've already told you no."

Thane fought the disappointment. June was far away. Missouri was even farther, but he was going to have to make them work.

The colonel wasn't done with him. "I've got another question for you, Carter. Is Lieutenant Michaels going to be able to keep serving as a platoon leader with you when I send you back to the 584th? Should we call her in here to ask?"

Thane had not and would not draw Chloe into it. "I have not said that I'm interested in Lieutenant Michaels, sir. I have not said she's the reason behind my request."

"Don't play games with me. It's obvious you've got the hots for someone in your company, and Phillips and Salvatore aren't it. The only female officer in the 584th is Michaels. She's new. You're the XO, the senior platoon leader. It would be a hell of a lot easier to move her instead of you."

"That would be grossly unfair to her, sir, since none of this is her idea. She doesn't know I've made this request. She'd be rightfully shocked if an order came down that made her move."

"Shocked? You expect me to believe you two haven't already canoodled around and decided it's love?"

Thane came close to laughing at that one, laughing in disgust. "Sir, we barely manage to be polite to one another. We only succeed in being civil about every third day."

The colonel seemed genuinely curious now. "You're going to all this trouble for a woman who doesn't even like you? What do you think the odds are that you'd ever win her over?"

"Optimistically, sir? I'd say about fifty-fifty."

"You're willing to upend your career for a fifty-fifty shot at a woman who may not even like you?"

"There's zero chance of success if I don't try, sir." Thane decided to take a risk and walk that line between disrespectful and bold. "But I can tell you where there is a one hundred percent chance of success. That's the S-3 shop. If I work for Major Nord more than sixty days, he can give me a rating, and I can guarantee I'll have given him nothing to say but good things. It won't hurt my career to add one more good review to my file before I hit the captain's course."

The colonel leaned forward, managing to get in Thane's face without leaving his seat. "Well, that isn't going to happen, Carter. You're not moving to the battalion S-3 shop."

Damn it. Thane had taken one last swing, and missed.

"Because you're moving to the brigade S-3 shop. This week. You've convinced me you aren't being stupid about your career, but I'm keeping my eye on you."

"Yes, sir," Thane answered automatically. The relief was dizzying, the happiness staggering.

"You're dismissed."

Thane stood, amazed he was still steady on his feet. "Good afternoon, sir."

"Before you go, let me make my policy clear. An officer on brigade staff is not in the same unit as a platoon leader in a line company. I've decided there is no conflict of interest there."

"Yes, sir." Thane headed for the door while he still had some semblance of military bearing.

"Oh, and Carter?"

He wiped the smile off his face before turning around. "Yes, sir?"

"Apparently my brigade is full of a bunch of sappy, damned romantics. Everyone seems to think you and Michaels would make a perfect couple. They're all rooting for you."

To hell with it. Thane smiled.

"Yes, sir."

He walked out of the office and down the brigade staff hall, but that was the end of his self-restraint. He slammed out of the entrance door and pulled his phone out of his pocket.

Yes, Ballerina, let's meet. ASAP.

Today, I am desperate for sanity.

Chloe wasn't going to get it.

The entire week had been crazy. Thane had been tapped to move into the brigade S-3 office even though he wouldn't make captain until May. It was a shock to everybody except Thane, apparently. The platoon leaders and platoon sergeants had hastily passed around a card to sign and had taken him to a restaurant in Killeen for a farewell lunch. Sergeant First Class Lloyd had proposed a toast that had choked everyone up.

Then they'd gone back to work. Thane had parked the chair with the squeaky wheel at his empty desk and left her with a rather intense, "I'll see you around, Chloe. I'm not going far."

But he was far, no longer part of the company. No longer part of the battalion. His office wasn't even in her building.

She sat at her desk, alone, and missed him like crazy.

But the craziest thing of all was that, in just a few hours, Drummer was going to become more than just a man stuck in her laptop.

She wasn't ready. She'd tried to stall. I can't get to Austin until Sunday at the earliest.

Then I'll come to you, Ballerina. Give me your address. I'll take you on a picnic. Thursday after work?

It was lucky that Drummer had chosen Thursday, because troops were dismissed at three instead of five every Thursday. Those extra two hours were supposed to be devoted to family time. Hers were going to be devoted to a picnic with Drummer.

She didn't have a thing to wear.

She looked over her civilian clothes, deliberately passing over anything blue or pink. She wasn't going to do that again. She had some pride left, plus enough self-preservation that she'd stopped just short of telling him her address. She'd told him to pick her up outside the complex's swimming pool, a safer area in public. He'd never know which apartment in which of the six buildings was hers, unless she decided to tell him.

Chloe dressed, then went out to her balcony and looked down at the pool. It was as blue as always, but empty. Even in Texas, the water in February was too chilly for swimming. The afternoon was warm, though, seventy degrees. She'd decided her yellow sundress would work with a navy cardigan over it. Her navy ballerina flats were practical for a picnic, but she did not wear her hair in a ballerina bun. She wasn't going to spend an hour on a floral updo again; Drummer had missed his chance to see that. She'd blown her hair dry and left it down.

It was time. She headed down to the pool, perhaps with a bit of military stoicism on her face. That was how she got through nerve-racking occasions, after all. Drummer should understand that she'd fall back on what had always served her well.

She waited outside the pool's chest-high fence and looked

for…someone. Drummer had refused to give her any description of himself. *You'll know me when you see me,* he'd written.

As she waited, she heard the growl of an engine built for power, excess power for the size of the sports car that held it. Thane's Mustang came in the complex's entrance. Pulled up to the pool.

And parked.

She wanted to die. The last person she wanted to witness this meeting with Drummer was Thane Carter. If Drummer turned out to be someone flaky, it would be humiliating. If she got stood up again, it would be too humiliating to explain why she was standing around in a dress. If Drummer—

Thane got out of his car. It was awful to have such a handsome nemesis. He looked fantastic in a burgundy knit shirt that clung nicely to strong shoulders, to his ripped arms—she did watch the man do push-ups every day at PT, which wasn't exactly a hardship. At least if Drummer turned out to be a creep, she knew Thane would pummel the guy. Of course, so would she, but if Thane got to him first, there wouldn't be much left for her to pummel, more's the pity, and *oh, my God, I am so not normal. What kind of girl thinks like that? What is Drummer going to say when he finds out I'm a soldier and a cop?*

"You look terrific, Chloe."

She pasted on a polite little smile. "Thanks."

She'd been hoping Drummer would hurry up and get here, but now she prayed he'd be late, just late enough to let Thane clear out of the parking lot and head up to his apartment.

Instead of walking away, Thane popped his trunk and took out a wicker suitcase. A picnic basket. He carried it right up to her—no, right past her, and he went in the gate to the pool.

She felt a little dazed, like she had when she'd gotten a concussion once. She was fine, only she was not, and the world seemed a little surreal. She turned to watch Thane as he carried the basket to that table, their table, the little one in the shade, and set it down. He undid the latches and opened it up, and from here, she could see the champagne bottle and the glasses neatly strapped into the lid.

A picnic basket. She should be thinking something significant right now. She knew she should, but it seemed she couldn't think at all as Thane walked back toward her.

He opened the gate again and stopped a little too close to her, his hands in the pockets of his jeans. "Hello, Ballerina."

Her knees buckled.

"Whoa." He was quick, grabbing her upper arm to keep her from falling, but she'd caught herself. She didn't faint. Of course she didn't faint, because she'd never fainted in her life and she wasn't going to start now. She shook off his hand and took a step back.

"It takes some getting used to, I know." He pushed the gate open. "Come and sit down. You're a little pale."

She was numb. Her lips felt numb, her fingers felt numb and tingly, and she let him escort her to the table like she was some fragile flower, a spun-sugar princess who might break.

"At least we know why the app matched us up. Under careers, I checked 'military officer.' You must have, too."

The reminder penetrated the numbness. She was a military officer, not a woman made out of spun sugar.

Instead of sitting down, she squared off with Thane. "What do you mean by saying you know 'it takes some getting used to'? How do you know that?"

He looked, for the first time, serious. Chagrined. He took a breath, ready to explain.

"You knew before I gave you my address yesterday. How long have you known?"

But again, she didn't wait for his answer. "*The Nutcracker.* You were *there*. You were there because you're… Oh, my God. You came, after all." She thought she might choke on the lump in her throat. Her eyes teared up. He'd come, he'd come, and she hadn't been a fool to believe Drummer would come.

The tears gave way to horror. "You came, but you didn't tell me who you were. You—you—you sat next to me in that lobby. You laughed at my pain. Oh, you incredible *jerk*."

She didn't realize her hand was in motion until Thane caught her wrist before her hand connected with his cheek. She gasped, shocked that she'd even tried to slap him.

She'd never felt so emotional, never been so out of control. No military training could prepare her for this horrible, horrible feeling. Her heart had been broken, and the man who'd broken it had sat next to her on the most miserable night of her life while he drank his whiskey.

She looked into those eyes, those same blue and gray irises she'd noticed that night. The same eyes she'd glared at over the roof of a police cruiser. The same eyes she'd laughed with when they'd pranked their platoon sergeants.

Thane closed his eyes and kissed the palm of the hand he'd captured. "I didn't laugh at you. I was as upset as you are now."

He let go of her wrist but clasped her fingers and held her hand as if she were a lady in a historical movie, and he, the gentleman. He kissed the back of her hand. "I didn't know what to do at first, either."

She instinctively tried to pull her hand back. They were in public.

He lowered her hand, but he didn't let go. She watched as he ran his thumb over her knuckles, a caress so innocent, so intimate.

"You kept pretending to be Drummer."

"Your letter. I couldn't ignore it. And I am Drummer."

"You've known for months. I didn't know who I was talking to. All those things I said about my coworker…" Her cheeks felt hot. "I called you arrogant. And things. Are you angry?"

He squeezed her hand gently. "It was a gift, really. What a gift it is, to see ourselves as others see us."

He smiled, looking at her expectantly. He was so handsome when he smiled, she almost forgot why those words sounded familiar. "Did you just quote Robbie Burns?"

"Ay, my online lass likes her Scottish poet."

Chloe's heart pounded. She couldn't sort out all her feelings. She could almost laugh, but she was mortified, too, a little sad that Drummer was not what she'd imagined, perhaps, and amazed that her very best friend all year could be this handsome man before her, an officer she had grudgingly admired even when she didn't want to.

He reached for her other hand and brought both of her hands up to kiss, watching her with those gray-blue eyes as he did.

"Thane, don't." He couldn't kiss her hands. He couldn't kiss her anywhere. She looked over her shoulder to see if anyone was coming up the walk.

"It's safe, Chloe. I did know what to do about that, at least." His smile turned a little devilish, so intimate, her fingers trembled in his. "The brigade commander has made his fraternization policy very clear. He said officers in line companies are free to date brigade staffers."

"He said that?"

Thane smiled at her and raised her hand not to his lips, but to the side of his face, gently drawing her knuckles along his cheek. He must have shaved recently, just for this. Just for her.

"You asked him," she breathed, though it was hard to breathe. "You asked the brigade commander. Oh, Thane, you didn't lose your position because of me?"

"Nope." He winked at her with a little of that arrogance she'd once lied and told Drummer she found unappealing. "I was going to be sent to the battalion S-3, anyway. He just promoted me to brigade S-3 instead and let me start twelve weeks early."

"Twelve weeks." She was absolutely mesmerized by him, by the way his hand felt warm and strong, by the way his mouth formed words, by the way his eyes never, ever left hers. "What do you need those twelve weeks for?"

He let go of her fingers to capture her whole hand and pressed the palm of her hand against the side of his face. "Do you realize we've never touched before?"

"That's not true." Her heart was still pounding, but it was steady. She was getting used to it, breathing through it. "The day we met, we sat side by side right at this pool with our feet in the water. Our feet brushed against each other. I nudged you with my shoulder when you made me laugh."

He looked so tenderly at her, she thought she would melt. "Such a little touch to live on, wasn't it? Such a little touch, but it kept us going for three months, here at Hood. Eight months online. Do you realize you've been my favorite person in the world for eight months?"

She didn't wipe the tears that trickled down her cheeks, because she didn't want to let go of Thane's hands. It was okay to cry a little; only Thane would see, and he would understand why she cried for a silly, wonderful, online love.

"We're really, really good at keeping up a long-distance relationship, Baby. That's a really, really good trait for a military couple to have." He tugged her closer, then let go of one hand so he could slide his arm around her waist and pull her close. The impact was exciting, energizing, awakening a whole new awareness. He felt as hard as he looked during PT, strong arm, hard thighs, but he felt warm and giving, too, a body she could press into, lie upon, rest against.

"But for these twelve weeks?" she asked, smiling against his mouth. Whether he'd brought his mouth to hers or she had to his didn't matter, because the kiss that followed was all she'd ever wanted. Strong, warm, giving—the best first kiss any couple could ever have.

He spoke with his lips against hers. "Now we've got

twelve weeks to get really, really good at being very, very close."

She laughed, they kissed, and he tasted so good and felt so very right, she knew the picnic was going to be eaten either by a red, red couch or in front of a massive TV.

After.

She ran her hand up his neck, sliding her fingers through his short hair. "And what happens at the end of twelve weeks?"

"Then you will be the one who pins the captain's bars on me, and I will be the one who puts a ring on your finger."

There may have been a tear trickling down his cheek as well, but it didn't matter, because only she was here to see it—and she could see nothing while kissing her best friend in the world.

* * * * *

MILLS & BOON

Coming next month

MISS WHITE AND THE SEVENTH HEIR
Jennifer Faye

Of all the bedrooms, why did she have to pick that one?

Trey frowned as he struggled to get all five suitcases up the stairs. The woman really needed to learn how to pack lighter.

At the top of the steps, he paused. It was a good thing he exercised daily. He rolled the cases back down the hallway to the very familiar bedroom. The door was still ajar.

"Sage, it's just me." He would have knocked but his hands were full trying to keep a hold on all of the luggage.

There was no response. Maybe she'd decided to explore the rest of the house. Or perhaps she was standing out on the balcony. It was one of his favorite spots to clear his head.

But two steps into the room, he stopped.

There was Sage stretched across his bed. Her long dark hair was splayed across the comforter. He knew he shouldn't stare, but he couldn't help himself. She was so beautiful. And the look on her face as she was sleeping was one of utter peace. It was a look he'd never noticed during her wakeful hours. If you knew her, you could see something was always weighing on her mind. And he'd hazard a guess that it went much deeper than the trouble with the magazine.

Though he hated to admit it, he was impressed with the new format that she'd rolled out for the magazine. But he wasn't ready to back down on his campaign to close the magazine's doors. None of it changed the fact that to hurt his father in the same manner that he'd hurt him, the magazine had to go. It had been his objective for so many years. He never thought he'd be in a position to make it happen—but now as the new CEO of QTR International, he was in the perfect position to make his father understand in some small way the pain his absence had inflicted on him.

Trey's thoughts returned to the gorgeous woman lying on his bed sound asleep. She was the innocent party— the bystander that would get hurt—and he had no idea how to protect her. The only thing he did know was that the longer he kept up this pretense of being her assistant instead of the heir to the QTR empire—the worse it was going to be when the truth finally won out—and it would. The truth always came to light—sometimes at the most inopportune times.

Continue reading
MISS WHITE AND THE SEVENTH HEIR
Jennifer Faye

Available next month
www.millsandboon.co.uk

LET'S TALK
Romance

For exclusive extracts, competitions
and special offers, find us online:

 facebook.com/millsandboon
 @millsandboonuk
 @millsandboon

Or get in touch on 0844 844 1351*

For all the latest titles coming soon, visit
millsandboon.co.uk/nextmonth